APHRA BEHN

LOVE-LETTERS BETWEEN A NOBLEMAN AND HIS SISTER

CLEAN BRIGHT CLASSICS

The Argument

In the time of the rebellion of the true Protestant *Huguenot* in *Paris*, under the conduct of the Prince of *Condé* (whom we will call *Cesario*) many illustrious persons were drawn into the association, amongst which there was one, whose quality and fortune (joined with his youth and beauty) rendered him more elevated in the esteem of the gay part of the world than most of that age. In his tender years (unhappily enough) he chanced to fall in love with a lady, whom we will call *Myrtilla*, who had charms enough to engage any heart; she had all the advantages of youth and nature; a shape excellent; a most agreeable stature, not too tall, and far from low, delicately proportioned; her face a little inclined round, soft, smooth and white; her eyes were blue, a little languishing, and full of love and wit; a mouth curiously made, dimpled, and full of sweetness; lips round, soft, plump and red; white teeth, firm and even; her nose a little *Roman*, and which gave a noble grace to her lovely face, her hair light brown; a neck and bosom delicately turned, white and rising; her arms and hands exactly shaped; to this a vivacity of youth engaging; a wit quick and flowing; a humour gay, and an air irresistibly charming; and nothing was wanting to complete the joys of the young *Philander*, (so we call our amorous hero) but *Myrtilla*'s heart, which the illustrious *Cesario* had before possessed; however, consulting her honour and her interest, and knowing all the arts as women do to feign a tenderness; she yields to marry him: while *Philander*, who scorned to owe his happiness to the commands of parents, or to chaffer for a beauty, with her consent steals her away, and marries her. But see how transitory is a violent passion; after being satiated, he slights the prize he had so dearly conquered; some say, the change was occasioned by her too visibly continued love to *Cesario*; but whatever it was, this was most certain, *Philander* cast his eyes upon a young maid, sister to *Myrtilla*, a beauty, whose early bloom promised wonders when come to perfection; but I will spare her picture here, *Philander* in the following epistles will often enough present it to your view: He loved and languished, long before he durst discover his pain; her being sister to his wife, nobly born, and of undoubted fame, rendered his passion too criminal to hope for a return, while the young lovely *Sylvia* (so we shall call the noble maid) sighed out her hours in the same pain and languishment for *Philander*, and knew not that it was love, till she betraying it innocently to the overjoyed lover and brother, he soon taught her to understand it was love — he pursues it, she permits it, and at last yields, when being discovered in the criminal intrigue, she flies with him; he absolutely quits *Myrtilla*, lives some time in a village near *Paris*, called St *Denis*, with this betrayed unfortunate, till being found out, and like to be apprehended, (one for the rape, the other for the flight) she is forced to marry a cadet, a creature of *Philander*'s, to bear the name of husband only to her, while *Philander* had the entire possession of her soul and body: still the *League* went forward, and all things were ready for a war in *Paris*; but it is not my business here to mix the rough relation of a war, with the soft affairs of love; let it suffice, the *Huguenots* were defeated, and the King got the day, and every rebel lay at the mercy of his sovereign. *Philander* was taken prisoner, made his escape to a little cottage near his own palace, not far from *Paris*, writes to *Sylvia* to come to him, which she does, and in spite of all the industry to re-seize him, he got away with *Sylvia*.

After their flight these letters were found in their cabinets, at their house at St *Denis*, where they both lived together, for the space of a year; and they are as exactly as possible placed in the order they were sent, and were those supposed to be written towards the latter end of their amours.

Chapter 1

To SYLVIA.

Though I parted from you resolved to obey your impossible commands, yet know, oh charming *Sylvia*! that after a thousand conflicts between love and honour, I found the god (too mighty for the idol) reign absolute monarch in my soul, and soon banished that tyrant thence. That cruel counsellor that would suggest to you a thousand fond arguments to hinder my noble pursuit; *Sylvia* came in view! her irresistible *Idea*! With all the charms of blooming youth, with all the attractions of heavenly beauty! Loose, wanton, gay, all flowing her bright hair, and languishing her lovely eyes, her dress all negligent as when I saw her last, discovering a thousand ravishing graces, round, white, small breasts, delicate neck, and rising bosom, heaved with sighs she would in vain conceal; and all besides, that nicest fancy can imagine surprising — Oh I dare not think on, lest my desires grow mad and raving; let it suffice, oh adorable *Sylvia*! I think and know enough to justify that flame in me, which our weak alliance of brother and sister has rendered so criminal; but he that adores *Sylvia*, should do it at an uncommon rate; 'tis not enough to sacrifice a single heart, to give you a simple passion, your beauty should, like itself, produce wondrous effects; it should force all obligations, all laws, all ties even of nature's self: you, my lovely maid, were not born to be obtained by the dull methods of ordinary loving; and 'tis in vain to prescribe me measures; and oh much more in vain to urge the nearness of our relation. What kin, my charming *Sylvia*, are you to me? No ties of blood forbid my passion; and what's a ceremony imposed on man by custom? What is it to my divine *Sylvia*, that the priest took my hand and gave it to your sister? What alliance can that create? Why should a trick devised by the wary old, only to make provision for posterity, tie me to an eternal slavery? No, no, my charming maid, 'tis nonsense all; let us, (born for mightier joys) scorn the dull *beaten road*, but let us love like the first race of men, nearest allied to God, promiscuously they loved, and possessed, father and daughter, brother and sister met, and reaped the joys of love without control, and counted it religious coupling, and 'twas encouraged too by heaven itself: therefore start not (too nice and lovely maid) at shadows of things that can but frighten fools. Put me not off with these delays; rather say you but dissembled love all this while, than now 'tis born, to die again with a poor fright of nonsense. A fit of honour! a phantom imaginary, and no more; no, no, represent me to your soul more favourably, think you see me languishing at your feet, breathing out my last in sighs and kind reproaches, on the pitiless *Sylvia*; reflect when I am dead, which will be the more afflicting object, the ghost (as you are pleased to call it) of your murdered honour, or the pale and bleeding one of

The lost PHILANDER.

I have lived a whole day, and yet no letter from Sylvia.

•••••••••••••••••••

To PHILANDER.

OH why will you make me own (oh too importunate *Philander*!) with what regret I made you promise to prefer my honour before your love?

I confess with blushes, which you might then see kindling in my face, that I was not at all pleased with the vows you made me, to endeavour to obey me, and I then even wished you would obstinately have denied obedience to my just commands; have pursued your criminal flame, and have left me raving on my undoing: for when you were gone, and I had leisure to look into my heart, alas! I found, whether you obliged or not, whether love or honour were preferred, I, unhappy I, was either way inevitably lost. Oh! what pitiless god, fond of his wondrous power, made us the objects of his almighty vanity? Oh why were we two made the first precedents of his new found revenge? For sure no brother ever loved a sister with so criminal a flame before: at least my inexperienced innocence never met with so fatal a story: and it is in vain (my too charming brother) to make me insensible of our alliance; to persuade me I am a stranger to all but your eyes and soul.

Alas, your fatally kind industry is all in vain. You grew up a brother with me; the title was fixed in my heart, when I was too young to understand your subtle distinctions, and there it thrived and spread; and it is now too late to transplant it, or alter its native property: who can graft a flower on a contrary stalk? The rose will bear no tulips, nor the hyacinth the poppy, no more will the brother the name of lover. Oh! spoil not the natural sweetness and innocence we now retain, by an endeavour fruitless and destructive; no, no, *Philander*, dress yourself in what charms you will, be powerful as love can make you in your soft argument — yet, oh yet, you are my brother still. — But why, oh cruel and eternal powers, was not *Philander* my lover before you destined him a brother? Or why, being a brother, did you, malicious and spiteful powers, destine him a lover? Oh, take either title from him, or from me a life, which can render me no satisfaction, since your cruel laws permit it not for *Philander*, nor his to bless the now

Unfortunate SYLVIA.

Wednesday morning.

. . . .

To PHILANDER.

After I had dismissed my page this morning with my letter, I walked (filled with sad soft thoughts of my brother *Philander*) into the grove, and commanding *Melinda* to retire, who only attended me, I threw myself down on that bank of grass where we last disputed the dear, but fatal business of our souls: where our prints (that invited me) still remain on the pressed greens: there with ten thousand sighs, with remembrance of the tender minutes we passed then, I drew your last letter from my bosom, and often kissed, and often read it over; but oh! who can conceive my torment, when I came to that fatal part of it, where you say you gave your hand to my sister? I found my soul agitated with a thousand different passions, but all insupportable, all mad and raving; sometimes I threw myself with fury on the ground, and pressed my panting heart to the earth; then rise in rage, and tear my heart, and hardly spare that face that taught you first to love; then fold my wretched arms to keep down rising sighs that almost rend my breast, I traverse swiftly the conscious grove; with my distracted show'ring eyes directed in vain to pitiless heaven, the lovely silent shade favouring my complaints, I cry aloud, Oh God! *Philander*'s, married, the lovely charming thing for whom I languish is married! — That fatal word's enough, I need not add to whom. Married is enough to make me curse my birth, my youth, my beauty, and my eyes that first betrayed me to the undoing object: curse on the charms you have flattered, for every fancied grace has helped my ruin on; now, like flowers that wither unseen and unpossessed in shades, they must die and be no more, they were to no end created, since *Philander* is married: married! Oh fate, oh hell, oh torture and confusion! Tell me not it is to my sister, that addition is needless and vain: to make me eternally wretched, there needs no more than that *Philander* is married! Than that the priest gave your hand away from me; to another, and not to me; tired out with life, I need no other pass-port than this repetition, *Philander* is married! 'Tis that alone is sufficient to lay in her cold tomb

The wretched and despairing Wednesday night, Bellfont. SYLVIA.

....

To SYLVIA.

Twice last night, oh unfaithful and unloving *Sylvia*! I sent the page to the old place for letters, but he returned the object of my rage, because without the least remembrance from my fickle maid: in this torment, unable to hide my disorder, I suffered myself to be laid in bed; where the restless torments of the night exceeded those of the day, and are not even by the languisher himself to be expressed; but the returning light brought a short slumber on its wings; which was interrupted by my atoning boy, who brought two letters from my adorable *Sylvia*: he waked me from dreams more agreeable than all my watchful hours could bring; for they are all tortured. —— And even the softest mixed with a thousand despairs, difficulties and disappointments, but these were all love, which gave a loose to joys undenied by honour! And this way, my charming *Sylvia*, you shall be mine, in spite of all the tyrannies of that cruel hinderer; honour appears not, my *Sylvia*, within the close-drawn curtains; in shades and gloomy light the phantom frights not, but when one beholds its blushes, when it is attended and adorned, and the sun sees its false beauties; in silent groves and grottoes, dark alcoves, and lonely recesses, all its formalities are laid aside; it was then and there methought my *Sylvia* yielded, with a faint struggle and a soft resistance; I heard her broken sighs, her tender whispering voice, that trembling cried — 'Oh! Can you be so cruel? — Have you the heart — Will you undo a maid, because she loves you? Oh! Will you ruin me, because you may? — — My faithless — — My unkind — —' then sighed and yielded, and made me happier than a triumphing god! But this was still a dream, I waked and sighed, and found it vanished all! But oh, my *Sylvia*, your letters were substantial pleasure, and pardon your adorer, if he tell you, even the disorder you express is infinitely dear to him, since he knows it all the effects of love; love, my soul! Which you in vain oppose; pursue it, dear, and call it not undoing, or else explain your fear, and tell me what your soft, your trembling heart gives that cruel title to? Is it undoing to love? And love the man you say has youth and beauty to justify that love? A man, that adores you with so submissive and perfect a resignation; a man, that did not only love first, but is resolved to die in that agreeable flame; in my creation I was formed for love, and destined for my *Sylvia*, and she for her *Philander*: and shall we, can we disappoint our fate? No, my soft charmer, our souls were touched with the same shafts of love before they had a being in our bodies, and can we contradict divine decree?

Or is it undoing, dear, to bless *Philander* with what you must some time or other sacrifice to some hated, loathed object, (for *Sylvia* can never love again;) and are those treasures for the dull conjugal lover to rifle? Was the beauty of divine shape created for the cold matrimonial embrace? And shall the eternal joys that *Sylvia* can dispense, be returned by the clumsy husband's careless, forced, insipid duties? Oh, my *Sylvia*, shall a husband (whose insensibility will call those raptures of joy! Those heavenly blisses! The drudgery of life) shall he I say receive them? While your *Philander*, with the very thought of the excess of pleasure the least possession would afford, faints over the paper that brings here his eternal vows.

Oh! Where, my *Sylvia*, lies the undoing then? My quality and fortune are of the highest rank amongst men, my youth gay and fond, my soul all soft, all love; and all *Sylvia*'s! I adore her, I am sick of love, and sick of life, till she yields, till she is all mine!

You say, my *Sylvia*, I am married, and there my happiness is shipwrecked; but *Sylvia*, I deny it, and will not have you think it: no, my soul was married to yours in its first creation; and only *Sylvia* is the wife of my sacred, my everlasting vows; of my solemn considerate thoughts, of my ripened judgement, my mature considerations. The rest are all repented and forgot, like the hasty follies of unsteady youth, like vows breathed in anger, and die perjured as soon as vented, and unregarded either of heaven or man. Oh! why should my soul suffer for ever, why eternal pain for the unheedy, short-lived sin of my unwilling lips? Besides, this fatal thing called wife, this unlucky sister, this *Myrtilla*, this stop to all my heaven, that breeds such fatal differences in our affairs, this *Myrtilla*, I say, first broke her marriage-vows to me; I blame her not, nor is it reasonable I should; she saw the young *Cesario*, and loved him. *Cesario*, whom the envying world in spite of prejudice must own, has irresistible charms, that godlike form, that sweetness in his face, that softness in his eyes and delicate mouth; and every beauty besides, that women dote on, and men envy: that lovely composition of man and angel! with the addition of his eternal youth and illustrious birth, was formed by heaven and nature for universal conquest! And who can love the charming hero at a cheaper rate than being undone? And she that would not venture fame, honour, and a marriage-vow for the glory of the young *Cesario*'s heart, merits not the noble victim; oh! would I could say so much for the young *Philander*, who would run a thousand times more hazards of life and fortune for the adorable *Sylvia*, than that amorous hero ever did for *Myrtilla*, though from that prince I learned some of my disguises for my thefts of love; for he, like *Jove*, courted in several shapes; I saw them all, and suffered the delusion to pass upon me; for I had seen the lovely *Sylvia*; yes, I had seen her, and loved her too: but honour kept me yet master of my vows; but when I knew her false, when I was once confirmed — when by my own soul I found the dissembled passion of hers, when she could no longer hide the blushes, or the paleness that seized at the approaches of my disordered rival, when I saw love dancing in her eyes, and her false heart beat with nimble motions, and soft trembling seized every limb, at the approach or touch of the royal lover, then I thought myself no longer obliged to conceal my flame for *Sylvia*; nay, ere I broke silence, ere I discovered the hidden treasure of my heart, I made her falsehood plainer yet: even the time and place of the dear assignations I discovered; certainty, happy certainty! broke the dull heavy chain, and I with joy submitted to my shameful freedom, and caressed my generous rival; nay, and by heaven I loved him for it, pleased at the resemblance of our souls; for we were secret lovers both, but more pleased that he loved *Myrtilla*; for that made way to my passion for the adorable *Sylvia*!

Let the dull, hot-brained, jealous fool upbraid me with cold patience: let the fond coxcomb, whose honour depends on the frail marriage-vow, reproach me, or tell me that my reputation depends on the feeble constancy of a wife, persuade me it is honour to fight for an irretrievable and unvalued prize, and that because my rival has taken leave to cuckold me, I shall give him leave to kill me too; unreasonable nonsense grown to custom. No, by heaven! I had gather *Myrtilla* should be false, (as she is) than wish and languish for the happy occasion; the sin is the same, only the act is more generous: believe me, my *Sylvia*, we have all false notions of virtue and honour, and surely this was taken up by some despairing husband in love with a fair jilting wife, and then I pardon him; I should have done as much: for only she that has my soul can engage my sword; she that I love, and myself, only commands and keeps my stock of honour: for *Sylvia*! the charming, the distracting *Sylvia*! I could fight for a glance or smile, expose my heart for her dearer fame, and wish no recompense, but breathing out my last gasp into her soft, white, delicate bosom. But for a wife! that stranger to my soul, and whom we wed for interest and necessity — a wife, light, loose, unregarding property, who for a momentary appetite will expose her fame, without the noble end of loving on; she that will abuse my bed, and yet return again to the loathed conjugal embrace, back to the arms so hated, and even strong fancy of the absent youth beloved, cannot so much as render supportable. Curse on her, and yet she kisses, fawns and dissembles on, hangs on his neck, and makes the sot believe:— damn her, brute; I'll whistle her off, and let her down the wind, as *Othello* says. No, I adore the wife, that, when the heart is gone, boldy and nobly pursues the conqueror, and generously owns the whore; — not poorly adds the nauseous sin of jilting to it: that I could have borne, at least commended; but this can never pardon; at worst then the world had said her passion had undone her, she loved, and love at worst is worthy of pity. No, no, *Myrtilla*, I forgive your love, but never can your poor dissimulation. One drives you but from the heart you value not, but the other to my eternal contempt. One deprives me but of thee, *Myrtilla*, but the other entitles me to a beauty more surprising, renders thee no part of me; and so leaves the lover free to *Sylvia*, without the brother.

Thus, my excellent maid, I have sent you the sense and truth of my soul, in an affair you have often hinted to me, and I take no pleasure to remember: I hope you will at least think my aversion reasonable; and that being thus indisputably free from all obligations to *Myrtilla* as a husband, I may be permitted to lay claim to *Sylvia*, as a lover, and marry myself more effectually by my everlasting vows, than the priest by his common method could do to any other woman less beloved; there being no other way at present left by heaven, to render me *Sylvia*'s.

Eternal happy lover and I die to see you.
PHILANDER.

●●●●●●●●●●●●●●●●●

To SYLVIA.

When I had sealed the enclosed, *Brilliard* told me you were this morning come from *Bellfont*, and with infinite impatience have expected seeing you here; which deferred my sending this to the old place; and I am so vain (oh adorable *Sylvia*) as to believe my fancied silence has given you disquiets; but sure, my *Sylvia* could not charge me with neglect; no, she knows my soul, and lays it all on chance, or some strange accident, she knows no business could divert me. No, were the nation sinking, the great senate of the world confounded, our glorious designs betrayed and ruined, and the vast city all in flames; like *Nero*, unconcerned, I would sing my everlasting song of love to *Sylvia*; which no time or fortune shall untune. I know my soul, and all its strength, and how it is fortified, the charming *Idea* of my young *Sylvia* will for ever remain there; the original may fade; time may render it less fair, less blooming in my arms, but never in my soul; I shall find thee there the same gay glorious creature that first surprised and enslaved me, believe me ravishing maid, I shall. Why then, oh why, my cruel *Sylvia* are my joys delayed? Why am I by your rigorous commands kept from the sight of my heaven, my eternal bliss? An age, my fair tormentor, is past; four tedious live-long days are numbered over, since I beheld the object of my lasting vows, my eternal wishes; how can you think, oh unreasonable *Sylvia*! that I could live so long without you? And yet I am alive; I find it by my pain, by torments of fears and jealousies insupportable; I languish and go downward to the earth; where you will shortly see me laid without your recalling mercy. It is true, I move about this unregarded world, appear every day in the great senate-house, at clubs, cabals, and private consultations; (for *Sylvia* knows all the business of my soul, even in politics of State as well as love) I say I appear indeed, and give my voice in public business; but oh my heart more kindly is employed; that and my thoughts are *Sylvia*'s! Ten thousand times a day I breathe that name, my busy fingers are eternally tracing out those six mystic letters; a thousand ways on every thing I touch, form words, and make them speak a thousand things, and all are *Sylvia* still; my melancholy change is evident to all that see me, which they interpret many mistaken ways; our party fancy I repent my league with them, and doubting I'll betray the cause, grow jealous of me, till by new oaths, new arguments, I confirm them; then they smile all, and cry I am in love; and this they would believe, but that they see all women that I meet or converse with are indifferent to me, and so can fix it no where; for none can guess it *Sylvia*; thus while I dare not tell my soul, no not even to *Cesario*, the stifled flame burns inward, and torments me so, that (unlike the thing I was) I fear *Sylvia* will lose her love, and lover too; for those few charms she said I had, will fade, and this fatal distance will destroy both soul and body too; my very reason will abandon me, and I shall rave to see thee; restore me, oh restore me then to *Bellfont*, happy *Bellfont*, still blest with *Sylvia*'s presence! permit me, oh permit me into those sacred shades, where I have been so often (too innocently) blest! Let me survey again the dear character of *Sylvia* on the smooth birch; oh when shall I sit beneath those boughs, gazing on the young goddess of the grove, hearing her sigh for love, touching her glowing small white hands, beholding her killing eyes languish, and her charming bosom rise and fall with short-breath'd uncertain breath; breath as soft and sweet as the restoring breeze that glides o'er the new-blown flowers: But oh what is it? What heaven of perfumes, when it inclines to the ravish'd *Philander*, and whispers love it dares not name aloud?

What power with-holds me then from rushing on thee, from pressing thee with kisses; folding thee in my transported arms, and following all the dictates of love without respect or awe! What is it, oh my *Sylvia*, can detain a love so violent and raving, and so wild; admit me, sacred maid, admit me again to those soft delights, that I may find, if possible, what divinity (envious of my bliss) checks my eager joys, my raging flame; while you too make an experiment (worth the trial) what 'tis makes *Sylvia* deny her

Impatient adorer,

PHILANDER.

My page is ill, and I am oblig'd to trust Brilliard *with these to the dear cottage of their rendezvous; send me your opinion of his fidelity: and ah! remember I die to see you.*

To PHILANDER.

Not yet? — not yet? oh ye dull tedious hours, when will you glide away? and bring that happy moment on, in which I shall at least hear from my *Philander*; eight and forty tedious ones are past, and I am here forgotten still; forlorn, impatient, restless every where; not one of all your little moments (ye undiverting hours) can afford me repose; I drag ye on, a heavy load; I count ye all, and bless ye when you are gone; but tremble at the approaching ones, and with a dread expect you; and nothing will divert me now; my couch is tiresome, my glass is vain; my books are dull, and conversation insupportable; the grove affords me no relief; nor even those birds to whom I have so often breath'd *Philander*'s, name, they sing it on their perching boughs; no, nor the reviewing of his dear letters, can bring me any ease. Oh what fate is reserved for me! For thus I cannot live; nor surely thus I shall not die. Perhaps *Philander*'s making a trial of virtue by this silence. Pursue it, call up all your reason, my lovely brother, to your aid, let us be wise and silent, let us try what that will do towards the cure of this too infectious flame; let us, oh let us, my brother, sit down here, and pursue the crime of loving on no farther. Call me sister — swear I am so, and nothing but your sister: and forbear, oh forbear, my charming brother, to pursue me farther with your soft bewitching passion; let me alone, let me be ruin'd with honour, if I must be ruin'd. — For oh! 'twere much happier I were no more, than that I should be more than *Philander*'s sister; or he than *Sylvia*'s brother: oh let me ever call you by that cold name, 'till that of lover be forgotten:— ha! — Methinks on the sudden, a fit of virtue informs my soul, and bids me ask you for what sin of mine, my charming brother, you still pursue a maid that cannot fly: ungenerous and unkind! Why did you take advantage of those freedoms I gave you as a brother? I smil'd on you; and sometimes kiss'd you too; — but for my sister's sake, I play'd with you, suffer'd your hands and lips to wander where I dare not now; all which I thought a sister might allow a brother, and knew not all the while the treachery of love: oh none, but under that intimate title of a brother, could have had the opportunity to have ruin'd me; that, that betray'd me; I play'd away my heart at a game I did not understand; nor knew I when 'twas lost, by degrees so subtle, and an authority so lawful, you won me out of all. Nay then too, even when all was lost, I would not think it love. I wonder'd what my sleepless nights, my waking eternal thoughts, and slumbering visions of my lovely brother meant: I wonder'd why my soul was continually fill'd with wishes and new desires; and still concluded 'twas for my sister all, 'till I discover'd the cheat by jealousy; for when my sister hung upon your neck, kiss'd, and caress'd that face that I ador'd, oh how I found my colour change, my limbs all trembled, and my blood enrag'd, and I could scarce forbear reproaching you; or crying out, 'Oh why this fondness, brother? Sometimes you perceiv'd my concern, at which you'd smile; for you who had been before in love, (a curse upon the fatal time) could guess at my disorder; then would you turn the wanton play on me: when sullen with my jealousy and the cause, I fly your soft embrace, yet wish you would pursue and overtake me, which you ne'er fail'd to do, where after a kind quarrel all was pardon'd, and all was well again: while the poor injur'd innocent, my sister, made herself sport at our delusive wars; still I was ignorant, 'till you in a most fatal hour inform'd me I was a lover. Thus was it with my heart in those blest days of innocence; thus it was won and lost; nor can all my stars in heav'n prevent, I doubt, prevent my ruin. Now you are sure of the fatal conquest, you scorn the trifling glory, you are silent now; oh I am inevitably lost, or with you, or without you: and I find by this little silence and absence of yours, that 'tis most certain I must either die, or be *Philander*'s

SYLVIA.

If Dorillus *come not with a letter, or that my page, whom I have sent to this cottage for one, bring it not, I cannot support my life: for oh*, Philander, *I have a thousand wild distracting fears, knowing how you are involv'd in the interest you have espoused with the young* Cesario: *how danger surrounds you, how your life and glory depend on the frail sacrifice of villains and rebels: oh give me leave to fear eternally your fame and life, if not your love; If* Sylvia *could command*, Philander *should be loyal as he's noble; and what generous maid would not suspect his vows to a mistress, who breaks 'em with his prince and master! Heaven preserve you and your glory.*

....

To Philander.
Another night, oh heavens, and yet no letter come! Where are you,

my *Philander*? What happy place contains you? If in heaven, why does not some posting angel bid me haste after you? If on earth, why does not some little god of love bring the grateful tidings on his painted wings? If sick, why does not my own fond heart by sympathy inform me? But that is all active, vigorous, wishing, impatient of delaying, silent, and busy in imagination. If you are false, if you have forgotten your poor believing and distracted *Sylvia*, why does not that kind tyrant death, that meagre welcome vision of the despairing, old and wretched, approach in dead of night, approach my restless bed, and toll the dismal tidings in my frighted listening ears, and strike me for ever silent, lay me for ever quiet, lost to the world, lost to my faithless charmer! But if a sense of honour in you has made you resolve to prefer mine before your love, made you take up a noble fatal resolution, never to tell me more of your passion; this were a trial, I fear my fond heart wants courage to bear; or is it a trick, a cold fit, only assum'd to try how much I love you? I have no arts, heaven knows, no guile or double meaning in my soul, 'tis all plain native simplicity, fearful and timorous as children in the night, trembling as doves pursu'd; born soft by nature, and made tender by love; what, oh! what will become of me then? Yet would I were confirm'd in all my fears: for as I am, my condition is more deplorable; for I'm in doubt, and doubt is the worst torment of the mind: oh *Philander*, be merciful, and let me know the worst; do not be cruel while you kill, do it with pity to the wretched *Sylvia*; oh let me quickly know whether you are at all, or are the most impatient and unfortunate

SYLVIA's.

I rave, I die for some relief.

....

To PHILANDER.

As I was going to send away this enclos'd, *Dorillus* came with two letters; oh, you cannot think, *Philander*, with how much reason you call me fickle maid; for could you but imagine how I am tormentingly divided, how unresolved between violent love and cruel honour, you would say 'twere impossible to fix me any where; or be the same thing for a moment together: there is not a short hour pass'd through the swift hand of time, since I was all despairing, raging love, jealous, fearful, and impatient; and now, now that your fond letters have dispers'd those demons, those tormenting counsellors, and given a little respite, a little tranquillity to my soul; like states luxurious grown with ease, it ungratefully rebels against the sovereign power that made it great and happy; and now that traitor honour heads the mutineers within; honour, whom my late mighty fears had almost famish'd and brought to nothing, warm'd and reviv'd by thy new-protested flames, makes war against almighty love! and I, who but now nobly resolv'd for love, by an inconstancy natural to my sex, or rather my fears, am turn'd over to honour's side: so the despairing man stands on the river's bank, design'd to plunge into the rapid stream, 'till coward-fear seizing his timorous soul, he views around once more the flowery plains, and looks with wishing eyes back to the groves, then sighing stops, and cries, I was too rash, forsakes the dangerous shore, and hastes away. Thus indiscreet was I, was all for love, fond and undoing love! But when I saw it with full tide flow in upon me, one glance of glorious honour makes me again retreat. I will —— I am resolv'd —— and must be brave! I cannot forget I am daughter to the great *Beralti*, and sister to *Myrtilla*, a yet unspotted maid, fit to produce a race of glorious heroes! And can *Philander*'s love set no higher value on me than base poor prostitution? Is that the price of his heart? — Oh how I hate thee now! or would to heaven I could. — Tell me not, thou charming beguiler, that *Myrtilla* was to blame; was it a fault in her, and will it be virtue in me? And can I believe the crime that made her lose your heart, will make me mistress of it? No, if by any action of hers the noble house of the *Beralti* be dishonour'd, by all the actions of my life it shall receive additions and lustre and glory! Nor will I think *Myrtilla*'s virtue lessen'd for your mistaken opinion of it, and she may be as much in vain pursu'd, perhaps, by the Prince *Cesario*, as *Sylvia* shall be by the young *Philander*: the envying world talks loud, 'tis true; but oh, if all were true that busy babbler says, what lady has her fame? What husband is not a cuckold? Nay, and a friend to him that made him so? And it is in vain, my too subtle brother, you think to build the trophies of your conquests on the ruin of both *Myrtilla*'s fame and mine: oh how dear would your inglorious passion cost the great unfortunate house of the *Beralti*, while you poorly ruin the fame of *Myrtilla*, to make way to the heart of *Sylvia*! Remember, oh remember once your passion was as violent for *Myrtilla*, and all the vows, oaths, protestations, tears and prayers you make and pay at my feet, are but the faint repetitions, the feeble echoes of what you sigh'd out at hers. Nay, like young *Paris* fled with the fair prize, your fond, your eager passion made it a rape. Oh perfidious! — Let me not call it back to my remembrance. — Oh let me die, rather than call to mind a time so fatal; when the lovely false *Philander* vow'd his heart, his faithless heart away to any maid but *Sylvia*:— oh let it not be possible for me to imagine his dear arms ever grasping any body with joy but *Sylvia*! And yet they did, with transports of love! Yes, yes, you lov'd! by heaven you lov'd this false, this perfidious *Myrtilla*; for false she is; you lov'd her, and I'll have it so; nor shall the sister in me plead her cause. She is false beyond all pardon; for you are beautiful as heaven itself can render you, a shape exactly form'd, not too low, nor too tall, but made to beget soft desire and everlasting wishes in all that look on you; but your face! your lovely face, inclining to round, large piercing languishing black eyes, delicate proportion'd nose, charming dimpled mouth, plump red lips, inviting and swelling, white teeth, small and even, fine complexion, and a beautiful turn! All which you had an art to order in so engaging a manner, that it charm'd all the beholders, both sexes were undone with looking on you; and I have heard a witty man of your party swear, your face gain'd more to the League and association than the cause, and has curs'd a thousand times the false *Myrtilla*, for preferring *Cesario*! (less beautiful) to the adorable *Philander*; to add to this, heaven! how you spoke, when ere you spoke of love! in that you far surpass'd the young *Cesario*! as young as he, almost as great and glorious; oh perfidious *Myrtilla*, oh false, oh foolish and ingrate! — That you abandon'd her was just, she was not worth retaining in your heart, nor could be worth defending with your sword:— but grant her false; oh *Philander*! — How does her perfidy entitle you to me? False as she is, you still are married to her; inconstant as she is, she is still your wife; and no breach of the nuptial vow can untie the fatal knot; and that is a mystery to common sense: sure she was born for mischief; and fortune, when she gave her you, designed the ruin of us all; but most particularly *The unfortunate* Sylvia.

······················

To Sylvia.

My soul's eternal joy, my *Sylvia*! what have you done, and oh how durst you, knowing my fond heart, try it with so fatal a stroke? What means this severe letter? and why so eagerly at this time? Oh the day! Is *Myrtilla's* virtue so defended? Is it a question now whether she is false or not? Oh poor, oh frivolous excuse! You love me not; by all that's good, you love me not; to try your power you have flatter'd and feign'd, oh woman! false charming woman! you have undone me, I rave and shall commit such extravagance that will ruin both: I must upbraid you, fickle and inconstant, I must, and this distance will not serve, 'tis too great; my reproaches lose their force; I burst with resentment, with injur'd love; and you are either the most faithless of your sex, or the most malicious and tormenting: oh I am past tricks, my *Sylvia*, your little arts might do well in a beginning flame, but to a settled fire that is arriv'd to the highest degree, it does but damp its fierceness, and instead of drawing me on, would lessen my esteem, if any such deceit were capable to harbour in the heart of *Sylvia*; but she is all divine, and I am mistaken in the meaning of what she says. Oh my adorable, think no more on that dull false thing a wife; let her be banish'd thy thoughts, as she is my soul; let her never appear, though but in a dream, to fright our solid joys, or true happiness; no, let us look forward to pleasures vast and unconfin'd, to coming transports, and leave all behind us that contributes not to that heaven of bliss: remember, oh *Sylvia*, that five tedious days are past since I sigh'd at your dear feet; and five days, to a man so madly in love as your *Philander*, is a tedious age: 'tis now six o'clock in the morning, *Brilliard* will be with you by eight, and by ten I may have your permission to see you, and then I need not say how soon I will present myself before you at *Bellfont*; for heaven's sake, my eternal blessing, if you design me this happiness, contrive it so, that I may see no body that belongs to *Bellfont*, but the fair, the lovely *Sylvia*; for I must be more moments with you, than will be convenient to be taken notice of, lest they suspect our business to be love, and that discovery yet may ruin us. Oh! I will delay no longer, my soul is impatient to see you, I cannot live another night without it; I die, by heaven, I languish for the appointed hour; you will believe, when you see my languid face, and dying eyes, how much and greater a sufferer in love I am.

My soul's delight, you may perhaps deny me from your fear; but oh, do not, though I ask a mighty blessing; *Sylvia's* company alone, silent, and perhaps by dark:— oh, though I faint with the thought only of so bless'd an opportunity, yet you shall secure me, by what vows, what imprecations or ties you please; bind my busy hands, blind my ravish'd eyes, command my tongue, do what you will; but let me hear your angel's voice, and have the transported joy of throwing my self at your feet; and if you please, give me leave (a man condemned eternally to love) to plead a little for my life and passion; let me remove your fears; and though that mighty task never make me entirely happy, at least it will be a great satisfaction to me to know, that 'tis not through my own fault that I am the

Most wretched
PHILANDER.

I have order'd Brilliard *to wait your commands at* Dorillus's *cottage, that he may not be seen at* Bellfont: *resolve to see me to-night, or I shall come without order, and injure both: my dear, damn'd wife is dispos'd of at a ball* Cesario *makes to-night; the opportunity will be lucky, not that I fear her jealousy, but the effects of it.*

·····················

To PHILANDER.

I tremble with the apprehension of what you ask: how shall I comply with your fond desires? My soul bodes some dire effect of this bold enterprise, for I must own (and blush while I do own it) that my soul yields obedience to your soft request, and even whilst

I read your letter, was diverted with the contrivance of seeing you: for though, as my brother, you have all the freedoms imaginable at *Bellfont*, to entertain and walk with me, yet it would be difficult and prejudicial to my honour, to receive you alone any where without my sister, and cause a suspicion, which all about me now are very far from conceiving, except *Melinda*, my faithful confidante, and too fatal counsellor; and but for this fear, I know, my charming brother, three little leagues should not five long days separate *Philander* from his *Sylvia*: but, my lovely brother, since you beg it so earnestly, and my heart consents so easily, I must pronounce my own doom, and say, come, my *Philander*, whether love or soft desire invites you; and take this direction in the management of this mighty affair. I would have you, as soon as this comes to your hands, to haste to *Dorillus*'s cottage, without your equipage, only *Brilliard*, whom I believe you may trust, both from his own discretion, and your vast bounties to him; wait there 'till you receive my commands, and I will retire betimes to my apartment, pretending not to be well; and as soon as the evening's obscurity will permit, *Melinda* shall let you in at the *garden-gate*, that is next the *grove*, unseen and unsuspected; but oh, thou powerful charmer, have a care, I trust you with my all: my dear, dear, my precious honour, guard it well; for oh I fear my forces are too weak to stand your shock of beauties; you have charms enough to justify my yielding; but yet, by heaven I would not for an empire: but what is dull empire to almighty love? The god subdues the monarch; 'tis to your strength I trust, for I am a feeble woman, a virgin quite disarm'd by two fair eyes, an angel's voice and form; but yet I'll die before I'll yield my honour; no, though our unhappy family have met reproach from the imagined levity of my sister, 'tis I'll redeem the bleeding honour of our family, and my great parents' virtues shall shine in me; I know it, for if it passes this test, if I can stand this temptation, I am proof against all the world; but I conjure you aid me if I need it: if I incline but in a languishing look, if but a wish appear in my eyes, or I betray consent but in a sigh; take not, oh take not the opportunity, lest when you have done I grow raging mad, and discover all in the wild fit. Oh who would venture on an enemy with such unequal force? What hardy

fool would hazard all at sea, that sees the rising storm come rolling on? Who but fond woman, giddy heedless woman, would thus expose her virtue to temptation? I see, I know my danger, yet I must permit it: love, soft bewitching love will have it so, that cannot deny what my feebler honour forbids; and though I tremble with fear, yet love suggests, it will be an age to night: I long for my undoing; for oh I cannot stand the batteries of your eyes and tongue; these fears, these conflicts I have a thousand times a-day; it is pitiful sometimes to see me; on one hand a thousand *Cupids* all gay and smiling present *Philander* with all the beauties of his sex, with all the softness in his looks and language those gods of love can inspire, with all the charms of youth adorn'd, bewitching all, and all transporting; on the other hand, a poor lost virgin languishing and undone, sighing her willing rape to the deaf shades and fountains, filling the woods with cries, swelling the murmuring rivulets with tears, her noble parents with a generous rage reviling her, and her betray'd sister loading her bow'd head with curses and reproaches, and all about her looking forlorn and sad. Judge, oh judge, my adorable brother, of the vastness of my courage and passion, when even this deplorable prospect cannot defend me from the resolution of giving you admittance into my apartment this night, nor shall ever drive you from the soul of your
SYLVIA.

....

To SYLVIA.

I have obey'd my *Sylvia*'s dear commands, and the dictates of my own impatient soul; as soon as I receiv'd them, I immediately took horse for *Bellfont*, though I knew I should not see my adorable *Sylvia* 'till eight or nine at night; but oh 'tis wondrous pleasure to be so much more near my eternal joy; I wait at *Dorillus*'s cottage the tedious approaching night that must shelter me in its kind shades, and conduct me to a pleasure I faint but with imagining; 'tis now, my lovely charmer, three o'clock, and oh how many tedious hours I am to languish here before the blessed one arrive! I know you love, my *Sylvia*, and therefore must guess at some part of my torment, which yet is mix'd with a certain trembling joy, not to be imagin'd by any but *Sylvia*, who surely loves *Philander*; if there be truth in beauty, faith in youth, she surely loves him much; and much more above her sex she is capable of love, by how much more her soul is form'd of a softer and more delicate composition; by how much more her wit's refin'd and elevated above her duller sex, and by how much more she is oblig'd; if passion can claim passion in return, sure no beauty was ever so much indebted to a slave, as *Sylvia* to *Philander*; none ever lov'd like me: judge then my pains of love, my joys, my fears, my impatience and desires; and call me to your sacred presence with all the speed of love, and as soon as it is duskish, imagine me in the meadow behind the grove, 'till when think me employed in eternal thoughts of *Sylvia*, restless, and talking to the trees of *Sylvia*, sighing her charming name, circling with folded arms my panting heart, (that beats and trembles the more, the nearer it approaches the happy *Bellfont*) and fortifying the feeble trembler against a sight so ravishing and surprising; I fear to be sustain'd with life; but if I faint in *Sylvia*'s arms, it will be happier far than all the glories of life without her.

Send, my angel, something from you to make the hours less tedious: consider me, love me, and be as impatient as I, that you may the sooner find at your feet your everlasting lover, PHILANDER.

From Dorillus's *cottage.*

•••••••••••••••••••

To PHILANDER.

I have at last recover'd sense enough to tell you, I have receiv'd your letter by *Dorillus*, and which had like to have been discover'd; for he prudently enough put it under the strawberries he brought me in a basket, fearing he should get no other opportunity to have given it me; and my mother seeing them look so fair and fresh, snatch'd the basket with a greediness I have not seen in her before; whilst she was calling to her page for a porcelain dish to put them out, *Dorillus* had an opportunity to hint to me what lay at the bottom: heavens! had you seen my disorder and confusion; what should I do? Love had not one invention in store, and here it was that all the subtlety of women abandon'd me. Oh heavens, how cold and pale I grew, lest the most important business of my life should be betray'd and ruin'd! but not to terrify you longer with fears of my danger, the dish came, and out the strawberries were pour'd, and the basket thrown aside on the bank where my mother sat, (for we were in the garden when we met accidentally *Dorillus* first with the basket) there were some leaves of fern put at the bottom between the basket and letter, which by good fortune came not out with the strawberries, and after a minute or two I took up the basket, and walking carelessly up and down the garden, gather'd here and there a flower, pinks and jessamine, and filling my basket, sat down again 'till my mother had eat her fill of the fruit, and gave me an opportunity to retire to my apartment, where opening the letter, and finding you so near, and waiting to see me, I had certainly sunk down on the floor, had not *Melinda* supported me, who only was by; something so new, and 'till now so strange, seiz'd me at the thought of so secret an interview, that I lost all my senses, and life wholly departing, I rested on *Melinda* without breath or motion; the violent effects of love and honour, the impetuous meeting tides of the extremes of joy and fear, rushing on too suddenly, overwhelm'd my senses; and it was a pretty while before I recover'd strength to get to my cabinet, where a second time I open'd your letter, and read it again with a thousand changes of countenance, my whole mass of blood was in that moment so discompos'd, that I chang'd from an ague to a fever several times in a minute: oh what will all this bring me to? And where will the raging fit end? I die with that thought, my guilty pen slackens in my trembling hand, and I languish and fall over the un-employ'd paper; —— oh help me, some divinity —— or if you did — I fear I should be angry: oh *Philander*! a thousand passions and distracted thoughts crowd to get out, and make their soft complaints to thee; but oh they lose themselves with mixing; they are blended in a confusion together, and love nor art can divide them, to deal them out in order; sometimes I would tell you of my joy at your arrival, and my unspeaking transports at the thought of seeing you so soon, that I shall hear your charming voice, and find you at my feet making soft vows anew, with all the passion of an impatient lover, with all the eloquence that sighs and cries, and tears from those lovely eyes can express; and sure that is enough to conquer any where, and to which coarse vulgar words are dull. The rhetoric of love is half-breath'd, interrupted words, languishing eyes, flattering speeches, broken sighs, pressing the hand, and falling tears: ah how do they not persuade, how do they not charm and conquer; 'twas thus, with these soft easy arts, that *Sylvia* first was won; for sure no arts of speaking could have talked my heart away, though you can speak like any god: oh whither am I driven? What do I say? 'Twas not my purpose, not my business here, to give a character of *Philander*, no nor to speak of love; but oh! like *Cowley*'s lute, my soul will sound to nothing but to love: talk what you will, begin what discourse you please, I end it all in love, because my soul is ever fix'd on *Philander*, and insensibly its biass leads to that subject; no, I did not when I began to write, think of speaking one word of my own weakness; but to have told you with what resolv'd courage, honour and virtue, I expect your coming; and sure so sacred a thing as love was not made to ruin these, and therefore in vain, my lovely brother, you will attempt it; and yet, oh heavens! I gave a private assignation, in my apartment, alone and at night; where silence, love and shades, are all your friends, where opportunity obliges your passion, while, heaven knows, not one of all these, nor any kind of power, is friend to me; I shall be left to you and all these tyrants expos'd, without other guards than this boasted virtue; which had need be wondrous to resist all these powerful enemies of its purity and repose. Alas I know not its strength, I never tried it yet; and this will be the first time it has ever been expos'd to your power; the first time I ever had courage to meet you as a lover, and let you in by stealth, and put myself unguarded into your hands: oh I die with the apprehension of approaching danger! and yet I have not power to retreat; I must on, love compels me, love holds me fast; the smiling flatterer promises a thousand joys, a thousand ravishing minutes of delight; all innocent and harmless as his mother's doves; but oh they bill and kiss, and do a thousand things I must forbid *Philander*; for I have often heard him say with sighs, that his complexion render'd him less capable of the soft play of love, than any other lover: I have seen him fly my very touches, yet swear they were the greatest joy on earth; I tempt him even with my looks from virtue: and when I ask the cause, or cry he is cold, he vows 'tis because he dares not endure my temptations; says his blood runs hotter and fiercer in his veins than any other's does; nor have the oft repeated joys reaped in the marriage bed, any thing abated that which he wish'd, but he fear'd would ruin me: thus, thus whole days we have sat and gaz'd, and sigh'd; but durst not trust our virtues with fond dalliance.

My page is come to tell me that Madam the Duchess of —— is come to *Bellfont*, and I am oblig'd to quit my cabinet, but with infinite regret, being at present much more to my soul's content employ'd; but love must sometimes give place to *devoir* and respect. *Dorillus* too waits, and tells *Melinda* he will not depart without something for his lord, to entertain him till the happy hour. The rustic pleas'd me with the concern he had for my *Philander*; oh my charming brother, you have an art to tame even savages, a tongue that would charm and engage wildness itself, to softness and gentleness, and give the rough unthinking, love; 'tis a tedious time to-night, how shall I pass the hours?

....

To SYLVIA.

Say, fond love, whither wilt thou lead me? Thou hast brought me from the noisy hurries of the town, to charming solitude; from crowded cabals, where mighty things are resolving, to lonely groves; to thy own abodes where thou dwell'st; gay and pleas'd among the rural swains in shady homely cottages; thou hast brought me to a grove of flowers, to the brink of purling streams, where thou hast laid me down to contemplate on *Sylvia*, to think my tedious hours away in the softest imagination a soul inspir'd by love can conceive, to increase my passion by every thing I behold; for every sound that meets the sense is thy proper music, oh love, and every thing inspires thy dictates; the winds around me blow soft, and mixing with wanton boughs, continually play and kiss; while those, like a coy maid in love, resist, and comply by turns; they, like a ravish'd vigorous lover, rush on with a transported violence, rudely embracing their spring-dress'd mistress, ruffling her native order; while the pretty birds on the dancing branches incessantly make love; upbraiding duller man with his defective want of fire: man, the lord of all! He to be stinted in the most valuable joy of life; is it not pity? Here is no troublesome honour, amongst the pretty inhabitants of the woods and streams, fondly to give laws to nature, but uncontrolled they play, and sing, and love; no parents checking their dear delights, no slavish matrimonial ties to restrain their nobler flame. No spies to interrupt their blest appointments; but every little nest is free and open to receive the young fledg'd lover; every bough is conscious of their passion, nor do the generous pair languish in tedious ceremony; but meeting look, and like, and love, embrace with their wingy arms, and salute with their little opening bills; this is their courtship, this the amorous compliment, and this only the introduction to all their following happiness; and thus it is with the flocks and herds; while scanted man, born alone for the fatigues of love, with industrious toil, and all his boasting arts of eloquence, his god-like image, and his noble form, may labour on a tedious term of years, with pain, expense, and hazard, before he can arrive at happiness, and then too perhaps his vows are unregarded, and all his sighs and tears are vain. Tell me, oh you fellow-lovers, ye amorous dear brutes, tell me, when ever you lay languishing beneath your coverts, thus for your fair she, and durst not approach for fear of honour? Tell me, by a gentle bleat, ye little butting rams, do you sigh thus for your soft, white ewes? Do you lie thus conceal'd, to wait the coming shades of night, 'till all the cursed spies are folded? No, no, even you are much more blest than man, who is bound up to rules, fetter'd by the nice decencies of honour.

My divine maid, thus were my thoughts employ'd, when from the farthest end of the grove, where I now remain, I saw *Dorillus* approach with thy welcome letter; he tells, you had like to have been surpris'd in making it up; and he receiv'd it with much difficulty: ah *Sylvia*, should any accident happen to prevent my seeing you to-night, I were undone for ever, and you must expect to find me stretch'd out, dead and cold under this oak, where now I lie writing on its knotty root. Thy letter, I confess, is dear; it contains thy soul, and my happiness; by this after-story of the surprise I long to be inform'd of, for from thence I may gather part of my fortune. I rave and die with fear of a disappointment; not but I would undergo a thousand torments and deaths for *Sylvia*; but oh consider me, and let me not suffer if possible; for know, my charming angel, my impatient heart is almost broke, and will not contain itself without being nearer my adorable maid, without taking in at my eyes a little comfort; no, I am resolv'd; put me not off with tricks, which foolish honour invents to jilt mankind with; for if you do, by heaven I will forget all considerations and respect, and force myself with all the violence of raging love into the presence of my cruel *Sylvia*; own her mine, and ravish my delight; nor shall the happy walls of *Bellfont* be of strength sufficient to secure her; nay, persuade me not, for if you make me mad and raving, this will be the effects on't. —— Oh pardon me, my sacred maid, pardon the wildness of my frantic love — I paused, took a turn or two in the lone path, consider'd what I had said, and found it was too much, too bold, too rude to approach my soft, my tender maid: I am calm, my soul, as thy bewitching smiles; hush, as thy secret sighs, and will resolve to die rather than offend my adorable virgin; only send me word what you think of my fate, while I expect it here on this kind mossy bed where now I lie; which I would not quit for a throne, since here I may hope the news may soonest arrive to make me happier than a god! which that nothing on my part may prevent, I here vow in the face of heaven, I will not abuse the freedom my *Sylvia* blesses me with; nor shall my love go beyond the limits of honour. *Sylvia* shall command with a frown, and fetter me with a smile; prescribe rules to my longing, ravish'd eyes, and pinion my busy, fond, roving hands, and lay at her feet, like a tame slave, her adoring

PHILANDER.

....

To PHILANDER.

Approach, approach, you sacred Queen of Night, and bring

Philander veil'd from all eyes but mine; approach at a fond lover's call, behold how I lie panting with expectation, tir'd out with your tedious ceremony to the God of Day; be kind, oh lovely night, and let the deity descend to his beloved *Thetis*'s arms, and I to my *Philander*'s; the sun and I must snatch our joys in the same happy hours; favour'd by thee, oh sacred, silent Night! See, see, the enamour'd sun is hasting on apace to his expecting mistress, while thou dull Night art slowly lingering yet. Advance, my friend! my goddess! and my confidante! hide all my blushes, all my soft confusions, my tremblings, transports, and eyes all languishing.

Oh *Philander*! a thousand things I have done to divert the tedious hours, but nothing can; all things are dull without thee. I am tir'd with every thing, impatient to end, as soon as I begin them; even the shades and solitary walks afford me now no ease, no satisfaction, and thought but afflicts me more, that us'd to relieve. And I at last have recourse to my kind pen: for while I write, methinks I am talking to thee; I tell thee thus my soul, while thou, methinks, art all the while smiling and listening by; this is much easier than silent thought, and my soul is never weary of this converse; and thus I would speak a thousand things, but that still, methinks, words do not enough express my soul; to understand that right, there requires looks; there is a rhetoric in looks; in sighs and silent touches that surpasses all; there is an accent in the sound of words too, that gives a sense and soft meaning to little things, which of themselves are of trivial value, and insignificant; and by the cadence of the utterance may express a tenderness which their own meaning does not bear; by this I wou'd insinuate, that the story of the heart cannot be so well told by this way, as by presence and conversation; sure *Philander* understands what I mean by this, which possibly is nonsense to all but a lover, who apprehends all the little fond prattle of the thing belov'd, and finds an eloquence in it, that to a sense unconcern'd would appear even approaching to folly: but *Philander*, who has the true notions of love in him, apprehends all that can be said on that dear subject; to him I venture to say any thing, whose kind and soft imaginations can supply all my wants in the description of the soul: will it not, *Philander*? Answer me:— But oh, where art thou?

I see thee not, I touch thee not; but when I haste with transport to embrace thee, 'tis shadow all, and my poor arms return empty to my bosom: why, oh why com'st thou not? Why art thou cautious, and prudently waitest the slow-pac'd night: oh cold, oh unreasonable lover, why? — But I grow wild, and know not what I say: impatient love betrays me to a thousand follies, a thousand rashnesses: I die with shame; but I must be undone, and it is no matter how, whether by my own weakness, *Philander*'s charms, or both, I know not; but so it is destin'd — oh *Philander*, it is two tedious hours love has counted since you writ to me, yet are but a quarter of a mile distant; what have you been doing all that live-long while? Are you not unkind? Does not *Sylvia* lie neglected and unregarded in your thoughts? Huddled up confusedly with your graver business of State, and almost lost in the ambitious crowd? Say, say, my lovely charmer, is she not? Does not this fatal interest you espouse, rival your *Sylvia*? Is she not too often remov'd thence to let in that haughty tyrant mistress? Alas, *Philander*, I more than fear she is: and oh, my adorable lover, when I look forward on our coming happiness, whenever I lay by the thoughts of honour, and give a loose to love; I run not far in the pleasing career, before that dreadful thought stopp'd me on my way: I have a fatal prophetic fear, that gives a check to my soft pursuit, and tells me that thy unhappy engagement in this League, this accursed association, will one day undo us both, and part for ever thee and thy unlucky *Sylvia*; yes, yes, my dear lord, my soul does presage an unfortunate event from this dire engagement; nor can your false reasoning, your fancied advantages, reconcile it to my honest, good-natur'd heart; and surely the design is inconsistent with love, for two such mighty contradictions and enemies, as love and ambition, or revenge, can never sure abide in one soul together, at least love can but share *Philander*'s heart; when blood and revenge (which he miscalls glory) rivals it, and has possibly the greater part in it: methinks, this notion enlarges in me, and every word I speak, and every minute's thought of it, strengthens its reason to me; and give me leave (while I am full of the jealousy of it) to express my sentiments, and lay before you those reasons, that love and I think most substantial ones; what you have hitherto desired of me, oh unreasonable *Philander*, and what I (out of modesty and honour) denied, I have reason to fear (from the absolute conquest you have made of my heart) that some time or other the charming thief may break in and rob me of; for fame and virtue love begins to laugh at. My dear unfortunate condition being thus, it is not impossible, oh *Philander*, but I may one day, in some unlucky hour, in some soft bewitching moment, in some spiteful, critical, ravishing minute, yield all to the charming *Philander*; and if so, where, oh where is my security, that I shall not be abandon'd by the lovely victor? For it is not your vows which you call sacred (and I alas believe so) that can secure me, though I, heaven knows, believe them all, and am undone; you may keep them all too, and I believe you will; but oh *Philander*, in these fatal circumstances you have engag'd yourself, can you secure me my lover? Your protestations you may, but not the dear protestor. Is it not enough, oh *Philander*, for my eternal unquiet, and undoing, to know that you are married and cannot therefore be entirely mine; is not this enough, oh cruel *Philander*? But you must espouse a fatal cause too, more pernicious than that of matrimony, and more destructive to my repose: oh give me leave to reason with you, and since you have been pleas'd to trust and afflict me with the secret, which, honest as I am, I will never betray; yet, yet give me leave to urge the danger of it to you, and consequently to me, if you pursue it; when you are with me, we can think, and talk, and argue nothing but the mightier business of love; and it is fit that I, so fondly, and fatally lov'd by you, should warn you of the danger. Consider, my lord, you are born noble, from parents of untainted loyalty; blest with a fortune few princes beneath sovereignty are masters of; blest with all-gaining youth, commanding beauty, wit, courage, bravery of mind, and all that renders men esteem'd and ador'd: what would you more? What is it, oh my charming brother then, that you set up for? Is it glory? Oh mistaken, lovely youth, that glory is but a glittering light, that flashes for a moment, and then disappears; it is a false bravery, that will bring an eternal blemish upon your honest fame and house; render your honourable name hated, detested and abominable in story to after ages; a traitor! the worst of titles, the most inglorious and shameful; what has the King, our good, our gracious monarch, done to *Philander*? How disoblig'd him? Or indeed, what injury to mankind? Who has he oppress'd? Where play'd the tyrant or the ravisher? What one cruel or angry thing has he committed in all the time of his fortunate and peaceable reign over us? Whose ox or whose ass has he unjustly taken? What orphan wrong'd, or widow's tears neglected? But all his life has been one continued miracle; all good, all gracious, calm and merciful: and this good, this god-like King, is mark'd out for slaughter, design'd a sacrifice to the private revenge of a few ambitious knaves and rebels, whose pretence is the public good, and doomed to be basely murdered. A murder! even on the worst of criminals, carries with it a cowardice so black and infamous, as the most abject wretches, the meanest spirited creature has an abhorrence for. What! to murder a man unthinking, unwarn'd, unprepar'd and undefended! oh barbarous! oh poor and most unbrave! What villain is there lost to all humanity, to be found upon the face of the earth, that, when done, dare own so hellish a deed as the murder of the meanest of his fellow subjects, much less the sacred person of the king; the Lord's anointed; on whose awful face 'tis impossible to look without that reverence wherewith one would behold a god! For 'tis most certain, that every glance from his piercing, wondrous eyes, begets a trembling adoration; for my part, I swear to you, *Philander*, I never approach his sacred person, but my heart beats, my blood runs cold about me, and my eyes overflow with tears of joy, while an awful confusion seizes me all over; and I am certain should the most harden'd of your bloody rebels look him in the face, the devilish instrument of death would drop from his sacrilegious hand, and leave him confounded at the feet of the royal forgiving sufferer; his eyes have in them something so fierce, so majestic, commanding, and yet so good and merciful, as would soften rebellion itself into repenting loyalty; and like *Caius Marius*, seem to say — 'Who is it dares hurt the King?'— They alone, like his guardian angels, defend his sacred person: oh! what pity it is, unhappy young man, thy education was not near the King.

'Tis plain, 'tis reasonable, 'tis honest, great and glorious to believe, what thy own sense (if thou wilt but think and consider) will instruct thee in, that treason, rebellion and murder, are far from the paths that lead to glory, which are as distant as hell from heaven. What is it then to advance? (Since I say 'tis plain, glory is never this way to be achiev'd.) Is it to add more thousands to those fortune has already so lavishly bestow'd on you? Oh my *Philander*, that's to double the vast crime, which reaches already to damnation: would your honour, your conscience, your Christianity, or common humanity, suffer you to enlarge your fortunes at the price of another's ruin; and make the spoils of some honest, noble, unfortunate family, the rewards of your treachery? Would you build your fame on such a foundation? Perhaps on the destruction of some friend or kinsman. Oh barbarous and mistaken greatness; thieves and robbers would scorn such outrages, that had but souls and sense.

Is it for addition of titles? What elevation can you have much greater than where you now stand fix'd? If you do not grow giddy with your fancied false hopes, and fall from that glorious height you are already arrived to, and which, with the honest addition of loyalty, is of far more value and lustre, than to arrive at crowns by blood and treason. This will last; to ages last: while t'other will be ridicul'd to all posterity, short liv'd and reproachful here, infamous and accursed to all eternity.

Is it to make *Cesario* king? Oh what is *Cesario* to my *Philander*? If a monarchy you design, then why not this king, this great, this good, this royal forgiver? This, who was born a king, and born your king; and holds his crown by right of nature, by right of law, by right of heaven itself; heaven who has preserved him, and confirmed him ours, by a thousand miraculous escapes and sufferings, and indulged him ours by ten thousand acts of mercy, and endeared him to us by his wondrous care and conduct, by securing of peace, plenty, ease and luxurious happiness, over all the fortunate limits of his blessed kingdoms: and will you? Would you destroy this wondrous gift of heaven? This god-like king, this real good we now possess, for a most uncertain one; and with it the repose of all the happy nation? To establish a king without law, without right, without consent, without title, and indeed without even competent parts for so vast a trust, or so glorious a rule? One who never oblig'd the nation by one single act of goodness or valour, in all the course of his life; and who never signaliz'd himself to the advantage of one man of all the kingdom: a prince unfortunate in his principles and morals; and whose sole, single ingratitude to His Majesty, for so many royal bounties, honours, and glories heap'd upon him, is of itself enough to set any honest generous heart against him. What is it bewitches you so? Is it his beauty? Then *Philander* has a greater title than *Cesario*; and not one other merit has he, since in piety, chastity, sobriety, charity and honour, he as little excels, as in gratitude, obedience and loyalty. What then, my dear *Philander*? Is it his weakness? Ah, there's the argument: you all propose, and think to govern so soft a king: but believe me, oh unhappy *Philander*! Nothing is more ungovernable than a fool; nothing more obstinate, wilful, conceited, and cunning; and for his gratitude, let the world judge what he must prove to his servants, who has dealt so ill with his lord and master; how he must reward those that present him with a crown, who deals so ungraciously with him who gave him life, and who set him up an happier object than a monarch: no, no, *Philander*; he that can cabal, and contrive to dethrone a father, will find it easy to discard the wicked and hated instruments, that assisted him to mount it; decline him then, oh fond and deluded *Philander*, decline him early; for you of all the rest ought to do so, and not to set a helping hand to load him with honours, that chose you out from all the world to load with infamy: remember that; remember *Myrtilla*, and then renounce him; do not you contribute to the adorning of his unfit head with a diadem, the most glorious of ornaments, who unadorned yours with the most inglorious of all reproaches. Think of this, oh thou unconsidering noble youth; lay thy hand upon thy generous heart, and tell it all the fears, all the reasonings of her that loves thee more than life. A thousand arguments I could bring, but these few unstudied (falling in amongst my softer thoughts) I beg you will accept of, till I can more at large deliver the glorious argument to your soul; let this suffice to tell thee, that, like *Cassandra*, I rave and prophesy in vain; this association will be the eternal ruin of *Philander*; for let it succeed or not, either way thou art undone; if thou pursuest it, I must infallibly fall with thee, if I resolve to follow thy good or ill fortune; for you cannot intend love and ambition, *Sylvia* and *Cesario* at once: no, persuade me not; the title to one or t'other must be laid down, *Sylvia* or *Cesario* must be abandon'd: this is my fix'd resolve, if thy too powerful arguments convince not in spite of reason, for they can do it; thou hast the tongue of an angel, and the eloquence of a god, and while I listen to thy voice, I take all thou say'st for wondrous sense. — Farewell; about two hours hence I shall expect you at the gate that leads into the garden grove — adieu! Remember

SYLVIA.

....

To SYLVIA.

How comes my charming *Sylvia* so skilled in the mysteries of State? Where learnt her tender heart the notions of rigid business? Where her soft tongue, formed only for the dear language of love, to talk of the concerns of nations and kingdoms? 'Tis true, when I gave my soul away to my dear counsellor, I reserved nothing to myself, not even that secret that so concerned my life, but laid all at her mercy; my generous heart could not love at a less rate, than to lavish all and be undone for *Sylvia*; 'tis glorious ruin, and it pleases me, if it advance one single joy, or add one demonstration of my love to *Sylvia*; 'tis not enough that we tell those we love all they love to hear, but one ought to tell them too, every secret that we know, and conceal no part of that heart one has made a present of to the person one loves; 'tis a treason in love not to be pardoned: I am sensible, that when my story is told (and this happy one of my love shall make up the greatest part of my history) those that love not like me will be apt to blame me, and charge me with weakness, for revealing so great a trust to a woman, and amongst all that I shall do to arrive at glory, that will brand me with feebleness; but *Sylvia*, when lovers shall read it, the men will excuse me, and the maids bless me! I shall be a fond admired precedent for them to point out to their remiss reserving lovers, who will be reproached for not pursuing my example. I know not what opinion men generally have of the weakness of women; but 'tis sure a vulgar error, for were they like my adorable *Sylvia*, had they had her wit, her vivacity of spirit, her courage, her generous fortitude, her command in every graceful look and action, they were most certainly fit to rule and reign; and man was only born robust and strong, to secure them on those thrones they are formed (by beauty, softness, and a thousand charms which men want) to possess. Glorious woman was born for command and dominion; and though custom has usurped us the name of rule over all; we from the beginning found ourselves (in spite of all our boasted prerogative) slaves and vassals to the almighty sex. Take then my share of empire, ye gods; and give me love! Let me toil to gain, but let *Sylvia* triumph and reign; I ask no more than the led slave at her chariot wheels, to gaze on my charming conqueress, and wear with joy her fetters! Oh how proud I should be to see the dear victor of my soul so elevated, so adorn'd with crowns and sceptres at her feet, which I had won; to see her smiling on the adoring crowd, distributing her glories to young waiting princes; there dealing provinces, and there a coronet. Heavens! methinks I see the lovely virgin in this state, her chariot slowly driving through the multitude that press to gaze upon her, she dress'd like *Venus*, richly gay and loose, her hair and robe blown by the flying winds, discovering a thousand charms to view; thus the young goddess looked, then when she drove her chariot down descending clouds, to meet the love-sick gods in cooling shades; and so would look my *Sylvia*! Ah, my soft, lovely maid; such thoughts as these fir'd me with ambition: for me, I swear by every power that made me love, and made thee wondrous fair, I design no more by this great enterprise than to make thee some glorious thing, elevated above what we have seen yet on earth; to raise thee above fate or fortune, beyond that pity of thy duller sex, who understand not thy soul, nor can ever reach the flights of thy generous love! No, my soul's joy, I must not leave thee liable to their little natural malice and scorn, to the impertinence of their reproaches. No, my *Sylvia*, I must on, the great design must move forward; though I abandon it, 'twill advance; it is already too far to put a stop to it; and now I am entered, it is in vain to retreat; if we are prosperous, it will to all ages be called a glorious enterprise; but if we fail, it will be base, horrid and infamous; for the world judges of nothing but by the success; that cause is always good that is prosperous, that is ill which is unsuccessful. Should I now retreat, I run many hazards; but to go on I run but one; by the first I shall alarm the whole cabal with a jealousy of my discovering, and those are persons of too great sense and courage, not to take some private way of revenge, to secure their own stakes; and to make myself uncertainly safe by a discovery, indeed, were to gain a refuge so ignoble, as a man of honour would scorn to purchase life at; nor would that baseness secure me. But in going on, oh *Sylvia*! when three kingdoms shall lie unpossess'd, and be exposed, as it were, amongst the raffling crowd, who knows but the chance may be mine, as well as any other's, who has but the same hazard, and throw for it? If the strongest sword must do it, (as that must do it) why not mine still? Why may not mine be that fortunate one? *Cesario* has no more right to it than *Philander*; 'tis true, a few of the rabble will pretend he has a better title to it, but they are a sort of easy fools, lavish in nothing but noise and nonsense; true to change and inconstancy, and will abandon him to their own fury for the next that cries Haloo: neither is there one part of fifty (of the fools that cry him up) for his interest, though they use him for a tool to work with, he being the only great man that wants sense enough to find out the cheat which they dare impose upon. Can any body of reason believe, if they had design'd him good, they would let him bare-fac'd have own'd a party so opposite to all laws of nature, religion, humanity, and common gratitude? When his interest, if design'd, might have been carried on better, if he had still dissembled and stay'd in Court: no, believe me, *Sylvia*, the politicians shew him, to render him odious to all men of tolerable sense of the party; for what reason soever they have who are disoblig'd (or at least think themselves so) to set up for liberty, the world knows *Cesario* renders himself the worst of criminals by it, and has abandon'd an interest more glorious and easy than empire, to side with and aid people that never did, or ever can oblige him; and he is so dull as to imagine that for his sake, who never did us service or good, (unless cuckolding us be good) we should venture life and fame to pull down a true monarch, to set up his bastard over us. *Cesario* must pardon me, if I think his politics are shallow as his parts, and that his own interest has undone him; for of what advantage soever the design may be to us, it really shocks one's nature to find a son engag'd against a father, and to him such a father. Nor, when time comes, shall I forget the ruin of *Myrtilla*. But let him hope on — and so will I, as do a thousand more, for ought I know; I set out as fair as they, and will start as eagerly; if I miss it now, I have youth and vigour sufficient for another race; and while I stand on fortune's wheel as she rolls it round, it may be my turn to be o'th' top; for when 'tis set in motion, believe me, *Sylvia*, it is not easily fix'd: however let it suffice, I am now in, past a retreat, and to urge it now to me, is but to put me into inevitable danger; at best it can but set me where I was; that is worse than death. When every fool is aiming at a kingdom, what man of tolerable pride and ambition can be unconcerned, and not put himself into a posture of catching, when a diadem shall be thrown among the crowd? It were insensibility, stupid dullness, not to lift a hand, or make an effort to snatch it as it flies: though the glorious falling weight should crush me, it is great to attempt; and if fortune do not favour fools, I have as fair a grasp for it as any other adventurer.

This, my *Sylvia*, is my sense of a business you so much dread; I may rise, but I cannot fall; therefore, my *Sylvia*, urge it no more; love gave me ambition, and do not divert the glorious effects of your wondrous charms, but let them grow, and spread, and see what they will produce for my lovely *Sylvia*, the advantages will most certainly be hers:— But no more: how came my love so dull to entertain thee so many minutes thus with reasons for an affair, which one soft hour with *Sylvia* will convince to what she would have it; believe me, it will, I will sacrifice all to her repose, nay, to her least command, even the life of

(My eternal pleasure) Your PHILANDER.

I have no longer patience, I must be coming towards the grove, though it will do me no good, more than knowing I am so much nearer to my adorable creature.

I conjure you burn this, for writing in haste I have not counterfeited my hand.

....

To SYLVIA. *Writ in a pair of tablets.*

My charmer, I wait your commands in the meadow behind the grove, where I saw *Dorinda*, *Dorillus* his daughter, entering with a basket of cowslips for *Sylvia*, unnecessarily offering sweets to the Goddess of the Groves, from whence they (with all the rest of their gaudy fellows of the spring) assume their ravishing odours. I take every opportunity of telling my *Sylvia* what I have so often repeated, and shall be ever repeating with the same joy while I live, that I love my *Sylvia* to death and madness; that my soul is on the rack, till she send me the happy advancing word. And yet believe me, lovely maid, I could grow old with waiting here the blessed moment, though set at any distance (within the compass of life, and impossible to be 'till then arriv'd to) but when I am so near approach'd it, love from all parts rallies and hastens to my heart for the mighty encounter, 'till the poor panting over-loaded victim dies with the pressing weight. No more — You know it, for it is, and will be eternally *Sylvia*'s.

POSTSCRIPT.

Remember, my adorable, it is now seven o'clock: I have my watch in my hand, waiting and looking on the slow pac'd minutes. Eight will quickly arrive, I hope, and then it is dark enough to hide me; think where I am, and who I am, waiting near Sylvia, *and her* Philander.

I think, my dear angel, you have the other key of these tablets, if not, they are easily broke open: you have an hour good to write in, Sylvia *and I shall wait unemployed by any thing but thought. Send me word how you were like to have been surpris'd; it may possibly be of advantage to me in this night's dear adventure. I wonder'd at the superscription of my letter indeed, of which* Dorillus *could give me no other account, than that you were surpris'd, and he receiv'd it with difficulty; give me the story now, do it in charity my angel. Besides, I would employ all thy moments, for I am jealous of every one that is not dedicated to* Sylvia's Philander.

....

To PHILANDER.

I have received your tablets, of which I have the key, and heaven only knows (for lovers cannot, unless they loved like *Sylvia*, and her *Philander*) what pains and pantings my heart sustain'd at every thought they brought me of thy near approach; every moment I start, and am ready to faint with joy, fear, and something not to be express'd that seizes me. To add to this, I have busied myself with dressing my apartment up with flowers, so that I fancy the ceremonious business of the light looks like the preparations for the dear joy of the nuptial bed; that too is so adorn'd and deck'd with all that's sweet and gay; all which possesses me with so ravishing and solemn a confusion, that it is even approaching to the most profound sadness itself. Oh *Philander*, I find I am fond of being undone; and unless you take a more than mortal care of me, I know this night some fatal mischief will befall me; what it is I know not, either the loss of *Philander*, my life, or my honour, or all together, which a discovery only of your being alone in my apartment, and at such an hour, will most certainly draw upon us: death is the least we must expect, by some surprise or other, my father being rash, and extremely jealous, and the more so of me, by how much more he is fond of me, and nothing would enrage him like the discovery of an interview like this; though you have liberty to range the house of *Bellfont* as a son, and are indeed at home there; but when you come by stealth, when he shall find his son and virgin daughter, the brother and the sister so retired, so entertained — What but death can ensue? Or what is worse, eternal shame? Eternal confusion on my honour? What excuse, what evasions, vows and protestations will convince him, or appease *Myrtilla*'s jealousy; *Myrtilla*, my sister, and *Philander*'s wife? Oh God! that cruel thought will put me into ravings; I have a thousand streams of killing reflections which flow from that original fountain! Curse on the alliance, that gave you a welcome to *Bellfont*. Ah *Philander*, could you not have stay'd ten short years longer? Alas, you thought that was an age in youth, but it is but a day in love: Ah, could not your eager youth have led you to a thousand diversions, a thousand times have baited in the long journey of life, without hurrying on to the last stage, to the last retreat, but the grave; and to me seem as irrecoverable, as impossible to retrieve thee! — Could no kind beauty stop thee on thy way, in charity or pity; *Philander* saw me then. And though *Myrtilla* was more fit for his caresses, and I but capable to please with childish prattle; oh could he not have seen a promising bloom in my face, that might have foretold the future conquests I was born to make? Oh! was there no prophetic charm that could bespeak your heart, engage it, and prevent that fatal marriage? You say, my adorable brother, we were destined from our creation for one another; that the decrees of heaven, or fate, or both, design'd us for this mutual passion: why then, oh why did not heaven, fate or destiny, do the mighty work, when first you saw my infant charms? But oh, *Philander*, why do I vainly rave? Why call in vain on time that's fled and gone? Why idly wish for ten years' retribution? That will not yield a day, an hour, a minute: no, no, 'tis past, 'tis past and flown for ever, as distant as a thousand years to me, as irrecoverable. Oh *Philander*, what hast thou thrown away? Ten glorious years of ravishing youth, of unmatch'd heavenly beauty, on one that knew not half the value of it! *Sylvia* was only born to set a rate upon it, was only capable of love, such love as might deserve it: oh why was that charming face ever laid on any bosom that knew not how to sigh, and pant, and heave at every touch of so much distracting beauty? Oh why were those dear arms, whose soft pressings ravish where they circle, destin'd for a body cold and dull, that could sleep insensibly there, and not so much as dream the while what the transporting pleasure signified; but unconcerned receive the wondrous blessing, and never knew its price, or thank'd her stars? She has thee all the day to gaze upon, and yet she lets thee pass her careless sight, as if there were no miracles in view: she does not see the little gods of love that play eternally in thy eyes; and since she never received a dart from thence, believes there's no artillery there. She plays not with thy hair, nor weaves her snowy fingers in the curls of jet, sets it in order, and adores its beauty: the fool with flaxen-wig had done as well for her; a dull, white coxcomb had made as good a property; a husband is no more, at best no more. Oh thou charming object of my eternal wishes, why wert thou thus dispos'd? Oh save my life, and tell me what indifferent impulse obliged thee to these nuptials: had *Myrtilla* been recommended or forc'd by the tyranny of a father into thy arms, or for base lucre thou hadst chosen her, this had excus'd thy youth and crime; obedience or vanity I could have pardon'd — but oh —'twas love; love, my *Philander*! thy raving love, and that which has undone thee was a rape rather than marriage; you fled with her. Oh heavens, mad to possess, you stole the unloving prize! — Yes, you lov'd her, false as you are, you did; perjur'd and faithless. Lov'd her? — Hell and confusion on the word; it was so — Oh *Philander*, I am lost —

This letter was found torn in pieces.

••••••••••••••••••

To Monsieur, the Count of —

My Lord, These pieces of paper, which I have put together as well as I could, were writ by my lady to have been sent by *Dorinda*, when on a sudden she rose in rage from her seat, tore first the paper, and then her robes and hair, and indeed nothing has escaped the violence of her passion; nor could my prayers or tears retrieve them, or calm her: 'tis however chang'd at last to mighty passions of weeping, in which employment I have left her on her repose, being commanded away. I thought it my duty to give your lordship this account, and to send the pieces of paper, that your lordship may guess at the occasion of the sudden storm which ever rises in that fatal quarter; but in putting them in order, I had like to have been surprised by my lady's father; for my Lord, the Count, having long solicited me for favours, and taking all opportunities of entertaining me, found me alone in my chamber, employ'd in serving your lordship; I had only time to hide the papers, and to get rid of him, having given him an assignation to-night in the garden grove, to give him the hearing to what he says he has to propose to me: pray heaven all things go right to your lordship's wish this evening, for many ominous things happen'd to-day. Madam, the Countess, had like to have taken a letter writ for your lordship to-day; for the Duchess of —— coming to make her a visit, came on a sudden with her into my lady's apartment, and surpris'd her writing in her dressing room, giving her only time to slip the paper into her combbox. The first ceremonies being pass'd, as Madam, the Duchess, uses not much, she fell to commend my lady's dressing-plate, and taking up the box, and opening it, found the letter, and laughing, cried, 'Oh, have I found you making love;' at which my lady, with an infinite confusion, would have retrieved it — but the Duchess not quitting her hold, cried —'Nay, I am resolved to see in what manner you write to a lover, and whether you have a heart tender or cruel?' At which she began to read aloud, my lady to blush and change colour a hundred times in a minute: I ready to die with fear; Madam the Countess, in infinite amazement, my lady interrupting every word the Duchess read, by prayers and entreaties, which heightened her curiosity, and being young and airy, regarded not the indecency to which she preferr'd her curiosity, who still laughing, cried she was resolv'd to read it out, and know the constitution of her heart; when my lady, whose wit never fail'd her, cried, 'I beseech you, madam, let us have so much complaisance for *Melinda* as to ask her consent in this affair, and then I am pleas'd you should see what love I can make upon occasion:' I took the hint, and with a real confusion, cried —'I implore you, madam, not to discover my weakness to Madam, the Duchess; I would not for the world — be thought to love so passionately, as your ladyship, in favour of *Alexis*, has made me profess, under the name of *Sylvia* to *Philander*'. This encouraged my lady, who began to say a thousand pleasant things of *Alexis*, *Dorillus* his son, and my lover, as your lordship knows, and who is no inconsiderable fortune for a maid, enrich'd only by your lordship's bounty. My lady, after this, took the letter, and all being resolv'd it should be read, she herself did it, and turned it so prettily into burlesque love by her manner of reading it, that made Madam, the Duchess, laugh extremely; who at the end of it, cried to my lady —'Well, madam, I am satisfied you have not a heart wholly insensible of love, that could so express it for another.' Thus they rallied on, till careful of my lover's repose, the Duchess urg'd the letter might be immediately sent away; at which my lady readily folding up the letter, writ '*For the Constant* Alexis', on the outside: I took it, and begg'd I might have leave to retire to write it over in my own hand; they

permitted me, and I carried it, after sealing it, to *Dorillus*, who waited
for it, and wondering to find his son's name on it, cried 'Mistress,
Melinda, I doubt you have mistook my present business; I wait for
a letter from my lady to my lord, and you give me one from yourself
to my son *Alexis*; 'twill be very welcome to *Alexis* I confess, but
at this time I had rather oblige my lord than my son:' I laughing
replied, he was mistaken, that *Alexis*, at this time, meant no other
than my lord, which pleas'd the good man extremely, who thought it
a good omen for his son, and so went his way satisfied; as every body
was, except the Countess, who fancied something more in it than
my lady's inditing for me; and after Madam the Duchess was gone,
she went ruminating and pensive to her chamber, from whence I am
confident she will not depart to-night, and will possibly set spies in
every corner; at least 'tis good to fear the worst, that we may prevent
all things that would hinder this night's assignation: as soon as the
coast is clear, I'll wait on your lordship, and be your conductor, and
in all things else am ready to shew myself,

My Lord,
Your lordship's most humble and most obedient servant,
MELINDA.

Sylvia *has given orders to wait on your lordship as soon as all is*
clear.

....

To MELINDA.

Oh *Melinda*, what have you told me? Stay me with an immediate
account of the recovery and calmness of my adorable weeping *Sylvia*,
or I shall enter *Bellfont* with my sword drawn, bearing down all
before me, 'till I make my way to my charming mourner: O God!
Sylvia in a rage! *Sylvia* in any passion but that of love? I cannot bear
it, no, by heaven I cannot; I shall do some outrage either on myself
or at *Bellfont*. Oh thou dear advocate of my tenderest wishes, thou
confidante of my never dying flame, thou kind administering maid,
send some relief to my breaking heart — haste and tell me, *Sylvia*
is calm, that her bright eyes sparkle with smiles, or if they languish,

say 'tis with love, with expecting joys; that her dear hands are no more employed in exercises too rough and unbecoming their native softness. O eternal God! tearing perhaps her divine hair, brighter than the sun's reflecting beams, injuring the heavenly beauty of her charming face and bosom, the joy and wish of all mankind that look upon her: oh charm her with prayers and tears, stop her dear fingers from the rude assaults; bind her fair hands; repeat *Philander* to her, tell her he's fainting with the news of her unkindness and outrage on her lovely self; but tell her too, I die adoring her; tell her I rave, I tear, I curse myself — for so I do; tell her I would break out into a violence that should set all *Bellfont* in a flame, but for my care of her. Heaven and earth should not restrain me — no, they should not —— But her least frown should still me, tame me, and make me a calm coward: say this, say all, say any thing to charm her rage and tears. Oh I am mad, stark-mad, and ready to run on business I die to think her guilty of: tell her how it would grieve her to see me torn and mangled; to see that hair she loves ruffled and diminish'd by rage, violated by my insupportable grief, myself quite bereft of all sense but that of love, but that of adoration for my charming, cruel insensible, who is possessed with every thought, with every imagination that can render me unhappy, borne away with every fancy that is in disfavour of the wretched *Philander*. Oh *Melinda*, write immediately, or you will behold me enter a most deplorable object of pity.

When I receiv'd yours, I fell into such a passion that I forc'd myself back to *Dorillus* his house, left my transports and hurried me to *Bellfont*, where I should have undone all: but as I can now rest no where, I am now returning to the meadow again, where I will expect your aid, or die.

From Dorillus *his cottage, almost nine o'clock.*

·····················

To PHILANDER.

I must own, my charming *Philander*, that my love is now arrived to that excess, that every thought which before but discompos'd me, now puts me into a violence of rage unbecoming my sex; or any thing but the mighty occasion of it, love, and which only had power to calm what it had before ruffled into a destructive storm: but like the anger'd sea, which pants and heaves, and retains still an uneasy motion long after the rude winds are appeas'd and hush'd to silence; my heart beats still, and heaves with the sensible remains of the late dangerous tempest of my mind, and nothing can absolutely calm me but the approach of the all-powerful *Philander*; though that thought possesses me with ten thousand fears, which I know will vanish all at thy appearance, and assume no more their dreadful shapes till thou art gone again: bring me then that kind cessation, bring me my *Philander*, and set me above the thoughts of cares, frights, or any other thoughts but those of tender love; haste then, thou charming object of my eternal wishes, and of my new desires; haste to my arms, my eyes, my soul — but oh, be wondrous careful there, do not betray the easy maid that trusts thee amidst all her sacred store.

'Tis almost dark, and my mother is retired to her chamber, my father to his cabinet, and has left all that apartment next the garden wholly without spies. I have, by trusty *Dorillus*, sent you a key *Melinda* got made to the door, which leads from the garden to the black-stairs to my apartment, so carefully locked, and the original key so closely guarded by my jealous father: that way I beg you to come; a way but too well known to *Philander*, and by which he has made many an escape to and from *Myrtilla*. Oh damn that thought, what makes it torturing me —— let me change it for those of *Philander*, the advantage will be as great as bartering hell for heaven; haste then, *Philander*: but what need I bid thee, love will lend thee his wings; thou who commandest all his artillery, put them on, and fly to thy languishing

SYLVIA.

Oh I faint with the dear thought of thy approach.

....

To the Charming SYLVIA.

With much ado, with many a sigh, a panting heart, and many a languishing look back towards happy *Bellfont*, I have recovered

Dorillus his farm, where I threw me on a bed, and lay without motion, and almost without life for two hours; till at last, through all my sighs, my great concern, my torment, my love and rage broke silence, and burst into all the different complaints both soft and mad by turns, that ever possessed a soul extravagantly seized with frantic love; ah, *Sylvia*, what did not I say? How did I not curse, and who except my charming maid? For yet my *Sylvia* is a maid: yes, yes, ye envying powers, she is, and yet the sacred and inestimable treasure was offered a trembling victim to the overjoyed and fancied deity, for then and there I thought myself happier than a triumphing god; but having overcome all difficulties, all the fatigues and toils of love's long sieges, vanquish'd the mighty phantom of the fair, the giant honour, and routed all the numerous host of women's little reasonings, passed all the bounds of peevish modesty; nay, even all the loose and silken counterscarps that fenced the sacred fort, and nothing stopped my glorious pursuit: then, then, ye gods, just then, by an over-transport, to fall just fainting before the surrendering gates, unable to receive the yielding treasure! Oh *Sylvia*! What *demon*, malicious at my glory, seized my vigour? What god, envious of my mighty joy, rendered me a shameful object of his raillery? Snatched my (till then) never failing power, and left me dying on thy charming bosom. Heavens, how I lay! Silent with wonder, rage and ecstasy of love, unable to complain, or rail, or storm, or seek for ease, but with my sighs alone, which made up all my breath; my mad desires remained, but all inactive, as age or death itself, as cold and feeble, as unfit for joy, as if my youthful fire had long been past, or *Sylvia* had never been blest with charms. Tell me, thou wondrous perfect creature, tell me, where lay the hidden witchcraft? Was *Sylvia*'s beauty too divine to mix with mortal joys? Ah no, 'twas ravishing, but human all. Yet sure 'twas so approaching to divinity, as changed my fire to awful adoration, and all my wanton heat to reverent contemplation. — But this is nonsense all, it was something more that gave me rage, despair and torments insupportable: no, it was no dull devotion, tame divinity, but mortal killing agony, unlucky disappointment, unnatural impotence. Oh! I am lost, enchanted by some magic spell: oh, what can *Sylvia* say? What can she think of my fond passion; she'll swear it is all a cheat, I had it not. No, it could not be; such tales I've often heard, as often laughed at too, of disappointed lovers; would *Sylvia* believe (as sure she may) mine was excess of passion: what! My *Sylvia*! being arrived to all the joy of love, just come to reap the glorious recompense, the full reward, the heaven for all my sufferings, do I lie gazing only, and no more? A dull, a feeble unconcerned admirer! Oh my eternal shame! — Curse on my youth; give me, ye powers, old age, for that has some excuse, but youth has none: 'tis dullness, stupid insensibility: where shall I hide my head when this lewd story's told? When it shall be confirmed, *Philander* the young, the brisk and gay *Philander*, who never failed the woman he scarce wished for, never baulked the amorous conceited old, nor the ill-favoured young, yet when he had extended in his arms the young, the charming fair and longing *Sylvia*, the untouched, unspotted, and till then, unwishing lovely maid, yielded, defenceless, and unguarded all, he wanted power to seize the trembling prey: defend me, heaven, from madness. Oh *Sylvia*, I have reflected on all the little circumstances that might occasion this disaster, and damn me to this degree of coldness, but I can fix on none: I had, it is true, for *Sylvia*'s sake, some apprehensions of fear of being surprised; for coming through the garden, I saw at the farther end a man, at least I fancied by that light it was a man; who perceiving the glimpse of something approach from the grove, made softly towards me, but with such caution, as if he feared to be mistaken in the person, as much as I was to approach him: and reminding what *Melinda* told me, of an assignation she had made to *Monsieur* the Count — imagined it him; nor was I mistaken when I heard his voice calling in low tone —'*Melinda*' — at which I mended my pace, and ere he got half way the garden recovered the door, and softly unlocking it, got in unperceived, and fastened it after me, well enough assured that he saw not which way I vanished: however, it failed not to alarm me with some fears on your dear account, that disturbed my repose, and which I thought then not necessary to impart to you, and which indeed all vanished at the sight of my adorable maid: when entering thy apartment, I beheld thee extended on a bed of roses, in garments, which, if possible, by their wanton loose negligence and gaiety, augmented thy natural charms: I trembling fell on my knees by your bed-side and gazed a while, unable to speak for transports of joy and love: you too were silent, and remained so, so long that I ventured to press your lips with mine, which all their eager kisses could not put in motion, so that I feared you fainted; a sudden fright, that in a moment changed my fever of love into a cold ague fit; but you revived me with a sigh again, and fired me anew, by pressing my hand, and from that silent soft encouragement, I, by degrees, ravished a thousand blisses; yet still between your tempting charming kisses, you would cry —'Oh, my *Philander*, do not injure me — be sure you press me not to the last joys of love — Oh have a care, or I am undone for ever: restrain your roving hands —— Oh whither would they wander? —— My soul, my joy, my everlasting charmer, oh whither would you go?'— Thus with a thousand cautions more, which did but raise what you designed to calm, you made me but the madder to possess: not all the vows you bid me call to mind, could now restrain my wild and headstrong passion; my raving, raging (but my soft) desire: no, *Sylvia*, no, it was not in the power of feeble flesh and blood to find resistance against so many charms; yet still you made me swear, still I protested, but still burnt on with the same torturing flame, till the vast pleasure even became a pain: to add to this, I saw, (yes, *Sylvia*, not all your art and modesty could hide it) I saw the ravishing maid as much inflamed as I; she burnt with equal fire, with equal languishment: not all her care could keep the sparks concealed, but it broke out in every word and look; her trembling tongue, her feeble fainting voice betrayed it all; sighs interrupting every syllable; a languishment I never saw till then dwelt in her charming eyes, that contradicted all her little vows; her short and double breathings heaved her breast, her swelling snowy breast, her hands that grasped me trembling as they closed, while she permitted mine unknown, unheeded to traverse all her beauties, till quite forgetting all I had faintly promised, and wholly abandoning my soul to joy, I rushed upon her, who, all fainting, lay beneath my useless weight, for on a sudden all my power was fled, swifter than lightning hurried through my enfeebled veins, and vanished all: not the dear lovely beauty which I pressed, the dying charms of that fair face and eyes, the clasps of those soft arms, nor the bewitching accent of her voice, that murmured love half smothered in her sighs, nor all my love, my vast, my mighty passion, could call my fugitive vigour back again: oh no, the more I looked — the more I touched and saw, the more I was undone. Oh pity me, my too I too lovely maid, do not revile the faults which you alone create. Consider all your charms at once exposed, consider every sense about me ravished, overcome with joys too mighty to be supported, no wonder if I fell a shameful sacrifice to the fond deity: consider how I waited, how I strove, and still I burnt on, and every tender touch still added fuel to the vigorous fire, which by your delay consumed itself in burning. I want philosophy to make this out, or faith to fix my unhappiness on any chance or natural accident; but this, my charming *Sylvia*, I am sure, that had I loved you less, I'd been less wretched: nor had we parted, *Sylvia*, on so ill terms, nor had I left you with an opinion so disadvantageous for *Philander*, but for that unhappy noise at your chamber-door, which alarming your fear, occasioned your recovery from that dear trance, to which love and soft desire had reduced you, and me from the most tormenting silent agony that disappointed joy ever possessed a fond expecting heart with. Oh heavens! to have my *Sylvia* in my power, favoured by silence, night and safe retreat! then, then, to lie a tame cold sigher only, as if my *Sylvia* gave that assignation alone by stealth, undressed, all loose and languishing, fit for the mighty business of the night, only to hear me prattle, see me gaze, or tell her what a pretty sight it was to see the moon shine through the dancing boughs. Oh damn my hardened dullness! — But no more — I am all fire and madness at the thought — but I was saying, *Sylvia*, we both recovered then when the noise alarmed us. I long to know whether you think we were betrayed, for on that knowledge rests a mighty part of my destiny: I hope we are not, by an accident that befell me at my going away, which (but for my untimely force of leaving my lovely *Sylvia*, which gave me pains insupportable) would have given me great diversion. You know our fear of being discovered occasioned my disguise, for you found it necessary I should depart, your fear had so prevailed, and that in *Melinda*'s night-gown and head-dress: thus attired, with much ado, I went and left my soul behind me, and finding no body all along the gallery, nor in my passage from your apartment into the garden, I was a thousand times about to return to all my joys; when in the midst of this almost ended dispute, I saw by the light of the moon (which was by good fortune under a cloud, and could not distinctly direct the sight) a man making towards me with cautious speed, which made me advance with the more haste to recover the grove, believing to have escaped him under the covert of the trees; for retreat I could not, without betraying which way I went; but just at the entrance of the thicket, he turning short made up to me, and I perceived it *Monsieur* the Count, who taking me for *Melinda*, whom it seems he expected, caught hold of my gown as I would have passed him, and cried, 'Now *Melinda*, I see you are a maid of honour — come, retire with me into the grove, where I have a present of a heart and something else to make you, that will be of more advantage to you than that of *Alexis*, though something younger.'— I all confounded knew not what to reply, nor how, lest he should find his mistake, at least, if he discovered not who I was: which silence gave him occasion to go on, which he did in this manner: 'What not a word, *Melinda*, or do you design I shall take your silence for consent? If so, come my pretty creature, let us not lose the hour love has given us;' at this he would have advanced, leading me by the hand, which he pressed and kissed very amorously: judge, my adorable *Sylvia*, in what a fine condition your *Philander* then was in. What should I do? To go had disappointed him worse than I was with thee before; not to go, betrayed me: I had much ado to hold my countenance, and unwilling to speak. While I was thus employed in thought, *Monsieur*—— pulling me (eager of joys to come,) and I holding back, he stopped and cried, 'Sure, *Melinda*, you came not hither to bring me a denial.' I then replied, whispering — 'Softly, sir, for heaven's sake' (sweetening my voice as much as possible) 'consider I am a maid, and would not be discovered for the world.' 'Who can discover us?' replied my lover, 'what I take from thee shall never be missed, not by *Alexis* himself upon thy wedding night; — Come — sweet child, come:—'—'With that I pulled back and whispered —'Heavens! Would you make a mistress of me?'— Says he —'A mistress, what would'st thou be a cherubin?' Then I replied as before —'I am no whore, sir,'—'No,' cries he, 'but I can quickly make thee one, I have my tools about me, sweet-heart; therefore let us lose no time, but fall to work:' this last raillery from the brisk old gentleman, had in spite of resolution almost made me burst out into a loud laughter, when he took more gravity upon him, and cried —'Come, come, *Melinda*, why all this foolish argument at this hour in this place, and after so much serious courtship; believe me, I'll be kind to thee for ever;' with that he clapped fifty guineas in a purse into one hand, and something else that shall be nameless into the other, presents that had been both worth *Melinda*'s acceptance: all this while was I studying an evasion; at last, to shorten my pleasant adventure, looking round, I cried softly, 'Are you sure, sir, we are safe — for heaven's sake step towards the garden door and see, for I would not be discovered for the world.'—'Nor I,' cried he —'but do not fear, all is safe:'—'However see' (whispered I) 'that my fear may not disturb your joys.' With that he went toward the house, and I slipping into the grove, got immediately into the meadow, where *Alexis* waited my coming with *Brilliard*; so I, left the expecting lover, I suppose, ranging the grove for his fled nymph, and I doubt will fall heavy on poor *Melinda*, who shall have the guineas, either to restore or keep, as she and the angry Count can agree: I leave the management of it to her wit and conduct.

This account I thought necessary to give my charmer, that she might prepare *Melinda* for the assault, who understanding all that passed between us, may so dispose of matters, that no discovery may happen by mistake, and I know my *Sylvia* and she can find a thousand excuses for the supposed *Melinda*'s flight. But, my adorable maid, my business here was not to give an account of my adventure only, nor of my ravings, but to tell my *Sylvia*, on what my life depends; which is, in a permission to wait on her again this ensuing night; make no excuse, for if you do, by all I adore in heaven and earth I'll end my life here where I received it. I will say no more, nor give your love instructions, but wait impatiently here the life or death of your PHILANDER.

'Tis six o'clock, and yet my eyes have not closed themselves to

sleep: Alexis *and* Brilliard *give me hopes of a kind return to this, and have brought their flute and violin to charm me into a slumber: if* Sylvia *love, as I am sure she does, she will wake me with a dear consent to see me; if not, I only wake to sleep for ever.*

· · · · · · · · · · · · · · · · · · ·

To My Fair CHARMER.

When I had sealed the enclosed, my page, whom I had ordered to come to me with an account of any business extraordinary, is this morning arrived with a letter from *Cesario*, which I have sent here enclosed, that my *Sylvia* may see how little I regard the world, or the mighty revolution in hand, when set in competition with the least hope of beholding her adorable face, or hearing her charming tongue when it whispers the soft dictates of her tender heart into my ravished soul; one moment's joy like that surmounts an age of dull empire. No, let the busy unregarded rout perish, the cause fall or stand alone for me: give me but love, love and my *Sylvia*; I ask no more of heaven; to which vast joy could you but imagine (O wondrous miracle of beauty!) how poor and little I esteem the valued trifles of the world, you would in return contemn your part of it, and live with me in silent shades for ever. Oh! *Sylvia*, what hast thou this night to add to the soul of thy
PHILANDER.

· · · · · · · · · · · · · · · · · · ·

To the Count of ——

I'll allow you, my dear, to be very fond of so much beauty as the world must own adorns the lovely *Sylvia*: I'll permit love too to rival me in your heart, but not out-rival glory; haste then, my dear, to the advance of that, make no delay, but with the morning's dawn let me find you in my arms, where I have something that will surprise you to relate to you: you were last night expected at —— It behoves you to give no umbrage to persons whose interest renders them enough jealous. We have two new advancers come in of youth and money, teach them not negligence; be careful, and let nothing hinder you from taking horse immediately, as you value the repose and fortune of,

My dear, Your CESARIO.

I called last night on you, and your page following me to my coach, whispered me — if I had any earnest business with you, he knew where to find you; I soon imagined where, and bid him call within an hour for this, and post with it immediately, though dark.

•••••••••••••••••••

To PHILANDER.

Ah! What have I done, *Philander*, and where shall I hide my guilty blushing face? Thou hast undone my eternal quiet: oh, thou hast ruin'd my everlasting repose, and I must never, never look abroad again: curse on my face that first debauched my virtue, and taught thee how to love; curse on my tempting youth, my shape, my air, my eyes, my voice, my hands, and every charm that did contribute to my fatal love, a lasting curse on all — but those of the adorable *Philander*, and those —— even in this raging minute, my furious passion dares not approach with an indecent thought: no, they are sacred all, madness itself would spare them, and shouldst thou now behold me as I sit, my hair dishevelled, ruffled and disordered, my eyes bedewing every word I write, when for each letter I let fall a tear; then (pressed with thought) starting, I dropped my pen, and fell to rave anew, and tear those garments whose loose negligence helped to betray me to my shameful ruin, wounding my breast, but want the resolution to wound it as I ought; which when I but propose, love stays the thought, raging and wild as it is, the conqueror checks it, with whispering only *Philander* to my soul; the dear name calms me to an easiness, gives me the pen into my trembling hand, and I pursue my silent soft complaint: oh! shouldst thou see me thus, in all these sudden different changes of passion, thou wouldst say, *Philander*, I were mad indeed, madness itself can find no stranger motions: and I would calmly ask thee, for I am calm again, how comes it, my adorable *Philander*, that thou canst possess a maid with so much madness? Who art thyself a miracle of softness, all sweet and all serene, the most of angel in thy composition that ever mingled with humanity; the very words fall so gently from thy tongue — are uttered with a voice so ravishingly soft, a tone so tender and so full of love, it would charm even frenzy, calm rude distraction, and wildness would become a silent listener; there's such a sweet serenity in thy face, such innocence and softness in thy eyes, should desert savages but gaze on thee, sure they would forget their native forest wildness, and be inspired with easy gentleness: most certainly this god-like power thou hast. Why then? Oh tell me in the agony of my soul, why must those charms that bring tranquillity and peace to all, make me alone a wild, unseemly raver? Why has it contrary effects on me? Oh! all I act and say is perfect madness: yet this is the least unaccountable part of my most wretched story; — oh! I must never behold thy lovely face again, for if I should, sure I should blush my soul away; no, no, I must not, nor ever more believe thy dear deluding vows; never thy charming perjured oaths, after a violation like to this. Oh heaven, what have I done? Yet by heaven I swear, I dare not ask my soul, lest it inform me how I was to blame, unless that fatal minute would instruct me how to revenge my wrongs upon my heart —— my fond betraying heart, despair and madness seize me, darkness and horror hide me from human sight, after an easiness like this; —— what to yield — to yield my honour? Betray the secrets of my virgin wishes? — My new desires, my unknown shameful flame. — Hell and Death! Where got I so much confidence? Where learned I the hardened and unblushing folly? To wish was such a fault, as is a crime unpardonable to own; to shew desire is such a sin in virtue as must deserve reproach from all the world; but I, unlucky I, have not only betrayed all these, but with a transport void of sense and shame, I yield to thy arms —— I'll not endure the thought —— by heaven! I cannot; there is something more than rage that animates that thought: some magic spell, that in the midst of all my sense of shame keeps me from true repentance; this angers me, and makes me know my honour but a phantom: now I could curse again my youth and love; but oh! When I have done, alas, *Philander*, I find myself as guilty as before; I cannot make one firm resolve against thee, or if I do, when I consider thee, they weigh not all one lovely hair of thine. It is all in vain, the charming cause remains, *Philander's* still as lovely as before; it is him I must remove from my fond eyes and heart, him I must banish from my touch, my smell, and every other sense; by heaven I cannot bear the mighty pressure, I cannot see his eyes, and touch his hands, smell the perfume every pore of his breathes forth, taste thy soft kisses, hear thy charming voice, but I am all on a flame: no, it is these I must exclaim on, not my youth, it is they debauch my soul, no natural propensity in me to yield, or to admit of such destructive fires. Fain I would put it off, but it will not do, I am the aggressor still; else why is not every living maid undone that does but touch or see thee? Tell me why? No, the fault is in me, and thou art innocent. — Were but my soul less delicate, were it less sensible of what it loves and likes in thee, I yet were dully happy; but oh, there is a nicety there so charmed, so apprehensive of thy beauties, as has betrayed me to unrest for ever:—— yet something I will do to tame this lewd betrayer of my right, and it shall plead no more in thy behalf; no more, no more disperse the joys which it conceives through every vein (cold and insensible by nature) to kindle new desires there. — No more shall fill me with unknown curiosity; no, I will in spite of all the perfumes that dwell about thee, in spite of all the arts thou hast of looking, of speaking, and of touching, I will, I say, assume my native temper, I will be calm, be cold and unconcerned, as I have been to all the World — but to *Philander*. — The almighty power he has is unaccountable:— by yonder breaking day that opens in the east, opens to see my shame — I swear — by that great ruler of the day, the sun, by that Almighty Power that rules them both, I swear — I swear, *Philander*, charming lovely youth! Thou art the first e'er kindled soft desires about my soul, thou art the first that ever did inform me that there was such a sort of wish about me. I thought the vanity of being beloved made up the greatest part of the satisfaction; it was joy to see my lovers sigh about me, adore and praise me, and increase my pride by every look, by every word and action; and him I fancied best I favoured most, and he past for the happy fortune; him I have suffered too to kiss and press me, to tell me all his tale of love, and sigh, which I would listen to with pride and pleasure, permitted it, and smiled him kind returns; nay, by my life, then thought I loved him too, thought I could have been content to have passed my life at this gay rate, with this fond hoping lover, and thought no farther than of being great, having rich coaches, shewing equipage, to pass my hours in dressing, in going to the operas and the tower, make visits where I list, be seen at balls; and having still the vanity to think the men would gaze and languish where I came, and all the women envy me; I thought no farther on — but thou, *Philander*, hast made me take new measures, I now can think of nothing but of thee, I loathe the sound of love from any other voice, and conversation makes my soul impatient, and does not only dull me into melancholy, but perplexes me out of all humour, out of all patient sufferance, and I am never so well pleased when from *Philander*, as when I am retired, and curse my character and figure in the world, because it permits me not to prevent being visited; one thought of thee is worth the world's enjoyment, I hate to dress, I hate to be agreeable to any eyes but thine; I hate the noise of equipage and crowds, and would be more content to live with thee in some lone shaded cottage, than be a queen, and hindered by that grandeur one moment's conversation with *Philander*: may'st thou despise and loathe me, a curse the greatest that I can invent, if this be any thing but real honest truth. No, no, *Philander*, I find I never lov'd till now, I understood it not, nor knew what those sighs and pressings meant which others gave me; yet every speaking glance thy eyes put on, inform my soul what it is they plead and languish for: if you but touch my hand, my breath grows faint and short, my blood glows in my face, and runs with an unusual warmth through every vein, and tells my heart what it is *Philander* ails, when he falls sighing on my bosom; oh then, I fear, I answer every look, and every sigh and touch, in the same silent but intelligible language, and understood, I fear, too well by thee: till now I never feared love as a criminal. Oh tell me not, mistaken foolish maids, true love is innocent, ye cold, ye dull, ye unconsidering lovers; though I have often heard it from the grave and wise, and preached myself that doctrine: I now renounce it all, it is false, by heaven! it is false, for now I love, and know it all a fiction; yes, and love so, as never any woman can equal me in love, my soul being all composed (as I have often said) of softer materials. Nor is it fancy sets my rates on beauty, there is an intrinsic value in thy charms, who surely none but I am able to understand, and to those that view thee not with my judging eyes, ugliness fancied would appear the same, and please as well. If all could love or judge like me, why does *Philander* pass so unregarded by a thousand women, who never sighed for him? What makes *Myrtilla*, who possesses all, looks on thee, feels thy kisses, hears thee speak, and yet wants sense to know how blessed she is, it is want of judgement all; and how, and how can she that judges ill, love well?

Granting my passion equal to its object, you must allow it infinite, and more in me than any other woman, by how much more my soul is composed of tenderness; and yet I say I own, for I may own it, now heaven and you are witness of my shame, I own with all this love, with all this passion, so vast, so true, and so unchangeable, that I have wishes, new, unwonted wishes, at every thought of thee I find a strange disorder in my blood, that pants and burns in every vein, and makes me blush, and sigh, and grow impatient, ashamed and angry; but when I know it the effects of love, I am reconciled, and wish and sigh anew; for when I sit and gaze upon thy eyes, thy languishing, thy lovely dying eyes, play with thy soft white hand, and lay my glowing cheeks to thine —— Oh God! What language can express my transport! All that is tender, all that is soft desire, seizes every trembling limb, and it is with pain concealed. — Yes, yes, *Philander*, it is the fatal truth, since thou hast found it, I confess it too, and yet I love thee dearly; long, long it was that I essayed to hide the guilty flame, if love be guilt; for I confess I did dissemble a coldness which I was not mistress of: there lies a woman's art, there all her boasted virtue, it is but well dissembling, and no more — but mine, alas, is gone, for ever fled; this, this feeble guard that should secure my honour, thou hast betrayed, and left it quite defenceless. Ah, what's a woman's honour when it is so poorly guarded! No wonder that you conquer with such ease, when we are only safe by the mean arts of base dissimulation, an ill as shameful as that to which we fall. Oh silly refuge! What foolish nonsense fond custom can persuade: Yet so it is; and she that breaks her laws, loses her fame, her honour and esteem.

Oh heavens! How quickly lost it is! Give me, ye powers, my fame, and let me be a fool; let me retain my virtue and my honour, and be a dull insensible — But, oh! Where is it? I have lost it all; it is irrecoverably lost: yes, yes, ye charming perjured man, it is gone, and thou hast quite undone me. —

What though I lay extended on my bed, undressed, unapprehensive of my fate, my bosom loose and easy of access, my garments ready, thin and wantonly put on, as if they would with little force submit to the fond straying hand: what then, *Philander*, must you take the advantage? Must you be perjured because I was tempting? It is true, I let you in by stealth by night, whose silent darkness favoured your treachery; but oh, *Philander*, were not your vows as binding by a glimmering taper, as if the sun with all his awful light had been a looker on? I urged your vows as you pressed on — but oh, I fear it was in such a way, so faintly and so feebly I upbraided you, as did but more advance your perjuries. Your strength increas'd, but mine alas declin'd; 'till I quite fainted in your arms, left you triumphant lord of all: no more my faint denials do persuade, no more my trembling hands resist your force, unregarded lay the treasure which you toil'd for, betrayed and yielded to the lovely conqueror — but oh tormenting —— when you saw the store, and found the prize no richer, with what contempt, (yes false, dear man) with what contempt you view'd the unvalu'd trophy: what, despised! Was all you call a heaven of joy and beauty exposed to view, and then neglected? Were all your prayers heard, your wishes granted, and your toils rewarded, the trembling victim ready for the sacrifice, and did you want devotion to perform it? And did you thus receive the expected blessing? —— Oh — by heaven I'll never see thee more, and it will be charity to thee, for thou hast no excuse in store that can convince my opinion that I am hated, loathed — I cannot bear that thought — or if I do, it shall only serve to fortify my fixed resolve never to see thee more. — And yet I long to hear thy false excuse, let it be quickly then; it is my disdain invites thee — to strengthen which, there needs no more than that you let me hear your poor defence. —— But it is a tedious time to that slow hour wherein I dare permit thee, but hope not to incline my soul to love: no, I am yet safe if I can stop but here, but here be wise, resolve and be myself.

SYLVIA.

....

To PHILANDER.

As my page was coming with the enclosed, he met *Alexis* at the gate with yours, and who would not depart without an answer to it; — to go or stay is the question. Ah, Philander! Why do you press a heart too ready to yield to love and you! Alas, I fear you guess too well my answer, and your own soul might save me the blushing trouble of a reply. I am plunged in, past hope of a retreat; and since my fate has pointed me out for ruin, I cannot fall more gloriously. Take then, *Philander*, to your dear arms, a maid that can no longer resist, who is disarmed of all defensive power: she yields, she yields, and does confess it too; and sure she must be more than mortal, that can hold out against thy charms and vows. Since I must be undone, and give all away; I'll do it generously, and scorn all mean reserves: I will be brave in love, and lavish all; nor shall *Philander* think I love him well, unless I do. Take, charming victor, then, what your own merits, and what love has given you; take, take, at last, the dear reward of all your sighs and tears, your vows and sufferings. But since, *Philander*, it is an age to night, and till the approach of those dear silent hours, thou knowest I dare not give thee admittance; I do conjure thee, go to *Cesario*, whom I find too pressing, not to believe the concerns great; and so jealous I am of thy dear safety, that every thing alarms my fears: oh! satisfy them then and go, it is early yet, and if you take horse immediately, you will be there by eight this morning; go, I conjure you; for though it is an unspeakable satisfaction to know you are so near me, yet I prefer your safety and honour to all considerations else. You may soon dispatch your affair, and render yourself time enough on the place appointed, which is where you last night waited, and it will be at least eight at night before it is possible to bring you to my arms. Come in your chariot, and do not heat yourself with riding; have a care of me and my life, in the preservation of all I love. Be sure you go, and do not, my

Philander, out of a punctilio of love, neglect your dear safety —— go then, *Philander*, and all the gods of love preserve and attend thee on thy way, and bring thee safely back to
  SYLVIA.

....

To SYLVIA.
  Oh thou most charming of thy sex! Thou lovely dear delight of my transported soul! thou everlasting treasure of my heart! What hast thou done? Given me an over-joy, that fails but very little of performing what grief's excess had almost finished before: eternal blessings on thee, for a goodness so divine, oh, thou most excellent, and dearest of thy sex! I know not what to do, or what to say. I am not what I was, I do not speak, nor walk, nor think as I was wont to do; sure the excess of joy is far above dull sense, or formal thinking, it cannot stay for ceremonious method. I rave with pleasure, rage with the dear thought of coming ecstasy. Oh *Sylvia, Sylvia, Sylvia*! My soul, my vital blood, and without which I could as well subsist — oh, my adorable, my *Sylvia*! Methinks I press thee, kiss thee, hear thee sigh, behold thy eyes, and all the wondrous beauty of thy face; a solemn joy has spread itself through every vein, sensibly through every artery of my heart, and I can think of nothing but of *Sylvia*, the lovely *Sylvia*, the blooming flowing *Sylvta*! And shall I see thee? Shall I touch thy hands, and press thy dear, thy charming body in my arms, and taste a thousand joys, a thousand ravishments? Oh God! shall I? Oh *Sylvia*, say; but thou hast said enough to make me mad, and I, forgetful of thy safety and my own, shall bring thy wild adoring slave to *Bellfont*, and throw him at thy feet, to pay his humble gratitude for this great condescension, this vast bounty.
  Ah, *Sylvia*! How shall I live till night? And you impose too cruelly upon me, in conjuring me to go to *Cesario*; alas! Does *Sylvia* know to what she exposes her *Philander*? Whose joy is so transporting, great, that when he comes into the grave cabal, he must betray the story of his heart, and, in lieu of the mighty business there in hand, be raving still on *Sylvia*, telling his joy to all the amazed listeners, and

answering questions that concern our great affair, with something of my love; all which will pass for madness, and undo me: no, give me leave to rave in silence, and unseen among the trees, they'll humour my disease, answer my murmuring joy, and echoes flatter it, repeat thy name, repeat that *Sylvia*'s mine! and never hurt her fame; while the cabals, business and noisy town will add confusion to my present transport, and make me mad indeed: no, let me alone, thou sacred lovely creature, let me be calm and quiet here, and tell all the insensibles I meet in the woods what *Sylvia* has this happy minute destined me: oh, let me record it on every bark, on every oak and beech, that all the world may wonder at my fortune, and bless the generous maid; let it grow up to ages that shall come, that they may know the story of our loves, and how a happy youth, they called *Philander*, was once so blest by heaven as to possess the charming, the adored and loved by all, the glorious *Sylvia*! a maid, the most divine that ever graced a story; and when the nymphs would look for an example of love and constancy, let them point out *Philander* to their doubted swains, and cry, 'Ah! love but as the young *Philander* did, and then be fortunate, and then reap all your wishes:' and when the shepherd would upbraid his nymph, let him but cry — 'See here what *Sylvia* did to save the young *Philander*;' but oh! There never will be such another nymph as *Sylvia*; heaven formed but one to shew the world what angels are, and she was formed for me, yes she was — in whom I would not quit my glorious interest to reign a monarch here, or any boasted gilded thing above! Take all, take all, ye gods, and give me but this happy coming night! Oh, *Sylvia*, *Sylvia*! By all thy promised joys I am undone if any accident should ravish this night from me: this night! No not for a lease of years to all eternity would I throw thee away: oh! I am all flame, all joyful fire and softness; methinks it is heaven where-ever I look round me, air where I tread, and ravishing music when I speak, because it is all of *Sylvia*—— let me alone, oh let me cool a little, or I shall by an excess of joyful thought lose all my hoped for bliss. Remove a little from me; go, my *Sylvia*, you are so excessive sweet, so wondrous dazzling, you press my senses even to pain — away — let me take air — let me recover breath: oh let me lay me down beneath some cooling shade, near some refreshing crystal murmuring spring, and fan the gentle air about me. I suffocate, I faint with this close loving, I must allay my joy or be undone — I will read thy cruel letters, or I will think of some sad melancholy hour wherein thou hast dismissed me despairing from thy presence: or while you press me now to be gone with so much earnestness, you have some lover to receive and entertain; perhaps it is only for the vanity to hear him tell his nauseous passion to you, breathe on your lovely face, and daub your garments with his fulsome embrace; but oh, by heaven, I cannot think that thought! And thou hast sworn thou canst not suffer it — if I should find thee false — but it is impossible. — Oh! Should I find *Foscario* visit thee, him whom thy parents favour, I should undo you all, by heaven I should — but thou hast sworn, what need *Philander* more? Yes, *Sylvia*, thou hast sworn and called heaven's vengeance down whenever thou gavest a look, or a dear smile in love to that pretending fop: yet from his mighty fortune there is danger in him — What makes that thought torment me now? — Be gone, for *Sylvia* loves me, and will preserve my life ——

I am not able, my adorable charmer, to obey your commands in going from the sight of happy *Bellfont*; no, let the great wheel of the vast design roll on —— or for ever stand still, for I will not aid its motion to leave the mightier business of my love unfinished; no, let fortune and the duller fools toil on —— for I'll not bate a minute of my joys with thee to save the world, much less so poor a parcel of it; and sure there is more solid pleasure even in these expecting hours I wait to snatch my bliss, than to be lord of all the universe without it: then let me wait, my *Sylvia*, in those melancholy shades that part *Bellfont* from *Dorillus*'s farm; perhaps my *Sylvia* may walk that way so unattended, that we might meet and lose ourselves for a few moments in those intricate retreats: ah *Sylvia*! I am dying with that thought —— oh heavens! What cruel destiny is mine? Whose fatal circumstances do not permit me to own my passion, and lay claim to *Sylvia*, to take her without control to shades and palaces, to live for ever with her, to gaze for ever on her, to eat, to loll, to rise, to play, to sleep, to act over all the pleasures and the joys of life with her — but it is in vain I rave, in vain employ myself in the fool's barren business, wishing — this thought has made me sad as death: oh, *Sylvia*! I can never be truly happy — adieu, employ thyself in writing to me, and remember my life bears date but only with thy faith and love.

PHILANDER.

Try, my adorable, what you can do to meet me in the wood this afternoon, for there I will live to-day.

....

To PHILANDER.

Obstinate *Philander*, I conjure you by all your vows, by all your sacred love, by those dear hours this happy night designed in favour of you, to go without delay to *Cesario*; 'twill be unsafe to disobey a prince in his jealous circumstances. The fatigue of the journey cannot be great, and you well know the torment of my fears! Oh! I shall never be happy, or think you safe, till you have quitted this fatal interest: go, my *Philander*—— and remember whatever toils you take will be rewarded at night in the arms of

SYLVIA.

....

To SYLVIA.

Whatever toils you take shall be rewarded in the arms of *Sylvia*—— by heaven, I am inspired to act wonders: yes, *Sylvia*, yes, my adorable maid, I am gone, I fly as swift as lightning, or the soft darts of love shot from thy charming eyes, and I can hardly stay to say —— adieu ——

....

To the Lady ——

Dear Child,

Long foreseeing the misery whereto you must arrive, by this fatal correspondence with my unhappy lord, I have often, with tears and prayers, implored you to decline so dangerous a passion: I have never yet acquainted our parents with your misfortunes, but I fear I must at last make use of their authority for the prevention of your ruin. It is not my dearest child, that part of this unhappy story that relates to me, that grieves me, but purely that of thine.

Consider, oh young noble maid, the infamy of being a prostitute! And yet the act itself in this fatal amour is not the greatest sin, but the manner, which carries an unusual horror with it; for it is a brother too, my child, as well as a lover, one that has lain by thy unhappy sister's side so many tender years, by whom he has a dear and lovely off-spring, by which he has more fixed himself to thee by relation and blood: consider this, oh fond heedless girl! And suffer not a momentary joy to rob thee of thy eternal fame, me of my eternal repose, and fix a brand upon our noble house, and so undo us all. —— Alas, consider, after an action so shameful, thou must obscure thyself in some remote corner of the world, where honesty and honour never are heard of: no, thou canst not shew thy face, but it will be pointed at for something monstrous; for a hundred ages may not produce a story so lewdly infamous and loose as thine. Perhaps (fond as you are) you imagine the sole joy of being beloved by him, will atone for those affronts and reproaches you will meet with in the censuring world: but, child, remember and believe me, there is no lasting faith in sin; he that has broke his vows with heaven and me, will be again perjured to heaven and thee, and all the world! —— He once thought me as lovely, lay at my feet, and sighed away his soul, and told such piteous stories of his sufferings, such sad, such mournful tales of his departed rest, his broken heart and everlasting love, that sure I thought it had been a sin not to have credited his charming perjuries; in such a way he swore, with such a grace he sighed, so artfully he moved, so tenderly he looked. Alas, dear child, then all he said was new, unusual with him, never told before, now it is a beaten road, it is learned by heart, and easily addressed to any fond believing woman, the tattered, worn out fragments of my trophies, the dregs of what I long since drained from off his fickle heart; then it was fine, then it was brisk and new, now palled and dull by being repeated often. Think, my child, what your victorious beauty merits, the victim of a heart unconquered by any but your eyes: alas, he has been my captive, my humble whining slave, disdain to put him on your fetters now; alas, he can say no new thing of his heart to thee, it is love at second hand, worn out, and all its gaudy lustre tarnished; besides, my child, if thou hadst no religion binding enough, no honour that could stay thy fatal course, yet nature should oblige thee, and give a check to the unreasonable enterprise. The griefs and dishonour of our noble parents, who have been eminent for virtue and piety, oh suffer them not to be regarded in this censuring world as the most unhappy of all the ráce of old nobility; thou art the darling child, the joy of all, the last hope left, the refuge of their sorrow, for they, alas, have had but unkind stars to influence their unadvised off-spring; no want of virtue in their education, but this last blow of fate must strike them dead; think, think of this, my child, and yet retire from ruin; haste, fly from destruction which pursues thee fast; haste, haste and save thy parents and a sister, or what is more dear, thy fame; mine has already received but too many desperate wounds, and all through my unkind lord's growing passion for thee, which was most fatally founded on my ruin, and nothing but my ruin could advance it; and when, my sister, thou hast run thy race, made thyself loathed, undone and infamous as hell, despis'd, scorn'd and abandon'd by all, lampoon'd, perhaps diseas'd; this faithless man, this cause of all will leave thee too, grow weary of thee, nauseated by use; he may perhaps consider what sins, what evils, and what inconveniencies and shames thou'st brought him to, and will not be the last shall loathe and hate thee: for though youth fancy it have a mighty race to run of pleasing vice and vanity, the course will end, the goal will be arrived to at the last, where they will sighing stand, look back, and view the length of precious time they've fool'd away; when traversed over with honour and discretion, how glorious were the journey, and with what joy the wearied traveller lies down and basks beneath the shades that end the happy course.

Forgive, dear child, this advice, and pursue it; it is the effect of my pity, not anger; nor could the name of rival ever yet have power to banish that of sister from my soul —— farewell, remember me; pray heaven thou hast not this night made a forfeit of thy honour, and that this which comes from a tender bleeding heart may have the fortune to inspire thee with grace to avoid all temptations for the future, since they must end in sorrows which is the eternal prayer of,

Dearest child,
Your affectionate Sister.

....

To PHILANDER.

Ask me not, my dearest brother, the reason of this sudden change, ask me no more from whence proceeds this strange coldness, or why this alteration; it is enough my destiny has not decreed me for *Philander*: alas, I see my error, and looking round about me, find nothing but approaching horror and confusion in my pursuit of love: oh whither was I going, to what dark paths, to what everlasting shades had smiling love betray'd me, had I pursued him farther? But I at last have subdued his force, and the fond charmer shall no more renew his arts and flatteries; for I'm resolv'd as heaven, as fix'd as fate and death, and I conjure you trouble my repose no more; for if you do (regardless of my honour, which if you loved you would preserve) I will do a deed shall free me from your importunities, that shall amaze and cool your vicious flame. No more — remember you have a noble wife, companion of your vows, and I have honour, both which are worth preserving, and for which, though you want generous love, you will find neither that nor courage wanting in *Sylvia*.

....

To SYLVIA.

Yes, my adorable *Sylvia*, I will pursue you no farther; only for all my pains, for all my sufferings, for my tormenting sleepless nights, and thoughtful anxious days; for all my faithless hopes, my fears, my sighs, my prayers and my tears, for my unequalled and unbounded passion, and my unwearied pursuits in love, my never-dying flame, and lastly, for my death; I only beg, in recompense for all, this last favour from your pity; That you will deign to view the bleeding wound that pierced the truest heart that ever fell a sacrifice to love; you will find my body lying beneath that spreading oak, so sacred to *Philander*, since it was there he first took into his greedy ravished soul, the dear, the soft confession of thy passion, though now forgotten and neglected all — make what haste you can, you will find there stretched out the mangled carcase of the lost

PHILANDER.

Ah Sylvia! *Was it for this that I was sent in such haste away this morning to* Cesario? *Did I for this neglect the world, our great affair, and all that Prince's interest, and fly back to* Bellfont *on the wings of love? Where in lieu of receiving a dear blessing from thy hand, do I find —— never see me more — good heaven — but, with my life, all my complaints are ended; only it would be, some ease, even in death, to know what happy rival it is has armed thy cruel hand against* Philander's *heart.*

....

To PHILANDER.

Stay, I conjure thee, stay thy sacrilegious hand; for the least wound it gives the lord of all my wishes, I'll double on my breast a thousand fold; stay then, by all thy vows, thy love, and all thy hopes, I swear thou hast this night a full recompense of all thy pains from yielding *Sylvia*; I do conjure thee stay —— for when the news arrives thou art no more, this poor, this lost, abandoned heart of mine shall fall a victim to thy cruelty: no, live, my *Philander*, I conjure thee, and receive all thou canst ask, and all that can be given by

SYLVIA.

....

To PHILANDER.

Oh, my charming *Philander*! How very ill have you recompensed my last lost commands? Which were that you should live; and yet at the same moment, while you are reading of the dear obligation, and while my page was waiting your kind return, you desperately exposed

your life to the mercy of this innocent rival, betraying unadvisedly at
the same time my honour, and the secret of your love, and where to
kill or to be killed, had been almost equally unhappy: it was well my
page told me you disarmed him in this rencounter; yet you, he says,
are wounded, some sacred drops of blood are fallen to the earth and
lost, the least of which is precious enough to ransom captive queens:
oh! Haste *Philander*, to my arms for cure, I die with fear there may
be danger —— haste, and let me bathe, the dear, the wounded part in
floods of tears, lay to my warm lips, and bind it with my torn hair: oh!
Philander, I rave with my concern for thee, and am ready to break all
laws of decency and duty, and fly without considering, to thy succour,
but that I fear to injure thee much more by the discovery, which
such an unadvised absence would make. Pray heaven the unlucky
adventure reach not *Bellfont; Foscario* has no reason to proclaim it,
and thou art too generous to boast the conquest, and my page was
the only witness, and he is as silent and as secret as the grave: but
why, *Philander*, was he sent me back without reply? What meant that
cruel silence —— say, my *Philander*, will you not obey me? —— Will
you abandon me? Can that dear tongue be perjured? And can you
this night disappoint your *Sylvia*? What have I done, oh obstinately
cruel, irreconcileable —— what, for my first offence? A little poor
resentment and no more? A little faint care of my gasping honour,
could that displease so much? Besides I had a cause, which you
shall see; a letter that would cool love's hottest fires, and turn it to
devotion; by heaven it was such a check —— such a surprise ——
but you yourself shall judge, if after that I could say less, than bid
eternally farewell to love — at least to thee — but I recanted soon; one
sad dear word, one soft resenting line from thee, gained love the day
again, and I despised the censures of the duller world: yes, yes, and
I confessed you had overcome, and did this merit no reply? I asked
the boy a thousand times what you said, how and in what manner
you received it, chid him, and laid your silent fault on him, till he
with tears convinced me, and said he found you hastening to the
grove — and when he gave you my commands —— you looked upon
him with such a wild and fixed regard, surveying him all over while
you were opening it —— as argued some unusual motion in you;

then cried, 'Be gone — I cannot answer flattery'—— Good heaven, what can you mean? But 'ere he got to the farther end of the grove, where still you walked a solemn death-like pace, he saw *Foscario* pass him unattended, and looking back saw your rencounter, saw all that happened between you, then ran to your assistance just as you parted; still you were roughly sullen, and neither took notice of his proffered service, nor that you needed it, although you bled apace; he offered you his aid to tie your wounds up —— but you replied —'Be gone, and do not trouble me'—— Oh, could you imagine I could live with this neglect? Could you, my *Philander*? Oh what would you have me do! If nothing but my death or ruin can suffice for my atonement, I will sacrifice either with joy; yes, I'll proclaim my passion aloud, proclaim it at *Bellfont*, own the dear criminal flame, fly to my Philander's aid and be undone; for thus I cannot, no, I will not live, I rave, I languish, faint and die with pain; say that you live, oh, say but that you live, say you are coming to the meadow behind the garden-grove, in order to your approach to my arms: oh, swear that all your vows are true; oh, swear that you are *Sylvia's*; and in return, I will swear that I am yours without reserve, whatever fate is destined for your

SYLVIA.

I die with impatience, either to see or hear from you; I fear it is yet too soon for the first —— oh therefore save me with the last, or I shall rave, and wildly betray all by coming to Dorillus *his farm, or seeking you where-ever you cruelly have hid yourself from*

SYLVIA.

....

To SYLVIA.

Ah, *Sylvia*, how have you in one day destroyed that repose I have been designing so many years! Oh, thou false —— but wondrous fair creature! Why did heaven ordain so much beauty, and so much perfidy, so much excellent wit, and so much cunning, (things inconsistent in any but in *Sylvia*) in one divine frame, but to undo mankind: yes, *Sylvia*, thou wert born to murder more believing men than the unhappy and undone *Philander*. Tell me, thou charming hypocrite, why hast thou thus deluded me? Why? oh, why was I made the miserable object of thy fatal vow-breach? What have I done, thou lovely, fickle maid, that thou shouldst be my murderer? And why dost thou call me from the grave with such dear soft commands as would awake the very quiet dead, to torture me anew, after my eyes (curse on their fatal sense) were too sure witnesses of thy infidelity? Oh, fickle maid, how much more kind it had been to have sent me down to earth, with plain heart-breaking truth, than a mean subtle falsehood, that has undone thy credit in my soul? Truth, though it were cruel, had been generous in thee; though thou wert perjured, false, forsworn —— thou shouldst not have added to it that yet baser sin of treachery: you might have been provoked to have killed your friend, but it were base to stab him unawares, defenceless and unwarned; smile in my face, and strike me to the heart; soothe me with all the tenderest marks of my passion —— nay, with an invitation too, that would have gained a credit in one that had been jilted over the world, flattered and ruined by all thy cozening sex, and all to send me vain and pleased away, only to gain a day to entertain another lover in. Oh, fantastic woman! destructive glorious thing, what needed this deceit? Hadst thou not with unwonted industry persuaded me to have hasted to *Cesario*, by heaven, I had dully lived the tedious day in traversing the flowery meads and silent groves, laid by some murmuring spring, had sigh'd away the often counted hours, and thought on *Sylvia*, till the blessed minute of my ravishing approach to her; had been a fond, believing and imposed on coxcomb, and never had dreamt the treachery, never seen the snake that basked beneath the gay, the smiling flowers; securely thou hadst cozened me, reaped the new joys, and made my rival sport at the expense of all my happiness: yes, yes, your hasty importunity first gave me jealousy, made me impatient with *Cesario*, and excuse myself to him by a hundred inventions; neglected all to hasten back, where all my joys, where all my killing fears and torments resided — but when I came —— how was I welcomed? With your confirming billet; yes, *Sylvia*, how! Let *Dorillus* inform you, between whose arms I fell dead, shame on me, dead — and the first thought my soul conceived when it returned, was, not to die in jest. I answered your commands, and hastened to the grove, where —— by all that is sacred, by thyself I swear (a dearer oath than heaven and earth can furnish me with) I did resolve to die; but oh, how soon my soft, my silent passion turned to loud rage, rage easier to be borne, to dire despair, to fury and revenge; for there I saw, *Foscario*, my young, my fair, my rich and powerful rival, he hasted through the grove, all warm and glowing from the fair false one's arms; the blushes which thy eyes had kindled were fresh upon his cheeks, his looks were sparkling with the new-blown fire, his heart so briskly burnt with a glad, peaceful smile dressed all his face, tricked like a bridegroom, while he perfum'd the air as he passed through it —— none but the man that loves and dotes like me is able to express my sense of rage: I quickly turned the sword from my own heart to send it to his elevated one, giving him only time to —— draw — that was the word, and I confess your spark was wondrous ready, brisk with success, vain with your new-given favours, he only cried —'If *Sylvia* be the quarrel — I am prepared ——' And he maintained your cause with admirable courage I confess, though chance or fortune luckily gave me his sword, which I would fain have rendered back, and that way would have died; but he refused to arm his hand anew against the man that had not took advantage of him, and thus we parted: then it was that malice supported me with life, and told me I should scorn to die for so perfidious and so ruinous a creature; but charming and bewitching still, it was then I borrowed so much calmness of my lessening anger to read the billet over, your page had brought me, which melted all the rough remaining part of rage away into tame languishment: ah, *Sylvia*! This heart of mine was never formed by nature to hold out long in stubborn sullenness; I am already on the excusing part, and fain would think thee innocent and just; deceive me prettily, I know thou canst soothe my fond heart, and ask how it could harbour a faithless thought of *Sylvia*— do — flatter me, protest a little, swear my rival saw thee not, say he was there by chance —— say any thing; or if thou sawest him, say with how cold a look he was received —— Oh, *Sylvia*, calm my soul, deceive it flatter it, and I shall still believe and love thee on —— yet shouldest thou tell me truth, that thou art false, by heaven I do adore thee so, I still should love thee on; should I have seen thee clasp him in thy arms, print kisses on his cheeks and lips, and more —— so fondly and so dotingly I love, I think I should forgive thee; for I swear by all the powers that pity frail mortality, there is no joy, no life, no heaven without thee! Be false! Be cruel, perjured, infamous, yet still I must adore thee; my soul was formed of nothing but of love, and all that love, and all that soul is *Sylvia*'s; but yet, since thou hast framed me an excuse, be kind and carry it on; —— to be deluded well, as thou canst do it, will be the same to innocence, as loving: I shall not find the cheat: I will come then —— and lay myself at thy feet, and seek there that repose, that dear content, which is not to be found in this vast world besides; though much of my heart's joy thou hast abated; and fixed a sadness in my soul that will not easily vanish —— oh *Sylvia*, take care of me, for I am in thy power, my life, my fame, my soul are all in thy hands, be tender of the victims, and remember if any action of thy life should shew a fading love, that very moment I perceive the change, you shall find dead at your feet the abandoned

PHILANDER.

Sad as death, I am going towards the meadow, in order to my approach towards Sylvia, *the world affording no repose to me, but when I am where the dear charmer is.*

·····················

To Philander *in the Meadow.*

And can you be jealous of me, *Philander*? I mean so poorly jealous as to believe me capable of falsehood, of vow-breach, and what is worse, of loving any thing but the adorable *Philander*? I could not once believe so cruel a thought could have entered into the imaginations of a soul so entirely possessed with *Sylvia*, and so great a judge of love. Abandon me, reproach me, hate me, scorn me, whenever I harbour any thing in mind so destructive to my repose and thine. Can I *Philander*, give you a greater proof of my passion; of my faithful, never-dying passion, than being undone for you? Have I any other prospect in all this soft adventure, but shame, dishonour,

reproach, eternal infamy and ever-lasting destruction, even of soul
and body? I tremble with fear of future punishment; but oh, love will
have no devotion (mixed with his ceremonies) to any other deity;
and yet, alas, I might have loved another, and have been saved, or
any maid but *Sylvia* might have possessed without damnation. But
it is a brother I pursue, it is a sister gives her honour up, and none
but *Canace*, that ever I read in story, was ever found so wretched
as to love a brother with so criminal a flame, and possibly I may
meet her fate. I have a father too as great as *Aeolus*, as angry and
revengeful where his honour is concerned; and you found, my dearest
brother, how near you were last night to a discovery in the garden.
I have some reason too to fear this night's adventure, for as ill fate
would have it (loaded with other thoughts) I told not *Melinda* of
your adventure last night with *Monsieur* the Count, who meeting her
early this morning, had like to have made a discovery, if he have not
really so already; she strove to shun him, but he cried out —'*Melinda*,
you cannot fly me by light, as you did last night in the dark —'She
turned and begged his pardon, for neither coming nor designing to
come, since she had resolved never to violate her vows to *Alexis*:
'Not coming?' cried he, 'not returning again, you meant, *Melinda*;
secure of my heart and my purse, you fled with both.' *Melinda*, whose
honour was now concerned, and not reminding your escape in her
likeness, blushing, she sharply denied the fact, and with a disdain
that had laid aside all respect, left him; nor can it be doubted, but
he fancied (if she spoke truth) there was some other intrigue of love
carried on at *Bellfont*. Judge, my charming *Philander*, if I have not
reason to be fearful of thy safety, and my fame; and to be jealous
that so wise a man as *Monsieur* did not take that parly to be held
with a spirit last night, or that it was an apparition he courted: but
if there be no boldness like that of love, nor courage like that of a
lover; sure there never was so great a heroine as *Sylvia*. Undaunted, I
resolve to stand the shock of all, since it is impossible for me to leave
Philander any doubt or jealousy that I can dissipate, and heaven
knows how far I was from any thought of seeing *Foscario*, when I
urged *Philander* to depart. I have to clear my innocence, sent thee
the letter I received two hours after thy absence, which falling into

my mother's hands, whose favourite he is, he had permission to make his visit, which within an hour he did; but how received by me, be thou the judge, whenever it is thy fate to be obliged to entertain some woman to whom thy soul has an entire aversion. I forced a complaisance against my nature, endured his racking courtship with a fortitude that became the great heart that bears thy sacred image; as martyrs do, I suffered without murmuring, or the least sign of the pain I endured — it is below the dignity of my mighty passion to justify it farther, let it plead its own cause, it has a thousand ways to do it, and those all such as cannot be resisted, cannot be doubted, especially this last proof of sacrificing to your repose the never more to be doubted

SYLVIA.

About an hour hence I shall expect you to advance.

....

To the Lady ——

Madam,

'Tis not always the divine graces wherewith heaven has adorned your resplendent beauties, that can maintain the innumerable conquests they gain, without a noble goodness; which may make you sensibly compassionate the poor and forlorn captives you have undone: but, most fair of your sex, it is I alone that have a destiny more cruel and severe, and find myself wounded from your very frowns, and secured a slave as well as made one; the very scorn from those triumphant stars, your eyes, have the same effects, as if they shined with the continual splendour of ravishing smiles; and I can no more shun their killing influence, than their all-saving aspects: and I shall expire contentedly, since I fall by so glorious a fate, if you will vouchsafe to pronounce my doom from that store-house of perfection, your mouth, from lips that open like the blushing rose, strow'd over with morning dew, and from a breath sweeter than holy incense; in order to which, I approach you, most excellent beauty, with this most humble petition, that you will deign to permit me to throw my unworthy self before the throne of your mercy, there to receive the sentence of my life or death; a happiness, though incomparably too great for so mean a vassal, yet with that reverence and awe I shall receive it, as I would the sentence of the gods, and which I will no more resist than I would the thunderbolts of *Jove*, or the revenge of angry *Juno*: for, madam, my immense passion knows no medium between life | and death, and as I never had the presumption to aspire to the glory of the first, I am not so abject as to fear I am wholly deprived of the glory of the last: I have too long lain convicted, extend your mercy, and put me now out of pain: you have often wrecked me to confess my promethean sin; spare the cruel vulture of despair, take him from my heart in pity, and either by killing words, or blasting lightning from those refulgent eyes, pronounce the death of,

Madam,
Your admiring slave,
FOSCARIO.

....

To SYLVIA.

My Everlasting Charmer,

I am convinc'd and pleas'd, my fears are vanish'd, and a heaven of solid joy is opened to my view, and I have nothing now in prospect but angel-brightness, glittering youth, dazzling beauty, charming sounds, and ravishing touches, and all around me ecstasies of pleasure, inconceivable transports without conclusion; *Mahomet* never fancied such a heaven, not all his paradise promised such lasting felicity, or ever provided there the recompense of such a maid as *Sylvia*, such a bewitching form, such soft, such glorious eyes, where the soul speaks and dances, and betrays love's secrets in every killing glance, a face, where every motion, every feature sweetly languishes, a neck all tempting — and her lovely breast inviting presses from the eager lips; such hands, such clasping arms, so white, so soft and slender! No, nor one of all his heavenly enjoyments, though promised years of fainting in one continued ecstasy, can make one moment's joy with charming *Sylvia*. Oh, I am wrapt (with bare imagination) with a much vaster pleasure than any other dull appointment can dispense — oh, thou blessing sent from heaven to ease my toils of life! Thou sacred dear delight of my fond doting heart, oh, whither wilt thou lead me, to what vast heights of love? Into extremes as fatal and as dangerous as those excesses were that rendered me so cold in your opinion. Oh, *Sylvia, Sylvia*, have a care of me, manage my overjoyed soul, and all its eager passions, chide my fond heart, be angry if I faint upon thy bosom, and do not with thy tender voice recall me, a voice that kills out-right, and calls my fleeting soul out of its habitation: lay not such charming lips to my cold cheeks, but let me lie extended at thy feet untouched, unsighed upon, unpressed with kisses: oh, change those tender, trembling words of love into rough sounds and noises unconcerned, and when you see me dying, do not call my soul to mingle with thy sighs; yet shouldst thou abate one word, one look or tear, by heaven I should be mad; oh, never let me live to see declension in thy love! No, no, my charmer, I cannot bear the least supposed decay in those dear fondnesses of thine; and sure none ever became a maid so well, nor ever were received with adorations, like to mine!

Pardon, my adorable *Sylvia*, the rashness of my passion in this rencounter with *Foscario*; I am satisfied he is too unhappy in your disfavour to merit the being so in mine; but it was sufficient I then saw a joy in his face, a pleased gaiety in his ooks to make me think my rage reasonable, and my quarrel ust; by the style he writes, I dread his sense less than his person; but you, my lovely maid, have said enough to quit me of my fears for both —— the night comes on — I cannot call it envious, though it rob me of the light that should assist me to finish this, since it will more gloriously repay me in a happier place — come on then, thou blest retreat of lovers, I forgive by interruptions here, since thou wilt conduct to the arms of *Sylvia* — the adoring

PHILANDER.

If you have any commands for me, this weeder of the gardens, whom I met in going in thither, will bring it back; I wait in the meadow, and date this from the dear primrose-bank, where I have sat with Sylvia.

....

To PHILANDER.

After the happy night.

'Tis done, yes, *Philander*, it is done, and after that, what will not love and grief oblige me to own to you? Oh, by what insensible degrees a maid in love may arrive to say any thing to her lover without blushing! I have known the time, the blest innocent time, when but to think I loved *Philander* would have covered my face with shame, and to have spoke it would have filled me with confusion — have made me tremble, blush, and bend my guilty eyes to earth, not daring to behold my charming conqueror, while I made that bashful confession — though now I am grown bold in love, yet I have known the time, when being at Court, and coming from the Presence, being offered some officious hand to lead me to my coach, I have shrunk back with my aversion to your sex, and have concealed my hands in my pockets to prevent their being touched;-a kiss would turn my stomach, and amorous looks (though they would make me vain) gave me a hate to him that sent them, and never any maid resolved so much as I to tread the paths of honour, and I had many precedents before me to make me careful: thus I was armed with resolution, pride and scorn, against all mankind; but alas, I made no defence against a brother, but innocently lay exposed to all his attacks of love, and never thought it criminal till it kindled a new desire about me, oh, that I should not die with shame to own it —— yet see (I say) how from one soft degree to another, I do not onlyconfess the shameful truth, but act it too; what with a brother — oh heavens! a crime so monstrous and so new —— but by all thy love, by those surprising joys so lately experienced —— I never will —— no, no, I never can —— repent it: oh incorrigible passion! oh harden'd love! At least I might have some remorse, some sighing after my poor departed honour; but why should I dissemble with the powers divine; that know the secrets of a soul doomed to eternal love? Yet I am mad, I rave and tear myself, traverse my guilty chamber in a disordered, but a soft confusion; and often opening the conscious curtains, survey the print where thou and I were last night laid, surveying it with a thousand tender sighs, and kiss and press thy dear forsaken side, imagine over all our solemn joys, every dear transport, all our ravishing repeated blisses; then almost fainting, languishing, cry —*Philander*, oh, my charming little god! Then lay me down in the dear place you pressed, still warm and fragrant with the sweet remains that thou hast left behind thee on the pillow. Oh, my soul's joy! My dear, eternal pleasure! What softness hast thou added to my heart within a few hours! But oh, *Philander*— if (as I've oft been told) possession, which makes women fond and doting, should make thee cold and grow indifferent — if nauseated with repeated joy, and having made a full discovery of all that was but once imaginary, when fancy rendered every thing much finer than experience, oh, how were I undone! For me, by all the inhabitants of heaven I swear, by thy dear charming self, and by thy vows —— thou so transcendest all fancy, all dull imagination, all wondering ideas of what man was to me, that I believe thee more than human! Some charm divine dwells in thy touches; besides all these, thy charming look, thy love, the beauties that adorn thee, and thy wit, I swear there is a secret in nature that renders thee more dear, and fits thee to my soul; do not ask it me, let it suffice, it is so, and is not to be told; yes, by it I know thou art the man created for my soul, and he alone that has the power to touch it; my eyes and fancy might have been diverted, I might have favoured this above the other, preferred that face, that wit, or shape, or air —— but to concern my soul, to make that capable of something more than love, it was only necessary that *Philander* should be formed, and formed just as he is; that shape, that face, that height, that dear proportion; I would not have a feature, not a look, not a hair altered, just as thou art, thou art an angel to me, and I, without considering what I am, what I might be, or ought, without considering the fatal circumstances of thy being married (a thought that shocks my soul whenever it enters) or whatever other thought that does concern my happiness or quiet, have fixed my soul to love and my *Philander*, to love thee with all thy disadvantages, and glory in my ruin; these are my firm resolves — these are my thoughts. But thou art gone, with all the trophies of my love and honour, gay with the spoils, which now perhaps are unregarded: the mystery is now revealed, the mighty secret is known, and now will be no wonder or surprise: But hear my vows: by all on which my life depends I swear —— if ever I perceive the least decay of love in thee, if ever thou breakest an oath, a vow, a word, if ever I see repentance in thy face, a coldness in thy eyes (which heaven divert) by that bright heaven I will die; you may believe me, since I had the courage and durst love thee, and after that durst sacrifice my fame, lose all to justify that love, will, when a change so fatal shall arrive, find courage too to die; yes, die *Philander*, assure thyself I will, and therefore have a care of

SYLVIA.

....

To PHILANDER.

OH, where shall I find repose, where seek a silent quiet, but in my last retreat, the grave! I say not this, my dearest *Philander*, that I do or ever can repent my love, though the fatal source of all: for already we are betrayed, our race of joys, our course of stolen delight is ended 'ere begun. I chid, alas, at morning's dawn, I chid you to be gone, and yet, heaven knows, I grasped you fast, and rather would have died than parted with you; I saw the day come on, and cursed its busy light, and still you cried, one blessed minute more, before I part with all the joys of life! And hours were minutes then, and day grew old upon us unawares, it was all abroad, and had called up all the household spies to pry into the secrets of our loves, and thou, by some tale-bearing flatterer, were seen in passing through the garden; the news was carried to my father, and a mighty consult has been held in my mother's apartment, who now refuses to see me; while I, possessed with love, and full of wonder at my new change, lulled with dear contemplation, (for I am altered much since yesterday, however thou hast charmed me) imagining none knew our theft of love, but only heaven and *Melinda*. But oh, alas, I had no sooner finished this enclosed, but my father entered my cabinet, but it was with such a look —— as soon informed me all was betrayed to him; a while he gazed on me with fierceness in his eyes, which so surprised and frighted me, that I, all pale and trembling, threw myself at his feet; he, seeing my disorder, took me up, and fixed so steadfast and so sad a look upon me, as would have broken any heart but mine, supported with *Philander*'s, image; I sighed and wept — and silently attended when the storm should fall, which turned into a shower so soft and piercing, I almost died to see it; at last delivering me a paper —'Here,' (cried he, with a sigh and trembling-interrupted voice) 'read what I cannot tell thee. Oh, *Sylvia*,' cried he, '— thou joy and hope of all my aged years, thou object of my dotage, how hast thou brought me to my grave with sorrow!' So left me with the paper in my hand: speechless, unmov'd a while I stood, till he awaked me by new sighs and cries; for passing through my chamber, by chance, or by design, he cast his melancholy eyes towards my bed, and saw the dear disorder there, unusual — then cried —'Oh, wretched *Sylvia*, thou art lost!' And left me almost fainting. The letter, I soon found, was one you'd sent from *Dorillus* his farm this morning, after you had parted from me, which has betrayed us all, but how it came into their hands I since have understood: for, as I said, you were seen passing through the garden, from thence (to be confirmed) they dogged you to the farm, and waiting there your motions, saw *Dorillus* come forth with a letter in his hand, which though he soon concealed, yet not so soon but it was taken notice of, when hastening to *Bellfont* the nearest way, they gave an account to *Monsieur*, my father, who going out to *Dorillus*, commanded him to deliver him the letter; his vassal durst not disobey, but yielded it with such dispute and reluctancy, as he durst maintain with a man so great and powerful; before *Dorillus* returned you had taken horse, so that you are a stranger to our misfortune — What shall I do? Where shall I seek a refuge from the danger that threatens us? A sad and silent grief appears throughout *Bellfont*, and the face of all things is changed, yet none knows the unhappy cause but *Monsieur* my father, and *Madam* my mother, *Melinda* and myself. *Melinda* and my page are both dismissed from waiting on me, as supposed confidants of this dear secret, and strangers, creatures of *Madam* the Countess, put about me. Oh *Philander*, what can I do? Thy advice, or I am lost: but how, alas, shall I either convey these to thee, or receive any thing from thee, unless some god of love, in pity of our miseries, should offer us his aid? I will try to corrupt my new boy, I see good nature, pity and generosity in his looks, he is well born too, and may be honest.

Thus far, *Philander*, I had writ when supper was brought me, for yet my parents have not deigned to let me come into their presence; those that serve me tell me *Myrtilla* is this afternoon arrived at *Bellfont*; all is mighty close carried in the Countess's apartment. I tremble with the thought of what will be the result of the great consultation: I have been tempting of the boy, but I perceive they have strictly charged him not to obey me; he says, against his will he shall betray me, for they will have him searched; but he has promised me to see one of the weeders, who working in the garden, into which my window opens, may from thence receive what I shall let down; if it be true, I shall get this fatal knowledge to you, that you may not only prepare for the worst, but contrive to set at liberty

The unfortunate SYLVIA.

My heart is ready to break, and my eyes are drowned in tears: oh Philander, *how much unlike the last will this fatal night prove! Farewell, and think of* Sylvia.

....

This was writ in the cover to both the foregoing letters to Philander.

Philander, all that I dreaded, all that I feared is fallen upon me: I have been arraigned, and convicted, three judges, severe as the three infernal ones, sat in condemnation on me, a father, a mother, and a sister; the fact, alas, was too clearly proved, and too many circumstantial truths appeared against me, for me to plead not guilty. But, oh heavens! Had you seen the tears, and heard the prayers, threats, reproaches and upbraidings — these from an injured sister, those my heartbroken parents; a tender mother here, a railing and reviling sister there — an angry father, and a guilty conscience — thou wouldst have wondered at my fortitude, my courage, and my resolution, and all from love! For surely I had died, had not thy love, thy powerful love supported me; through all the accidents of life and fate, that can and will support me; in the midst of all their clamours and their railings I had from that a secret and soft repose within, that whispered me, *Philander* loves me still; discarded and renounced by my fond parents; love still replies, *Philander* still will own thee; thrown from thy mother's and thy sister's arms, *Philander*'s still are open to receive thee: and though I rave and almost die to see them grieve, to think that I am the fatal cause who makes so sad confusion in our family; (for, oh, 'tis piteous to behold my sister's sighs and tears, my mother's sad despair, my father's raging and his weeping, by melancholy turns;) yet even these deplorable objects, that would move the most obdurate, stubborn heart to pity and repentance, render not mine relenting; and yet I am wondrous pitiful by nature, and I can weep and faint to see the sad effects of my loose, wanton love, yet cannot find repentance for the dear charming sin; and yet, should'st thou behold my mother's languishment, no bitter words proceeding from her lips, no tears fall from her downcast eyes, but silent and sad as death she sits, and will not view the light; should'st thou, I say, behold it, thou would'st, if not repent, yet grieve that thou hadst loved me: sure love has quite confounded nature in me, I could not else behold this fatal ruin without revenging it upon my stubborn heart; a thousand times a day I make new vows against the god of love, but it is too late, and I am as often perjured —— oh, should the gods revenge the broken vows of lovers, what love-sick man, what maid betrayed like me, but would be damned a thousand times? For every little love-quarrel, every kind resentment makes us swear to love no more; and every smile, and every flattering softness from the dear injurer, makes us perjured: let all the force of virtue, honour, interest join with my suffering parents to persuade me to cease to love *Philander*, yet let him but appear, let him but look on me with those dear charming eyes, let him but sigh, or press me to his fragrant cheek, fold me — and cry —'Ah, *Sylvia*, can you quit me? — nay, you must not, you shall not, nay, I know you cannot, remember you are mine — There is such eloquence in those dear words, when uttered with a voice so tender and so passionate, that I believe them irresistible — alas, I find them so — and easily break all the feebler vows I make against thee; yes, I must be undone, perjured, forsworn, incorrigible, unnatural, disobedient, and any thing, rather than not *Philander*'s — Turn then, my soul, from these domestic, melancholy objects, and look abroad, look forward for a while on charming prospects; look on *Philander*, the dear, the young, the amorous *Philander*, whose very looks infuse a tender joy throughout the soul, and chase all cares, all sorrows and anxious thoughts from thence, whose wanton play is softer I than that of young-fledged angels, and when he looks, and sighs, and speaks, and touches, he is a very god: where art thou, oh miracle of youth, thou charming dear undoer! Now thou hast gained the glory of the conquest, thou slightest the rifled captive: what, not a line? Two tedious days are past, and no kind power relieves me with a word, or any tidings of *Philander*— and yet thou mayest have sent — but I shall never see it, till they raise up fresh witnesses against me — I cannot think thee wavering or forgetful; for if I did, surely thou knowest my heart so well, thou canst not think it would live to think another thought. Confirm my kind belief, and send to me ——

There is a gate well known to thee through which thou passest to *Bellfont*, it is in the road about half a league from hence, an old man opens it, his daughter weeds in the garden, and will convey this to thee as I have ordered her; by the same messenger thou mayest return thine, and early as she comes I'll let her down a string, by which way unperceived I shall receive them from her: I will say no more, nor instruct you how you shall preserve your

SYLVIA.

••••••••••••••••••

To SYLVIA.

That which was left in her hands by Monsieur, *her father, in her cabinet.*

My adorable Sylvia,

I can no more describe to thee the torment with which I part from *Bellfont*, than I can that heaven of joy I was raised to last night by the transporting effects of thy wondrous love; both are to excess, and both killing, but in different kinds. Oh, *Sylvia*, by all my unspeakable raptures in thy arms, by all thy charms of beauty, too numerous and too ravishing for fancy to imagine — I swear —— by this last night, by this dear new discovery, thou hast increased my love to that vast height, it has undone my peace — all my repose is gone — this dear, dear night has ruined me, it has confirmed me now I must have *Sylvia*, and cannot live without her, no not a day, an hour —— to save the world, unless I had the entire possession of my lovely maid: ah, *Sylvia*, I am not that indifferent dull lover that can be raised by one beauty to an appetite, and satisfy it with another; I cannot carry the dear flame you kindle to quench it in the embraces of *Myrtilla*; no, by the eternal powers, he that pretends to love, and loves at that coarse rate, needs fear no danger from that passion, he never was born to love, or die for love; *Sylvia*, *Myrtilla* and a thousand more were all the same to such a dull insensible; no, *Sylvia*, when you find I can return back to the once left matrimonial bed, despise me, scorn me: swear (as then thou justly may'st) I love not *Sylvia*: let the hot brute drudge on (he who is fired by nature, not by love, whom any body's kisses can inspire) and ease the necessary heats of youth; love is a nobler fire, which nothing can allay but the dear she that raised it; no, no, my purer stream shall never run back to the fountain, whence it is parted, nay it cannot, it were as possible to love again, where one has ceased to love, as carry the desire and wishes back; by heaven, to me there is nothing so unnatural; no, *Sylvia*, it is you I must possess, you have completed my undoing now, and I must die unless you give me all —— but oh, I am going from thee —— when are we like to meet —— oh, how shall I support my absent hours! Thought will destroy me, for it will be all on thee, and those at such a distance will be insupportable. —— What shall I do without thee? If after all the toils of dull insipid life I could return and lay me down by thee, *Herculean* labours would be soft and easy —— the harsh fatigues of war, the dangerous hurries of affairs of State, the business and the noise of life, I could support with pleasure, with wondrous satisfaction, could treat *Myrtilla* too with that respect, that generous care, as would become a husband. I could be easy every where, and every one should be at ease with me; now I shall go and find no *Sylvia* there, but sigh and wander like an unknown thing, on some strange foreign shore; I shall grow peevish as a new wean'd child, no toys, no bauble of the gaudy world will please my wayward fancy: I shall be out of humour, rail at every thing, in anger shall demand, and sullenly reply to every question asked and answered, and when I think to ease my soul by a retreat, a thousand soft desires, a thousand wishes wreck me, pain me to raving, till beating the senseless floor with my feet —— I cried aloud —'My *Sylvia!*'— thus, thus, my charming dear, the poor *Philander* is employed when banished from his heaven! If thus it used to be when only that bright outside was adored, judge now my pain, now thou hast made known a thousand graces more — oh, pity me —— for it is not in thy power to guess what I shall now endure in absence of thee; for thou hast charmed my soul to an excess too mighty for a patient suffering: alas, I die already ——

I am yet at *Dorillus* his farm, lingering on from one swift minute to the other, and have not power to go; a thousand looks all languishing I've cast from eyes all drowned in tears towards *Bellfont*, have sighed a thousand wishes to my angel, from a sad breaking heart — love will not let me go — and honour calls me — alas, I must away; when shall we meet again? Ah, when my *Sylvia*? — Oh charming maid — thou'lt see me shortly dead, for thus I cannot live; thou must be mine, or I must be no more — I must away — farewell — may all the softest joys of heaven attend thee — adieu — fail not to send a hundred times a day, if possible; I've ordered *Alexis* to do nothing but wait for all that comes, and post away with what thou sendest to me —— again adieu, think on me —— and till thou callest me to thee, imagine nothing upon earth so wretched as *Sylvia*'s own

PHILANDER.

Know, my angel, that passing through the garden this morning, I met Erasto ——*I fear he saw me near enough to know me, and will give an account of it; let me know what happens* —— *adieu half dead, just taking horse to go from* Sylvia.

To PHILANDER.

Written in a leaf of a table-book.

I have only time to say, on Thursday I am destined a sacrifice to

Foscario, which day finishes the life of
     SYLVIA.

··················

To SYLVIA.
     From Dorillus *his farm.*
     Raving and mad at the news your billet brought me, I (without
considering the effects that would follow) am arrived at *Bellfont*; I
have yet so much patience about me, to suffer myself to be concealed
at *Dorillus* his cottage; but if I see thee not to-night, or find no hopes
of it —— by heaven I'll set Bellfont all in a flame but I will have
my *Sylvia*; be sure I'll do it — What? To be married — Sylvia to be
married — and given from *Philander*— Oh, never think it, forsworn
fair creature — What? Give *Foscario* that dear charming body? Shall
he be grasped in those dear naked arms? Taste all thy kisses, press
thy snowy breasts, command thy joys, and rifle all thy heaven? Furies
and hell environ me if he do —— Oh, Sylvia, faithless, perjured,
charming *Sylvia*— and canst thou suffer it — Hear my vows, oh fickle
angel — hear me, thou faithless ravisher! That fatal moment that
the daring priest offers to join your hands, and give thee from me,
I will sacrifice your lover; by heaven I will, before the altar, stab
him at your feet; the holy place, nor the numbers that attend ye,
nor all your prayers nor tears, shall save his heart; look to it, and
be not false —— yet I'll trust not thy faith; no, she that can think
but falsely, and she that can so easily be perjured —— for, but to
suffer it is such a sin — such an undoing sin — that thou art surely
damned! And yet, by heaven, that is not all the ruin shall attend thee;
no, lovely mischief, no —— you shall not escape till the damnation
day; for I will rack thee, torture thee and plague thee, those few
hours I have to live, (if spiteful fate prevent my just revenge upon
Foscario) and when I am dead — as I shall quickly be killed by thy
cruelty — know, thou fair murderer, I will haunt thy sight, be ever
with thee, and surround thy bed, and fright thee from the ravisher;
fright all thy loose delights, and check thy joys —— Oh, I am mad!
—— I cannot think that thought, no, thou shalt never advance so far

in wickedness, I will save thee, if I can —— Oh, my adorable, why dost thou torture me? How hast thou sworn so often and so loud that heaven I am sure has heard thee, and will punish thee? How didst thou swear that happy blessed night, in which I saw thee last, clasped in my arms, weeping with eager love, with melting softness on my bosom —— remember how thou swor'st —— oh, that dear night — let me recover strength — and then I will tell thee more — I must repeat the story of that night, which thou perhaps (oh faithless!) hast forgot — that glorious night, when all the heavens were gay, and every favouring power looked down and smiled upon our thefts of love, that gloomy night, the first of all my joys, the blessedest of my life — trembling and fainting I approach your chamber, and while you met and grasped me at the door, taking my trembling body in your arms-remember how I fainted at your feet, and what dear arts you used to call me back to life — remember how you kissed and pressed my face — Remember what dear charming words you spoke — and when I did recover, how I asked you with a feeble doubtful voice —'Ah, *Sylvia*, will you still continue thus, thus wondrous soft and fond? Will you be ever mine, and ever true?'— What did you then reply, when kneeling on the carpet where I lay, what *Sylvia*, did you vow? How invoke heaven? How call its vengeance down if ever you loved another man again, if ever you touched or smiled on any other, if ever you suffered words or acts of love but from *Philander*? Both heaven and hell thou didst awaken with thy oaths, one was an angry listener to what it knew thou'dst break, the other laughed to know thou would'st be perjured, while only I, poor I, was all the while a silent fond believer; your vows stopped all my language, as your kisses did my lips, you swore and kissed, and vowed and clasped my neck — Oh charming flatterer! Oh artful, dear beguiler! Thus into life, and peace, and fond security, you charmed my willing soul! It was then, my *Sylvia*, (certain of your heart, and that it never could be given away to any other) I pressed my eager joys, but with such tender caution — such fear and fondness, such an awful passion, as overcame your faint resistance; my reasons and my arguments were strong, for you were mine by love, by sacred vows, and who could lay a better claim to *Sylvia*? How oft I cried

—'Why this resistance, *Sylvia*? My charming dear, whose are you? Not *Philander*'s? And shall *Philander* not command his own —— you must —— ah cruel ——' then a soft struggle followed, with half-breathed words, with sighs and trembling hearts, and now and then —'Ah cruel and unreasonable'— was softly said on both sides; thus strove, thus argued — till both lay panting in each other's arms, not with the toil, but rapture; I need not say what followed after this — what tender showers of strange endearing mixtures 'twixt joy and shame, 'twixt love and new surprise, and ever when I dried your eyes with kisses, unable to repeat any other language than —'Oh my *Sylvia*! Oh my charming angel!' While sighs of joy, and close grasping thee — spoke all the rest — while every tender word, and every sigh was echoed back by thee; you pressed me — and you vowed you loved me more than ever yet you did; then swore anew, and in my bosom, hid your charming blushing face, then with excess of love would call on heaven, 'Be witness, oh ye powers' (a thousand times ye cried) 'if ever maid e'er loved like *Sylvia*— punish me strangely, oh eternal powers, if ever I leave *Philander*, if ever I cease to love him; no force, no art, not interest, honour, wealth, convenience, duty, or what other necessary cause — shall ever be of force to make me leave thee ——' Thus hast thou sworn, oh charming, faithless flatterer, thus betwixt each ravishing minute thou would'st swear — and I as fast believed — and loved thee more —— Hast thou forgot it all, oh fickle charmer, hast thou? Hast thou forgot between each awful ceremony of love, how you cried out 'Farewell the world and mortal cares, give me *Philander*, heaven, I ask no more'— Hast thou forgot all this? Did all the live-long night hear any other sound but those our mutual vows, of invocations, broken sighs, and soft and trembling whispers? Say, had we any other business for the tender hours? Oh, all ye host of heaven, ye stars that shone, and all ye powers the faithless lovely maid has sworn by, be witness how she is perjur'd; revenge it all, ye injured powers, revenge it, since by it she has undone the faithfullest youth, and broke the tenderest heart — that ever fell a sacrifice to love; and all ye little weeping gods of love, revenge your murdered victim — your

PHILANDER.

....

To PHILANDER.

In the leaves of a table-book.

On, my *Philander*, how dearly welcome, and how needless were thy kind reproaches! Which I will not endeavour to convince by argument, but such a deed as shall at once secure thy fears now and for the future. I have not a minute to write in; place, my dear *Philander*, your chariot in St *Vincent's* Wood, and since I am not able to fix the hour of my flight, let it wait there my coming; it is but a little mile from *Bellfont, Dorillus* is suspected there, remove thyself to the high-way-gate cottage — there I'll call on thee ——'twas lucky, that thy fears, or love, or jealousy brought thee so near me, since I'd resolv'd before upon my flight. Parents and honour, interest and fame, farewell — I leave you all to follow my *Philander*— Haste the chariot to the thickest part of the wood, for I am impatient to be gone, and shall take the first opportunity to fly to my *Philander*—— Oh, love me, love me, love me!

Under pretence of reaching the jessamine which shades my window, I unperceived let down and receive what letters you send by the honest weeder; by her send your sense of my flight, or rather your direction, for it is resolved already.

....

To SYLVIA.

My lovely Angel,

So careful I will be of this dear mighty secret, that I will only say, *Sylvia* shall be obeyed; no more —— nay, I'll not dare to think of it, lest in my rapture I should name my joy aloud, and busy winds should bear it to some officious listener, and undo me; no more, no more, my *Sylvia*, extremes of joy (as grief) are ever dumb: let it suffice, this blessing which you proffer I had designed to ask, as soon as you'd convinced me of your faith; yes, *Sylvia*, I had asked it though it was a bounty too great for any mortal to conceive heaven should bestow upon him; but if it do, that very moment I'll resign the world, and barter all for love and charming *Sylvia*. Haste, haste, my life; my arms, my bosom and my soul are open to receive the lovely fugitive; haste, for this moment I am going to plant myself where you directed. *Adieu*.

·····················

To PHILANDER.
   After her flight.
   Ah, *Philander*, how have you undone a harmless poor unfortunate? Alas, where are you? Why would you thus abandon me? Is this the soul, the bosom, these the arms that should receive me? I'll not upbraid thee with my love, or charge thee with my undoing; it was all my own, and were it yet to do, I should again be ruined for *Philander*, and never find repentance, no not for a thought, a word or deed of love, to the dear false forsworn; but I can die, yes, hopeless, friendless — left by all, even by *Philander*— all but resolution has abandoned me, and that can lay me down, whenever I please, in safe repose and peace: but oh, thou art not false, or if thou be'st, oh, let me hear it from thy mouth, see thy repented love, that I may know there is no such thing on earth, as faith, as honesty, as love or truth; however, be thou true, or be thou false, be bold and let me know it, for thus to doubt is torture worse than death. What accident, thou dear, dear man, has happened to prevent thee from pursuing my directions, and staying for me at the gate? Where have I missed thee, thou joy of my soul? By what dire mistake have I lost thee? And where, oh, where art thou, my charming lover? I sought thee every where, but like the languishing abandoned mistress in the *Canticles* I sought thee, but I found thee not, no bed of roses would discover thee: I saw no print of thy dear shape, nor heard no amorous sigh that could direct me — I asked the wood and springs, complained and called on thee through all the groves, but they confessed thee not; nothing but echoes answered me, and when I cried 'Philander'— cried — 'Philander'; thus searched I till the coming night, and my increasing fears made me resolve for flight, which soon we did, and soon arrived at *Paris*, but whither then to go, heaven knows, I could

not tell, for I was almost naked, friendless and forlorn; at last, consulting *Brilliard* what to do, after a thousand revolutions, he concluded to trust me with a sister he had, who was married to a *Guidon* of the *Guard de Corps*; he changed my name, and made me pass for a fortune he had stolen; but oh, no welcomes, nor my safe retreat were sufficient to repose me all the ensuing night, for I had no news of *Philander*, no, not a dream informed me; a thousand fears and jealousies have kept me waking, and *Brilliard*, who has been all night in pursuit of thee, is now returned successless and distracted as thy *Sylvia*, for duty and generosity have almost the same effects in him, with love and tenderness and jealousy in me; and since *Paris* affords no news of thee, (which sure it would if thou wert in it, for oh, the sun might hide himself with as much ease as great *Philander*) he is resolved to search St *Vincent*'s Wood, and all the adjacent cottages and groves; he thinks that you, not knowing of my escape, may yet be waiting thereabouts; since quitting the chariot for fear of being seen, you might be so far advanced into the wood, as not to find the way back to the thicket where the chariot waited: it is thus he feeds my hope, and flatters my poor heart, that fain would think thee true — or if thou be'st not — but cursed be all such thoughts, and far from *Sylvia*'s soul; no, no, thou art not false, it cannot be, thou art a god, and art unchangeable: I know, by some mistake, thou art attending me, as wild and impatient as I; perhaps you thinkest me false, and thinkest I have not courage to pursue my love, and fly; and, thou perhaps art waiting for the hour wherein thou thinkest I will give myself away to *Foscario*: oh cruel and unkind! To think I loved so lightly, to think I would attend that fatal hour; no, *Philander*, no faithless, dear enchanter: last night, the eve to my intended wedding-day, having reposed my soul by my resolves for flight, and only waiting the lucky minute for escape, I set a willing hand to every thing that was preparing for the ceremony of the ensuing morning; with that pretence I got me early to my chamber, tried on a thousand dresses, and asked a thousand questions, all impertinent, which would do best, which looked most gay and rich, then dressed my gown with jewels, decked my apartment up, and left nothing undone that might secure 'em both of my being pleased, and of my stay; nay, and to give the less suspicion, I undressed myself even to my under-petticoat and night-gown; I would not take a jewel, not a pistole, but left my women finishing my work, and carelessly and thus undressed, walked towards the garden, and while every one was busy in their office, getting myself out of sight, posted over the meadow to the wood as swift as *Daphne* from the god of day, till I arrived most luckily where I found the chariot waiting; attended by *Brilliard*; of whom, when I (all fainting and breathless with my swift flight) demanded his lord, he lifted me into the chariot, and cried, 'a little farther, *Madam*, you will find him; for he, for fear of making a discovery, took yonder shaded path'— towards which we went, but no dear vision of my love appeared — And thus, my charming lover, you have my kind adventure; send me some tidings back that you are found, that you are well, and lastly that you are mine, or this, that should have been my wedding-day, will see itself that of the death of

SYLVIA.

Paris, *Thursday, from my bed, for want of clothes, or rather news from* Philander.

....

To SYLVIA.

My life, my *Sylvia*, my eternal joy, art thou then safe! And art thou reserved for *Philander*? Am I so blest by heaven, by love, and my dear charming maid? Then let me die in peace, since I have lived to see all that my soul desires in *Sylvia*'s being mine; perplex not thy soft heart with fears or jealousies, nor think so basely, so poorly of my love, to need more oaths or vows; yet to confirm thee, I would swear my breath away; but oh, it needs not here; —— take then no care, my lovely dear, turn not thy charming eyes or thoughts on afflicting objects; oh think not on what thou hast abandoned, but what thou art arrived to; look forward on the joys of love and youth, for I will dedicate all my remaining life to render thine serene and glad; and yet, my *Sylvia*, thou art so dear to me, so wondrous precious to my soul, that in my extravagance of love, I fear I shall grow a troublesome and wearying coxcomb, shall dread every look thou givest away from me — a smile will make me rave, a sigh or touch make me commit a murder on the happy slave, or my own jealous heart, but all the world besides is *Sylvia*'s, all but another lover; but I rave and run too fast away; ages must pass a tedious term of years before I can be jealous, or conceive thou can'st be weary of *Philander*— I will be so fond, so doting, and so playing, thou shalt not have an idle minute to throw away a look in, or a thought on any other; no, no, I have thee now, and will maintain my right by dint and force of love — oh, I am wild to see thee — but, *Sylvia*, I am wounded — do not be frighted though, for it is not much or dangerous, but very troublesome, since it permits me not to fly to *Sylvia*, but she must come to me in order to it. *Brilliard* has a bill on my goldsmith in *Paris* for a thousand pistoles to buy thee something to put on; any thing that is ready, and he will conduct thee to me, for I shall rave myself into a fever if I see thee not to-day — I cannot live without thee now, for thou art my life, my everlasting charmer: I have ordered *Brilliard* to get a chariot and some unknown livery for thee, and I think the continuance of passing for what he has already rendered thee will do very well, till I have taken farther care of thy dear safety, which will be as soon as I am able to rise; for most unfortunately, my dear *Sylvia*, quitting the chariot in the thicket for fear of being seen with it, and walking down a shaded path that suited with the melancholy and fears of unsuccess in thy adventure; I went so far, as ere I could return to the place where I left the chariot it was gone — it seems with thee; I know not how you missed me — but possessed myself with a thousand false fears, sometimes that in thy flight thou mightest be pursued and overtaken, seized in the chariot and returned back to *Bellfont*; or that the chariot was found seized on upon suspicion, though the coachman and *Brilliard* were disguised past knowledge —— or if thou wert gone, alas I knew not whither; but that was a thought my doubts and fears would not suffer me to ease my soul with; no, I (as jealous lovers do) imagined the most tormenting things for my own repose. I imagined the chariot taken, or at least so discovered as to be forced away without thee: I imagined that thou wert false —— heaven forgive me, false, my *Sylvia*, and hadst changed thy mind; mad with this thought (which I fancied most reasonable, and fixt it in my soul) I raved about the wood, making a thousand vows to be revenged on all; in order to it I left the thicket, and betook myself to the high road of the wood, where I laid me down among the fern, close hid, with sword ready, waiting for the happy bridegroom, who I knew (it being the wedding eve) would that way pass that evening; pleased with revenge, which now had got even the place of love, I waited there not above a little hour but heard the trampling of a horse, and looking up with mighty joy, I found it *Foscario*'s; alone he was, and unattended, for he'd outstripped his equipage, and with a lover's haste, and full of joy, was making towards *Bellfont*; but I (now fired with rage) leaped from my cover, cried, 'Stay, *Foscario*, ere you arrive to *Sylvia*, we must adjust an odd account between us'—— at which he stopping, as nimbly alighted; — in fine, we fought, and many wounds were given and received on both sides, till his people coming up, parted us, just as we were fainting with loss of blood in each other's arms; his coach and chariot were amongst his equipage; into the first his servants lifted him, when he cried out with a feeble voice, to have me, who now lay bleeding on the ground, put into the chariot, and to be safely conveyed where- ever I commanded, and so in haste they drove him towards *Bellfont*, and me, who was resolved not to stir far from it, to a village within a mile of it; from whence I sent to *Paris* for a surgeon, and dismissed the chariot, ordering, in the hearing of the coachman, a litter to be brought me immediately, to convey me that night to *Paris*; but the surgeon coming, found it not safe for me to be removed, and I am now willing to live, since *Sylvia* is mine; haste to me then, my lovely maid, and fear not being discovered, for I have given order here in the *cabaret* where I am, if any inquiry is made after me, to say, I went last night to *Paris*. Haste, my love, haste to my arms, as feeble as they are, they'll grasp thee a dear welcome: I will say no more, nor prescribe rules to thy love, that can inform thee best what thou must do to save the life of thy most passionate adorer,

PHILANDER.

To PHILANDER.

I have sent *Brilliard* to see if the coast be clear, that we may come with safety; he brings you, instead of *Sylvia*, a young cavalier that will be altogether as welcome to *Philander*, and who impatiently waits his return at a little cottage at the end of the village.

••••••••••••••••••

To SYLVIA.

From the Bastille.

I know my *Sylvia* expected me at home with her at dinner to-day, and wonders how I could live so long as since morning without the eternal joy of my soul; but know, my *Sylvia*, that a trivial misfortune is now fallen upon me, which in the midst of all our heaven of joys, our softest hours of life, has so often changed thy smiles into fears and sighings, and ruffled thy calm soul with cares: nor let it now seem strange or afflicting, since every day for these three months we have been alarmed with new fears that have made thee uneasy even in *Philander*'s arms; we knew some time or other the storm would fall on us, though we had for three happy months sheltered ourselves from its threatening rage; but love, I hope, has armed us both; for me — let me be deprived of all joys, (but those my charmer can dispense) all the false world's respect, the dull esteem of fools and formal coxcombs, the grave advice of the censorious wise, the kind opinion of ill-judging women, no matter, so my *Sylvia* remain but mine.

I am, my *Sylvia*, arrested at the suit of *Monsieur* the Count, your father, for a rape on my lovely maid: I desire, my soul, you will immediately take coach and go to the Prince *Cesario*, and he will bail me out. I fear not a fair trial; and, *Sylvia*, thefts of mutual love were never counted felony; I may die for love, my *Sylvia*, but not for loving — go, haste, my *Sylvia*, that I may be no longer detained from the solid pleasure and business of my soul — haste, my loved dear — haste and relieve

PHILANDER.

Come not to me, lest there should be an order to detain my dear.

· · · · · · · · · · · · · · · · · · ·

To PHILANDER.

I am not at all surprised, my *Philander*, at the accident that has befallen thee, because so long expected, and love has so well fortified my heart, that I support our misfortunes with a courage worthy of her that loves and is beloved by the glorious *Philander*; I am armed for the worst that can befall me, and that is my being rendered a public shame, who have been so in the private whispers of all the Court for near these happy three months, in which I have had the wondrous satisfaction of being retired from the world with the charming *Philander*; my father too knew it long since, at least he could not hinder himself from guessing it, though his fond indulgence suffered his justice and his anger to sleep, and possibly had still slept, had not *Myrtilla*'s spite and rage (I should say just resentment, but I cannot) roused up his drowsy vengeance: I know she has plied him with her softening eloquence, her prayers and tears, to win him to consent to make a public business of it; but I am entered, love has armed my soul, and I'll pursue my fortune with that height of fortitude as shall surprise the world; yes, *Philander*, since I have lost my honour, fame and friends, my interest and my parents, and all for mightier love, I'll stop at nothing now; if there be any hazards more to run, I will thank the spiteful Fates that bring them on, and will even tire them out with my unwearied passion. Love on, *Philander*, if thou darest, like me; let 'em pursue me with their hate and vengeance, let prisons, poverty and tortures seize me, it shall not take one grain of love away from my resolved heart, nor make me shed a tear of penitence for loving thee; no, *Philander*, since I know what a ravishing pleasure it is to live thine, I will never quit the glory of dying also thy

SYLVIA.

Cesario, *my dear, is coming to be your bail; with* Monsieur *the Count of —— I die to see you after your suffering for* Sylvia.

· · · · · · · · · · · · · · · · · · ·

To SYLVIA.

BELIEVE me, charming *Sylvia*, I live not those hours I am absent from thee, thou art my life, my soul, and my eternal felicity; while you believe this truth, my *Sylvia*, you will not entertain a thousand fears, if I but stay a moment beyond my appointed hour; especially when *Philander*, who is not able to support the thought that any thing should afflict his lovely baby, takes care from hour to hour to satisfy her tender doubting heart. My dearest, I am gone into the city to my advocate's, my trial with *Monsieur* the Count, your father, coming on to-morrow, and it will be at least two tedious hours ere I can bring my adorable her
PHILANDER.

....

To SYLVIA.

I was called on, my dearest child, at my advocate's by *Cesario*; there is some great business this evening debated in the cabal, which is at *Monsieur* —— in the city; *Cesario* tells me there is a very diligent search made by *Monsieur* the Count, your father, for my *Sylvia*; I die if you are taken, lest the fright should hurt thee; if possible, I would have thee remove this evening from those lodgings, lest the people, who are of the royal party, should be induced through malice or gain to discover thee; I dare not come myself to wait on thee, lest my being seen should betray thee, but I have sent *Brilliard* (whose zeal for thee shall be rewarded) to conduct thee to a little house in the *Faubourg St Germain*, where lives a pretty woman, and mistress to *Chevalier Tomaso*, called *Belinda*, a woman of wit, and discreet enough to understand what ought to be paid to a maid of the quality and character of *Sylvia*; she already knows the stories of our loves; thither I'll come to thee, and bring *Cesario* to supper, as soon as the cabal breaks up. Oh, my *Sylvia*, I shall one day recompense all thy goodness, all thy bravery, thy love and thy suffering for thy eternal lover and slave,
PHILANDER.

••••••••••••••••••

To PHILANDER.

So hasty I was to obey *Philander*'s commands, that by the unwearied care and industry of the faithful *Brilliard*, I went before three o'clock disguised away to the place whither you ordered us, and was well received by the very pretty young woman of the house, who has sense and breeding as well as beauty: but oh, *Philander*, this flight pleases me not; alas, what have I done? my fault is only love, and that sure I should boast, as the most divine passion of the soul; no, no, *Philander*, it is not my love's the criminal, no, not the placing it on *Philander* the crime, but it is thy most unhappy circumstances, thy being married, and that was no crime to heaven till man made laws, and can laws reach to damnation? If so, curse on the fatal hour that thou wert married, curse on the priest that joined ye, and curst be all that did contribute to the undoing ceremony —— except *Philander*'s tongue, that answered yes — oh, heavens! Was there but one dear man of all your whole creation that could charm the soul of *Sylvia*! And could ye — oh, ye wise all-seeing powers that knew my soul, could ye give him away? How had my innocence offended ye? Our hearts you did create for mutual love, how came the dire mistake?

Another would have pleased the indifferent *Myrtilla*'s soul as well, but mine was fitted for no other man; only *Philander*, the adored *Philander*, with that dear form, that shape, that charming face, that hair, those lovely speaking eyes, that wounding softness in his tender voice, had power to conquer *Sylvia*; and can this be a sin? Oh, heavens, can it? Must laws, which man contrived for mere conveniency, have power to alter the divine decrees at our creation? — Perhaps they argue to-morrow at the bar, that *Myrtilla* was ordained by heaven for *Philander*; no, no, he mistook the sister, it was pretty near he came, but by a fatal error was mistaken; his hasty youth made him too negligently stop before his time at the wrong woman, he should have gazed a little farther on — and then it had been *Sylvia*'s lot —— It is fine divinity they teach, that cry marriages are made in heaven — folly and madness grown into grave custom; should an unheedy youth in heat of blood take up with the first convenient she that offers, though he be an heir to some grave politician, great and rich, and she the outcast of the common stews, coupled in height of wine, and sudden lust, which once allayed, and that the sober morning wakes him to see his error, he quits with shame the jilt, and owns no more the folly; shall this be called a heavenly conjunction? Were I in height of youth, as now I am, forced by my parents, obliged by interest and honour, to marry the old, deformed, diseased, decrepit Count *Anthonio*, whose person, qualities and principles I loathe, and rather than suffer him to consummate his nuptials, suppose I should (as sure I should) kill myself, it were blasphemy to lay this fatal marriage to heaven's charge —— curse on your nonsense, ye imposing gownmen, curse on your holy cant; you may as well call rapes and murders, treason and robbery, the acts of heaven; because heaven suffers them to be committed. Is it heaven's pleasure therefore, heaven's decree? A trick, a wise device of priests, no more —— to make the nauseated, tired-out pair drag on the careful business of life, drudge for the dull-got family with greater satisfaction, because they are taught to think marriage was made in heaven; a mighty comfort that, when all the joys of life are lost by it: were it not nobler far that honour kept him just, and that good nature made him reasonable provision? Daily experience proves to us, no couple live with less content, less ease, than those who cry heaven joins? Who is it loves less than those that marry? And where love is not, there is hate and loathing at best, disgust, disquiet, noise and repentance: no, *Philander*, that's a heavenly match when two souls touched with equal passion meet, (which is but rarely seen)— when willing vows, with serious considerations, are weighed and made, when a true view is taken of the soul, when no base interest makes the hasty bargain, when no conveniency or design, or drudge, or slave, shall find it necessary, when equal judgements meet that can esteem the blessings they possess, and distinguish the good of either's love, and set a value on each other's merits, and where both understand to take and pay; who find the beauty of each other's minds and rate them as they ought; whom not a formal ceremony binds, (with which I've nought to do, but dully give a cold consenting affirmative) but well considered vows from soft inclining hearts, uttered with love, with joy, with dear delight, when heaven is called to witness; she is thy wife, *Philander* he is my husband; this is the match, this heaven designs and means; how then, oh how came I to miss *Philander*? Or he his

SYLVIA.

Since I writ this, which I designed not an invective against marriage, when I began, but to inform thee of my being where you directed; but since I write this, I say, the house where I am is broken open with warrants and officers for me, but being all undressed and ill, the officer has taken my word for my appearance to-morrow, it seems they saw me when I went from my lodgings, and pursued me; haste to me, for I shall need your counsel.

·····················

To SYLVIA.

My eternal joy, my affliction is inexpressible at the news you send me of your being surprised; I am not able to wait on thee yet — not being suffered to leave the cabal, I only borrow this minute to tell thee the sense of my advocate in this case; which was, if thou should be taken, there was no way, no law to save thee from being ravished from my arms, but that of marrying thee to some body whom I can trust; this we have often discoursed, and thou hast often vowed thou'lt do any thing rather than kill me with a separation; resolve then, oh thou charmer of my soul, to do a deed, that though the name would fright thee, only can preserve both thee and me; it is — and though it have no other terror in it than the name, I faint to speak it — to marry, *Sylvia*; yes, thou must marry; though thou art mine as fast as heaven can make us, yet thou must marry; I have pitched upon the property, it is *Brilliard*, him I can only trust in this affair; it is but joining hands — no more, my *Sylvia* — *Brilliard* is a gentleman, though a *cadet*, and may be supposed to pretend to so great a happiness, and whose only crime is want of fortune; he is handsome too, well made, well bred, and so much real esteem he has for me, and I have so obliged him, that I am confident he will pretend no farther than to the honour of owning thee in Court; I'll time him from it, nay, he dares not do it, I will trust him with my life — but oh, *Sylvia* is more — think of it, and this night we will perform it, there being no other way to keep *Sylvia* eternally

PHILANDER's.

•••••••••••••••••••

To SYLVIA.

Now, my adorable *Sylvia*, you have truly need of all that heroic bravery of mind I ever thought thee mistress of; for *Sylvia*, coming from thee this morning, and riding full speed for *Paris*, I was met, stopped, and seized for high-treason by the King's messengers, and possibly may fall a sacrifice to the anger of an incensed monarch. My *Sylvia*, bear this last shock of fate with a courage worthy thy great and glorious soul; 'tis but a little separation, *Sylvia*, and we shall one day meet again; by heaven, I find no other sting in death but parting with my *Sylvia*, and every parting would have been the same; I might have died by thy disdain, thou might'st have grown weary of thy *Philander*, have loved another, and have broke thy vows, and tortured me to death these crueller ways: but fate is kinder to me, and I go blest with my *Sylvia*'s, love, for which heaven may do much, for her dear sake, to recompense her faith, a maid so innocent and true to sacred love; expect the best, my lovely dear, the worst has this comfort in it, that I shall die my charming *Sylvia*'s

PHILANDER.

•••••••••••••••••••

To PHILANDER.

I'LL, only say, thou dear supporter of my soul, that if *Philander* dies, he shall not go to heaven without his *Sylvia*— by heaven and earth I swear it, I cannot live without thee, nor shall thou die without thy

SYLVIA.

....

To SYLVIA.

SEE, see my adorable angel, what care the powers above take of divine innocence, true love and beauty; oh, see what they have done for their darling *Sylvia*; could they do less?

Know, my dear maid, that after being examined before the King, I was found guilty enough to be committed to the *Bastille*, (from whence, if I had gone, I had never returned, but to my death;) but the messenger, into whose hands I was committed, refusing other guards, being alone with me in my own coach, I resolved to kill, if I could no other way oblige him to favour my escape; I tried with gold before I shewed my dagger, and that prevailed, a way less criminal, and I have taken sanctuary in a small cottage near the sea-shore, where I wait for *Sylvia*; and though my life depend upon my flight, nay, more, the life of *Sylvia*, I cannot go without her; dress yourself then, my dearest, in your boy's clothes, and haste with *Brilliant*, whither this seaman will conduct thee, whom I have hired to set us on some shore of safety; bring what news you can learn of *Cesario*; I would not have him die poorly after all his mighty hopes, nor be conducted to a scaffold with shouts of joys, by that uncertain beast the rabble, who used to stop his chariot-wheels with fickle adorations whenever he looked abroad — by heaven, I pity him; but *Sylvia*'s presence will chase away all thoughts, but those of love, from

PHILANDER.

I need not bid thee haste.

The End of the first Part.

Chapter 2

At the end of the first part of these letters, we left *Philander* impatiently waiting on the sea-shore for the approach of the lovely *Sylvia*; who accordingly came to him dressed like a youth, to secure herself from a discovery. They stayed not long to caress each other, but he taking the welcome maid in his arms, with a transported joy bore her to a small vessel, that lay ready near the beach; where, with only *Brilliard* and two men servants, they put to sea, and passed into *Holland*, landing at the nearest port; where, after having refreshed themselves for two or three days, they passed forwards towards the *Brill*, *Sylvia* still remaining under that amiable disguise: but in their passage from town to town, which is sometimes by coach, and other times by boat, they chanced one day to encounter a young *Hollander* of a more than ordinary gallantry for that country, so degenerate from good manners, and almost common civility, and so far short of all the good qualities that made themselves appear in this young nobleman. He was very handsome, well made, well dressed, and very well attended; and whom we will call *Octavio*, and who, young as he was, was one of the *States* of *Holland*; he spoke admirable good *French*, and had a vivacity and quickness of wit unusual with the natives of that part of the world, and almost above all the rest of his sex: *Philander* and *Sylvia* having already agreed for the cabin of the vessel that was to carry them to the next stage, *Octavio* came too late to have any place there but amongst the common crowd; which the master of the vessel, who knew him, was much troubled at, and addressed himself as civilly as he could to *Philander*, to beg permission for one stranger of quality to dispose of himself in the cabin for that day: *Philander* being well enough pleased, so to make an acquaintance with some of power of that country, readily consented; and *Octavio* entered with an address so graceful and obliging, that at first sight he inclined *Philander*'s, heart to a friendship with him; and on the other side the lovely person of *Philander*, the quality that appeared in his face and mien, obliged *Octavio* to become no less his admirer. But when he saluted *Sylvia*, who appeared to him a youth of quality, he was extremely charmed with her pretty gaiety, and an unusual air and life in her address and motion; he felt a secret joy and pleasure play about his soul, he knew not why, and was almost angry, that he felt such an emotion for a youth, though the most lovely that he ever saw. After the first compliments, they fell into discourse of a thousand indifferent things, and if he were pleased at first sight with the two lovers, he was wholly charmed by their conversation, especially that of the amiable youth; who well enough pleased with the young stranger, or else hitherto having met nothing so accomplished in her short travels; and indeed despairing to meet any such; she put on all her gaiety and charms of wit, and made as absolute a conquest as it was possible for her supposed sex to do over a man, who was a great admirer of the other; and surely the lovely maid never appeared so charming and desirable as that day; they dined together in the cabin; and after dinner reposed on little mattresses by each other's side, where every motion, every limb, as carelessly she lay, discovered a thousand graces, and more and more enflamed the now beginning lover; she could not move, nor smile, nor speak, nor order any charm about her, but had some peculiar grace that began to make him uneasy; and from a thousand little modesties, both in her blushes and motions, he had a secret hope she was not what she seemed, but of that sex whereof she discovered so many softnesses and beauties; though to what advantage that hope would amount to his repose, was yet a disquiet he had not considered nor felt: nor could he by any fondness between them, or indiscretion of love, conceive how the lovely strangers were allied; he only hoped, and had no thoughts of fear, or any thing that could check his new beginning flame. While thus they passed the afternoon, they asked a thousand questions, of lovers, of the country and manners, and their security and civility to strangers; to all which *Octavio* answered as a man, who would recommend the place and persons purely to oblige their stay; for now self-interest makes him say all things in favour of it; and of his own friendship, offers them all the service of a man in power, and who could make an interest in those that had more than himself; much he protested, much he offered, and yet no more than he designed to make good on all occasions, which they received with an acknowledgement that plainly discovered a generosity and quality above the common rate of men; so that finding in each other occasions for love and friendship, they mutually professed it, and nobly entertained it. *Octavio* told his name and quality, left nothing unsaid that might confirm the lovers of his sincerity. This begot a confidence in *Philander*, who in return told him so much of his circumstances, as sufficed to let him know he was a person so unfortunate to have occasioned the displeasure of his king against him, and that he could not continue with any repose in that kingdom, whose monarch thought him no longer fit for those honours he had before received: *Octavio* renewed his protestations of serving him with his interest and fortune, which the other receiving with all the gallant modesty of an unfortunate man, they came ashore, where *Octavio*'s coaches and equipage waiting his coming to conduct him to his house, he offered his new friends the best of them to carry them to their lodging, which he had often pressed might be his own palace; but that being refused as too great an honour, he would himself see them placed in some one, which he thought might be most suitable to their quality; they excused the trouble, but he pressed too eagerly to be denied, and he conducted them to a merchant's house not far from his own, so love had contrived for the better management of this new affair of his heart, which he resolved to pursue, be the fair object of what sex soever: but after having well enough recommended them to the care of the merchant, he thought it justice to leave them to their rest, though with abundance of reluctancy; so took his leave of both the lovely strangers, and went to his own home. And after a hasty supper got himself up to bed: not to sleep; for now he had other business: love took him now to task, and asked his heart a thousand questions. Then it was he found the idea of that fair unknown had absolute possession there: nor was he at all displeased to find he was a captive; his youth and quality promise his hopes a thousand advantages above all other men: but when he reflected on the beauty

of Philander, on his charming youth and conversation, and every
grace that adorns a conqueror, he grew inflamed, disordered,
restless, angry, and out of love with his own attractions; considered
every beauty of his own person, and found them, or at least thought
them infinitely short of those of his now fancied rival; yet it was a
rival that he could not hate, nor did his passion abate one thought of
his friendship for Philander, but rather more increased it, insomuch
that he once resolved it should surmount his love if possible, at
least he left it on the upper-hand, till time should make a better
discovery. When tired with thought we'll suppose him asleep, and see
how our lovers fared; who being lodged all on one stair-case (that
is, Philander, Sylvia, and Brilliard) it was not hard for the lover to
steal into the longing arms of the expecting *Sylvia*; no fatigues of
tedious journeys, and little voyages, had abated her fondness, or his
vigour; the night was like the first, all joy! All transport! *Brilliard*
lay so near as to be a witness to all their sighs of love, and little
soft murmurs, who now began from a servant to be permitted as an
humble companion; since he had had the honour of being married
to *Sylvia*, though yet he durst not lift his eyes or thoughts that way;
yet it might be perceived he was melancholy and sullen whenever he
saw their dalliances; nor could he know the joys his lord nightly stole,
without an impatience, which, if but minded or known, perhaps had
cost him his life. He began, from the thoughts she was his wife, to
fancy fine enjoyment, to fancy authority which he durst not assume,
and often wished his lord would grow cold, as possessing lovers do,
that then he might advance his hope, when he should even abandon
or slight her: he could not see her kissed without blushing with
resentment; but if he has assisted to undress him for her bed, he was
ready to die with anger, and would grow sick, and leave the office to
himself: he could not see her naked charms, her arms stretched out
to receive a lover, with impatient joy, without madness; to see her
clasp him fast, when he threw himself into her soft, white bosom, and
smother him with kisses: no, he could not bear it now, and almost
lost his respect when he beheld it, and grew saucy unperceived. And
it was in vain that he looked back upon the reward he had to stand for
that necessary cypher a husband. In vain he considered the reasons

why, and the occasion wherefore; he now seeks precedents of usurped dominion, and thinks she is his wife, and has forgot that he is her creature, and *Philander*'s vassal. These thoughts disturbed him all the night, and a certain jealousy, or rather curiosity to listen to every motion of the lovers, while they were employed after a different manner.

Next day it was debated what was best to be done, as to their conduct in that place; or whether *Sylvia* should yet own her sex or not; but she, pleased with the cavalier in herself, begged she might live under that disguise, which indeed gave her a thousand charms to those which nature had already bestowed on her sex; and Philander was well enough pleased she should continue in that agreeable dress, which did not only add to her beauty, but gave her a thousand little privileges, which otherwise would have been denied to women, though in a country of much freedom. Every day she appeared in the Tour, she failed not to make a conquest on some unguarded heart of the fair sex: not was it long ere she received *billets-doux* from many of the most accomplished who could speak and write *French*. This gave them a pleasure in the midst of her unlucky exile, and she failed not to boast her conquests to Octavio, who every day gave all his hours to love, under the disguise of friendship, and every day received new wounds, both from her conversation and beauty, and every day confirmed him more in his first belief, that she was a woman; and that confirmed his love. But still he took care to hide his passion with a gallantry, that was natural to him, and to very few besides; and he managed his eyes, which were always full of love, so equally to both, that when he was soft and fond it appeared more his natural humour, than from any particular cause. And that you may believe that all the arts of gallantry, and graces of good management were more peculiarly his than another's, his race was illustrious, being descended from that of the Princes of *Orange*, and great birth will shine through, and shew itself in spite of education and obscurity: but *Octavio* had all those additions that render a man truly great and brave; and this is the character of him that was next undone by our unfortunate and fatal beauty. At this rate for some time they lived thus disguised under feigned names, *Octavio* omitting nothing that might oblige them in the highest degree, and hardly any thing was talked of but the new and beautiful strangers, whose conquests in all places over the ladies are well worthy, both for their rarity and comedy, to be related entirely by themselves in a novel. *Octavio* saw every day with abundance of pleasure the little revenges of love, on those women's hearts who had made before little conquests over him, and strove by all the gay presents he made a young *Fillmond* (for so they called *Sylvia*,) to make him appear unresistible to the ladies; and while *Sylvia* gave them new wounds, *Octavio* failed not to receive them too among the crowd, till at last he became a confirmed slave, to the lovely unknown; and that which was yet more strange, she captivated the men no less than the women, who often gave her *serenades* under her window, with songs fitted to the courtship of a boy, all which added to their diversion: but fortune had smiled long enough, and now grew weary of obliging, she was resolved to undeceive both sexes, and let them see the errors of their love; for *Sylvia* fell into a fever so violent, that *Philander* no longer hoped for her recovery, insomuch that she was obliged to own her sex, and take women servants out of decency. This made the first discovery of who and what they were, and for which every body languished under a secret grief. But *Octavio*, who now was not only confirmed she was a woman, but that she was neither wife to *Philander*, nor could in almost all possibility ever be so; that she was his mistress, gave him hope that she might one day as well be conquered by him; and he found her youth, her beauty, and her quality, merited all his pains of lavish courtship. And now there remains no more than the fear of her dying to oblige him immediately to a discovery of his passion, too violent now by his new hope to be longer concealed, but decency forbids he should now pursue the dear design; he waited and made vows for her recovery; visited her, and found *Philander* the most deplorable object that despair and love could render him, who lay eternally weeping on her bed, and no counsel or persuasion could remove him thence; but if by chance they made him sensible it was for her repose, he would depart to ease his mind by new torments, he would rave and tear his delicate hair, sigh and weep upon *Octavio*'s bosom, and a thousand times begin to unfold the story, already known to the generous rival; despair, and hopes of pity from him, made him utter all: and one day, when by the advice of the physician he was forced to quit the chamber to give her rest, he carried *Octavio* to his own, and told him from the beginning, all the story of his love with the charming *Sylvia*, and with it all the story of his fate: *Octavio* sighing (though glad of the opportunity) told him his affairs were already but too well known, and that he feared his safety from that discovery, since the States had obliged themselves to harbour no declared enemy to the *French* King. At this news our young unfortunate shewed a resentment that was so moving, that even *Octavio*, who felt a secret joy at the thoughts of his departure, could no longer refrain from pity and tenderness, even to a wish that he were less unhappy, and never to part from *Sylvia*: but love soon grew again triumphant in his heart, and all he could say was, that he would afford him the aids of all his power in this encounter; which, with the acknowledgements of a lover, whose life depended on it, he received, and parted with him, who went to learn what was decreed in Council concerning him. While *Philander* returned to *Sylvia*, the most dejected lover that ever fate produced, when he had not sighed away above an hour, but received a billet by *Octavio*'s page from his lord; he went to his own apartment to read it, fearing it might contain something too sad for him to be able to hold his temper at the reading of, and which would infallibly have disturbed the repose of *Sylvia*, who shared in every cruel thought of *Philander*'s: when he was alone he opened it, and read this.

OCTAVIO *to* PHILANDER.

My Lord,

I had rather die than be the ungrateful messenger of news, which I am sensible will prove too fatal to you, and which will be best expressed in fewest words: it is decreed that you must retire from the United Provinces in four and twenty hours, if you will save a life that is dear to me and *Sylvia*, there being no other security against your being rendered up to the King of *France*. Support it well, and hope all things from the assistance of your

OCTAVIO.

From the Council, Wednesday.

Philander having finished the reading of this, remained a while wholly without life or motion, when coming to himself, he sighed and cried — 'Why — farewell trifling life — if of the two extremes one must be chosen, rather than I'll abandon *Sylvia*, I'll stay and be delivered up a victim to incensed *France*— It is but a life — at best I never valued thee — and now I scorn to preserve thee at the price of *Sylvia*'s tears!' Then taking a hasty turn or two about his chamber, he pausing cried — 'But by my stay I ruin both *Sylvia* and myself, her life depends on mine; and it is impossible hers can be preserved when mine is in danger: by retiring I shall shortly again be blessed with her sight in a more safe security, by staying I resign myself poorly to be made a public scorn to *France*, and the cruel murderer of *Sylvia*.' Now, it was after an hundred turns and pauses, intermixed with sighs and ravings, that he resolved for both their safeties to retire; and having a while longer debated within himself how, and where, and a little time ruminated on his hard pursuing fate, grown to a calm of grief, (less easy to be borne than rage) he hastes to *Sylvia*, whom he found something more cheerful than before, but dares not acquaint her with the commands he had to depart —— But silently he views her, while tears of love and grief glide unperceivably from his fine eyes, his soul grows tenderer at every look, and pity and compassion joining to his love and his despair, set him on the wreck of life; and now believing it less pain to die than to leave *Sylvia*, resolves to disobey, and dare the worst that shall befall him; he had some glimmering hope, as lovers have, that some kind chance will prevent his going, or being delivered up; he trusts much to the friendship of *Octavio*, whose power joined with that of his uncle, (who was one of the *States* also, and whom he had an ascendant over, as his nephew and his heir) might serve him; he therefore ventures to move him to compassion by this following letter.

PHILANDER *to* OCTAVIO.

I know, my lord, that the exercise of virtue and justice is so innate to your soul, and fixed to the very principle of a generous commonwealth's man, that where those are in competition, it is neither birth, wealth, or glorious merit, that can render the unfortunate condemned by you, worthy of your pity or pardon: your very sons and fathers fall before your justice, and it is crime enough to offend (though innocently) the least of your wholesome laws, to fall under the extremity of their rigour. I am not ignorant neither how flourishing this necessary tyranny, this lawful oppression renders your State; how safe and glorious, how secure from enemies at home, (those worst of foes) and how feared by those abroad: pursue then, sir, your justifiable method, and still be high and mighty, retain your ancient Roman virtue, and still be great as *Rome* herself in her height of glorious commonwealths; rule your stubborn natives by her excellent examples, and let the height of your ambition be only to be as severely just, as rigidly good as you please; but like her too, be pitiful to strangers, and dispense a noble charity to the distressed, compassionate a poor wandering young man, who flies to you for refuge, lost to his native home, lost to his fame, his fortune, and his friends; and has only left him the knowledge of his innocence to support him from falling on his own sword, to end an unfortunate life, pursued every where, and safe no where; a life whose only refuge is *Octavio*'s goodness; nor is it barely to preserve this life that I have recourse to that only as my sanctuary, and like an humble slave implore your pity: oh, *Octavio*, pity my youth, and intercede for my stay yet a little longer: yourself makes one of the illustrious number of the grave, the wise and mighty Council, your uncle and relations make up another considerable part of it, and you are too dear to all, to find a refusal of your just and compassionate application. Oh! What fault have I committed against you, that I should not find a safety here; as well as those charged with the same crime with me, though of less quality? Many I have encountered here of our unlucky party, who find a safety among you: is my birth a crime? Or does the greatness of that augment my guilt? Have I broken any of your laws, committed any outrage? Do they suspect me for a spy to *France*! Or do I hold any correspondence with that ungrateful nation? Does my religion, principle, or opinion differ from yours? Can I design the subversion of your glorious State? Can I plot, cabal, or mutiny alone? Oh charge me with some offence, or yourselves of injustice. Say, why am I denied my length of earth amongst you, if I die? Or why to breathe the open air, if I live, since I shall neither oppress the one, nor infect the other? But on the contrary am ready with my sword, my youth and blood to serve you, and bring my little aids on all occasions to yours: and should be proud of the glory to die for you in battle, who would deliver me up a sacrifice to *France*. Oh! where, *Octavio*, is the glory or virtue of this *punctilio*? For it is no other: there are no laws that bind you to it, no obligatory article of Nations, but an unnecessary compliment made a *nemine contradicente* of your senate, that argues nothing but ill nature, and cannot redound to any one's advantage; an ill nature that's levelled at me alone; for many I found here, and many shall leave under the same circumstances with me; it is only me whom you have marked out the victim to atone for all: well then, my lord, if nothing can move you to a safety for this unfortunate, at least be so merciful to suspend your cruelty a little, yet a little, and possibly I shall render you the body of *Philander*, though dead, to send into *France*, as the trophy of your fidelity to that Crown: oh yet a little stay your cruel sentence, till my lovely sister, who pursued my hard fortunes, declare my fate by her life or death: oh, my lord, if ever the soft passion of love have touched your soul, if you have felt the unresistible force of young charms about your heart, if ever you have known a pain and pleasure from fair eyes, or the transporting joys of beauty, pity a youth undone by love and ambition, those powerful conquerors of the young —— pity, oh pity a youth that dies, and will ere long no more complain upon your rigours. Yes, my lord, he dies without the force of a terrifying sentence, without the grim reproaches of an angry judge, without the soon consulted arbitrary —— guilty of a severe and hasty jury, without the ceremony of the scaffold, axe, and hangman, and the clamours of inconsidering crowds; all which melancholy ceremonies render death so terrible, which else would fall like gentle slumbers upon the eye-lids, and which in field I would encounter with that joy I would the sacred thing I love! But oh, I fear my fate is in the lovely *Sylvia*, and in her dying eyes you may read it, in her languishing face you will see how near it is approached. Ah, will you not suffer me to attend it there? By her dear side I shall fall as calmly as flowers from their stalks, without regret or pain: will you, by forcing me to die from her, run me to a madness? To wild distraction? Oh think it sufficient

that I die here before half my race of youth be run, before the light
be half burnt out, that might have conducted me to a world of glory!
Alas, she dies=-the lovely *Sylvia* dies; she is sighing out a soul to
which mine is so entirely fixed, that they must go upward together;
yes, yes, she breathes it sick into my bosom, and kindly gives mine
its disease of death: let us at least then die in silence quietly; and
if it please heaven to restore the languished charmer, I will resign
myself up to all your rigorous honour; only let me bear my treasure
with me, while we wander over the world to seek us out a safety in
some part of it, where pity and compassion is no crime, where men
have tender hearts, and have heard of the god of love; where politics
are not all the business of the powerful, but where civility and good
nature reign.

Perhaps, my lord, you will wonder I plead no weightier argument
for my stay than love, or the griefs and tears of a languishing maid:
but, oh! they are such tears as every drop would ransom lives, and
nothing that proceeds from her charming eyes can be valued at a less
rate! In pity to her, to me, and your amorous youths, let me bear her
hence: for should she look abroad as her own sex, should she appear
in her natural and proper beauty, alas they were undone. Reproach
not (my lord) the weakness of this confession, and which I make with
more glory than could I boast myself lord of all the universe: if it
appear a fault to the more grave and wise, I hope my youth will plead
something for my excuse. Oh say, at least, it was pity that love had
the ascendant over *Philander*'s soul, say it was his destiny, but say
withal, that it put no stop to his advance to glory; rather it set an edge
upon his sword, and gave wings to his ambition! — Yes, try me in
your Councils, prove me in your camps, place me in any hazard — but
give me love! And leave me to wait the life or death of *Sylvia*, and
then dispose as you please, my lord, of your unfortunate
PHILANDER.

....

OCTAVIO *to* PHILANDER.
My Lord,

I am much concerned, that a request so reasonable as you have made, will be of so little force with these arbitrary tyrants of State; and though you have addressed and appealed to me as one of that grave and rigid number, (though without one grain of their formalities, and I hope age, which renders us less gallant, and more envious of the joys and liberties of youth, will never reduce me to so dull and thoughtless a Member of State) yet I have so small and single a portion of their power, that I am ashamed of my incapacity of serving you in this great affair. I bear the honour and the name, it is true, of glorious sway; but I can boast but of the worst and most impotent part of it, the title only; but the busy, absolute, mischievous politician finds no room in my soul, my humour, or constitution; and plodding restless power I have made so little the business of my gayer and more careless youth, that I have even lost my right of rule, my share of empire amongst them. That little power (whose unregarded loss I never bemoaned till it rendered me incapable of serving *Philander*) I have stretched to the utmost bound for your stay; insomuch that I have received many reproaches from the wiser coxcombs, have made my youth's little debauches hinted on, and judgements made of you (disadvantageous) from my friendship to you; a friendship, which, my lord, at first sight of you found a being in my soul, and which your wit, your goodness, your greatness, and your misfortunes have improved to all the degrees of it: though I am infinitely unhappy that it proves of no use to you here, and that the greatest testimony I can now render of it, is to warn you of your approaching danger, and hasten your departure, for there is no safety in your stay. I just now heard what was decreed against you in Council, which no pleading, nor eloquence of friendship had force enough to evade. Alas, I had but one single voice in the number, which I sullenly and singly gave, and which unregarded passed. Go then, my lord, haste to some place where good breeding and humanity reigns: go and preserve *Sylvia*, in providing for your own safety; and believe me, till she be in a condition to pursue your fortunes, I will take such care that nothing shall be wanting to her recovery here, in order to her following after you. I am, alas, but too sensible of all the pains you must endure by such a separation; for

I am neither insensible, nor incapable of love, or any of its violent effects: go then, my lord, and preserve the lovely maid in your flight, since your stay and danger will serve but to hasten on her death: go and be satisfied she shall find a protection suitable to her sex, her innocence, her beauty, and her quality; and that wherever you fix your stay, she shall be resigned to your arms by, my lord, your eternal friend and humble servant,

OCTAVIO.

Lest in this sudden remove you should want money, I have sent you several Bills of Exchange to what place soever you arrive, and what you want more (make no scruple to use me as a friend and) command.

After this letter finding no hopes, but on the contrary a dire necessity of departing, he told *Brilliard* his misfortune, and asked his counsel in this extremity of affairs. *Brilliard*, (who of a servant was become a rival) you may believe, gave him such advice as might remove him from the object he adored. But after a great deal of dissembled trouble, the better to hide his joy, he gave his advice for his going, with all the arguments that appeared reasonable enough to *Philander*; and at every period urged, that his life being dear to *Sylvia*, and on which hers so immediately depended, he ought no longer to debate, but hasten his flight: to all which counsel our amorous hero, with a soul ready to make its way through his trembling body, gave a sighing unwilling assent. It was now no longer a dispute, but was concluded he must go; but how was the only question. How should he take his farewell? How he should bid adieu, and leave the dear object of his soul in an estate so hazardous? He formed a thousand sad ideas to torment himself with fancying he should never see her more, that he should hear that she was dead, though now she appeared on this side the grave, and had all the signs of a declining disease. He fancied absence might make her cold, and abate her passion to him; that her powerful beauty might attract adorers, and she being but a woman, and no part angel but her form, 'twas not expected she should want her sex's frailties. Now he could consider how he had won her, how by importunity and opportunity she had at last yielded to him, and therefore might

to some new gamester, when he was not by to keep her heart in
continual play: then it was that all the despair of jealous love, the
throbs and piercing of a violent passion seized his timorous and
tender heart, he fancied her already in some new lover's arms, and
ran over all these soft enjoyments he had with her; and fancied with
tormenting thought, that so another would possess her; till racked
with tortures, he almost fainted on the repose on which he was set:
but *Brilliard* roused and endeavoured to convince him, told him he
hoped his fear was needless, and that he would take all the watchful
care imaginable of her conduct, be a spy upon her virtue, and from
time to time give him notice of all that should pass! Bid him consider
her quality, and that she was no common mistress whom hire could
lead astray; and that if from the violence of her passion, or her most
severe fate, she had yielded to the most charming of men, he ought
as little to imagine she could be again a lover, as that she could find
an object of equal beauty with that of *Philander*. In fine, he soothed
and flattered him into so much ease, that he resolves to take his
leave for a day or two, under pretence of meeting and consulting
with some of the rebel party; and that he would return again to her
by that time it might be imagined her fever might be abated, and
Sylvia in a condition to receive the news of his being gone for a
longer time, and to know all his affairs. While *Brilliard* prepared all
things necessary for his departure, *Philander* went to *Sylvia*; from
whom, having been absent two tedious hours, she caught him in
her arms with a transport of joy, reproached him with want of love,
for being absent so long: but still the more she spoke soft sighing
words of love, the more his soul was seized with melancholy, his sighs
redoubled, and he could not refrain from letting fall some tears upon
her bosom —— which *Sylvia* perceiving, with a look and a trembling
in her voice, that spoke her fears, she cried, 'Oh *Philander*! These
are unusual marks of your tenderness; oh tell me, tell me quickly
what they mean.' He answered with a sigh, and she went on —'It is
so, I am undone, it is your lost vows, your broken faith you weep;
yes, *Philander*, you find the flower of my beauty faded, and what
you loved before, you pity now, and these be the effects of it.' Then
sighing, as if his soul had been departing on her neck, he cried, 'By

heaven, by all the powers of love, thou art the same dear charmer that thou wert;' then pressing her body to his bosom, he sighed anew as if his heart were breaking —'I know' (says she) '*Philander*, there is some hidden cause that gives these sighs their way, and that dear face a paleness. Oh tell me all; for she that could abandon all for thee, can dare the worst of fate: if thou must quit me —— oh *Philander*, if it must be so, I need not stay the lingering death of a feeble fever; I know a way more noble and more sudden.' Pleased at her resolution, which almost destroyed his jealousy and fears, a thousand times he kissed her, mixing his grateful words and thanks with sighs; and finding her fair hands (which he put often to his mouth) to increase their fires, and her pulse to be more high and quick, fearing to relapse her into her (abating) fever, he forced a smile, and told her, he had no griefs, but what she made him feel, no torments but her sickness, nor sighs but for her pain, and left nothing unsaid that might confirm her he was still more and more her slave; and concealing his design in favour of her health, he ceased not vowing and protesting, till he had settled her in all the tranquillity of a recovering beauty. And as since her first illness he had never departed from her bed, so now this night he strove to appear in her arms with all that usual gaiety of love that her condition would permit, or his circumstances could feign, and leaving her asleep at day-break (with a force upon his soul that cannot be conceived but by parting lovers) he stole from her arms, and retiring to his chamber, he soon got himself ready for his flight, and departed. We will leave *Sylvia*'s ravings to be expressed by none but herself, and tell you that after about fourteen days' absence, *Octavio* received this letter from *Philander*.

PHILANDER *to* OCTAVIO.

Being safely arrived at *Cologne*, and by a very pretty and lucky adventure lodged in the house of the best quality in the town, I find myself much more at ease than I thought it possible to be without *Sylvia*, from whom I am nevertheless impatient to hear; I hope absence appears not so great a bugbear to her as it was imagined: for I know not what effects it would have on me to hear her griefs exceeded a few sighs and tears: those my kind absence has taught me to allow and bear without much pain, but should her love transport her to extremes of rage and despair, I fear I should quit my safety here, and give her the last proof of my love and my compassion, throw myself at her feet, and expose my life to preserve hers. Honour would oblige me to it. I conjure you, my dear *Octavio*, by all the friendship you have vowed me, (and which I no longer doubt) let me speedily know how she bears my absence, for on that knowledge depends a great deal of the satisfaction of my life; carry her this enclosed which I have writ her, and soften my silent departure, which possibly may appear rude and unkind, plead my pardon, and give her the story of my necessity of offending, which none can so well relate as yourself; and from a mouth so eloquent to a maid so full of love, will soon reconcile me to her heart. With her letter I send you a bill to pay her 2000 patacons, which I have paid *Vander Hanskin* here, as his letter will inform you, as also those bills I received of you at my departure, having been supplied by an *English* merchant here, who gave me credit. It will be an age, till I hear from you, and receive the news of the health of *Sylvia*, than which two blessings nothing will be more welcome to, generous *Octavio*, your

PHILANDER.

Direct your letters for me to your merchant Vander Hanskin.

....

PHILANDER *to* SYLVIA.

There is no way left to gain my *Sylvia*'s pardon for leaving her, and leaving her in such circumstances, but to tell her it was to preserve a life which I believed entirely dear to her; but that unhappy crime is too severely punished by the cruelties of my absence: believe me, lovely *Sylvia*, I have felt all your pains, I have burnt with your fever, and sighed with your oppressions; say, has my pain abated yours? Tell me, and hasten my health by the assurance of your recovery, or I have fled in vain from those dear arms to save my life, of which I know not what account to give you, till I receive from you the knowledge of your perfect health, the true state of mine. I can only say I sigh, and have a sort of a being in *Cologne*, where I have some more assurance of protection than I could hope I from those interested brutes, who sent me from you; yet brutish as they are, I know thou art safe from their clownish outrages. For were they senseless as their fellow-monsters of the sea, they durst not profane so pure an excellence as thine; the sullen boars would jouder out a welcome to thee, and gape, I and wonder at thy awful beauty, though they want the tender sense to know to what use it was made. Or if I doubted their humanity, I cannot the friendship of *Octavio*, since he has given me too good a proof of it, to leave me any fear that he has not in my absence pursued those generous sentiments for *Sylvia*, which he vowed to *Philander*, and of which this first proof must be his relating the necessity of my absence, to set me well with my adorable maid, who, better than I, can inform her; and that I rather chose to quit you only for a short space, than reduce myself to the necessity of losing you eternally. Let the satisfaction this ought to give you retrieve your health and beauty, and put you into a condition of restoring to me all my joys; that by pursuing the dictates of your love, you may again bring the greatest happiness on earth to the arms of your

PHILANDER.

POSTSCRIPT.

My affairs here are yet so unsettled, that I can take no order for your coming to me; but as soon as I know where I can fix with safety, I shall make it my business and my happiness: adieu. Trust Octavio *with your letters only.*

This letter *Octavio* would not carry himself to her, who had omitted no day, scarce an hour, wherein he saw not or sent not to the charming *Sylvia*; but he found in that which *Philander* had writ to him an air of coldness altogether unusual with that passionate lover, and infinitely short in point of tenderness to those he had formerly seen of his, and from what he had heard him speak; so that he no longer doubted (and the rather because he hoped it) but that *Philander* found an abatement of that heat, which was wont to inspire at a more amorous rate: this appearing declension he could not conceal from *Sylvia*, at least to let her know he took notice of it; for he knew her love was too quick-sighted and sensible to pass it unregarded; but he with reason thought, that when she should find others observe the little slight she had put on her, her pride (which is natural to women in such cases) would decline and lessen her love for his rival. He therefore sent his page with the letters enclosed in this from himself.

OCTAVIO *to* SYLVIA.

Madam,

From a little necessary debauch I made last night with the Prince, I am forced to employ my page in those duties I ought to have performed myself: he brings you, madam, a letter from *Philander*, as mine, which I have also sent you, informs me; I should else have doubted it; it is, I think, his character, and all he says of *Octavio* confesses the friend, but where he speaks of *Sylvia* sure he disguises the lover: I wonder the mask should be put on now to me, to whom before he so frankly discovered the secrets of his amorous heart. It is a mystery I would fain persuade myself he finds absolutely necessary to his interest, and I hope you will make the same favourable constructions of it, and not impute the lessened zeal wherewith he treats the charming *Sylvia* to any possible change or coldness, since I am but too fatally sensible, that no man can arrive at the glory of being beloved by you, that had ever power to shorten one link of that dear chain that holds him, and you need but survey that adorable face, to confirm your tranquillity; set a just value on your charms, and you need no arguments to secure your everlasting empire, or to establish it in what heart you please. This fatal truth I learned from your fair eyes, ere they discovered to me your sex, and you may as soon change to what I then believed you, as I from adoring what I now find you: if all then, madam, that do but look on you become your slaves, and languish for you, love on, even without hope, and die, what must *Philander* pay you, who has the mighty blessing of your love, your vows, and all that renders the hours of amorous youth, sacred, glad, and triumphant? But you know the conquering power of your charms too well to need either this daring confession, or a defence of *Philander*'s virtue from, madam, your obedient slave,

OCTAVIO.

Sylvia had no sooner read this with blushes, and a thousand fears, and trembling of what was to follow in *Philander*'s letters both to

Octavio and to herself, but with an indignation agreeable to her haughty soul, she cried —'How — slighted! And must *Octavio* see it too! By heaven, if I should find it true, he shall not dare to think it.' Then with a generous rage she broke open *Philander*'s, letter; and which she soon perceived did but too well prove the truth of *Octavio*'s suspicion, and her own fears. She repeated it again and again, and still she found more cause of grief and anger; love occasioned the first, and pride the last; and, to a soul perfectly haughty, as was that of *Sylvia*, it was hard to guess which had the ascendant: she considered *Octavio* to all the advantages that thought could conceive in one, who was not a lover of him; she knew he merited a heart, though she had none to give him; she found him charming without having a tenderness for him; she found him young and amorous without desire towards him; she found him great, rich, powerful and generous without designing on him; and though she knew her soul free from all passion, but that for *Philander*, nevertheless she blushed and was angry, that he had thoughts no more advantageous to the power of those charms, which she wish'd might appear to him above her sex, it being natural to women to desire conquests, though they hate the conquered; to glory in the triumph, though they despise the slave: and she believed, while *Octavio* had so poor a sense of her beauty as to believe it could be forsaken, he would adore it less: and first, to satisfy her pride, she left the softer business of her heart to the next tormenting hour, and sent him this careless answer by his page, believing, if she valued his opinion; and therefore dissembled her thoughts, as women in those cases ever do, who when most angry seem the most galliard, especially when they have need of the friendship of those they flatter.

SYLVIA *to* OCTAVIO.

Is it indeed, *Octavio*, that you believe *Philander* cold, or would you make that a pretext to the declaration of your own passion? We *French* ladies are not so nicely tied up to the formalities of virtue, but we can hear love at both ears: and if we receive not the addresses of both, at least we are perhaps vain enough not to be displeased to find we make new conquests. But you have made your attack with so ill conduct, that I shall find force enough without more aids to repulse you. Alas, my lord, did you believe my heart was left unguarded when *Philander* departed? No, the careful charming lover left a thousand little gods to defend it, of no less power than himself; young deities, who laugh at all your little arts and treacheries, and scorn to resign their empire to any feeble *Cupids* you can draw up against them: your thick foggy air breeds love too dull and heavy for noble flights, nor can I stoop to them. The *Flemish* boy wants arrows keen enough for hearts like mine, and is a bungler in his art, too lazy and remiss, rather a heavy *Bacchus* than a *Cupid*, a bottle sends him to his bed of moss, where he sleeps hard, and never dreams of *Venus*.

How poorly have you paid yourself, my lord, (by this pursuit of your discovered love) for all the little friendship you have rendered me! How well you have explained, you can be no more a lover than a friend, if one may judge the first by the last! Had you been thus obstinate in your passion before *Philander* went, or you had believed me abandoned, I should perhaps have thought that you had loved indeed, because I should have seen you durst, and should have believed it true, because it ran some hazards for me, the resolution of it would have reconciled me then to the temerity of it, and the greatest demonstration you could have given of it, would have been the danger you would have ran and contemned, and the preference of your passion above any other consideration. This, my lord, had been generous and like a lover; but poorly thus to set upon a single woman in the disguise of a friend, in the dark silent melancholy hour of absence from *Philander*, then to surprise me, then to bid me deliver! to pad for hearts! It is not like *Octavio*, *Octavio* that *Philander* made his friend, and for whose dear sake, my lord, I will no farther reproach you, but from a goodness, which, I hope, you will merit, I will forgive an offence, which your ill-timing has rendered almost inexcusable, and expect you will for the future consider better how you ought to treat

SYLVIA.

As soon as she had dismissed the page, she hasted to her business of love, and again read over *Philander*'s, letter, and finding still new occasion for fear, she had recourse to pen and paper for a relief of that heart which no other way could find; and after having wiped the tears from her eyes, she writ this following letter.

SYLVIA *to* PHILANDER.

Yes, *Philander*, I have received your letter, and but I found my name there, should have hoped it was not meant for *Sylvia*! Oh! It is all cold — short — short and cold as a dead winter's day. It chilled my blood, it shivered every vein. Where, oh where hast thou lavished out all those soft words so natural to thy soul, with which thou usedst to charm; so tuned to the dear music of thy voice? What is become of all the tender things, which, as I used to read, made little nimble pantings in my heart, my blushes rise, and tremblings in my blood, adding new fire to the poor burning victim! Oh where are all thy pretty flatteries of love, that made me fond and vain, and set a value on this trifling beauty? Hast thou forgot thy wondrous art of loving? Thy pretty cunnings, and thy soft deceivings? Hast thou forgot them all? Or hast thou forgot indeed to love at all? Has thy industrious passion gathered all the sweets, and left the rifled flower to hang its withered head, and die in I shades neglected? For who will prize it now, now when all its I perfumes are fled? Oh my *Philander*, oh my charming fugitive! Was it not enough you left me, like false *Theseus*, on the shore, on the forsaken shore, departed from my fond, my clasping arms; where I believed you safe, secure and pleased, when sleep and night, that favoured you and ruined me, had rendered them incapable of their dear loss! Oh was it not enough, that when I found them empty and abandoned, and the place cold where you had lain, and my poor trembling bosom unpossessed of that dear load it bore, that I almost expired with my first fears? Oh, if *Philander* loved, he would have thought that cruelty enough, without the sad addition of a growing coldness: I awaked, I missed thee, and I called aloud, '*Philander*! my *Philander*!' But no Philander heard; then drew the close-drawn curtains, and with a hasty and busy view surveyed the chamber over; but oh! In vain I viewed, and called yet louder, but none appeared to my assistance but *Antonet* and *Brilliard*, to torture me with dull excuses, urging a thousand feigned and frivolous reasons to satisfy my fears: but I, who loved, who doted even to madness, by nature soft, and timorous as a dove, and fearful as a criminal escaped, that dreads each little noise, fancied

their eyes and guilty looks confessed the treasons of their hearts
and tongues, while they, more kind than true, strove to convince my
killing doubts, protested that you would return by night, and feigned
a likely story to deceive. Thus between hope and fear I languished
out a day; oh heavens! A tedious day without *Philander*: who would
have thought that such a dismal day should not, with the end of its
reign, have finished that of my life! But then *Octavio* came to visit
me, and who till then I never wished to see, but now I was impatient
for his coming, who by degrees told me that you were gone — I
never asked him where, or how, or why; that you were gone was
enough to possess me of all I feared, your being apprehended and
sent into *France*, your delivering yourself up, your abandoning me;
all, all I had an easy faith for, without consulting more than that thou
wert gone — that very word yet strikes a terror to my soul, disables
my trembling hand, and I must wait for reinforcements from some
kinder thoughts. But, oh! From whence should they arrive? From
what dear present felicity, or prospect of a future, though never so
distant, and all those past ones serve but to increase my pain; they
favour me no more, they charm and please no more, and only present
themselves to my memory to complete the number of my sighs and
tears, and make me wish that they had never been, though even
with *Philander*? Oh! say, thou monarch of my panting soul, how hast
thou treated *Sylvia*, to make her wish that she had never known a
tender joy with thee? Is it possible she should repent her loving thee,
and thou shouldst give her cause! Say, dear false charmer, is it? But
oh, there is no lasting faith in sin! —— Ah — What have I done?
How dreadful is the scene of my first debauch, and how glorious
that never to be regained prospect of my virgin innocence, where
I sat enthroned in awful virtue, crowned with shining honour, and
adorned with unsullied reputation, till thou, O tyrant *Love*, with a
charming usurpation invaded all my glories; and which I resigned
with greater pride and joy than a young monarch puts them on. Oh!
Why then do I repent? As if the vast, the dear expense of pleasures
past were not enough to recompense for all the pains of love to come?
But why, oh why do I treat thee as a lover lost already? Thou art
not, canst not; no, I will not believe it, till thou thyself confess it:

nor shall the omission of a tender word or two make me believe thou hast forgot thy vows. Alas, it may be I mistake thy cares, thy hard fatigues of life, thy present ill circumstances (and all the melancholy effects of thine and my misfortunes) for coldness and declining love. Alas, I had forgot my poor my dear *Philander* is now obliged to contrive for life as well as love, thou perhaps (fearing the worst) are preparing eloquence for a council table; and in thy busy and guilty imaginations haranguing it to the grave judges, defending thy innocence, or evading thy guilt: feeing advocates, excepting juries, and confronting witnesses, when thou shouldst be giving satisfaction to my fainting love-sick heart: sometimes in thy labouring fancy the horror of a dreadful sentence for an ignominious death, strikes upon thy tender soul with a force that frights the little god from thence, and I am persuaded there are some moments of this melancholy nature, wherein your *Sylvia* is even quite forgotten, and this too she can think just and reasonable, without reproaching thy heart with a declining passion, especially when I am not by to call thy fondness up, and divert thy more tormenting hours: but oh, for those soft minutes thou hast designed for love, and hast dedicated to *Sylvia,* *Philander* should dismiss the dull formalities of rigid business, the pressing cares of dangers, and have given a loose to softness. Could my *Philander* imagine this short and unloving letter sufficient to atone for such an absence? And has *Philander* then forgotten the pain with which I languished, when but absent from him an hour? How then can he imagine I can live, when distant from him so many leagues, and so many days? While all the scanty comfort I have for life is, that one day we might meet again; but where, or when, or how-thou hast not love enough so much as to divine; but poorly leavest me to be satisfied by *Octavio*, committing the business of thy heart, the once great importance of thy soul, the most necessary devoirs of thy life, to be supplied by another. Oh *Philander*, I have known a blessed time in our reign of love, when thou wouldst have thought even all thy own power of too little force to satisfy the doubting soul of *Sylvia*: tell me, *Philander*, hast thou forgot that time? I dare not think thou hast, and yet (O God) I find an alteration, but heaven divert the omen: yet something whispers to my soul, I am undone!

Oh, where art thou, my *Philander*? Where is thy heart? And what has it been doing since it begun my fate? How can it justify thy coldness, and thou this cruel absence, without accounting with me for every parting hour? My charming dear was wont to find me business for all my lonely absent ones; and writ the softest letters — loading the paper with fond vows and wishes, which ere I had read over another would arrive, to keep eternal warmth about my soul; nor wert thou ever wearied more with writing, than I with reading, or with sighing after thee; but now — oh! There is some mystery in it I dare not understand. Be kind at least and satisfy my fears, for it is a wondrous pain to live in doubt; if thou still lovest me, swear it over anew! And curse me if I do not credit thee. But if thou art declining — or shouldst be sent a shameful victim into *France*— oh thou deceiving charmer, yet be just, and let me know my doom: by heaven this last will find a welcome to me, for it will end the torment of my doubts and fears of losing thee another way, and I shall have the joy to die with thee, die beloved, and die

Thy SYLVIA.

Having read over this letter, she feared she had said too much of her doubts and apprehensions of a change in him; for now she flies to all the little stratagems and artifices of lovers, she begins to consider the worst, and to make the best of that; but quite abandoned she could not believe herself, without flying into all the rage that disappointed woman could be possessed with. She calls *Brilliard*, shews him his lord's letters, and told him, (while he read) her doubts and fears; he being thus instructed by herself in the way how to deceive her on, like fortune-tellers, who gather people's fortune from themselves, and then return it back for their own divinity; tells her he saw indeed a change! Glad to improve her fear, and feigns a sorrow almost equal to hers: 'It is evident,' says he, 'it is evident, that he is the most ungrateful of his sex! Pardon, madam,' (continued he, bowing) 'if my zeal for the most charming creature on earth, make me forget my duty to the best of masters and friends.' 'Ah, *Brilliard*,' cried she, with an air of languishment that more enflamed him, 'have a care, lest that mistaken zeal for me should make you profane virtue, which has not, but on this occasion, shewed that it wanted angels for its guard. Oh, *Brilliard*, if he be false — if the dear man be perjured, take, take, kind heaven, the life you have preserved but for a greater proof of your revenge'—— and at that word she sunk into his arms, which he hastily extended as she was falling, both to save her from harm, and to give himself the pleasure of grasping the loveliest body in the world to his bosom, on which her fair face declined, cold, dead, and pale; but so transporting was the pleasure of that dear burden, that he forgot to call for, or to use any aid to bring her back to life, but trembling with his love and eager passion, he took a thousand joys, he kissed a thousand times her lukewarm lips, sucked her short sighs, and ravished all the sweets, her bosom (which was but guarded with a loose night-gown) yielded his impatient touches. Oh heaven, who can express the pleasures he received, because no other way he ever could arrive to so much daring? It was all beyond his hope; loose were her robes, insensible the maid, and love had made him insolent, he roved, he kissed, he gazed, without control, forgetting all respect of persons, or of place, and quite despairing by fair means to win her, resolves to take this lucky opportunity; the door he knew was fast, for the counsel she had to ask him admitted of no lookers-on, so that at his entrance she had secured the pass for him herself, and being near her bed, when she fell into his arms, at this last daring thought he lifts her thither, and lays her gently down, and while he did so, in one minute ran over all the killing joys he had been witness to, which she had given *Philander*; on which he never paus'd, but urged by a *Cupid* altogether malicious and wicked, he resolves his cowardly conquest, when some kinder god awakened *Sylvia*, and brought *Octavio* to the chamber door; who having been used to a freedom, which was permitted to none but himself, with *Antonet* her woman, waiting for admittance, after having knocked twice softly, *Brittiard* heard it, and redoubled his disorder, which from that of love, grew to that of surprise; he knew not what to do, whether to refuse answering, or to re-establish the reviving sense of *Sylvia*; in this moment of perplexing thought he failed not however to set his hair in order, and adjust him, though there were no need of it, and stepping to the door (after having raised *Sylvia*, leaning her head on her hand on the bed-side,) he gave admittance to *Octavio*; but, oh heaven, how was he surprised when he saw it was *Octavio*? His heart with more force than before redoubled its beats, that one might easily perceive every stroke by the motion of his cravat; he blushed, which, to a complexion perfectly fair, as that of *Brilliard* (who wants no beauty, either in face or person) was the more discoverable, add to this his trembling, and you may easily imagine what a figure he represented himself to *Octavio*; who almost as much surprised as himself to find the goddess of his vows and devotions with a young *Endymion* alone, a door shut to, her gown loose, which (from the late fit she was in, and *Brilliard*'s rape upon her bosom) was still open, and discovered a world of unguarded beauty, which she knew not was in view, with some other disorders of her headcloths, gave him in a moment a thousand false apprehensions: *Antonet* was no less surprised; so that all had their part of amazement but the innocent *Sylvia*, whose eyes were beautified with a melancholy calm, which almost set the generous lover at ease, and took away his new fears; however, he could not choose but ask *Brilliard* what the matter was with him, he looked so out of countenance, and trembled so? He told him how *Sylvia* had been, and what extreme frights she had possessed him with, and told him the occasion, which the lovely *Sylvia* with her eyes and sighs assented to, and *Brilliard* departed; how well pleased you may imagine, or with what gusto he left her to be with the lovely *Octavio*, whom he perceived too well was a lover in the disguise of a friend. But there are in love those wonderful lovers who can quench the fire one beauty kindles with some other object, and as much in love as *Brilliard* was, he found *Antonet* an antidote that dispelled the grosser part of it; for she was in love with our amorous friend, and courted him with that passion those of that country do almost all handsome strangers; and one convenient principle of the religion of that country is, to think it no sin to be kind while they are single women, though otherwise (when wives) they are just enough, nor does a woman that manages her affairs thus discreetly meet with any reproach; of this humour was our *Antonet*, who pursued her lover out, half jealous there might be some amorous intrigue between her lady and him, which she sought in vain by all the feeble arts of her country's sex to get from him; while on the

other side he believing she might be of use in the farther discovery
he desired to make between *Octavio* and *Sylvia*, not only told her she
herself was the object of his wishes, but gave her substantial proofs
on it, and told her his design, after having her honour for security
that she would be secret, the best pledge a man can take of a woman:
after she had promised to betray all things to him, she departed to her
affairs, and he to giving his lord an account of *Sylvia*, as he desired,
in a letter which came to him with that of *Sylvia*; and which was thus:

PHILANDER *to* BRILLIARD.

I doubt not but you will wonder that all this time you have not
heard of me, nor indeed can well excuse it, since I have been in a
place whence with ease I could have sent every post; but a new affair
of gallantry has engaged my thoughtful hours, not that I find any
passion here that has abated one sigh for *Sylvia*; but a man's hours
are very dull, when undiverted by an intrigue of some kind or other,
especially to a heart young and gay as mine is, and which would
not, if possible, bend under the fatigues of more serious thought
and business; I should not tell you this, but that I would have you
say all the dilatory excuses that possibly you can to hinder *Sylvia*'s
coming to me, while I remain in this town, where I design to make
my abode but a short time, and had not stayed at all, but for this
stop to my journey, and I scorn to be vanquished without taking my
revenge; it is a sally of youth, no more — a flash, that blazes for a
while, and will go out without enjoyment. I need not bid you keep
this knowledge to yourself, for I have had too good a confirmation
of your faith and friendship to doubt you now, and believe you have
too much respect for *Sylvia* to occasion her any disquiet. I long to
know how she takes my absence, send me at large of all that passes,
and give your letters to *Octavio*, for none else shall know where I
am, or how to send to me: be careful of *Sylvia*, and observe her with
diligence, for possibly I should not be extravagantly afflicted to find
she was inclined to love me less for her own ease and mine, since
love is troublesome when the height of it carries it to jealousies, little
quarrels, and eternal discontents; all which beginning lovers prize,
and pride themselves on every distrust of the fond mistress, since it
is not only a demonstration of love in them, but of power and charms

in us that occasion it. But when we no longer find the mistress so desirable, as our first wishes form her, we value less their opinion of our persons, and only endeavour to render it agreeable to new beauties, and adorn it for new conquests; but you, *Brilliard*, have been a lover, and understand already this philosophy. I need say no more then to a man who knows so well my soul, but to tell him I am his constant friend.

PHILANDER.

This came as *Brilliard's* soul could wish, and had he sent him word he had been chosen King of *Poland*, he could not have received the news with so great joy, and so perfect a welcome. How to manage this to his best advantage was the business he was next to consult, after returning an answer; now he fancied himself sure of the lovely prize, in spite of all other oppositions: 'For' (says he, in reasoning the case) 'if she can by degrees arrive to a coldness to *Philander*, and consider him no longer as a lover, she may perhaps consider me as a husband; or should she receive *Octavio's* addresses, when once I have found her feeble, I will make her pay me for keeping of every secret.' So either way he entertained a hope, though never so distant from reason and probability; but all things seem possible to longing lovers, who can on the least hope resolve to out-wait even eternity (if possible) in expectation of a promised blessing; and now with more than usual care he resolved to dress, and set out all his youth and beauty to the best advantage; and being a gentleman well born, he wanted no arts of dressing, nor any advantage of shape or mien, to make it appear well: pleased with this hope, his art was now how to make his advances without appearing to have designed doing so. And first to act the hypocrite with his lord was his business; for he considered rightly, if he should not represent *Sylvia's* sorrows to the life, and appear to make him sensible of them, he should not be after credited if he related any thing to her disadvantage; for to be the greater enemy, you ought to seem to be the greatest friend. This was the policy of his heart, who in all things was inspired with fanatical notions. In order to this, being alone in his chamber, after the defeat he had in that of *Sylvia's*, he writ this letter.

BRILLIARD *to* PHILANDER.

My Lord,

You have done me the honour to make me your confidant in an affair that does not a little surprise me; since I believed, after *Sylvia*, no mortal beauty could have touched your heart, and nothing but your own excuses could have sufficed to have made it reasonable; and I only wish, that when the fatal news shall arrive to *Sylvia*'s ear (as for me it never shall) that she may think it as pardonable as I do; but I doubt it will add abundance of grief to what she is already possessed of, if but such a fear should enter in her tender thoughts. But since it is not my business, my lord, to advise or counsel, but to obey, I leave you to all the success of happy love, and will only give you an account how affairs stand here, since your departure.

That morning you left the *Brill*, and *Sylvia* in bed, I must disturb your more serene thoughts with telling you, that her first surprise and griefs at the news of your departure were most deplorable, where raging madness and the softer passion of love, complaints of grief, and anger, sighs, tears and cries were so mixed together, and by turns so violently seized her, that all about her wept and pitied her: it was sad, it was wondrous sad, my lord, to see it: nor could we hope her life, or that she would preserve it if she could; for by many ways she attempted to have released herself from pain by a violent death, and those that strove to preserve that, could not hope she would ever have returned to sense again: sometimes a wild extravagant raving would require all our aid, and then again she would talk and rail so tenderly —— and express her resentment in the kindest softest words that ever madness uttered, and all of her *Philander*, till she has set us all a weeping round her; sometimes she'd sit as calm and still as death, and we have perceived she lived only by sighs and silent tears that fell into her bosom; then on a sudden wildly gaze upon us with eyes that even then had wondrous charms, and frantically survey us all, then cry aloud, 'Where is my Lord *Philander*! —— Oh, bring me my *Philander*, *Brilliard*: Oh, *Antonet*, where have you hid the treasure of my soul?' Then, weeping floods of tears, would sink all fainting in our arms. Anon with trembling words and sighs she'd cry ——'But oh, my dear *Philander* is no more, you have surrendered him to *France*—— Yes, yes, you have given him up, and he must

die, publicly die, be led a sad victim through the joyful crowd —
reproached, and fall ingloriously ——' Then rave again, and tear her
lovely hair, and act such wildness — so moving and so sad, as even
infected the pitying beholders, and all we could do, was gently to
persuade her grief, and soothe her raving fits; but so we swore, so
heartily we vowed that you were safe, that with the aid of *Octavio*,
who came that day to visit her, we made her capable of hearing a
little reason from us. *Octavio* kneeled, and begged she would but
calmly hear him speak, he pawned his soul, his honour, and his
life, *Philander* was as safe from any injury, either from *France*, or
any other enemy, as he, as she, or heaven itself. In fine, my lord,
he vowed, he swore, and pleaded, till she with patience heard him
tell his story, and the necessity of your absence; this brought her
temper back, and dried her eyes, then sighing, answered him ——
that if for your safety you were fled, she would forgive your cruelty
and your absence, and endeavour to be herself again: but then she
would a thousand times conjure him not to deceive her faith, by all
the friendship that he bore *Philander*, not to possess her with false
hopes; then would he swear anew; and as he swore, she would behold
him with such charming sadness in her eyes that he almost forgot
what he would say, to gaze upon her, and to pass his pity. But, if
with all his power of beauty and of rhetoric he left her calm, he was
no sooner gone, but she returned to all the tempests of despairing
love, to all the unbelief of faithless passion, would neither sleep, nor
eat, nor suffer day to enter; but all was sad and gloomy as the vault
that held the *Ephesian* matron, nor suffered she any to approach her
but her page, and Count *Octavio*, and he in the midst of all was well
received: not that I think, my lord, she feigned any part of that close
retirement to entertain him with any freedom, that did not become
a woman of perfect love and honour; though I must own, my lord,
I believe it impossible for him to behold the lovely *Sylvia*, without
having a passion for her. What restraint his friendship to you may
put upon his heart or tongue I know not, but I conclude him a lover,
though without success; what effects that may have upon the heart
of *Sylvia*, only time can render an account of: and whose conduct I
shall the more particularly observe from a curiosity natural to me, to

see if it may be possible for *Sylvia* to love again, after the adorable *Philander*, which levity in one so perfect would cure me of the disease of love, while I lived amongst the fickle sex: but since no such thought can yet get possession of my belief, I humbly beg your lordship will entertain no jealousy, that may be so fatal to your repose, and to that of *Sylvia*; doubt not but my fears proceed perfectly from the zeal I have for your lordship, for whose honour and tranquillity none shall venture so far as, my lord, your lordship's most humble and obedient servant,

BRILLIARD.

POSTSCRIPT.

My lord, the groom shall set forward with your coach horses tomorrow morning, according to your order.

Having writ this, he read it over; not to see whether it were witty or eloquent, or writ up to the sense of so good a judge as *Philander*, but to see whether he had cast it for his purpose; for there his masterpiece was to be shewn; and having read it, he doubted whether the relation of *Sylvia*'s griefs were not too moving, and whether they might not serve to revive his fading love, which were intended only as a demonstration of his own pity and compassion, that from thence the deceived lover might with the more ease entertain a belief in what he hinted of her levity, when he was to make that out, as he now had but touched upon it, for he would not have it thought the business of malice to *Sylvia*, but duty and respect to *Philander*: that thought reconciled him to the first part without alteration; and he fancied he had said enough in the latter, to give any man of love and sense a jealousy which might inspire a young lover in pursuit of a new mistress, with a revenge that might wholly turn to his advantage; for now every ray gave him light enough to conduct him to hope, and he believed nothing too difficult for his love, nor what his invention could not conquer: he fancied himself a very *Machiavel* already, and almost promised himself the charming *Sylvia*. With these thoughts he seals up his letters, and hastes to *Sylvia*'s chamber for her farther commands, having in his politic transports forgotten he had left *Octavio* with her. *Octavio*, who no sooner had seen *Brilliard* quit the chamber all trembling and disordered, after having given him entrance, but the next step was to the feet of the new recovered languishing beauty, who not knowing any thing of the freedom the daring husband lover had taken, was not at all surprised to hear *Octavio* cry (kneeling before her) 'Ah madam, I no longer wonder you use *Octavio* with such rigour;' then sighing declined his melancholy eyes, where love and jealousy made themselves too apparent; while she believing he had only reproached her want of ceremony at his entrance, checking herself, she started from the bed, and taking him by the hand to raise him, she cried, 'Rise, my lord, and pardon the omission of that respect which was not wanting but with even life itself.' *Octavio* answered, 'Yes, madam, but you took care, not to make the world absolutely unhappy in your eternal loss, and therefore made choice of such a time to die in, when you were sure of a skilful person at hand to bring you back to life'—'My lord ——' said she (with an innocent wonder in her eyes, and an ignorance that did not apprehend him) 'I mean, *Brilliard*,' said he, 'whom I found sufficiently disordered to make me believe he took no little pains to restore you to the world again.' This he spoke with such an air, as easily made her imagine he was a lover to the degree of jealousy, and therefore (beholding him with a look that told him her disdain before she spoke) she replied hastily, 'My lord, if *Brilliard* have expressed, by any disorder or concern, his kind sense of my sufferings, I am more obliged to him for it, than I am to you for your opinion of my virtue; and I shall hereafter know how to set a value both on the one and the other, since what he wants in quality and ability to serve me, he sufficiently makes good with his respect and duty.' At that she would have quitted him, but he (still kneeling) held her train of her gown, and besought her, with all the eloquence of moving and petitioning love, that she would pardon the effect of a passion that could not run into less extravagancy at a sight so new and strange, as that she should in a morning, with only her night-gown thrown loosely about her lovely body, and which left a thousand charms to view, alone receive a man into her chamber, and make fast the door upon them, which when (from his importunity) it was opened he found her all ruffled, and almost fainting on her bed, and a young blushing youth start from her arms, with trembling limbs, and a heart that beat time to the tune of active love, faltering in his speech, as if scarce yet he had recruited the sense he had so happily lost in the amorous encounter: with that, surveying of herself, as she stood, in a great glass, which she could not hinder herself from doing, she found indeed her night-linen, her gown, and the bosom of her shift in such disorder, as, if at least she had yet any doubt remaining that *Brilliard* had not treated her well, she however found cause enough to excuse *Octavio*'s opinion: weighing all the circumstances together, and adjusting her linen and gown with blushes that almost appeared criminal, she turned to *Octavio*, who still held her, and still begged her pardon, assuring him, upon her honour, her love to *Philander*, and her friendship for him, that she was perfectly innocent, and that *Brilliard*, though he should have quality and all other advantages which he wanted to render him acceptable, yet there was in nature something which compelled her to a sort of coldness and disgust to his person; for she had so much the more abhorrence to him as he was a husband, but that was a secret to *Octavio*; but she continued speaking — and cried, 'No, could I be brought to yield to any but *Philander*, I own I find charms enough in *Octavio* to make a conquest; but since the possession of that dear man is all I ask of heaven, I charge my soul with a crime, when I but hear love from any other, therefore I conjure you, if you have any satisfaction in my conversation, never to speak of love more to me, for if you do, honour will oblige me to make vows against seeing you: all the freedoms of friendship I will allow, give you the liberties of a brother, admit you alone by night, or any way but that of love; but that is a reserve of my soul which is only for *Philander*, and the only one that ever shall be kept from *Octavio*.' She ended speaking, and raised him with a smile; and he with a sigh told her, she must command: then she fell to telling him how she had sent for *Brilliard*, and all the discourse that passed; with the reason of her falling into a swoon, in which she continued a moment or two; and while she told it she blushed with a secret fear, that in that trance some freedoms might be taken which she durst not confess: but while she spoke, our still more passionate lover devoured her with his eyes, fixed his very soul upon her charms of speaking and looking, and was a thousand times (urged by transporting passion) ready to break all her dictates, and vow himself her eternal slave; but he feared the result, and therefore kept himself within the bounds of seeming friendship; so that after a thousand things she said of *Philander*, he took his leave to go to dinner; but as he was going out he saw *Brilliard* enter, who, as I said, had forgot he left *Octavio* with her; but in a moment recollecting himself, he blushed at the apprehension, that they might make his disorder the subject of their discourse; so what with that, and the sight of the dear object of his late disappointed pleasures, he had much ado to assume an assurance to approach; but *Octavio* passed out, and gave him a little release. *Sylvia*'s confusion was almost equal to his, for she looked on him as a ravisher; but how to find that truth which she was very curious to know, she called up all the arts of women to instruct her in; by threats she knew it was in vain, therefore she assumed an artifice, which indeed was almost a stranger to her heart, that of jilting him out of a secret which she knew he wanted generosity to give handsomely; and meeting him with a smile, which she forced, she cried, 'How now, *Brilliard*, are you so faint-hearted a soldier, you cannot see a lady die without being terrified?' 'Rather, madam,' (replied he blushing anew) 'so soft-hearted, I cannot see the loveliest person in the world fainting in my arms, without being disordered with grief and fear, beyond the power of many days to resettle again.' At which she approached him, who stood near the door, and shutting it, she took him by the hand, and smiling, cried, 'And had you no other business for your heart but grief and fear, when a fair lady throws herself into your arms? It ought to have had some kinder effect on a person of *Brilliard*'s youth and complexion.' And while she spoke this she held him by the wrist, and found on the sudden his pulse to beat more high, and his heart to heave his bosom with sighs, which now he no longer took care to hide, but with a transported joy, he cried, 'Oh madam, do not urge me to a confession that must undo me, without making it criminal by my discovery of it; you know I am your slave ——' when she with a pretty wondering smile, cried —'What, a lover too, and yet so dull!' 'Oh charming *Sylvia*,' (says he, and falling on his knees) 'give my profound respect a kinder name:' to which she answered —

'You that know your sentiments may best instruct me by what name to call them, and you *Brilliard* may do it without fear —— You saw I did not struggle in your arms, nor strove I to defend the kisses which you gave ——' 'Oh heavens,' cried he, transported with what she said, 'is it possible that you could know of my presumption, and favour it too? I will no longer then curse those unlucky stars that sent *Octavio* just in the blessed minute to snatch me from my heaven, the lovely victim lay ready for the sacrifice, all prepared to offer; my hands, my eyes, my lips were tired with pleasure, but yet they were not satisfied; oh there was joy beyond those ravishments, of which one kind minute more had made me absolute lord:' 'Yes, and the next,' said she, 'had sent this to your heart'—— snatching a penknife that lay on her toilet, where she had been writing, which she offered so near to his bosom, that he believed himself already pierced, so sensibly killing her words, her motion, and her look; he started from her, and she threw away the knife, and walked a turn or two about the chamber, while he stood immovable, with his eyes fixed on the earth, and his thoughts on nothing but a wild confusion, which he vowed afterwards he could give no account of. But as she turned she beheld him with some compassion, and remembering how he had it in his power to expose her in a strange country, and own her for a wife, she believed it necessary to hide her resentments; and cried, '*Brilliard*, for the friendship your lord has for you I forgive you; but have a care you never raise your thoughts to a presumption of that nature more: do not hope I will ever fall below *Philander*'s love; go and repent your crime —— and expect all things else from my favour ——' At this he left her with a bow that had some malice in it, and she returned into her dressing-room. — After dinner *Octavio* writes her this letter, which his page brought.

OCTAVIO *to* SYLVIA.

Madam,

'Tis true, that in obedience to your commands, I begged your pardon for the confession I made you of my passion: but since you could not but see the contradiction of my tongue in my eyes, and hear it but too well confirmed by my sighs, why will you confine me to the formalities of a silent languishment, unless to increase my flame with my pain?

You conjure me to see you often, and at the same time forbid me speaking my passion, and this bold intruder comes to tell you now, it is impossible to obey the first, without disobliging the last; and since the crime of adoring you exceeds my disobedience in not waiting on you, be pleased at least to pardon that fault, which my profound respect to the lovely *Sylvia* makes me commit; for it is impossible to see you, and not give you an occasion of reproaching me: if I could make a truce with my eyes, and, like a mortified capuchin, look always downwards, not daring to behold the glorious temptations of your beauty, yet you wound a thousand ways besides; your touches inflame me, and your voice has music in it, that strikes upon my soul with ravishing tenderness; your wit is unresistible and piercing; your very sorrows and complaints have charms that make me soft without the aid of love: but pity joined with passion raises a flame too mighty for my conduct! And I in transports every way confess it: yes, yes, upbraid me, call me traitor and ungrateful, tell me my friendship is false; but, *Sylvia*, yet be just, and say my love was true, say only he had seen the charming *Sylvia*; and who is he that after that would not excuse the rest in one so absolutely born to be undone by love, as is her destined slave,

OCTAVIO.

POSTSCRIPT.

Madam, among some rarities I this morning saw, I found these trifles Florio *brings you, which because uncommon I presume to send you.*

Sylvia, notwithstanding the seeming severity of her commands, was well enough pleased to be disobeyed; and women never pardon any fault more willingly than one of this nature, where the crime gives so infallible a demonstration of their power and beauty; nor can any of their sex be angry in their hearts for being thought desirable; and it was not with pain that she saw him obstinate in his passion, as you may believe by her answering his letters, nor ought any lover to despair when he receives denial under his mistress's own hand, which she sent in this to *Octavio*.

SYLVIA *to* OCTAVIO.

You but ill judge of my wit, or humour, *Octavio*, when you send me such a present, and such a billet, if you believe I either receive the one, or the other, as you designed: in obedience to me you will no more tell me of your love, and yet at the same time you are breaking your word from one end of the paper to the other. Out of respect to me you will see me no more, and yet are bribing me with presents, believing you have found out the surest way to a woman's heart. I must needs confess, *Octavio*, there is great eloquence in a pair of bracelets of five thousand crowns: it is an argument to prove your passion, that has more prevailing reason in it, than either *Seneca* or *Tully* could have urged; nor can a lover write or speak in any language so significant, and very well to be understood, as in that silent one of presenting. The malicious world has a long time agreed to reproach poor women with cruel, unkind, insensible, and dull; when indeed it is those men that are in fault who want the right way of addressing, the true and secret arts of moving, that sovereign remedy against disdain. It is you alone, my lord, like a young *Columbus*, that have found the direct, unpractised way to that little and so much desired world, the favour of the fair; nor could love himself have pointed his arrows with any thing more successful for his conquest of hearts: but mine, my lord, like *Scæva*'s shield, is already so full of arrows, shot from *Philander*'s eyes, it has no room for any other darts: take back your presents then, my lord, and when you make them next be sure you first consider the receiver: for know, *Octavio*, maids of my quality ought to find themselves secure from addresses of this nature, unless they first invite. You ought to have seen advances in my freedoms, consenting in my eyes, or (that usual vanity of my sex) a thousand little trifling arts of affectation to furnish out a conquest, a forward complaisance to every gaudy coxcomb, to fill my train with amorous cringing captives, this might have justified your pretensions; but on the contrary, my eyes and thoughts, which never strayed from the dear man I love, were always bent to earth when gazed upon by you; and when I did but fear you looked with love, I entertained you with *Philander*'s, praise, his wondrous beauty, and his wondrous love, and left nothing untold that might confirm you how much impossible it was, I ever should love again, that I might leave you no room for hope; and since my story has been so unfortunate to alarm the whole world with a conduct so fatal, I made no scruple of telling you with what joy and pride I was undone; if this encourage you, if *Octavio* have sentiments so meanly poor of me, to think, because I yielded to *Philander*, his hopes should be advanced, I banish him for ever from my sight, and after that disdain the little service he can render the never to be altered

SYLVIA.

This letter she sent him back by his page, but not the bracelets, which were indeed very fine, and very considerable: at the same time she threatened him with banishment, she so absolutely expected to be disobeyed in all things of that kind, that she dressed herself that day to advantage, which since her arrival she had never done in her own habits: what with her illness, and *Philander*'s absence, a careless negligence had seized her, till roused and weakened to the thoughts of beauty by *Octavio*'s love, she began to try its force, and that day dressed. While she was so employed, the page hastes with the letter to his lord, who changed colour at the sight of it ere he received it; not that he hoped it brought love, it was enough she would but answer, though she railed: 'Let her' (said he opening it) 'vow she hates me: let her call me traitor, and unjust, so she take the pains to tell it this way;' for he knew well those that argue will yield, and only she that sends him back his own letters without reading them can give despair. He read therefore without a sigh, nor complained he on her rigours; and because it was too early yet to make his visit, to shew the impatience of his love, as much as the reality and resolution of it, he bid his page wait, and sent her back this answer.

OCTAVIO *to* SYLVIA.

Fair angry *Sylvia*, how has my love offended? Has its excess betrayed the least part of that respect due to your birth and beauty? Though I am young as the gay ruddy morning, and vigorous as the gilded sun at noon, and amorous as that god, when with such haste he chased young *Daphne* over the flowery plain, it never made me guilty of a thought that *Sylvia* might not pity and allow. Nor came that trifling present to plead for any wish, or mend my eloquence, which you with such disdain upbraid me with; the bracelets came not to be raffled for your love, nor pimp to my desires: youth scorns those common aids; no, let dull age pursue those ways of merchandise, who only buy up hearts at that vain price, and never make a barter, but a purchase. Youth has a better way of trading in love's markets, and you have taught me too well to judge of, and to value beauty, to dare to bid so cheaply for it: I found the toy was gay, the work was neat, and fancy new; and know not any thing they would so well adorn as *Sylvia*'s lovely hands: I say, if after this I should have been the mercenary fool to have dunned you for return, you might have used me thus —— Condemn me ere you find me sin in thought! That part of it was yet so far behind it was scarce arrived in wish. You should have stayed till it approached more near, before you damned it to eternal silence. To love, to sigh, to weep, to pray, and to complain; why one may be allowed it in devotion; but you, nicer than heaven itself, make that a crime, which all the powers divine have never decreed one. I will not plead, nor ask you leave to love; love is my right, my business, and my province; the empire of the young, the vigorous, and the bold; and I will claim my share; the air, the groves, the shades are mine to sigh in, as well as your *Philander*'s; the echoes answer me as willingly, when I complain, or name the cruel *Sylvia*; fountains receive my tears, and the kind spring's reflection agreeably flatters me to hope, and makes me vain enough to think it just and reasonable I should pursue the dictates of my soul —— love on in spite of opposition, because I will not lose my privileges; you may forbid me naming it to you, in that I can obey, because I can; but not to love! Not to adore the fair! And not to languish for you, were as impossible as for you not to be lovely, not to be the most charming of your sex. But I am so far from a pretending fool, because you have been possessed, that often that thought comes cross my soul, and checks my advancing love; and I would buy that thought off with almost all my share of future bliss! Were I a god, the first great miracle should be to form you a maid again: for oh, whatever reasons flattering love can bring to make it look like just, the world! The world, fair *Sylvia*, still will censure, and say —— you were to blame; but it was that fault alone that made you mortal, we else should have adored you as a deity, and so have lost a generous race of young succeeding heroes that may be born of you! Yet had *Philander* loved but half so well as I, he would have kept your glorious fame entire; but since alone for *Sylvia* I love *Sylvia*, let her be false to honour, false to love, wanton and proud, ill-natured, vain, fantastic, or what is worse — let her pursue her love, be constant, and still dote upon *Philander*— yet still she will be the *Sylvia* I adore, that *Sylvia* born eternally to enslave

OCTAVIO.

This he sent by *Florio* his page, at the same time that she expected the visit of his lord, and blushed with a little anger and concern at the disappointment; however she hasted to read the letter, and was pleased with the haughty resolution he made in spite of her, to love on as his right by birth; and she was glad to find from these positive resolves that she might the more safely disdain, or at least assume a tyranny which might render her virtue glorious, and yet at the same time keep him her slave on all occasions when she might have need of his service, which, in the circumstances she was in, she did not know of what great use it might be to her, she having no other design on him, bating the little vanity of her sex, which is an ingredient so intermixed with the greatest virtues of women-kind, that those who endeavour to cure them of that disease rob them of a very considerable pleasure, and in most it is incurable: give *Sylvia* then leave to share it with her sex, since she was so much the more excusable, by how much a greater portion of beauty she had than any other, and had sense enough to know it too; as indeed whatever other knowledge they want, they have still enough to set a price on beauty, though they do not always rate it; for had *Sylvia* done that, she had been the happiest of her sex: but as she was she waited the coming of *Octavio*, but not so as to make her quit one sad thought for *Philanders* love and vanity, though they both reigned in her soul; yet the first surmounted the last, and she grew to impatient ravings whenever she cast a thought upon her fear that *Philander* grew cold; and possibly pride and vanity had as great a share in that concern of hers as love itself, for she would oft survey herself in her glass, and cry, 'Gods! Can this beauty be despised? This shape! This face! This youth! This air! And what's more obliging yet, a heart that adores the fugitive, that languishes and sighs after the dear runaway. Is it possible he can find a beauty,' added she, 'of greater perfection —— But oh, it is fancy sets the rate on beauty, and he may as well love a third time as he has a second. For in love, those that once break the rules and laws of that deity, set no bounds to their treasons and disobedience. Yes, yes ——' would she cry, 'He that could leave *Myrtilla*, the fair, the young, the noble, chaste and fond *Myrtilla*, what after that may he not do to *Sylvia*, on whom he has less ties, less obligations? Oh wretched maid —— what has thy fondness done, he is satiated now with thee, as before with *Myrtilla*, and carries all those dear, those charming joys, to some new beauty, whom his looks have conquered, and whom his soft bewitching vows will ruin.' With that she raved and stamped, and cried aloud, 'Hell —— fires —— tortures —— daggers —— racks and poison —— come all to my relief! Revenge me on the perjured lovely devil —— But I will be brave —— I will be brave and hate him ——' This she spoke in a tone less fierce, and with great pride, and had not paused and walked above a hasty turn or two, but *Octavio*, as impatient as love could make him, entered the chamber, so dressed, so set out for conquest, that I wonder at nothing more than that *Sylvia* did not find him altogether charming, and fit for her revenge, who was formed by nature for love, and had all that could render him the dotage of women: but where a heart is prepossessed, all that is beautiful in any other man serves but as an ill comparison to what it loves, and even *Philander*'s likeness, that was not indeed *Philander*, wanted the secret to charm. At *Octavio*'s entrance she was so fixed on her revenge of love, that she did not see him, who presented himself as so proper an instrument, till he first sighing spoke, 'Ah, *Sylvia*, shall I never see that beauty easy more? Shall I never see it reconciled to content, and a soft calmness fixed upon those eyes, which were formed for looks all tender and serene; or are they resolved' (continued he, sighing) 'never to appear but in storms when I approach?' 'Yes,' replied she, 'when there is a calm of love in yours that raises it.' 'Will you confine my eyes,' said he, 'that are by nature soft? May not their silent language tell you my heart's sad story?' But she replied with a sigh, 'It is not generously done, *Octavio*, thus to pursue a poor unguarded maid, left to your care, your promises of friendship. Ah, will you use *Philander* with such treachery?' 'Sylvia,' said he,'my flame is so just and reasonable, that I dare even to him pronounce I love you; and after that dare love you on ——' 'And would you' (said she) 'to satisfy a little short lived passion, forfeit those vows you have made of friendship to *Philander*? 'That heart that loves you, Sylvia,' (he replied) 'cannot be guilty of so base a thought; *Philander* is my friend, and as he is so, shall know the dearest secrets of my soul. I should believe myself indeed ungrateful' (continued he) 'wherever I loved, should I not tell *Philander*; he told me frankly all his soul, his loves, his griefs, his treasons, and escapes, and in return I will pay him back with mine.' 'And do you imagine' (said she) 'that he would permit your love?' 'How should he hinder me?' (replied he.) 'I do believe' (said she) 'he'd forget all his safety and his friendship, and fight you.' 'Then I'd defend myself,' (said he) 'if he were so ungrateful.' While they thus argued, *Sylvia* had her thoughts apart, on the little stratagems that women in love sometimes make use of; and *Octavio* no sooner told her he would send *Philander* word of his love, but she imagined that such a knowledge might retrieve the heart of her lover, if indeed it were on the wing, and revive the dying embers in his soul, as usually it does from such occasions; and on the other side, she thought that she might more allowably receive *Octavio*'s addresses, when they were with the permission of *Philander*, if he could love so well to permit it; and if he could not, she should have the joy to undeceive her fears of his inconstancy, though she banished for ever the agreeable *Octavio*; so that on *Octavio*'s farther urging the necessity of his giving *Philander* that sure mark of his friendship she permitted him to write, which he immediately did on her table, where there stood a little silver escritoire which contained all things for this purpose.

OCTAVIO *to* PHILANDER.

My Lord,

Since I have vowed you my eternal friendship, and that I absolutely believe myself honoured with that of yours, I think myself obliged by those powerful ties to let you know my heart, not only now as that friend from whom I ought to conceal nothing, but as a rival too, whom in honour I ought to treat as a generous one: perhaps you will be so unkind as to say I cannot be a friend and a rival at the same time, and that almighty love, that sets the world at odds, chases all things from the heart where that reigns, to establish itself the more absolutely there; but, my lord, I avow mine a love of that good nature, that can endure the equal sway of friendship, where like two perfect friends they support each other's empire there; nor can the glory of one eclipse that of the other, but both, like the notion we have of the deity, though two distinct passions, make but one in my soul; and though friendship first entered, 'twas in vain, I called it to my aid, at the first soft invasion of *Sylvia*'s power; and you my charming friend, are the most oblig'd to pity me, who already know so well the force of her beauty. I would fain have you think, I strove at first with all my reason against the irresistible lustre of her eyes: and at the first assaults of love, I gave him not a welcome to my bosom, but like slaves unused to fetters, I grew sullen with my chains, and wore them for your sake uneasily. I thought it base to look upon the mistress of my friend with wishing eyes; but softer love soon furnished me with arguments to justify my claim, since love is not the choice but the face of the soul, who seldom regards the object lov'd as it is, but as it wishes to have it be, and then kind fancy makes it soon the same. Love, that almighty creator of something from nothing, forms a wit, a hero, or a beauty, virtue, good humour, honour, any excellence, when oftentimes there is neither in the object, but where the agreeing world has fixed all these; and since it is by all resolved, (whether they love or not) that this is she, you ought no more, *Philander*, to upbraid my flame, than to wonder at it: it is enough I tell you that it is *Sylvia* to justify my passion; nor is it a crime that I confess I love, since it can never rob *Philander* of the least part of what I have vowed him: or if his mere honour will believe me guilty of a fault, let this atone for all, that if I wrong my friend in loving *Sylvia*, I right him in despairing; for oh, I am repulsed with all the rigour of the coy and fair, with all the little malice of the witty sex, and all the love of *Sylvia* to *Philander*—— There, there is the stop to all my hopes and happiness, and yet by heaven I love thee, oh thou favoured rival!

After this frank confession, my *Philander*, I should be glad to hear your sentiment, since yet, in spite of love, in spite of beauty, I am resolved to die *Philander*'s constant friend,

OCTAVIO.

After he had writ this, he gave it to *Sylvia*: 'See charming creature' (said he in delivering it) 'if after this you either doubt my love, or what I dare for *Sylvia*.' 'I neither receive it' (said she) 'as a proof of the one or the other; but rather that you believe, by this frank confession, to render it as a piece of gallantry and diversion to *Philander*; for no man of sense will imagine that love true, or arrived to any height, that makes a public confession of it to his rival.' 'Ah, *Sylvia*,' answered he, 'how malicious is your wit, and how active to turn its pointed mischief on me! Had I not writ, you would have said I durst not; and when I make a declaration of it, you call it only a slight piece of gallantry: but, *Sylvia*, you have wit enough to try it a thousand ways, and power enough to make me obey; use the extremity of both, so you recompense me at last with a confession that I was at least found worthy to be numbered in the crowd of your adorers.' *Sylvia* replied, 'He were a dull lover indeed, that would need instructions from the wit of his mistress to give her proofs of his passion; whatever opinion you have of my sense, I have too good a one of *Octavio*'s to believe, that when he is a lover he will want aids to make it appear; till then we will let that argument alone, and consider his address to *Philander*.' She then read over the letter he had writ, which she liked very well for her purpose; for at this time our young *Dutch hero* was made a property of in order to her revenge on *Philander*: she told him, he had said too much both for himself and her. He told her, he had declared nothing with his pen, that he would not make good with his sword. 'Hold, sir,' said she, 'and do not imagine from the freedom you have taken in owning your passion to *Philander*, that I shall allow it here: what you declare to the world is your own crime; but when I hear it, it is no longer yours but mine; I therefore conjure you, my lord, not to charge my soul with so great a sin against *Philander*, and I confess to you, I shall be infinitely troubled to be obliged to banish you my sight for ever.' He heard her, and answered with a sigh; for she went from him to the table, and sealed her letter, and gave it him to be enclosed to *Philander*, and left him to consider on her last words, which he did not lay to heart, because he fancied she spoke this as women do that will be won with industry: he, in standing up as she went from him, saw himself in the great glass, and bid his person answer his heart, which from every view he took was reinforced with new hope, for he was too good a judge of beauty not to find it in every part of his own amiable person, nor could he imagine from *Sylvia*'s eyes, which were naturally soft and languishing, (and now the more so from her fears and jealousies) that she meant from her heart the rigours she expressed: much he allowed for his short time of courtship, much to her sex's modesty, much from her quality, and very much from her love, and imagined it must be only time and assiduity, opportunity and obstinate passion, that were capable of reducing her to break her faith with *Philander*; he therefore endeavour'd by all the good dressing, the advantage of lavish gaiety, to render his person agreeable, and by all the arts of gallantry to charm her with his conversation, and when he could handsomely bring in love, he failed not to touch upon it as far as it would be permitted, and every day had the vanity to fancy he made some advances; for indeed every day more and more she found she might have use for so considerable a person, so that one may very well say, never any passed their time better than *Sylvia* and *Octavio*, though with different ends. All he had now to fear was from the answer *Philander*'s letter should bring, for whom he had, in spite of love, so entire a friendship, that he even doubted whether (if *Philander* could urge reasons potent enough) he should not choose to die and quit Sylvia, rather than be false to friendship; one post passed, and another, and so eight successive ones, before they received one word of answer to what they sent; so that *Sylvia*, who was the most impatient of her sex, and the most in love, was raving and acting all the extravagance of despair, and even *Octavio* now became less pleasing, yet he failed not to visit her every day, to send her rich presents, and to say all that a fond lover, or a faithful friend might urge for her relief: at last *Octavio* received this following letter.

PHILANDER *to* OCTAVIO.

You have shewed, *Octavio*, a freedom so generous, and so beyond the usual measures of a rival, that it were almost injustice in me not to permit you to love on; if *Sylvia* can be false to me, and all her vows, she is not worth preserving; if she prefer *Octavio* to *Philander*, then he has greater merit, and deserves her best: but if on the contrary she be just, if she be true, and constant, I cannot fear his love will injure me, so either way *Octavio* has my leave to love the charming *Sylvia*; alas, I know her power, and do not wonder at thy fate! For it is as natural for her to conquer, as 'tis for youth to yield; oh, she has fascination in her eyes! A spell upon her tongue, her wit's a philtre, and her air and motion all snares for heedless hearts; her very faults have charms, her pride, her peevishness, and her disdain, have unresisted power. Alas, you find it every day — and every night she sweeps the tour along and shews the beauty, she enslaves the men, and rivals all the women! How oft with pride and anger I have seen it; and was the unconsidering coxcomb then to rave and rail at her, to curse her charms, her fair inviting and perplexing charms, and bullied every gazer: by heaven I could not spare a smile, a look, and she has such a lavish freedom in her humour, that if you chance to love as I have done — it will surely make thee mad; if she but talked aloud, or put her little affectation on, to show the force of beauty, oh God! How lost in rage! How mad with jealousy, was my fond breaking heart! My eyes grew fierce, and clamorous my tongue! And I have scarce contained myself from hurting what I so much adored; but then the subtle charmer had such arts to flatter me to peace again — to clasp her lovely arms about my neck — to sigh a thousand dear confirming vows into my bosom, and kiss, and smile, and swear — and take away my rage — and then — oh my *Octavio*, no human fancy can present the joy of the dear reconciling moment, where little quarrels raised the rapture higher, and she was always new. These are the wondrous pains, and wondrous pleasures that love by turns inspires, till it grows wise by time and repetition, and then the god assumes a serious gravity, enjoyment takes off the uneasy keenness of the passion, the little jealous quarrels rise no more; quarrels, the very feathers of love's darts, that send them with more swiftness to the heart; and when they cease, your transports lessen too, then we grow reasonable, and consider; we love with prudence then, as fencers fight with foils; a sullen brush perhaps sometimes or so;

but nothing that can touch the heart, and when we are arrived to love at that dull, easy rate, we never die of that disease; then we have recourse to all the little arts, the aids of flatterers, and dear dissimulation, (that help-meet to the lukewarm lover) to keep up a good character of constancy, and a right understanding.

Thus, *Octavio*, I have ran through both the degrees of love; which I have taken so often, that I am grown most learned and able in the art; my easy heart is of the constitution of those, whom frequent sickness renders apt to take relapses from every little cause, or wind that blows too fiercely on them; it renders itself to the first effects of new surprising beauty, and finds such pleasure in beginning passion, such dear delight of fancying new enjoyment, that all past loves, past vows and obligations, have power to bind no more; no pity, no remorse, no threatening danger invades my amorous course; I scour along the flow'ry plains of love, view all the charming prospect at a distance, which represents itself all gay and glorious! And long to lay me down, to stretch and bask in those dear joys that fancy makes so ravishing: nor am I one of those dull whining slaves, whom quality or my respect can awe into a silent cringer, and no more; no, love, youth, and oft success has taught me boldness and art, desire and cunning to attack, to search the feeble side of female weakness, and there to play love's engines; for women will be won, they will, *Octavio*, if love and wit find any opportunity.

Perhaps, my friend, you are wondering now, what this discourse, this odd discovery of my own inconstancy tends to? Then since I cannot better pay you back the secret you had told me of your love, than by another of my own; take this confession from thy friend —— I love! —— languish! And am dying —— for a new beauty. To you, *Octavio*, you that have lived twenty dull tedious years, and never understood the mystery of love, till *Sylvia* taught you to adore, this change may seem a wonder; you that have lazily run more than half your youth's gay course of life away, without the pleasure of one nobler hour of mine; who, like a miser, hoard your sacred store, or scantily have dealt it but to one, think me a lavish prodigal in love, and gravely will reproach me with inconstancy —— but use me like a friend, and hear my story.

It happened in my last day's journey on the road I overtook a man of quality, for so his equipage confessed; we joined and fell into discourse of many things indifferent, till, from a chain of one thing to another, we chanced to talk of *France*, and of the factions there, and I soon found him a *Cesarian*; for he grew hot with his concern for that prince, and fiercely owned his interest: this pleased me, and I grew familiar with him; and I pleased him so well in my devotion for *Cesario*, that being arrived at *Cologne* he invites me home to his palace, which he begged I would make use of as my own during my stay at *Cologne*. Glad of the opportunity I obeyed, and soon informed myself by a *Spanish* page (that waited on him) to whom I was obliged; he told me it was the Count of *Clarinau*, a *Spaniard* born, and of quality, who for some disgust at Court retired hither; that he was a person of much gravity, a great politician, and very rich; and though well in years was lately married to a very beautiful young lady, and that very much against her consent; a lady whom he had taken out of a monastery, where she had been pensioned from a child, and of whom he was so fond and jealous, he never would permit her to see or be seen by any man: and if she took the air in her coach, or went to church, he obliged her to wear a veil. Having learned thus much of the boy, I dismissed him with a present; for he had already inspired me with curiosity, that prologue to love, and I knew not of what use he might be hereafter; a curiosity that I was resolved to satisfy, though I broke all the laws of hospitality, and even that first night I felt an impatience that gave me some wonder. In fine, three days I languished out in a disorder that was very nearly allied to that of love. I found myself magnificently lodged; attended with a formal ceremony; and indeed all things were as well as I could imagine, bating a kind opportunity to get a sight of this young beauty: now half a lover grown, I sighed and grew oppressed with thought, and had recourse to groves, to shady walks and fountains, of which the delicate gardens afforded variety, the most resembling nature that ever art produced, and of the most melancholy recesses, fancying there, in some lucky hour, I might encounter what I already so much adored in *Idea*, which still I formed just as my fancy wished; there, for the first two days I walked and sighed, and told my new-born passion to every gentle wind that played among the boughs; for yet no lady bright appeared beneath them, no visionary nymph the groves afforded; but on the third day, all full of love and stratagem, in the cool of the evening, I passed into a thicket near a little rivulet, that purled and murmured through the glade, and passed into the meads; this pleased and fed my present amorous humour, and down I laid myself on the shady brink, and listened to its melancholy glidings, when from behind me I heard a sound more ravishing, a voice that sung these words:

> Alas, in vain, you pow'rs above,
>   You gave me youth, you gave me charms,
> And ev'ry tender sense of love;
>   To destine me to old *Phileno*'s arms.
> Ah how can youth's gay spring allow
> The chilling kisses of the winter's snow!
>
> All night I languish by his side,
>   And fancy joys I never taste;
> As men in dreams a feast provide,
>
>   And waking find, with grief they fast.
> Either, ye gods, my youthful fires allay,
> Or make the old *Phileno* young and gay.
>
> Like a fair flower in shades obscurity,
>   Though every sweet adorns my head,
> Ungather'd, unadmired I lie,
>   And wither on my silent gloomy bed,
> While no kind aids to my relief appear,
> And no kind bosom makes me triumph there.

By this you may easily guess, as I soon did, that the song was sung by Madam the Countess of *Clarinau*, as indeed it was; at the very beginning of her song my joyful soul divined it so! I rose, and advanced by such slow degrees, as neither alarmed the fair singer, nor hindered me the pleasure of hearing any part of the song, till I approached so near as (behind the shelter of some jessamine that divided us) I, unseen, completed those wounds at my eyes, which I had received before at my ears. Yes, *Ociavio*, I saw the lovely *Clarinau* leaning on a pillow made of some of those jessamines which favoured me, and served her for a canopy. But, oh my friend! How shall I present her to thee in that angel form she then appeared to me? All young! All ravishing as new-born light to lost benighted travellers; her face, the fairest in the world, was adorned with curls of shining jet, tied up — I know not how, all carelessly with scarlet ribbon mixed with pearls; her robe was gay and rich, such as young royal brides put on when they undress for joys; her eyes were black, the softest heaven ever made; her mouth was sweet, and formed for all delight; so red her lips, so round, so graced with dimples, that without one other charm, that was enough to kindle warm desires about a frozen heart; a sprightly air of wit completed all, increased my flame, and made me mad with love: endless it were to tell thee all her beauties: nature all over was lavish and profuse, let it suffice, her face, her shape, her mien, had more of angel in them than humanity! I saw her thus all charming! Thus she lay! A smiling melancholy dressed her eyes, which she had fixed upon the rivulet, near which I found her lying; just such I fancied famed *Lucretia* was, when *Tarquin* first beheld her; nor was that royal ravisher more inflamed than I, or readier for the encounter. Alone she was, which heightened my desires; oh gods! Alone lay the young lovely charmer, with wishing eyes, and all prepared for love! The shade was gloomy, and the tell-tale leaves combined so close, they must have given us warning if any had approached from either side! All favoured my design, and I advanced; but with such caution as not to inspire her with a fear, instead of that of love! A slow, uneasy pace, with folded arms, love in my eyes, and burning in my heart —— at my approach she scarce contained her cries, and rose surprised and blushing, discovering to me such a proportioned height — so lovely and majestic — that I stood gazing on her, all lost in wonder, and gave her time to dart her eyes at me, and every look pierced deeper to my soul, and I had no sense but love, silent admiring love! Immovable I stood,

and had no other motion but that of a heart all panting, which lent a
feeble trembling to my tongue, and even when I would have spoke to
her, it sent a sigh up to prevent my boldness; and oh, *Octavio*, though
I have been bred in all the saucy daring of a forward lover, yet now I
wanted a convenient impudence; awed with a haughty sweetness in
her look, like a Fauxbrave after a vigorous onset, finding the danger
fly so thick around him, sheers off, and dares not face the pressing
foe, struck with too fierce a lightning from her eyes, whence the gods
sent a thousand winged darts, I veiled my own, and durst not play
with fire: while thus she hotly did pursue her conquest, and I stood
fixed on the defensive part, I heard a rustling among the thick-grown
leaves, and through their mystic windings soon perceived the good
old Count of *Clarinau* approaching, muttering and mumbling to old
Dormina, the dragon appointed to guard this lovely treasure, and
which she having left alone in the thicket, and had retired but at an
awful distance, had most extremely disobliged her lord. I only had
time enough in this little moment to look with eyes that asked a
thousand pities, and told her in their silent language how loath they
were to leave the charming object, and with a sigh —— I vanished
from the wondering fair one, nimble as lightning, silent as a shade,
to my first post behind the jessamines; that was the utmost that I
could persuade my heart to do. You may believe, my dear *Octavio*,
I did not bless the minute that brought old *Clarinau* to that dear
recess, nor him, nor my own fate; and to complete my torment, I
saw him (after having gravely reproached her for being alone without
her woman) yes, I saw him fall on her neck, her lovely snowy neck,
and loll and kiss, and hang his tawny withered arms on her fair
shoulders, and press his nauseous load upon *Calista*'s body, (for so
I heard him name her) while she was gazing still upon the empty
place, whence she had seen me vanish; which he perceiving, cried
—'My little fool, what is it thou gazest on, turn to thy known old
man, and buss him soundly ——' When putting him by with a disdain,
that half made amends for the injury he had done me by coming,
'Ah, my lord,' cried she, 'even now, just there I saw a lovely vision, I
never beheld so excellent a thing:' 'How,' cried he, 'a vision, a thing
— What vision? What thing? Where? How? And when ——' 'Why

there,' said she, 'with my eyes, and just now is vanished behind yon jessamines.' With that I drew my sword — for I despaired to get off unknown; and being well enough acquainted with the jealous nature of the Spaniards, which is no more than see and stab, I prepared to stand on my defence till I could reconcile him, if possible, to reason; yet even in that moment I was more afraid of the injury he might do the innocent fair one, than of what he could do to me: but he not so much as dreaming she meant a man by her lovely vision, fell a kissing her anew, and beckoning *Dormina* off to pimp at distance, told her, 'The grove was so sweet, the river's murmurs so delicate, and she was so curiously dressed, that all together had inspired him with a love-fit;' and then assaulting her anew with a sneer, which you have seen a satyr make in pictures, he fell to act the little tricks of youth, that looked so goatish in him — instead of kindling it would have damped a flame; which she resisted with a scorn so charming gave me new hope and fire, when to oblige me more, with pride, disdain, and loathing in her eyes, she fled like *Daphne* from the ravisher; he being bent on love pursued her with a feeble pace, like an old wood-god chasing some coy nymph, who winged with fear out-strips the flying wind, and though a god he cannot overtake her; and left me fainting with new love, new hope, new jealousy, impatience, sighs and wishes, in the abandoned grove. Nor could I go without another view of that dear place in which I saw her lie. I went — and laid me down just on the print which her fair body made, and pressed, and kissed it over a thousand times with eager transports, and even fancied fair *Calista* there; there 'twas I found the paper with the song which I have sent you; there I ran over a thousand stratagems to gain another view; no little statesman had more plots and arts than I to gain this object I adored, the soft idea of my burning heart, now raging wild, abandoned all to love and loose desire; but hitherto my industry is vain; each day I haunt the thickest groves and springs, the flowery walks, close arbours; all the day my busy eyes and heart are searching her, but no intelligence they bring me in: in fine, *Octavio*, all that I can since learn is, that the bright *Calista* had seen a vision in the garden, and ever since was so possessed with melancholy, that she had not since quitted her chamber; she is daily pressing the Count to permit her to go into the garden, to see if she can again encounter the lovely *phantom*, but whether, from any description she hath made of it, (or from any other cause) he imagines how it was, I know not; but he endeavours all he can to hinder her, and tells her it is not lawful to tempt heaven by invoking an apparition; so that till a second view eases the torments of my mind, there is nothing in nature to be conceived so raving mad as I; as if my despair of finding her again increased my impatient flame, instead of lessening it.

After this declaration, judge, *Octavio*, who has given the greatest proofs of his friendship, you or I; you being my rival, trust me with the secret of loving my mistress, which can no way redound to your disadvantage; but I, by telling you the secrets of my soul, put it into your power to ruin me with *Sylvia*, and to establish yourself in her heart; a thought I yet am not willing to bear, for I have an ambition in my love, that would not, while I am toiling for empire here, lose my dominion in another place: but since I can no more rule a woman's heart, than a lover's fate, both you and *Sylvia* may deceive my opinion in that, but shall never have power to make me believe you less my friend, than I am your

PHILANDER.

POSTSCRIPT.

The enclosed I need not oblige you to deliver; you see I give you opportunity.

Octavio no sooner arrived to that part of the letter which named the Count of *Clarinau*, but he stopped, and was scarce able to proceed, for the charming *Calista* was his sister, the only one he had, who having been bred in a nunnery, was taken then to be married to this old rich count, who had a great fortune: before he proceeded, his soul divined this was the new amour that had engaged the heart of his friend; he was afraid to be farther convinced, and yet a curiosity to know how far he had proceeded, made him read it out with all the disorder of a man jealous of his honour, and nicely careful of his fame; he considered her young, about eighteen, married to an old, ill-favoured, jealous husband, no parents but himself to right her wrongs, or revenge her levity; he knew, though she wanted no wit, she did art, for being bred without the conversation of men, she had not learnt the little cunnings of her sex; he guessed by his own soul that hers was soft and apt for impression; he judged from her confession to her husband of the vision, that she had a simple innocence, that might betray a young beauty under such circumstances; to all this he considered the charms of *Philander* unresistible, his unwearied industry in love, and concludes his sister lost. At first he upbraids *Philander*, and calls him ungrateful, but soon thought it unreasonable to accuse himself of an injustice, and excused the frailty of *Philander*, since he knew not that she whom he adored was sister to his friend; however, it failed not to possess him with inquietude that exercised all his wit, to consider how he might prevent an irreparable injury to his honour, and an intrigue that possibly might cost his sister her life, as well as fame. In the midst of all these torments he forgot not the more important business of his love: for to a lover, who has his soul perfectly fixed on the fair object of its adoration, whatever other thoughts fatigue and cloud his mind, that, like a soft gleam of new sprung light, darts in and spreads a glory all around, and like the god of day, cheers every drooping vital; yet even these dearer thoughts wanted not their torments. At first he strove to atone for the fears of *Calista*, with those of imagining *Philander* false to *Sylvia*: 'Well,' cried he ——'If thou be'st lost, *Calista*, at least thy ruin has laid a foundation for my happiness, and every triumph *Philander* makes of thy virtue, it the more secures my empire over *Sylvia*; and since the brother cannot be happy, but by the sister's being undone, yield thou, O faithless fair one, yield to *Philander*, and make me blest in *Sylvia*! And thou' (continued he) 'oh perjured lover and inconstant friend, glut thy insatiate flame —— rifle *Calista* of every virtue heaven and nature gave her, so I may but revenge it on thy *Sylvia*!' Pleased with this joyful hope he traverses his chamber; glowing and blushing with new kindling fire, his heart that was all gay, diffused a gladness, that expressed itself in every feature of his lovely face; his eyes, that were by nature languishing, shone now with an unusual air of briskness, smiles graced his mouth, and dimples dressed his face, insensibly his busy fingers trick and dress, and set his hair, and without designing it, his feet are bearing him to *Sylvia*, till he stopped short and wondered whither he was going, for yet it was not time to make his visit —'Whither, fond heart,' (said he) 'O whither wouldst thou hurry this slave to thy soft fires!' And now returning back he paused and fell to thought — He remembered how impatiently *Sylvia* waited the return of the answer he writ to him, wherein he owned his passion for that beauty. He knew she permitted him to write it, more to raise the little brisk fires of jealousy in *Philander*, and to set an edge on his blunted love, than from any favours she designed *Octavio*; and that on this answer depended all her happiness, or the confirmation of her doubts, and that she would measure *Philander*'s love by the effects she found there of it: so that never lover had so hard a game to play, as our new one. He knew he had it now in his power to ruin his rival, and to make almost his own terms with his fair conqueress, but he considered the secret was not rendered him for so base an end, nor could his love advance itself by ways so false, dull and criminal — Between each thought he paused, and now resolves she must know he sent an answer to his letter; for should she know he had, and that he should refuse her the sight of it, he believed with reason she ought to banish him for ever her presence, as the most disobedient of her slaves. He walks and pauses on — but no kind thought presents itself to save him; either way he finds himself undone, and from the most gay, and most triumphing lover on the earth, he now, with one desirous thought of right reasoning, finds he is the most miserable of all the creation! He reads the superscription of that *Philander* writ to *Sylvia*, which was enclosed in his, and finds it was directed only —'For *Sylvia*', which would plainly demonstrate it came not so into *Holland*, but that some other cover secured it; so that never any but *Octavio*, the most nice in honour, had ever so great a contest with love and friendship: for his noble temper was not one of those that could sacrifice his friend to his little lusts, or his more solid passion, but truly brave, resolves now rather to die than to confess *Philander*'s secret; to evade which he sent her letter by his page, with one from himself, and commanded him to tell her, that he was going to receive some commands from the Prince of *Orange*, and that he would wait on her himself in the evening. The page obeys, and *Octavio* sent him with a sigh, and eyes that languishingly told him he did it with regret.

The page hastening to *Sylvia*, finds her in all the disquiet of an expecting lover; and snatching the papers from his hand, the first she saw was that from *Philander*, at which she trembled with fear and joy, for hope, love and despair, at once seized her, and hardly able to make a sign with her hand, for the boy to withdraw, she sank down into her chair, all pale, and almost fainting; but re-assuming her courage, she opened it, and read this.

PHILANDER *to* SYLVIA.

Ah, *Sylvia*! Why all these doubts and fears? why at this distance do you accuse your lover, when he is incapable to fall before you, and undeceive your little jealousies. Oh, *Sylvia*, I fear this first reproaching me, is rather the effects of your own guilt, than any that love can make you think of mine. Yes, yes, my *Sylvia*, it is the waves that roll and glide away, and not the steady shore. 'Tis you begin to unfasten from the vows that hold you, and float along the flattering tide of vanity. It is you, whose pride and beauty scorning to be confined, give way to the admiring crowd, that sigh for you. Yes, yes, you, like the rest of your fair glorious sex, love the admirer though you hate the coxcomb. It is vain! it is great! And shews your beauty's power —— Is it possible, that for the safety of my life I cannot retire, but you must think I am fled from love and *Sylvia*? Or is it possible that pitying tenderness that made me incapable of taking leave of her should be interpreted as false — and base — and that an absence of thirty days, so forc'd, and so compelled, must render me inconstant — lost — ungrateful —— as if that after *Sylvia* heaven ever made a beauty that could charm me?

You charge my letter with a thousand faults, it is short, it is cold, and wants those usual softnesses that gave them all their welcome, and their graces. I fear my *Sylvia* loves the flatterer, and not the man, the lover only, not *Philander*: and she considers him not for himself, but the gay, glorious thing he makes of her! Ah! too self-interested! Is that your justice? You never allow for my unhappy circumstances; you never think how care oppresses me, nor what my love contributes to that care. How business, danger, and a thousand ills, take up my harrassed mind: by every power! I love thee still, my *Sylvia*, but time has made us more familiar now, and we begin to leave off ceremony, and come to closer joys to join our interests now, as people fixed, resolved to live and die together; to weave our thoughts and be united stronger. At first we shew the gayest side of love, dress and be nice in every word and look, set out for conquest all; spread every art, use every stratagem — But when the toil is past, and the dear victory gained, we then propose a little idle rest, a little easy slumber: we then embrace, lay by the gaudy shew, the plumes and gilded equipage of love, the trappings of the conqueror, and bring the naked lover to your arms; we shew him then uncased with all his little disadvantages; perhaps the flowing hair, (those ebony curls you have so often combed and dressed, and kissed) are then put up, and shew a fiercer air, more like an antique *Roman* than *Philander*: and shall I then, because I want a grace, be thought to love you less? Because the embroidered coat, the point and garniture's laid by, must I put off my passion with my dress? No, *Sylvia*, love allows a thousand little freedoms, allows me to unbosom all my secrets; tell thee my wants, my fears, complaints and dangers, and think it great relief if thou but sigh and pity me: and oft thy charming wit has aided me, but now I find thee adding to my pain. O where shall I unload my weight of cares, when *Sylvia*, who was wont to sigh and weep, and suffer me to ease the heavy burden, now grows displeased and peevish with my moans, and calls them the effects of dying love! Instead of those dear smiles, that fond bewitching prattle, that used to calm my roughest storm of grief, she now reproaches me with coldness, want of concern, and lover's rhetoric: and when I seem to beg relief and shew my soul's resentment, it is then I'm false; it is my aversion, or the effects of some new kindling flame: is this fair dealing, *Sylvia*? Can I not spare a little sigh from love, but you must think I rob you of your due? If I omit a tender name, by which I used to call you, must I be thought to lose that passion that taught me such endearments? And must I never reflect upon the ruin both of my fame and fortune, but I must run the risk of losing *Sylvia* too? Oh cruelty of love! Oh too, too fond and jealous maid, what crimes thy innocent passion can create, when it extends beyond the bounds of reason! Ah too, too nicely tender *Sylvia*, that will not give me leave to cast a thought back on my former glory; yet even that loss I could support with tameness and content, if I believed my suffering reached only to my heart; but *Sylvia*, if she love, must feel my torments too, must share my loss, and want a thousand ornaments, my sinking fortune cannot purchase her: believe me, charming creature, if I should love you less, I have a sense so just of what you have suffered for *Philander*, I'd be content to be a galley-slave, to give thy beauty, birth and love their due; but as I am thy faithful lover still, depend upon that fortune heaven has left me; which if thou canst (as thou hast often sworn) then thou would'st submit to be cheerful still, be gay and confident, and do not judge my heart by little words; my heart — too great and fond for such poor demonstrations.

You ask me, *Sylvia*, where I am, and what I do; and all I can say is, that at present I am safe from any fears of being delivered up to *France*, and what I do is sighing, dying, grieving; I want my *Sylvia*; but my circumstances yet have nothing to encourage that hope; when I resolve where to settle, you shall see what haste I will make to have you brought to me: I am impatient to hear from you, and to know how that dear pledge of our soft hours advances. I mean, what I believe I left thee possessed of, a young *Philander*: cherish it, *Sylvia*, for that is a certain obligation to keep a dying fire alive; be sure you do it no hurt by your unnecessary grief, though there needs no other tie but that of love to make me more entirely

Your PHILANDER.

If *Sylvia*'s fears were great before she opened the letter, what were her pains when all those fears were confirmed from that never-failing mark of a declining love, the coldness and alteration of the style of letters, that first symptom of a dying flame! 'O where,' said she, 'where, oh perjured charmer, is all that ardency that used to warm the reader? Where is all that natural innocence of love that could not, even to discover and express a grace in eloquence, force one soft word, or one passion? Oh,' continued she, 'he is lost and gone from *Sylvia* and his vows; some other has him all, clasps that dear body, hangs upon that face, gazes upon his eyes, and listens to his voice, when he is looking, sighing, swearing, dying, lying and damning of himself for some new beauty — He is, I will not endure it; aid me, *Antonet*! Oh, where is the perjured traitor!' *Antonet*, who was waiting on her, seeing her rise on the sudden in so great a fury, would have stayed her hasty turns and ravings, beseeching her to tell her what was the occasion, and by a discovery to ease her heart; but she with all the fury imaginable flung from her arms, and ran to the table, and snatching up a penknife, had certainly sent it to her heart, had not *Antonet* stepped to her and caught her hand, which she resisted not, and blushing resigned, with telling her, she was ashamed of her own cowardice; 'For,' said she, 'if it had designed to have been brave, I had sent you off, and by a noble resolution have freed this slave within' (striking her breast) 'from a tyranny which it should disdain to suffer under:' with that she raged about the chamber with broken words and imperfect threatenings, unconsidered imprecations, and unheeded vows and oaths; at which *Antonet* redoubled her petition to know the cause; and she replied —'*Philander*! The dear, the soft, the fond and charming *Philander* is now no more the same. O, *Antonet*,' said she, 'didst thou but see this letter compared to those of heretofore, when love was gay and young, when new desire dressed his soft eyes in tears, and taught his tongue the harmony of angels; when every tender word had more of passion, than volumes of this forced, this trifling business; Oh thou wouldst say I were the wretchedest thing that ever nature made — Oh, thou wouldst curse as I do — not the dear murderer, but thy frantic self, thy mad, deceived, believing, easy self; if thou wert so undone —' Then while she wept she gave *Antonet* liberty to speak, which was to persuade her, her fears were vain; she urged every argument of love she had been witness to, and could not think it possible he could be false. To all which the still weeping *Sylvia* lent a willing ear; for lovers are much inclined to believe every thing they wish. *Antonet*, having a little calmed her, continued telling her, that to be better convinced of his love, or his perfidy, she ought to have patience till *Octavio* should come to visit her; 'For you have forgotten, madam,' said she, 'that the generous rival has sent him word he is your lover:' for *Antonet* was waiting at the reading of that letter, nor was there any thing the open-hearted *Sylvia* concealed from that servant; and women who have made a breach in their honour, are seldom so careful of their rest of fame, as those who have a stock entire; and *Sylvia* believed after she had entrusted the secret of one amour to her discretion, she might conceal none. 'See, madam,' says *Antonet*, 'here is a letter yet unread:' *Sylvia*, who had been a great while impatient for the return of *Octavio*'s answer from *Philander*, expecting from thence the confirmation of all her doubts, hastily snatched the letter out of *Antonet*'s hand, and read it, hoping to have found something there to have eased her soul one way or other; a soul the most raging and haughty by nature that ever possessed a body: the words were these.

OCTAVIO *to* SYLVIA.

At least you will pity me, oh charming *Sylvia*, when you shall call to mind the cruel services I am obliged to render you, to be the messenger of love from him, whom beauty and that god plead so strongly for already in your heart.

If, after this, you can propose a torture that yet may speak my passion and obedience in any higher measure, command and try my fortitude; for I too well divine, O rigorous beauty, the business of your love-sick slave will be only to give you proofs how much he does adore you, and never to taste a joy, even in a distant hope; like lamps in urns my lasting fire must burn, without one kind material to supply it. Ah *Sylvia*, if ever it be thy wretched fate to see the lord of all your vows given to another's arms —— when you shall see in those soft eyes that you adore, a languishment and joy if you but name another beauty to him; —— when you behold his blushes fade and rise at the approaches of another mistress —— hear broken sighs and unassured replies, whenever he answers some new conqueress; tremblings, and pantings seizing every part at the warm touch as of a second charmer: ah, *Sylvia*, do but do me justice then, and sighing say — I pity poor *Octavio*.

Take here a letter from the blest *Philander*, which I had brought myself, but cannot bear the torment of that joy that I shall see advancing in your eyes when you shall read it over — no — it is too much that I imagine all! Yet bless that patient fondness of my passion that makes me still your slave, and your adorer,

OCTAVIO.

....

At finishing this, the jealous fair one redoubled her tears with such violence, that it was in vain her woman strove to abate the flowing tide by all the reasonable arguments she could bring to her aid; and *Sylvia*, to increase it, read again the latter part of the ominous letter; which she wet with the tears that streamed from her bright eyes. 'Yes, yes,' (cried she, laying the letter down) 'I know, *Octavio*, this is no prophecy of yours, but a known truth: alas, you know too well the fatal time is already come, when I shall find these changes in *Philander*!' 'Ah madam,' replied *Antonet*, 'how curious are you to search out torment for your own heart, and as much a lover as you are, how little do you understand the arts and politics of love! Alas, madam,' continued she, 'you yourself have armed my Lord *Octavio* with these weapons that wound you: the last time he writ to my lord *Philander*, he found you possessed with a thousand fears and jealousies; of these he took advantage to attack his rival: for what man is there so dull, that would not assault his enemy in that part where the most considerable mischief may be done him? It is now *Octavio*'s interest, and his business, to render *Philander* false, to give you all the umbrage that is possible of so powerful a rival, and to say any thing that may render him hateful to you, or at least to make him love you less.' 'Away,' (replied *Sylvia* with an uneasy smile) 'how foolish are thy reasonings; for were it possible I could love *Philander* less, is it to be imagined that should make way for *Octavio* in my heart, or any after that dear deceiver?' 'No doubt of it,' replied *Antonet*, 'but that very effect it would have on your heart; for love in the soul of a witty person is like a skein of silk; to unwind it from the bottom, you must wind it on another, or it runs into confusion, and becomes of no use, and then of course, as one lessens the other increases, and what *Philander* loses in love, *Octavio*, or some one industrious lover, will most certainly gain.' 'Oh,' replied *Sylvia*, 'you are a great philosopher in love.' 'I should, madam,' cried *Antonet*, 'had I but had a good memory, for I had a young churchman once in love with me, who has read many a philosophical lecture to me upon love; among the rest, he used to say the soul was all composed of love. I used to ask him then, if it were formed of so soft materials, how it came to pass that we were no oftener in love, or why so many

were so long before they loved, and others who never loved at all?'
'No question but he answered you wisely,' said *Sylvia* carelessly, and
sighing, with her thoughts but half attentive. 'Marry, and so he did,'
cried *Antonet*, 'at least I thought so then, because I loved a little.
He said, love of itself was inactive, but it was informed by object;
and then too that object must depend on fancy; (for souls, though
all love, are not to love all.) Now fancy, he said, was sometimes nice,
humorous, and fantastic, which is the reason we so often love those of
no merit, and despise those that are most excellent; and sometimes
fancy guides us to like neither; he used to say, women were like
misers, though they had always love in store, they seldom cared to
part with it, but on very good interest and security, *cent per cent*
most commonly, heart for heart at least; and for security, he said, we
were most times too unconscionable, we asked vows at least, at worst
matrimony —' Half angry, *Sylvia* cried —'And what is all this to my
loving again?' 'Oh madam,' replied *Antonet*, 'he said a woman was
like a gamester, if on the winning hand, hope, interest, and vanity
made him play on, besides the pleasure of the play itself; if on the
losing, then he continued throwing at all to save a stake at last, if not
to recover all; so either way they find occasion to continue the game.'
'But oh,' said *Sylvia* sighing, 'what shall that gamester set, who has
already played for all he had, and lost it at a cast?' 'O, madam,' replied
Antonet,'the young and fair find credit every where, there is still a
prospect of a return, and that gamester that plays thus upon the tick
is sure to lose but little; and if they win it is all clear gains.' 'I find,'
said *Sylvia*, 'you are a good manager in love; you are for the frugal
part of it.' 'Faith, madam,' said *Antonet*, 'I am indeed of that opinion,
that love and interest always do best together, as two most excellent
ingredients in that rare art of preserving of beauty. Love makes us
put on all our charms, and interest gives us all the advantage of dress,
without which beauty is lost, and of little use. Love would have us
appear always new, always gay, and magnificent, and money alone
can render us so; and we find no women want lovers so much as
those who want petticoats, jewels, and all the necessary trifles of
gallantry. Of this last opinion I find you yourself to be; for even when
Octavio comes, on whose heart you have no design, I see you dress

to the best advantage, and put on many, to like one: why is this, but that even unknown to yourself, you have a secret joy and pleasure in gaining conquests, and of being adored, and thought the most charming of your sex?' 'That is not from the inconstancy of my heart,' cried *Sylvia*, 'but from the little vanity of our natures.' 'Oh, madam,' replied *Antonet*, 'there is no friend to love like vanity; it is the falsest betrayer of a woman's heart of any passion, not love itself betrays her sooner to love than vanity or pride; and madam, I would I might have the pleasure of my next wish, when I find you not only listening to the love of *Octavio*, but even approving it too.' 'Away,' replied *Sylvia*, in frowning, 'your mirth grows rude and troublesome — Go bid the page wait while I return an answer to what his lord has sent me.' So sitting at the table she dismissed *Antonet*, and writ this following letter.

SYLVIA *to* OCTAVIO.

I find, *Octavio*, this little gallantry of yours, of shewing me the lover, stands you in very great stead, and serves you upon all occasions for abundance of uses; amongst the rest, it is no small obligation you have to it, for furnishing you with handsome pretences to keep from those who importune you, and from giving them that satisfaction by your counsel and conversation, which possibly the unfortunate may have need of sometimes; and when you are pressed and obliged to render me the friendship of your visits, this necessary ready love of yours is the only evasion you have for the answering a thousand little questions I ask you of *Philander*; whose heart I am afraid you know much better than *Sylvia* does. I could almost wish, *Octavio*, that all you tell me of your passion were true, that my commands might be of force sufficient to compel you to resolve my heart in some doubts that oppress it. And indeed if you would have me believe the one, you must obey me in the other; to which end I conjure you to hasten to me, for something of an unusual coldness in *Philander*'s letter, and some ominous divinations in yours, have put me on a rack of thought; from which nothing but confirmation can relieve me; this you dare not deny, if you value the repose of SYLVIA.

She read it over; and was often about to tear it, fancying it was too kind: but when she considered it was from no other inclination of her heart than that of getting the secrets out of his, she pardoned herself the little levity she found it guilty of; all which, considering as the effects of the violent passion she had for *Philander*, she found it easy to do; and sealing it she gave it to *Antonet* to deliver to the page, and set herself down to ease her soul of its heavy weight of grief by her complaints to the dear author of her pain; for when a lover is insupportably afflicted, there is no ease like that of writing to the person loved; and that, all that comes uppermost in the soul: for true love is all unthinking artless speaking, incorrect disorder, and without method, as 'tis without bounds or rules; such were *Sylvia*'s unstudied thoughts, and such her following letter.

SYLVIA *to* PHILANDER.

Oh my *Philander*, how hard it is to bring my soul to doubt, when I consider all thy past tender vows, when I reflect how thou hast loved and sworn. Methinks I hear the music of thy voice still whispering in my bosom; methinks the charming softness of thy words remains like lessening echoes of my soul, whose distant voices by degrees decay, till they be heard no more! Alas, I've read thy letter over and over, and turned the sense a thousand several ways, and all to make it speak and look like love — Oh I have flattered it with all my heart. Sometimes I fancied my ill reading spoiled it, and then I tuned my voice to softer notes, and read it over again; but still the words appeared too rough and harsh for any moving air; I which way soever I changed, which way soever I questioned it of love, it answered in such language — as others would perhaps interpret love, or something like it; but I, who've heard the very god himself speak from thy wondrous lips, and known him guide thy pen, when all the eloquence of moving angels flowed from thy charming tongue! When I have seen thee fainting at my feet, (whilst all heaven opened in thy glorious face) and now and then sigh out a trembling word, in which there was contained more love, more soul, than all the arts of speaking ever found; what sense? Oh what reflections must I make on this decay, this strange — this sudden alteration in thee? But that the cause is fled, and the effect is ceased, the god retired, and all the oracles silenced! Confess — oh thou eternal conqueror of my soul, whom every hour, and every tender joy, renders more dear and lovely — tell me why (if thou still lovest me, and lovest as well) does love not dictate to thee as before? Dost thou want words? Oh then begin again, I repeat the old ones over ten thousand times; such repetitions are love's rhetoric! How often have I asked thee in an hour, when my fond soul was doting on thy eyes, when with my arms clasping thy yielding neck, my lips imprinting kisses on thy cheeks, and taking in the breath that sighed from thine? How often have I asked this little but important question of thee? 'Does my *Philander* love me?' Then kiss thee for thy 'Yes' and sighs, and ask again; and still my soul was ravished with new joy, when thou wouldst answer, 'Yes, I love thee dearly!' And if I thought you spoke it with a tone that seemed less soft and fervent than I wished, I asked so often, till I made thee answer in such a voice as I would wish to hear it; all this had been impertinent and foolish in any thing but love, to any but a lover: but oh — give me the impertinence of love! Talk little nonsense to me all the day, and be as wanton as a playing *Cupid*, and that will please and charm my love-sick heart better than all fine sense and reasoning.

Tell me, *Philander*, what new accident, what powerful misfortune has befallen thee, greater than what we have experienced yet, to drive the little god out of thy heart, and make thee so unlike my soft *Philander*? What place contains thee, or what pleasures ease thee, that thou art now contented to live a tedious day without thy *Sylvia*? How then the long long age of forty more, and yet thou livest, art patient, tame and well; thou talkest not now of ravings, or of dying, but look'st about thee like a well pleased conqueror after the toils of battle — oh, I have known a time — but let me never think upon it more! It cannot be remembered without madness! What, think thee fallen from love! To think, that I must never hear thee more pouring thy soul out in soft sighs of love? A thousand dear expressions by which I knew the story of thy heart, and while you tell it, bid me feel it panting — never to see thy eyes fixed on my face — till the soft showers of joy would gently fall and hang their shining dew upon thy looks, then in a transport snatch me to thy bosom, and sigh a thousand times ere thou couldst utter —'Ah *Sylvia*, how I love thee'— oh the dear eloquence those few short words contain, when they are sent with lovers' accents to a soul all languishing! But now — alas, thy love is more familiar grown — oh take the other part of the proverb too, and say it has bred contempt, for nothing less than that your letter shews, but more it does, and that is indifference, less to be borne than hate, or any thing —

At least be just, and let me know my doom: do not deceive the heart that trusted all thy vows, if thou be'st generous — if thou lettest me know — thy date of love — is out (for love perhaps as life has dates) and equally uncertain, and thou no more canst stay the one than the other; yet if thou art so kind for all my honour lost, my youth undone, my beauty tarnished, and my lasting vows, to let me fairly know thou art departing, my worthless life will be the only loss: but if thou still continuest to impose upon my easy faith, and I should any other way learn my approaching fate — look to it *Philander* — she that had the courage to abandon all for love and faithless thee, can, when she finds herself betrayed and lost, nobly revenge the ruin of her fame, and send thee to the other world with SYLVIA.

She having writ this, read it over, and fancied she had not spoke half the sense of her soul — fancied if she were again to begin, she could express herself much more to the purpose she designed, than she had done. She began again, and writ two or three new ones, but they were either too kind or too rough; the first she feared would shew a weakness of spirit, since he had given her occasion of jealousy; the last she feared would disoblige if all those jealousies were false; she therefore tore those last she had writ, and before she sealed up the first she read *Philander*'s, letter again, but still ended it with fears that did not lessen those she had first conceived; still she thought she had more to say, as lovers do, who are never weary of speaking or writing to the dear object of their vows; and having already forgotten what she had just said before — and her heart being by this time as full as ere she began, she took up her complaining pen, and made it say this in the covert of the letter.

Oh *Philander*! Oh thou eternal charmer of my soul, how fain I would repent me of the cruel thoughts I have of thee! When I had finished this enclosed I read again thy chilling letter, and strove with all the force of love and soft imagination, to find a dear occasion of asking pardon for those fears which press my breaking heart: but oh, the more I read, the more they strike upon my tenderest part

— something so very cold, so careless and indifferent you end your letter with — I will not think of it — by heaven it makes me rave — and hate my little power, that could no longer keep thee soft and kind. Oh if those killing fears (bred by excess of love) are vainly taken up, in pity, my adorable — in pity to my tortured soul convince them, redress the torment of my jealous doubts, and either way confirm me; be kind to her that dies and languishes for thee, return me all the softness that first charmed me, or frankly tell me my approaching fate. Be generous or be kind to the unfortunate and undone

SYLVIA.

She thought she had ended here, but here again she read *Philander*'s letter, as if on purpose to find new torments out for a heart too much pressed already; a sour that is always mixed with the sweets of love, a pain that ever accompanies the pleasure. Love else were not to be numbered among the passions of men, and was at first ordained in heaven for some divine motion of the soul, till *Adam*, with his loss of *Paradise*, debauched it with jealousies, fears and curiosities, and mixed it with all that was afflicting; but you'll say he had reason to be jealous, whose woman, for want of other seducers, listened to the serpent, and for the love of change, would give way even to a devil; this little love of novelty and knowledge has been entailed upon her daughters ever since, and I have known more women rendered unhappy and miserable from this torment of curiosity, which they bring upon themselves, than have ever been undone by less villainous men. One of this humour was our haughty and charming *Sylvia*, whose pride and beauty possessing her with a belief that all men were born to die her slaves, made her uneasy at every action of the lover (whether beloved or not) that did but seem to slight her empire: but where indeed she loved and doted, as now in *Philander*, this humour put her on the rack at every thought or fancy that he might break his chains, and having laid the last obligation upon him, she expected him to be her slave for ever, and treated him with all the haughty tyranny of her sex, in all those moments when softness was not predominant in her soul. She was chagrin at every thing, if but displeased with one thing; and while she gave torments to others, she failed not to feel them the most sensibly herself; so that still searching for new occasion of quarrel with *Philander*, she drew on herself most intolerable pains, such as doubting lovers feel after long hopes and confirmed joy; she reads and weeps, and when she came to that part of it that inquired of the health and being of the pledge of love — she grew so tender that she was almost fainting in her chair, but recovering from the soft reflection, and finding she had said nothing of it already, she took her pen again and writ.

You ask me, oh charming *Philander*, how the pledge of our soft hours thrives: alas, as if it meant to brave the worst of fate! It does advance my sorrows, and all your cruelties have not destroyed that: but I still bear about me the destiny of many a sighing maid, that this (who will, I am sure, be like *Philander*) will ruin with his looks.

Thou sacred treasure of my soul, forgive me, if I have wronged thy love, *adieu*.

She made an end of writing this, just when *Antonet* arrived, and told her *Octavio* was alighted at the gate, and coming to visit her, which gave her occasion to say this of him to *Philander*.

I think I had not ended here, but that *Octavio*, the bravest and the best of friends, is come to visit me. The only satisfaction I have to support my life in *Philander*'s absence. Pay him those thanks that are due to him from me; pay him for all the generous cares he has taken of me; beyond a friend! Almost *Philander* in his blooming passion, when it was all new and young, and full of duty, could not have rendered me his service with a more awful industry: sure he was made for love and glorious friendship. Cherish him then, preserve him next your soul, for he is a jewel fit for such a cabinet: his form, his parts, and every noble action, shews us the royal race from whence he sprung, and the victorious *Orange* confesses him his own in every virtue, and in every grace; nor can the illegitimacy eclipse him: sure he was got in the first heat of love, which formed him so a *hero*— but no more. *Philander* is as kind a judge as

SYLVIA.

She had no sooner finished this and sealed it, but *Octavio* came into the chamber, and with such an air, with such a grace and mien he approached her — with all the languishment of soft trembling love in his face, which with the addition of the dress he was that day in, (which was extremely rich and advantageous, and altogether such as pleases the vanity of women,) I have since heard the charming *Sylvia* say, in spite of her tenderness for *Philander*, she found a soft emotion in her soul, a kind of pleasure at his approach, which made her blush with some kind of anger at her own easiness. Nor could she have blushed in a more happy season; for *Octavio* saw it, and it served at once to add a lustre to her paler beauty, and to betray some little kind sentiment, which possessed him with a joy that had the same effects on him: *Sylvia* saw it; and the care she took to hide her own, served but to increase her blushes, which put her into a confusion she had much ado to reclaim: she cast her eyes to earth, and leaning her cheek on her hand, she continued on her seat without paying him that usual ceremony she was wont to do; while he stood speechless for a moment, gazing on her with infinite satisfaction: when she, to assume a formality as well as she could, rose up and cried, (fearing he had seen too much) '*Octavio*, I have been considering after what manner I ought to receive you? And while I was so, I left those civilities unpaid, which your quality and my good manners ought to have rendered you.' 'Ah, madam,' replied he sighing, 'if you would receive me as I merited, and you ought, at least you would receive me as the most passionate lover that ever adored you.' 'I was rather believing,' said *Sylvia*, 'that I ought to have received you as my foe; since you conceal from me so long what you cannot but believe I am extremely impatient of hearing, and what so nearly concerns my repose.' At this, he only answering with a sigh, she pursued, 'Sure, *Octavio*, you understand me: *Philander*'s answer to the letter of your confessing passion, has not so long been the subject of our discourse and expectation, but you guess at what I mean?' *Octavio*, who on all occasions wanted not wit, or reply, was here at a loss what to answer; notwithstanding he had considered before what he would say: but let those in love fancy, and make what fine speeches they please, and believe themselves furnished with abundance of eloquent harangues, at the sight of the dear object they lose them all, and love teaches them a dialect much more prevailing, without the expense of duller thought: and they leave unsaid all they had so floridly formed before, a sigh a thousand things with more success: love, like poetry, cannot be taught, but uninstructed flows without painful study, if it be true; it is born in the soul, a noble inspiration, not a science! Such was *Octavio*'s, he thought it dishonourable to be guilty of the meanness of a lie; and say he had no answer: he thought it rude to say he had one and would not shew it *Sylvia*; and he believed it the height of ungenerous baseness to shew it. While he remained this moment silent, *Sylvia*, whose love, jealousy, and impatience endured no delay, with a malicious half smile, and a tone all angry, scorn in her eyes, and passion on her tongue, she cried —'It is well, *Octavio*, that you so early let me know, you can be false, unjust, and faithless; you knew your power, and in pity to that youth and easiness you found in me, have given a civil warning to my heart. In this I must confess,' continued she, 'you have given a much greater testimony of your friendship for *Philander*, than your passion for *Sylvia*, and I suppose you came not here to resolve yourself which you should prefer; that was decided ere you arrived, and this visit I imagine was only to put me out of doubt: a piece of charity you might have spared.' She ended this with a scorn, that had a thousand charms, because it gave him a little hope; and he answered with a sigh, 'Ah, madam, how very easy you find it to entertain thoughts disadvantageous of me: and how small a fault your wit and cruelty can improve to a crime! You are not offended at my friendship for *Philander*. I know you do not value my life, and my repose so much, as to be concerned who, or what shares this heart that adores you! No, it has not merited that glory; nor dare I presume to hope, you should so much as wish my passion for *Sylvia*, should surmount my friendship to *Philander*.' 'If I did,' replied she with a scorn, 'I perceive I might wish in vain.' 'Madam,' answered he, 'I have too divine an opinion of the justice of the charming *Sylvia* to believe I ought, or could make my approaches to her heart, by ways so base and ungenerous, the result of even tolerated treason is to hate the traitor.' 'Oh, you are very nice, *Octavio*,' replied *Sylvia*, 'in your punctilio to *Philander*; but I perceive you are not so tender in those you ought to have for *Sylvia*: I find honour in you men, is only what you please to make it; for at the same time you think it ungenerous to betray *Philander*, you believe it no breach of honour to betray the eternal repose of *Sylvia*. You have promised *Philander* your friendship; you have avowed yourself my lover, my slave, my friend, my every thing; and yet not one of these has any tie to oblige you to my interest: pray tell me,' continued she, 'when you last writ to him; was it not in order to receive an answer from him? And was not I to see that answer? And here you think it no dishonour to break your word or promise; by which I find your false notions of virtue and honour, with which you serve yourselves, when interest, design, or self-love makes you think it necessary.' 'Madam,' replied *Octavio*, 'you are pleased to pursue your anger, as if indeed I had disobeyed your command, or refused to shew you what you imagine I have from *Philander*:' 'Yes, I do,' replied she hastily; 'and wonder why you should have a greater friendship for *Philander*, than for *Sylvia*; especially if it be true that you say, you have joined love to friendship: or are you of the opinion of those that cry, they cannot be a lover and a friend of the same object.' 'Ah, madam,' cried our perplexed lover, 'I beg you to believe, I think it so much more my duty and inclination to serve and obey *Sylvia*, than I do *Philander*, that I swear to you, oh charming conqueress of my soul, if *Philander* have betrayed *Sylvia*, he has at the same time betrayed *Octavio*, and that I would revenge it with the loss of my life: in injuring the adorable *Sylvia*, believe me, lovely maid, he injures so much more than a friend, as honour is above the inclinations; if he wrong you, by heaven he cancels all! He wrongs my soul, my honour, mistress, and my sister:' fearing he had said too much, he stopped and sighed at the word sister, and casting down his eyes, blushing with shame and anger, he continued. 'Oh give me leave to say a sister, madam, lest mistress had been too daring and presumptuous, and a title that would not justify my quarrel half so well, since it would take the honour from my just resentment, and blast it with the scandal of self-interest or jealous revenge.' 'What you say,' replied she, 'deserves abundance of acknowledgement; but if you would have me believe you, you ought to hide nothing from me; and he, methinks, that was so daring to confess his passion to *Philander*, may after that, venture on any discovery: in short, *Octavio*, I demand to see the return you have from *Philander*, for possibly —' said she, sweetening her charming face into a smile designed, 'I should not be displeased to find I might with more freedom receive your addresses, and on the coldness of *Philander*'s reasoning may depend a great part of your fate, or fortune: come, come, produce your credentials, they may recommend your heart more effectually than all the fine things you can say; you know how the least appearance of a slight from a lover may advance the pride of a mistress; and pride in this affair will be your best advocate.' Thus she insinuated with all her female arts, and put on all her charms of looks and smiles, sweetened her mouth, softened her voice and eyes, assuming all the tenderness and little affectations her subtle sex was capable of, while he lay all ravished and almost expiring at her feet; sometimes transported with imagined joys in the possession of the dear flattering charmer, he was ready to unravel all the secrets of *Philander*'s letter; but honour yet was even above his passion, and made him blush at his first hasty thought; and now he strove to put her off with all the art he could, who had so very little in his nature, and whose real love and perfect honour had set him above the little evasions of truth, who scorned in all other cases the baseness and cowardice of a lie; and so unsuccessful now was the little honest cheat, which he knew not how to manage well, that it was soon discovered to the witty, jealous, and angry *Sylvia*: so that after all the rage a passionate woman could express, who believed herself injured by the only two persons in the world from whom she expected most adoration; she had recourse to that natural and softening aid of her sex, her tears; and having already reproached *Octavio* with all the malice of a defeated woman, she now continued it in so moving a manner, that our *hero* could no longer remain unconquered by that powerful way of charming, but unfixed to all he had resolved, gave up, at least, a part of the secret, and owned he had a letter from *Philander*; and after this confession knowing very well he could not keep her from the sight of it; no, though an empire were rendered her to buy it off; his wit was next employed how he should defend the sense of it, that she might not think *Philander* false. In order to this, he, forcing a smile, told her, that *Philander* was the most malicious of his sex, and had contrived the best stratagem in the world to find whether *Sylvia* still loved, or

Octavio retained his friendship for him: 'And but that,' continued he, 'I know the nature of your curious sex to be such, that if I should persuade you not to see it, it would but the more inflame your desire of seeing it; I would ask no more of the charming *Sylvia*, than that she would not oblige me to shew what would turn so greatly to my own advantage: if I were not too sensible, it is but to entrap me, that *Philander* has taken this method in his answer. Believe me, adorable *Sylvia*, I plead against my own life, while I beg you not to put my honour to the test, by commanding me to shew this letter, and that I join against the interest of my own eternal repose while I plead thus.' She hears him with a hundred changes of countenance. Love, rage, and jealousy swell in her fierce eyes, her breath beats short, and she was ready to burst into speaking before he had finished what he had to say; she called up all the little discretion and reason love had left her to manage herself as she ought in this great occasion; she bit her lips, and swallowed her rising sighs; but he soon saw the storm he had raised, and knew not how to stand the shock of its fury; he sighs, he pleads in vain, and the more he endeavours to excuse the levity of *Philander*, the more he rends her heart, and sets her on the rack; and concluding him false, she could no longer contain her rage, but broke out into all the fury that madness can inspire, and from one degree to another wrought her passion to the height of lunacy: she tore her hair, and bit his hands that endeavoured to restrain hers from violence; she rent the ornaments from her fair body, and discovered a thousand charms and beauties; and finding now that both his strength and reason were too weak to prevent the mischiefs he found he had brought on her, he calls for help: when *Brilliard* was but too ready at hand, with *Antonet*, and some others who came to his assistance. *Brilliard*, who knew nothing of the occasion of all this, believed it the second part of his own late adventure, and fancied that *Octavio* had used some violence to her; upon this he assumes the authority of his lord, and secretly that of a husband or lover, and upbraiding the innocent *Octavio* with his brutality, they fell to such words as ended in a challenge the next morning, for *Brilliard* appeared a gentleman, companion to his lord; and one whom *Octavio* could not well refuse: this was not carried so silently but *Antonet*, busy as she was about her raving lady, heard the appointment, and *Octavio* quitted the chamber almost as much disturbed as *Sylvia*, whom, with much ado they persuaded him to leave; but before he did so, he on his knees offered her the letter, and implored her to receive it; so absolutely his love had vanquished his nobler part, that of honour. But she attending no motions but those of her own rage, had no regard either to *Octavio*'s proffer, or his arguments of excuse; so that he went away with the letter in all the extremity of disorder. This last part of his submission was not seen by *Brilliard*; who immediately left the chamber, upon receiving *Octavio*'s answer to his challenge; so that *Sylvia* was now left with her woman only; who by degrees brought her to more calmness; and *Brilliard*, impatient to hear the reproaches he hoped she would give *Octavio* when she was returned to reason, being curious of any thing that might redound to his disadvantage, whom he took to be a powerful rival, returned again into her chamber: but in lieu of hearing what he wished, *Sylvia* being recovered from her passion of madness, and her soul in a state of thinking a little with reason, she misses *Octavio* in the crowd, and with a voice her rage had enfeebled to a languishment, she cried — surveying carefully those about her, 'Oh where is *Octavio*? Where is that angel man: he who of all his kind can give me comfort?' 'Madam,' replied *Antonet*, 'he is gone; while he was here, he kneeled and prayed in vain, but for a word, or look; his tears are yet remaining wet upon your feet, and all for one sensible reply, but rage had deafened you; what has he done to merit this?' 'Oh *Antonet*,' cried *Sylvia*——'It was what he would not do, that makes me rave; run, haste and fetch him back —— but let him leave his honour all behind: tell him he has too much consideration for *Philander*, and none for my repose. Oh, *Brilliard* —— Have I no friend in view dares carry a message from me to *Octavio*? Bid him return, oh instantly return —— I die, I languish for a sight of him —— descending angels would not be so welcome —— Why stand ye still —— have I no power with you —— Will none obey ——' Then running hastily to the chamber door, she called her page to whom she cried ——'Haste, haste, dear youth, and find *Octavio* out, and bring him to me instantly: tell him I die to see him.' The boy, glad of so kind a message to so liberal a lover, runs on his errand, while she returns to her chamber, and endeavours to recollect her senses against *Octavio*'s coming as much as possibly she could: she dismisses her attendant with different apprehensions; sometimes *Brilliard* believed this was the second part of her first raving, and having never seen her thus, but for *Philander*, concludes it the height of tenderness and passion for *Octavio*; but because she made so public a declaration of it, he believed he had given her a philtre, which had raised her flame so much above the bounds of modesty and discretion; concluding it so, he knew the usual effects of things of that nature, and that nothing could allay the heat of such a love but possession; and easily deluded with every fancy that flattered his love, mad, stark-mad, by any way to obtain the last blessing with *Sylvia*, he consults with *Antonet* how to get one of *Octavio*'s letters out of her lady's cabinet, and feigning many frivolous reasons, which deluded the amorous maid, he persuaded her to get him one, which she did in half an hour after; for by this time *Sylvia* being in as much tranquillity as it was possible a lover could be in, who had the hopes of knowing all the secrets of the false betrayer, she had called *Antonet* to dress her; which she resolved should be in all the careless magnificence that art or nature could put on; to charm *Octavio* wholly to obedience, whom she had sent for, and whom she expected! But she was no sooner set to her toilet, but *Octavio*'s page arrived with a letter from his master, which she greedily snatched, and read this:

OCTAVIO *to* SYLVIA.

By this time, oh charming *Sylvia*, give me leave to hope your rage is abated, and your reason returned, and that you will hear a little from the most unfortunate of men, whom you have reduced to this miserable extremity of losing either the adorable object of his soul, or his honour: if you can prefer a little curiosity that will serve but to afflict you, before either that or my repose, what esteem ought I to believe you have for the unfortunate *Octavio*: and if you hate me, as it is evident, if you compel me to the extremity of losing my repose or honour, what reason or argument have I to prefer so careless a fair one above the last? It is certain you neither do nor can love me now; and how much below that hope shall the exposed and abandoned *Octavio* be, when he shall pretend to that glory without his honour? Believe me, charming maid, I would sacrifice my life, and my entire fortune at your least command to serve you; but to render you a devoir that must point me out the basest of my sex, is what my temper must resist in spite of all the violence of my love; and I thank my happier stars, that they have given me resolution enough, rather to fall a sacrifice to the last, than be guilty of the breach of the first: this is the last and present thought and pleasure of my soul; and lest it should, by the force of those divine ideas which eternally surround it, be soothed and flattered from its noble principles, I will to-morrow put myself out of the hazard of temptation, and divert if possible, by absence, to the campaign, those soft importunate betrayers of my liberty, that perpetually solicit in favour of you: I dare not so much as bid you adieu, one sight of that bright angel's face would undo me, unfix my nobler resolution, and leave me a despicable slave, sighing my unrewarded treason at your insensible feet: my fortune I leave to be disposed by you; but the more useless necessary I will for ever take from those lovely eyes, you can look on nothing with joy, but the happy *Philander*: if I have denied you one satisfaction, at least I have given you this other, of securing you eternally from the trouble and importunity of, madam, your faithful

    OCTAVIO.

    This letter to any other less secure of her power than was our fair subject, would have made them impatient and angry; but she found that there was something yet in her power, the dispensation of which could soon recall him from any resolution he was able to make of absenting himself. Her glass stood before her, and every glance that way was an assurance and security to her heart; she could not see that beauty, and doubt its power of persuasion. She therefore took her pen, and writ him this answer, being in a moment furnished with all the art and subtlety that was necessary on this occasion.

    SYLVIA *to* Octavio.

    My Lord,

    Though I have not beauty enough to command your heart; at least allow me sense enough to oblige your belief, that I fancy and resent all that the letter contains which you have denied me, and that I am not of that sort of women, whose want of youth or beauty renders so constant to pursue the ghost of a departed love: it is enough to justify my honour, that I was not the first aggressor. I find myself pursued by too many charms of wit, youth, and gallantry, to bury myself beneath the willows, or to whine away my youth by murmuring rivers, or betake me to the last refuge of a declining beauty, a monastery: no, my lord, when I have revenged and recompensed myself for the injuries of one inconstant, with the joys a thousand imploring lovers offer, it will be time to be weary of a world, which yet every day presents me new joys; and I swear to you, *Octavio*, that it was more to recompense what I owed your passion, that I desired a convincing proof of *Philander*'s falsehood, than for any other reason, and you have too much wit not to know it; for what other use could I make of the secret? If he be false he is gone, unworthy of me, and impossible to be retrieved; and I would as soon dye my sullied garments, and wear them over again, as take to my embraces a reformed lover, the native first lustre of whose passion is quite extinct, and is no more the same; no, my lord, she must be poor in beauty, that has recourse to shifts so mean; if I would know the secret, by all that is good it were to hate him heartily, and to dispose of my person to the best advantage; which in honour I cannot do, while I am unconvinced of the falseness of him with whom I exchanged a thousand vows of fidelity; but if he unlink the chain, I am at perfect liberty; and why by this delay you should make me lose my time, I am not able to conceive, unless you fear I should then take you at your word, and expect the performance of all the vows of love you have made me —— If that be it — my pride shall be your security, or if other recompense you expect, set the price upon your secret, and see at what rate I shall purchase the liberty it will procure me; possibly it may be such as may at once enfranchise me, and revenge me on the perjured ingrate, than which nothing can be a greater satisfaction to

SYLVIA.

She seals this letter with a wafer, and giving it to *Antonet* to give the page, believing she had writ what would not be in vain to the quick-sighted *Octavio*; *Antonet* takes both that and the other which

Octavio had sent, and left her lady busy in dressing her head, and went to *Brilliard*'s chamber, who thought every moment an age till she came, so vigorous he was on his new design. That which was sent to *Octavio*, being sealed with a wet wafer, he neatly opens, as it was easy to do, and read, and sealed again, and *Antonet* delivered it to the page. After receiving what pay *Brilliard* could force himself to bestow upon her, some flatteries of dissembled love, and some cold kisses, which even imagination could not render better, she returned to her lady, and he to his stratagem, which was to counterfeit a letter from *Octavio*; she having in hers given him a hint, by bidding him set a price upon the secret, which he had heard was that of a letter from *Philander*, with all the circumstances of it, from the faithless *Antonet*, whom love had betrayed; and after blotting much paper to try every letter through the alphabet, and to produce them like those of *Octavio*, which was not hard for a lover of ingenuity, he fell to the business of what he would write; and having finished it to his liking, his next trouble was how to convey it to her; for *Octavio* always sent his by his page, whom he could trust. He now was certain of love between them; for though he often had persuaded *Antonet* to bring him letters, yet she could not be wrought on till now to betray her trust; and what he long apprehended, he found too true on both sides, and now he waited but for an opportunity to send it seasonably, and in a lucky minute. In the mean time *Sylvia* adorns herself for an absolute conquest, and disposing herself in the most charming, careless, and tempting manner she could devise, she lay expecting her coming lover, on a repose of rich embroidery of gold on blue satin, hung within-side with little amorous pictures of *Venus* descending in her chariot naked to *Adonis*, she embracing, while the youth, more eager of his rural sports, turns half from her in a posture of pursuing his dogs, who are on their chase: another of *Armida*, who is dressing the sleeping warrior up in wreaths of flowers, while a hundred little Loves are playing with his gilded armour; this puts on his helmet too big for his little head, that hides his whole face; another makes a hobby-horse of his sword and lance; another fits on his breast-piece, while three or four little *Cupids* are seeming to heave and help him to hold it an end, and all turned the emblems of the hero into ridicule. These, and some either of the like nature, adorned the pavilion of the languishing fair one, who lay carelessly on her side, her arm leaning on little pillows of point of *Venice*, and a book of amours in her other hand. Every noise alarmed her with trembling hope that her lover was come, and I have heard she said, she verily believed, that acting and feigning the lover possessed her with a tenderness against her knowledge and will; and she found something more in her soul than a bare curiosity of seeing *Octavio* for the letter's sake: but in lieu of her lover, she found herself once more approached with a billet from him, which brought this.

OCTAVIO *to* SYLVIA.

Ah, *Sylvia*, he must be more than human that can withstand your charms; I confess my frailty, and fall before you the weakest of my sex, and own I am ready to believe all your dear letter contains, and have vanity enough to wrest every hopeful word to my own interest, and in favour of my own heart: what will become of me, if my easy faith should only flatter me, and I with shame should find it was not meant to me, or if it were, it was only to draw me from a virtue which has been hitherto the pride and beauty of my youth, the glory of my name, and my comfort and refuge in all extremes of fortune; the eternal companion, guide and counsellor of all my actions: yet this good you only have power to rob me of, and leave me exposed to the scorn of all the laughing world; yet give me love! Give me but hope in lieu of it, and I am content to divest myself of all besides.

Perhaps you will say I ask too mighty a rate for so poor a secret. But even in that there lies one of my own, that will more expose the feebleness of my blood and name, than the discovery will me in particular, so that I know not what I do, when I give you up the knowledge you desire. Still you will say all this is to enhance its value, and raise the price: and oh, I fear you have taught my soul every quality it fears and dreads in yours, and learnt it to chaffer for every thought, if I could fix upon the rate to sell it at: and I with shame confess I would be mercenary, could we but agree upon the price; but my respect forbids me all things but silent hope, and that, in spite of me and all my reason, will predominate; for the rest I will wholly resign myself, and all the faculties of my soul, to the charming arbitrator of my peace, the powerful judge of love, the adorable *Sylvia*; and at her feet render all she demands; yes, she shall find me there to justify all the weakness this proclaims; for I confess, oh too too powerful maid, that you have absolutely subdued

Your OCTAVIO.

She had no sooner read this letter, but *Antonet*, instead of laying it by, carried it to *Brilliard*, and departed the chamber to make way for *Octavio*, who she imagined was coming to make his visit, and left *Sylvia* considering how she should manage him to the best advantage, and with most honour acquit herself of what she had made him hope; but instead of his coming to wait on her, an unexpected accident arrived to prevent him; for a messenger from the Prince came with commands that he should forthwith come to His Highness, the messenger having command to bring him along with him: so that not able to disobey, he only begged time to write a note of business, which was a billet to *Sylvia* to excuse himself till the next day; for it being five leagues to the village where the Prince waited his coming, he could not return that night; which was the business of the note, with which his page hasted to *Sylvia*. *Brilliard*, who was now a vigilant lover, and waiting for every opportunity that might favour his design, saw the page arrive with the note; and, as it was usual, he took it to carry to his conqueress; but meeting *Antonet* on the stairs, he gave her what he had before counterfeited with such art, after he had opened what *Octavio* had sent, and found fortune was wholly on his side, he having learned from the page besides, that his lord had taken coach with Monsieur —— to go to His Highness, and would not return that night: *Antonet*, not knowing the deceit, carried her lady the forged letter, who opened it with eager haste, and read this.

To the Charming SYLVIA.

Madam,

Since I have a secret, which none but I can unfold, and that you have offered at any rate to buy it of me, give me leave to say, that you, fair creature, have another secret, a joy to dispense, which none but you can give the languishing *Octavio*: if you dare purchase this of mine, with that infinitely more valuable one of yours, I will be as secret as death, and think myself happier than a fancied god! Take what methods you please for the payment, and what time, order me, command me, conjure me, I will wait, watch, and pay my duty at all hours, to snatch the most convenient one to reap so ravishing a blessing. I know you will accuse me with all the confidence and rudeness in the world: but oh! consider, lovely *Sylvia*, that that passion which could change my soul from all the course of honour, has power to make me forget that nice respect your beauty awes me with, and my passion is now arrived at such a height, it obeys no laws but its own; and I am obstinately bent on the pursuit of that vast pleasure I fancy to find in the dear, the ravishing arms of the adorable *Sylvia*: impatient of your answer, I am, as love compels me, madam, your slave,

OCTAVIO.

The page, who waited no answer, was departed: but *Sylvia*, who believed he attended, was in a thousand minds what to say or do: she blushed, as she read, and then looked pale with anger and disdain, and, but that she had already given her honour up, it would have been something more surprising: but she was used to questions of that nature, and therefore received this with so much the less concern; nevertheless, it was sufficient to fill her soul with a thousand agitations; but when she would be angry, the consideration of what she had writ to him, to encourage him to this boldness, stopped her rage: when she would take it ill, she considered his knowledge of her lost fame, and that took off a great part of her resentment on that side; and in midst of all she was raving for the knowledge of *Philander*'s secret. She rose from the bed, and walked about the room in much disorder, full of thought and no conclusion; she is ashamed to consult of this affair with *Antonet*, and knows not what to fix on: the only thing she was certain of, and which was fully and undisputably resolved in her soul, was never to consent to so false an action, never to buy the secret at so dear a rate; she abhors *Octavio*, whom she regards no more as that fine thing which before she thought him; and a thousand times she was about to write her despite and contempt, but still the dear secret stayed her hand, and she was fond of the torment: at last *Antonet*, who was afflicted to know the cause of this disorder, asked her lady if *Octavio* would not come; 'No,' replied *Sylvia*, blushing at the name, 'nor never shall the ungrateful man dare to behold my face any more.' 'Jesu,' replied *Antonet*, 'what has he done, madam, to deserve this severity?' For he was a great benefactor to *Antonet*, and had already by his gifts and presents made her a fortune for a burgomaster. 'He has,' said *Sylvia*, 'committed such an impudence as deserves death from my hand:' this she spoke in rage, and walked away cross the chamber. 'Why, madam,' cried *Antonet*,'does he deny to give you the letter?' 'No,' replied *Sylvia*, 'but asks me such a price for it, as makes me hate myself, that am reduced by my ill conduct to addresses of that nature:' 'Heavens, madam, what can he ask you to afflict you so!' 'The presumptuous man,' said she, (in rage) 'has the impudence to ask what never man, but *Philander*, was ever possessed of ——' At this, *Antonet* laughed —'Good lord, madam,' said she, 'and are you angry at such desires in men towards you? I believe you are the first lady in the world that was ever offended for being desirable: can any thing proclaim your beauty more, or your youth, or wit? Marry, madam, I wish I were worthy to be asked the question by all the fine dancing, dressing, song-making fops in town.' 'And you would yield,' replied *Sylvia*. 'Not so neither,' replied *Antonet*, 'but I would spark myself, and value myself the more upon it.' 'Oh,' said *Sylvia*, 'she that is so fond of hearing of love, no doubt but will find some one to practise it with.' 'That is as I should find myself inclined,' replied *Antonet*. *Sylvia* was not so intent on *Antonet*'s raillery, but she employed all her thought the while on what she had to do: and those last words of *Antonet*'s jogged a thought that ran on to one very advantageous, at least her present and first apprehension of it was such: and she turned to *Antonet*, with a face more gay than it was the last minute, and cried, 'Prithee, good wench, tell me what sort of man would soonest incline you to a yielding:' 'If you command me, madam, to be free with your ladyship,' replied *Antonet*, 'I must confess there are two sorts of men that would most villainously incline me: the first is he that would make my fortune best; the next, he that would make my pleasure; the young, the handsome, or rather the well-bred and good-humoured; but above all, the man of wit.' 'But what would you say, *Antonet*,' replied *Sylvia*, 'if all these made up in one man should make his addresses to you?' 'Why then most certainly, madam,' replied *Antonet*, 'I should yield him my honour, after a reasonable siege.' This though the wanton young maid spoke possibly at first more to put her lady in good humour, than from any inclination she had to what she said; yet after many arguments upon that subject, *Sylvia*, cunning enough to pursue her design, brought the business more home, and told her in plain terms, that *Octavio* was the man who had been so presumptuous as to ask so great a reward as the possession of herself for the secret she desired; and, after a thousand little subtleties, having made the forward girl confess with blushes she was not a maid, she insinuated into her an opinion, that what she had done already (without any other motive than that of love, as she confessed, in which interest had no part) would make the trick the easier to do again, especially if she brought to her arms a person of youth, wit, gallantry, beauty, and all the charming qualities that adorn a man, and that besides she should find it turn to good account; and for her secrecy she might depend upon it, since the person to whose embraces she should submit herself, should not know but that she herself was the woman: 'So that,' says *Sylvia*, 'I will have all the infamy, and you the reward every way with unblemished honour.' While she spoke, the willing maid gave an inward pleasing attention, though at first she made a few faint modest scruples: nor was she less joyed to hear it should be *Octavio*, whom she knew to be rich, and very handsome; and she immediately found the humour of inconstancy seize her; and *Brilliard* appeared a very husband lover in comparison of this new brisker man of quality; so that after some pros and cons the whole matter was thus concluded on between these two young persons, who neither wanted wit nor beauty; and both crowed over the little contrivance, as a most diverting piece of little malice, that should serve their present turn, and make them sport for the future. The next thing that was considered was a letter which was to be sent in answer, and that *Sylvia* being to write with her own hand begot a new doubt, insomuch as the whole business was at a stand: for when it came to that point that she herself was to consent, she found the project look with a face so foul, that she a hundred times resolved and unresolved. But *Philander* filled her soul, revenge was in her view, and that one thought put her on new resolves to pursue the design, let it be never so base and dishonourable: 'Yes,' cried she at last, 'I can commit no action that is not more just, excusable and honourable, than that which *Octavio* has done to me, who uses me like a common mistress of the town, and dares ask me that which he knows he durst not do, if he had not mean and abject thoughts of me; his baseness deserves death at my hand, if I had courage to give it him, and the least I can do is to deceive the deceiver. Well then, give me my escritoire,' says she; so, sitting down, she writ this, not without abundance of guilt and confusion; for yet a certain honour, which she had by birth, checked the cheat of her pen.

....

SYLVIA *to* OCTAVIO.

The price, *Octavio*, which you have set upon your secret, I (more generous than you) will give your merit, to which alone it is due: if I should pay so high a price for the first, you would believe I had the less esteem for the last, and I would not have you think me so poor in spirit to yield on any other terms. If I valued *Philander* yet — after his confirmed inconstancy, I would have you think I scorn to yield a body where I do not give a soul, and am yet to be persuaded there are any such brutes amongst my sex; but as I never had a wish but where I loved, so I never extended one till now to any but *Philander*; yet so much my sense of shame is above my growing tenderness, that I could wish you would be so generous to think no more of what you seem to pursue with such earnestness and haste. But lest I should retain any sort of former love for *Philander*, whom I am impatient to rase wholly from my soul, I grant you all you ask, provided you will be discreet in the management: *Antonet* therefore shall only be trusted with the secret; the outward gate you shall find at twelve only shut to, and *Antonet* wait you at the stairs-foot to conduct you to me; come alone. I blush and gild the paper with their reflections, at the thought of an encounter like this, before I am half enough secured of your heart. And that you may be made more absolutely the master of mine, send me immediately *Philander*'s letter enclosed, that if any remains of chagrin possess me, they may be totally vanquished by twelve o'clock.

SYLVIA.

She having, with much difficulty, writ this, read it to her trusty confidante; for this was the only secret of her lady's she was resolved never to discover to *Brilliard*, and to the end he might know nothing of it she sealed the letter with wax: but before she sealed it, she told her lady, she thought she might have spared abundance of her blushes, and have writ a less kind letter; for a word of invitation or consent would have served as well. To which *Sylvia* replied, her anger against him was too high not to give him all the defeat imaginable, and the greater the love appeared, the greater would be the revenge when he should come to know (as in time he should) how like a false friend she had treated him. This reason, or any at that time would have served *Antonet*, whose heart was set upon a new adventure, and in such haste she was (the night coming on a-pace) to know how she should dress, and what more was to be done, that she only went out to call the page, and meeting *Brilliard* (who watched every body's motion) on the stair-case, he asked her what that was; and she said, to send by *Octavio*'s page: 'You need not look in it,' said she (when he snatched it hastily out of her hand:) 'For I can tell you the contents, and it is sealed so, it must be known if you unrip it.' 'Well, well,' said he, 'if you tell it me, it will satisfy my curiosity as well; therefore I'll give it the page.' She returns in again to her lady, and he to his own chamber to read what answer the dear object of his desire had sent to his forged one: so opening it, he found it such as his soul wished, and was all joy and ecstasy; he views himself a hundred times in the glass, and set himself in order with all the opinion and pride, as if his own good parts had gained him the blessing; he enlarged himself as he walked, and knew not what to do, so extremely was he ravished with his coming joy; he blessed himself, his wit, his stars, his fortune; then read the dear obliging letter, and kissed it all over, as if it had been meant to him; and after he had forced himself to a little more serious consideration, he bethought himself of what he had to do in order to this dear appointment: he finds in her letter, that in the first place he was to send her the letter from *Philander*: I told you before he took *Octavio*'s letter from the page, when he understood his lord was going five leagues out of town to the prince. *Octavio* could not avoid his going, and wrote to *Sylvia*; in which he sent her the letter *Philander* writ, wherein was the first part of the confession of his love to Madam the Countess of *Clarinau*: generously *Octavio* sent it without terms; but *Brilliard* slid his own forged one into *Antonet*'s hand in lieu of it, and now he read that from *Philander*, and wondered at his lord's inconstancy; yet glad of the opportunity to take *Sylvia*'s heart a little more off from him, he soon resolved she should have the letter, but being wholly mercenary, and fearing that either when once she had it, it might make her go back from her promised assignation, or at least put her out of humour, so as to spoil a great part of the entertainment he designed: he took the pains to counterfeit another billet to her, which was this.

······················

To SYLVIA.

  Madam,

  Since we have begun to chaffer, you must give me leave to make the best of the advantage I find I have upon you; and having violated my honour to *Philander*, allow the breach of it in some degree on other occasions; not but I have all the obedience and adoration for you that ever possessed the soul of a most passionate and languishing lover: but, fair *Sylvia*, I know not whether, when you have seen the secret of the false *Philander*, you may not think it less valuable than you before did, and so defraud me of my due. Give me leave, oh wondrous creature! to suspect even the most perfect of your sex; and to tell you, that I will no sooner approach your presence, but I will resign the paper you so much wish. If you send me no answer, I will come according to your directions: if you do, I must obey and wait, though with that impatience that never attended a suffering lover, or any but, divine creature, your OCTAVIO.

  This he sealed, and after a convenient distance of time carried as from the page to *Antonet*, who was yet contriving with her lady, to whom she gives it, who read it with abundance of impatience, being extremely angry at the rudeness of the style, which she fancied much altered from what it was; and had not her rage blinded her, she might easily have perceived the difference too of the character, though it came as near to the like as possible so short a practice could produce; she took it with the other, and tore it in pieces with rage, and swore she would be revenged; but, after calmer thoughts, she took up the pieces to keep to upbraid him with, and fell to weeping for anger, defeat and shame; but the *April* shower being past, she returned to her former resentment, and had some pleasure amidst all her torment of fears, jealousies, and sense of *Octavio*'s disrespect in the thoughts of revenge; in order to which she contrives how *Antonet* shall manage herself, and commanding her to bring out some fine point linen, she dressed up *Antonet*'s head with them, and put her on a shift, laced with the same; for though she intended no light should be in the chamber when *Octavio* should enter, she knew he understood by his touch the difference of fine things from other. In fine, having dressed her exactly as she herself used to be when she received *Octavio*'s visits in bed, she embraced her, and fancied she was much of her own shape and bigness, and that it was impossible to find the deceit: and now she made *Antonet* dress her up in her clothes, and mobbing her sarsenet hood about her head, she appeared so like *Antonet* (all but the face) that it was not easy to distinguish them: and night coming on they both long for the hour of twelve, though with different designs; and having before given notice that *Sylvia* was gone to bed, and would receive no visit that night, they were alone to finish all their business: this while *Brilliard* was not idle, but having a fine bath made, he washed and perfumed his body, and after dressed himself in the finest linen perfumed that he had, and made himself as fit as possible for his design; nor was his shape, which was very good, or his stature, unlike to that of *Octavio*: and ready for the approach, he conveys himself out of the house, telling his footman he would put himself to bed after his bathing, and, locking his chamber door, stole out; and it being dark, many a longing turn he walked, impatient till all the candles were out in every room of the house: in the mean time, he employed his thoughts on a thousand things, but all relating to *Sylvia*; sometimes the treachery he shewed in this action to his lord, caused short-lived blushes in his face, which vanished as soon, when he considered his lord false to the most beautiful of her sex: sometimes he accused and cursed the levity of *Sylvia* that could yield to *Octavio*, and was as jealous as if she had indeed been to have received that charming lover; but when his thought directed him to his own happiness, his pulse beat high, his blood flushed apace in his cheeks, his eyes languished with love, and his body with a feverish fit! In these extremes, by turns, he passed at least three tedious hours, with a striking watch in his hand; and when it told it was twelve, he advanced near the door, but finding it shut walked yet with greater impatience, every half minute going to the door; at last he found it yield to his hand that pushed it: but oh, what mortal can express his joy! His heart beats double, his knees tremble, and a feebleness seizes every limb; he breathes nothing but short sighs, and is ready in the dark hall to fall on the floor, and was forced to lean on the rail that begins the stairs to take a little courage: while he was there recruiting himself, intent on nothing but his vast joy; *Octavio*, who going to meet the Prince, being met halfway by that young *hero*, was dispatched back again without advancing to the end of his five leagues, and impatient to see *Sylvia*, after *Philander*'s letter that he had sent her, or at least impatient to hear how she took it, and in what condition she was, he, as soon as he alighted, went towards her house in order to have met *Antonet*, or her page, or some that could inform him of her welfare; though it was usual for *Sylvia* to sit up very late, and he had often made her visits at that hour: and *Brilliard*, wholly intent on his adventure, had left the door open; so that *Octavio* perceiving it, believed they were all up in the back rooms where *Sylvia*'s apartment was towards a garden, for he saw no light forward. But he was no sooner entered (which he did without noise) but he heard a soft breathing, which made him stand in the hall: and by and by he heard the soft tread of some body descending the stairs: at this he approaches near, and the hall being a marble floor, his tread was not heard; when he heard one cry with a sigh —'Who is there?' And another replied, 'It is I! Who are you?' The first replied, 'A faithful and an impatient lover.' 'Give me your hand then,' replied the female voice, 'I will conduct you to your happiness.' You may imagine in what surprise *Octavio* was at so unexpected an adventure, and, like a jealous lover, did not at all doubt but the happiness expected was *Sylvia*, and the impatient lover some one, whom he could not imagine, but raved within to know, and in a moment ran over in his thoughts all the men of quality, or celebrated beauty, or fortune in the town, but was at as great a loss as at first thinking: 'But be thou who thou wilt,' cried he to himself; 'traitor as thou art, I will by thy death revenge myself on the faithless fair one.' And taking out his sword, he had advanced towards the stairs-foot, when he heard them both softly ascend; but being a man of perfect good nature, as all the brave and witty are, he reflected on the severe usage he had from *Sylvia*, notwithstanding all his industry, his vast expense, and all the advantages of nature. This thought made him, in the midst of all his jealousy and haste, pause a little moment; and fain he would have persuaded himself, that what he heard was the errors of his sense; or that he dreamed, or that it was at least not to *Sylvia*, to whom this ascending lover was advancing: but to undeceive him of that favourable imagination, they were no sooner on the top of the stairs, but he not being many steps behind could both hear and see, by the ill light of a great sash-window on the stair-case, the happy lover enter the chamber-door of *Sylvia*, which he knew too well to be mistaken, not that he could perceive who, or what they were, but two persons not to be distinguished. Oh what human fancy, (but that of a lover to that degree that was our young hero,) can imagine the amazement and torture of his soul, wherein a thousand other passions reigned at once, and, maugre all his courage and resolution, forced him to sink beneath their weight? He stood holding himself up by the rails of the stair-case, without having the power to ascend farther, or to shew any other signs of life, but that of sighing; had he been a favoured lover, had he been a known declared lover to all the world, had he but hoped he had had so much interest with the false beauty, as but to have been designed upon for a future love or use, he would have rushed in, and have made the guilty night a covert to a scene of blood; but even yet he had an awe upon his soul for the perjured fair one, though at the same time he resolved she should be the object of his hate; for the nature of his honest soul abhorred an action so treacherous and base: he begins in a moment from all his good thoughts of her to think her the most jilting of her sex; he knew, if interest could oblige her, no man in *Holland* had a better pretence to her than himself; who had already, without any return, even so much as hope, presented her the value of eight or ten thousand pounds in fine plate and jewels: if it were looser desire, he fancied himself to have appeared as capable to have served her as any man; but oh! he considers there is a fate in things, a destiny in love that elevates and advances the most mean, deformed or abject, and debases and condemns the most worthy and magnificent: then he wonders at her excellent art of dissembling for *Philander*; he runs in a minute over all her passions of rage, jealousy, tears and softness; and now he hates the whole sex, and thinks them all like *Sylvia*, than whom nothing could appear more despicable to his present thought, and with a smile, while yet his heart was insensibly breaking, he fancies himself a very coxcomb, a cully, an imposed on fool, and a conceited fop; values *Sylvia* as a common fair jilt, whose whole design was to deceive the world, and make herself a fortune at the price of her honour; one that receives all kind bidders, and that he being too lavish, and too modest, was reserved the cully on purpose to be undone and jilted out of all his fortune! This thought was so perfectly fixed in him, that he recovered out of his excess of pain, and fancied himself perfectly cured of his blind passion, resolves to leave her to her beastly entertainment, and to depart; but before he did so, *Sylvia*, (who had conducted the amorous spark to the bed, where the expecting lady lay dressed rich and sweet to receive him) returned out of the chamber, and the light being a little more favourable to his eyes, by his being so long in the dark, he perceived it *Antonet*, at least such a sort of figure as he fancied her, and to confirm him saw her go into that chamber where he knew she lay; he saw her perfect dress, and all confirmed him; this brought him back almost to his former confusion; but yet he commands his passion, and descended the stairs, and got himself out of the hall into the street; and *Sylvia*, remembering the street-door was open, went and shut it, and returned to *Antonet*'s chamber with the letter which *Brilliard* had given to *Antonet*, as she lay in the bed, believing it *Sylvia*: for that trembling lover was no sooner entered the chamber, and approached the bed-side, but he kneeled before it, and offered the price of his happiness, this letter, which she immediately gave to *Sylvia*, unperceived, who quitted the room: and now with all the eager haste of impatient love she strikes a light, and falls to reading the sad contents; but as she read, she many times fainted over the paper, and as she has since said, it was a wonder she ever recovered, having no body with her. By that time she had finished it, she was so ill she was not able to get herself into bed, but threw herself down on the place where she sat, which was the side of it, in such agony of grief and despair, as never any soul was possessed of, but *Sylvia*'s, wholly abandoned to the violence of love and despair: it is impossible to paint a torment to express hers by; and though she had vowed to *Antonet* it should not at all affect her, being so prepossessed before; yet when she had the confirmation of her fears, and heard his own dear soft words addressed to another object, saw his transports, his impatience, his languishing industry and endeavour to obtain the new desire of his soul, she found her resentment above rage, and given over to a more silent and less supportable torment, brought herself into a high fever, where she lay without so much as calling for aid in her extremity; not that she was afraid the cheat she had put on *Octavio* would be discovered; for she had lost the remembrance that any such prank was played; and in this multitude of thoughts of more concern, had forgot all the rest of that night's action.

Octavio this while was traversing the street, wrapped in his cloak, just as if he had come from horse; for he was no sooner gone from the door, but his resenting passion returned, and he resolved to go up again, and disturb the lovers, though it cost him his life and fame: but returning hastily to the door, he found it shut; at which being enraged, he was often about to break it open, but still some unperceivable respect for *Sylvia* prevented him; but he resolved not to stir from the door, till he saw the fortunate rogue come out, who had given him all this torment. At first he cursed himself for being so much concerned for *Sylvia* or her actions to waste a minute, but flattering himself that it was not love to her, but pure curiosity to know the man who was made the next fool to himself, though the more happy one, he waited all night; and when he began to see the day break, which he thought a thousand years; his eye was never off from the door, and wondered at their confidence, who would let the day break upon them; 'but the close-drawn curtains there,' cried he, 'favour the happy villainy.' Still he walked on, and still he might for any rival that was to appear, for a most unlucky accident prevented *Brilliard*'s coming out, as he doubly intended to do; first, for the better carrying on of his cheat of being *Octavio*; and next that he had challenged *Octavio* to fight; and when he knew his error, designed to have gone this morning, and asked him pardon, if he had been returned; but the amorous lover over night, ordering himself for the encounter to the best advantage, had sent a note to a doctor, for something that would encourage his spirits; the doctor came, and opening a little box, wherein was a powerful medicine, he told him that a dose of those little flies would make him come off with wondrous honour in the battle of love; and the doctor being gone to call for a glass of sack, the doctor having laid out of the box what he thought requisite on a piece of paper, and leaving the box open, our spark thought if such a dose would encourage him so, a greater would yet make him do greater wonders; and taking twice the quantity out of the box, puts them into his pocket, and having drank the first with full directions, the doctor leaves him; who was no sooner gone, but he takes those out of his pocket, and in a glass of sack drinks them down; after this he bathes and dresses, and believes himself a very *Hercules*, that could have got at least twelve sons that happy night; but he was no sooner laid in bed with the charming *Sylvia*, as he thought, but he was taken with intolerable gripes and pains, such as he had never felt before, insomuch that he was not able to lie in the bed: this enrages him; he grows mad and ashamed; sometimes he had little intermissions for a moment of ease, and then he would plead softly by her bed-side, and ask ten thousand pardons; which being easily granted he would go into bed again, but then the pain would seize him anew, so that after two or three hours of distraction he was forced to dress and retire: but, instead of going down he went softly up to his own chamber, where he sat him down, and cursed the world, himself and his hard fate; and in this extremity of pain, shame and grief, he remained till break of day: by which time *Antonet*, who was almost as violently afflicted, got her coats on, and went to her own chamber, where she found her lady more dead than alive. She immediately shifted her bed-linen, and made her bed, and conducted her to it, without endeavouring to divert her with the history of her own misfortune; and only asked her many questions concerning her being thus ill: to which the wretched *Sylvia* only answered with sighs; so that *Antonet* perceived it was the letter that had disordered her, and begged she might be permitted to see it; she gave her leave, and *Antonet* read it; but no sooner was she come to that part of it which named the Countess of *Clarinau*, but she asked her lady if she understood who that person was, with great amazement: at this *Sylvia* was content to speak, pleased a little that she should have an account of her rival. 'No,' said she, 'dost thou know her?' 'Yes, madam,' replied *Antonet*, 'particularly well; for I have served her ever since I was a girl of five years old, she being of the same age with me, and sent at six years old both to a monastery; for she being fond of my play her father sent me at that age with her, both to serve and to divert her with babies and baubles; there we lived seven years together, when an old rich *Spaniard*, the Count of *Clarinau*, fell in love with my lady, and married her from the monastery, before she had seen any part of the world beyond those sanctified walls. She cried bitterly to have had me to *Cologne* with her, but he said I was too young now for her service, and so sent me away back to my own town, which is this; and here my lady was born too, and is sister to —— ' Here she stopped, fearing to tell; which *Sylvia* perceiving, with a briskness (which her indisposition one would have thought could not have allowed) sat up in bed, and cried, 'Ha! sister to whom? Oh, how thou wouldst please me to say to *Octavio*.' 'Why, madam, would it please you?' said the blushing maid. 'Because,' said *Sylvia*, 'it would in part revenge me on his bold addresses to me, and he would also be obliged, in honour to his family, to revenge himself on *Philander*.' 'Ah, madam,' said she, 'as to his presumption towards you, fortune has sufficiently revenged it;' at this she hung down her head, and looked very foolishly. 'How,' said *Sylvia*, smiling and rearing herself yet more in her bed, 'is any misfortune arrived to *Octavio*? Oh, how I will triumph and upbraid the daring man! —— tell me quickly what it is; for nothing would rejoice me more than to hear he were punished a little.' Upon this *Antonet* told her what an unlucky night she had, how *Octavio* was seized, and how he departed; by which *Sylvia* believed he had made some discovery of the cheat that was put upon him; and that he only feigned illness to get himself loose from her embraces; and now she falls to considering how she shall be revenged on both her lovers: and the best she can pitch upon is that of setting them both at odds, and making them fight and revenge themselves on one another; but she, like a right woman, could not dissemble her resentment of jealousy, whatever art she had to do so in any other point; but mad to ease her soul that was full, and to upbraid *Philander*, she writes him a letter; but not till she had once more, to make her stark-mad, read his over again, which he sent *Octavio*.

SYLVIA *to* PHILANDER.

Yes, perjured villain, at last all thy perfidy is arrived to my knowledge; and thou hadst better have been damned, or have fallen, like an ungrateful traitor, as thou art, under the public shame of dying by the common executioner, than have fallen under the grasp of my revenge; insatiate as thy lust, false as thy treasons to thy prince, fatal as thy destiny, loud as thy infamy, and bloody as thy party. Villain, villain, where got you the courage to use me thus, knowing my injuries and my spirit? Thou seest, base traitor, I do not fall on thee with treachery, as thou hast with thy king and mistress; to which thou hast broken thy holy vows of allegiance and eternal love! But thou that hast broken the laws of God and nature! What could I expect, when neither religion, honour, common justice nor law could bind thee to humanity? Thou that betrayest thy prince, abandonest thy wife, renouncest thy child, killest thy mother, ravishest thy sister, and art in open rebellion against thy native country, and very kindred and brothers. Oh after this, what must the wretch expect who has believed thee, and followed thy abject fortunes, the miserable out-cast slave, and contempt of the world? What could she expect but that the villain is still potent in the unrepented, and all the lover dead and gone, the vice remains, and all the virtue vanished! Oh, what could I expect from such a devil, so lost in sin and wickedness, that even those for whom he ventured all his fame, and lost his fortune, lent like a state-cully upon the public faith, on the security of rogues, knaves and traitors; even those, I say, turned him out of their councils for a reprobate too lewd for the villainous society? Oh cursed that I was, by heaven and fate, to be blind and deaf to all thy infamy, and suffer thy adorable bewitching face and tongue to charm me to madness and undoing, when that was all thou hadst left thee, thy false person, to cheat the silly, easy, fond, believing world into any sort of opinion of thee; for not one good principle was left, not one poor virtue to guard thee from damnation, thou hadst but one friend left thee, one true, on real friend, and that was wretched *Sylvia*; she, when all abandoned thee but the executioner, fled with thee, suffered with thee, starved with thee, lost her fame and honour with thee, lost her friends, her parents, and all her beauty's hopes for thee; and, in lieu of all, found only the accusation of all the good, the hate of all the virtuous, the reproaches of her kindred, the scorn of all chaste maids, and curses of all honest wives; and in requital had only thy false vows, thy empty love, thy faithless embraces, and cold dissembling kisses. My only comfort was, (ah miserable comfort,) to fancy they were true; now that it is departed too, and I have nothing but a brave revenge left in the room of all! In which I will be as merciless and irreligious as even thou hast been in all thy actions; and there remains about me only this sense of honour yet, that I dare tell thee of my bold design, a bravery thou hast never shewed to me, who takest me unawares, stabb'st me without a warning of the blow; so would'st thou serve thy king hadst thou but power; and so thou servest thy mistress. When I look back even to thy infancy, thy life has been but one continued race of treachery, and I, (destined thy evil genius) was born for thy tormentor; for thou hast made a very fiend of me, and I have hell within; all rage, all torment, fire, distraction, madness; I rave, I burn, I tear myself and faint, am still a dying, but can never fall till I have grasped thee with me: oh, I should laugh in flames to see thee howling by: I scorn thee, hate thee, loathe thee more than ever I have loved thee; and hate myself so much for ever loving thee, (to be revenged upon the filthy criminal) I will expose myself to all the world, cheat, jilt and flatter all as thou hast done, and having not one sense or grain of honour left, will yield the abandoned body thou hast rifled to every asking fop: nor is that all, for they that purchase this shall buy it at the price of being my *bravoes*. And all shall aid in my revenge on thee; all merciless and as resolved as I; as I! The injured

    SYLVIA.

Having shot this flash of the lightning of her soul, and finished her rant, she found herself much easier in the resolves on revenge she had fixed there: she scorned by any vain endeavour to recall him from his passion; she had wit enough to have made those eternal observations, that love once gone is never to be retrieved, and that it was impossible to cease loving, and then again to love the same person; one may believe for some time one's love is abated, but when it comes to a trial, it shews itself as vigorous as in its first shine, and finds its own error; but when once one comes to love a new object, it can never return with more than pity, compassion, or civility for the first: this is a most certain truth which all lovers will find, as most wives may experience, and which our *Sylvia* now took for granted, and gave him over for dead to all but her revenge. Though fits of softness, weeping, raving, and tearing, would by turns seize the distracted abandoned beauty, in which extremities she has recourse to scorn and pride, too feeble to aid her too often: the first thing she resolved on, by the advice of her reasonable counsellor, was to hear love at both ears, no matter whether she regard it or not, but to hear all, as a remedy against loving one in particular; for it is most certain, that the use of hearing love, or of making love (though at first without design) either in women or men, shall at last unfix the most confirmed and constant resolution. 'And since you are assured,' continued *Antonet*, 'that sighs nor tears bring back the wandering lover, and that dying for him will be no revenge on him, but rather a kind assurance that you will no more trouble the man who is already weary of you, you ought, with all your power, industry and reason, rather to seek the preservation of that beauty, of that fine humour, to serve you on all occasions, either of revenge or love, than by a foolish and insignificant concern and sorrow reduce yourself to the condition of being scorned by all, or at best but pitied.' 'How pitied!' cried the haughty *Sylvia*. 'Is there any thing so insupportable to our sex as pity!' 'No surely,' replied the servant, 'when 'tis accompanied by love: oh what blessed comfort 'tis to hear people cry —"she was once charming, once a beauty." Is any thing more grating, madam?' At this rate she ran on, and left nothing unsaid that might animate the angry *Sylvia* to love anew, or at least to receive and admit of love; for in that climate the air naturally breeds spirits avaricious, and much inclines them to the love of money, which they will gain at any price or hazard; and all this discourse to *Sylvia*, was but to incline the revengeful listening beauty to admit of the addresses of *Octavio*, because she knew he would make her fortune. Thus was the unhappy maid left by her own unfortunate conduct, encompassed in on every side with distraction; and she was pointed out by fate to be made the most wretched of all her sex; nor had she left one faithful friend to advise or stay her youth in its hasty advance to ruin; she hears the persuading eloquence of the flattering maid, and finds now nothing so prevalent on her soul as revenge, and nothing soothes it more; and among all her lovers, or those at least that she knew adored her, none was found so proper an instrument as the noble *Octavio*, his youth, his wit, his gallantry, but above all his fortune pleads most powerfully with her; so that she resolves upon the revenge, and fixes him the man; whom she now knew by so many obligations was obliged to serve her turn on *Philander*: thus *Sylvia* found a little tranquillity, such as it was, in hope of revenge, while the passionate *Octavio* was wrecked with a thousand pains and torments, such as none but jilted lovers can imagine; and having a thousand times resolved to hate her, and as often to love on, in spite of all —— after a thousand arguments against her, and as many in favour of her, he arrived only to this knowledge, that his love was extreme, and that he had no power over his heart; that honour, fame, interest, and whatever else might oppose his violent flame, were all too weak to extinguish the least spark of it, and all the conquest he could get of himself was, that he suffered all his torment, all the hell of raging jealousy grown to confirmation, and all the pangs of absence for that whole day, and had the courage to live on the rack without easing one moment of his agony by a letter or billet, which in such cases discharges the burden and pressures of the love-sick heart; and *Sylvia*, who dressed, and suffered herself wholly to be carried away by her vengeance, expected him with as much impatience as ever she did the coming of the once adorable *Philander*, though with a different passion; but all the live-long day passed in expectation of him, and no lover appeared; no not so much as a billet, nor page at her up-rising to ask her health; so that believing he had been very ill indeed, from what *Antonet* told her of his being so all night, and fearing now that it was no discovery of the cheat put upon him by the exchange of the maid for the mistress, but real sickness, she resolved to send to him, and the rather because *Antonet* assured her he was really sick, and in a cold damp sweat all over his face and hands which she touched, and that from his infinite concern at the defeat, the extreme respect he shewed her in midst of all the rage at his own disappointment, and every circumstance, she knew it was no feigned thing for any discovery he had made: on this confirmation, from a maid cunning enough to distinguish truth from flattery, she writ *Octavio* this letter at night.

SYLVIA *to* OCTAVIO.

After such a parting from a maid so entirely kind to you, she might at least have hoped the favour of a billet from you, to have informed her of your health; unless you think that after we have surrendered all, we are of the humour of most of your sex, who despise the obliger; but I believed you a man above the little crimes and levities of your race; and I am yet so hard to be drawn from that opinion, I am willing to flatter myself, that 'tis yet some other reason that has hindered you from visiting me since, or sending me an account of your recovery, which I am too sensible of to believe was feigned, and which indeed has made me so tender, that I easily forgive all the disappointment I received from it, and beg you will not afflict yourself at any loss you sustained by it, since I am still so much the same I was, to be as sensible as before of all the obligations I have to you; send me word immediately how you do, for on that depends a great part of the happiness of

SYLVIA.

You may easily see by this letter she was not in a humour of either writing love or much flattery; for yet she knew not how she ought to resent this absence in all kinds from *Octavio*, and therefore with what force she could put upon a soul, too wholly taken up with the thoughts of another, more dear and more afflicting, she only writ this to fetch one from him, that by it she might learn part of his sentiment of her last action, and sent her page with it to him; who, as was usual, was carried directly up to *Octavio*, whom he found in a gallery, walking in a most dejected posture, without a band, unbraced, his arms a-cross his open breast, and his eyes bent to the floor; and not taking any notice when the pages entered, his own was forced to pull him by the sleeve before he would look up, and starting from a thousand thoughts that oppressed him almost to death, he gazed wildly about him, and asked their business: when the page delivered him the letter, he took it, but with such confusion as he had much ado to support himself; but resolving not to shew his feebleness to her page, he made a shift to get a wax-light that was on the table, and read it; and was not much amazed at the contents, believing she was pursuing the business of her sex and life, and jilting him on; (for such was his opinion of all women now); he forced a smile of scorn, though his soul were bursting, and turning to the page gave him a liberal reward, as was his daily use when he came, and mustered up so much courage as to force himself to say —'Child, tell your lady it requires no answer; you may tell her too, that I am in perfect good health —' He was oppressed to speak more, but sighs stopped him, and his former resolution, wholly to abandon all correspondence with her, checked his forward tongue, and he walked away to prevent himself from saying more: while the page, who wondered at this turn of love, after a little waiting, departed; and when *Octavio* had ended his walk, and turned, and saw him gone, his heart felt a thousand pangs not to be borne or supported; he was often ready to recall him, and was angry the boy did not urge him for an answer. He read the letter again, and wonders at nothing now after her last night's action, though all was riddle to him: he found it was writ to some happier man than himself, however he chanced to have it by mistake; and turning to the outside, viewed the superscription, where there happened to be none at all, for *Sylvia* writ in haste, and when she did it, it was the least of her thoughts: and now he believed he had found out the real mystery, that it was not meant to him; he therefore calls his page, whom he sent immediately after that of *Sylvia*, who being yet below (for the lads were laughing together for a moment) he brought him to his distracted lord; who nevertheless assumed a mildness to the innocent boy, and cried, 'My child, thou hast mistaken the person to whom thou shouldst have carried the letter, and I am sorry I opened it; pray return it to the happy man it was meant to,' giving him the letter. 'My lord,' replied the boy, 'I do not use to carry letters to any but your lordship: it is the footmen's business to do that to other persons.' 'It is a mistake, where ever it lies,' cried *Octavio*, sighing, 'whether in thee, or thy lady ——' So turning from the wondering boy he left him to return with his letter to his lady, who grew mad at the relation of what she heard from the page, and notwithstanding the torment she had upon her soul, occasioned by *Philander*, she now found she had more to endure, and that in spite of all her love-vows and resentments, she had something for *Octavio* to which she could not give a name; she fancies it all pride, and concern for the indignity put on her beauty: but whatever it was, this slight of his so wholly took up her soul, that she had for some time quite forgot *Philander*, or when she did think on him it was with less resentment than of this affront; she considers *Philander* with some excuse now; as having long been possessed of a happiness he might grow weary of; but a new lover, who had for six months incessantly lain at her feet, imploring, dying, vowing, weeping, sighing, giving and acting all things the most passionate of men was capable of, or that love could inspire, for him to be at last admitted to the possession of the ravishing object of his vows and soul, to be laid in her bed, nay in her very arms (as she imagined he thought) and then, even before gathering the roses he came to pluck, before he had begun to compose or finished his nosegay, to depart the happy paradise with a disgust, and such a disgust, as first to oblige him to dissemble sickness, and next fall even from all his civilities, was a contempt she was not able to bear; especially from him, of whom all men living, she designed to make the greatest property of, as most fit for her revenge of all degrees and sorts: but when she reflected with reason, (which she seldom did, for either love or rage blinded that) she could not conceive it possible that *Octavio* could be fallen so suddenly from all his vows and professions, but on some very great provocation: sometimes she thinks he tempted her to try her virtue to *Philander*, and being a perfect honourable friend, hates her for her levity; but she considers his presents, and his unwearied industry, and believes he would not at that expense have bought a knowledge which could profit neither himself nor *Philander*; then she believes some disgusted scent, or something about *Antonet*, might disoblige him; but having called the maid, conjuring her to tell her whether any thing passed between her and *Octavio*; she again told her lady the whole truth, in which there could be no discovery of infirmity there; she embraced her, she kissed her bosom, and found her touches soft, her breath and bosom sweet as any thing in nature could be; and now lost almost in a confusion of thought, she could not tell what to imagine; at last she being wholly possessed that all the fault was not in *Octavio*, (for too often we believe as we hope) she concludes that *Antonet* has told him all the cheat she put upon him: this last thought pleased her, because it seemed the most probable, and was the most favourable to herself; and a thought that, if true, could not do her any injury with him. This set her heart a little to rights, and she grew calm with a belief, that if so it was, as now she doubted not, a sight of her, or a future hope from her, would calm all his discontent, and beget a right understanding; she therefore resolves to write to him, and own her little fallacy: but before she did so, *Octavio*, whose passion was violent as ever in his soul, though it was oppressed with a thousand torments, and languished under as many feeble resolutions, burst at last into all its former softness, and he resolves to write to the false fair one, and upbraid her with her last night's infidelity; nor could he sleep till he had that way charmed his senses, and eased his sick afflicted soul. It being now ten at night, and he retired to his chamber, he set himself down and writ this.

OCTAVIO *to* SYLVIA.

Madam,

You have at last taught me a perfect knowledge of myself; and in one unhappy night made me see all the follies and vanities of my soul, which self-love and fond imagination had too long rendered that way guilty; long long! I have played the fop as others do, and shewed the gaudy monsieur, and set a value on my worthless person for being well dressed, as I believed, and furnished out for conquest, by being the gayest coxcomb in the town, where, even as I passed, perhaps, I fancied I made advances on some wishing hearts, and vain, with but imaginary victory, I still fooled on —— and was at last undone; for I saw *Sylvia*, the charming faithless *Sylvia*, a beauty that one would have thought had had the power to have cured the fond disease of self-conceit and foppery, since love, they say, is a remedy against those faults of youth; but still my vanity was powerful in me, and even this beauty too I thought it not impossible to vanquish, and still dressed on, and took a mighty care to shew myself — a blockhead, curse upon me, while you were laughing at my industry, and turned the fancying fool to ridicule, oh, he deserved it well, most wondrous well, for but believing any thing about him could merit but a serious thought from *Sylvia*. *Sylvia*! whose business is to laugh at all; yet love, that is my sin and punishment, reigns still as absolutely in my soul, as when I wished and hoped and longed for mighty blessings you could give; yes, I still love! Only this wretchedness is fixed to it, to see those errors which I cannot shun; my love is as high, but all my wishes gone; my passion still remains entire and raving, but no desire; I burn, I die, but do not wish to hope; I would be all despair, and, like a martyr, am vain and proud even in suffering. Yes, *Sylvia*— when you made me wise, you made me wretched too: before, like a false worshipper, I only saw the gay, the gilded side of the deceiving idol; but now it is fallen —— discovers all the cheat, and shews a god no more; and it is in love as in religion too, there is nothing makes their votaries truly happy but being well deceived: for even in love itself, harmless and innocent, as it is by nature, there needs a little art to hide the daily discontents and torments, that fears, distrusts and jealousies create; a little soft dissimulation is needful; for where the lover is easy, he is most constant. But oh, when love itself is defective too, and managed by design and little interest, what cunning, oh what cautions ought the fair designer then to call to her defence; yet I confess your plot —— still charming *Sylvia*, was subtly enough contrived, discreetly carried on —— the shades of night, the happy lover's refuge, favoured you too; it was only fate was cruel, fate that conducted me in an unlucky hour; dark as it was, and silent too the night, I saw —— Yes, faithless fair, I saw I was betrayed; by too much faith, by too much love undone, I saw my fatal ruin and your perfidy; and, like a tame ignoble sufferer, left you without revenge!

I must confess, oh thou deceiving fair one, I never could pretend to what I wished, and yet methinks, because I know my heart, and the entire devotion, that is paid you, I merited at least not to have been imposed upon; but after so dishonourable an action, as the betraying the secret of my friend, it was but just that I should be betrayed, and you have paid me well, deservedly well, and that shall make me silent, and whatsoever I suffer, however I die, however I languish out my wretched life, I'll bear my sighs where you shall never hear them, nor the reproaches my complaints express: live thou a punishment to vain, fantastic, hoping youth, live, and advance in cunning and deceit, to make the fond believing men more wise, and teach the women new arts of falsehood, till they deceive so long, that man may hate, and set as vast a distance between sex and sex, as I have resolved (oh *Sylvia*) thou shalt be for ever from OCTAVIO.

This letter came just as *Sylvia* was going to write to him, of which she was extremely glad; for all along there was nothing expressed that could make her think he meant any other than the cheat she put upon him in *Antonet* instead of herself: and it was some ease to her mind to be assured of the cause of his anger and absence, and to find her own thought confirmed, that he had indeed discovered the truth of the matter: she knew, since that was all, she could easily reconcile him by a plain confession, and giving him new hopes; she therefore writes this answer to him, which she sent by his page, who waited for it.

SYLVIA *to* OCTAVIO.

I own, too angry, and too nice *Octavio*, the crime you charge me with; and did believe a person of your gallantry, wit and gaiety, would have passed over so little a fault, with only reproaching me pleasantly; I did not expect so grave a reproof, or rather so serious an accusation. Youth has a thousand follies to answer for, and cannot *Octavio* pardon one sally of it in *Sylvia*? I rather expected to have seen you early here this morning, pleasantly rallying my little perfidy, than to find you railing at a distance at it; calling it by a thousand names that does not merit half this malice: and sure you do not think me so poor in good nature, but I could, some other coming hour, have made you amends for those you lost last night, possibly I could have wished myself with you at the same time; and had I, perhaps, followed my inclination, I had made you happy as you wished; but there were powerful reasons that prevented me. I conjure you to let me see you, where I will make a confession of my last night's sin, and give such arguments to convince you of the necessity of it, as shall absolutely reconcile you to love, hope, and SYLVIA.

It being late, she only sent this short billet: and not hoping that night to see him, she went to bed, after having inquired the health of *Brilliard*, who she heard was very ill; and that young defeated lover, finding it impossible to meet *Octavio* as he had promised, not to fight him, but to ask his pardon for his mistake, made a shift, with much ado, to write him a note, which was this:

My Lord,

I confess my yesterday's rudeness, and beg you will give me a pardon before I leave the world; for I was last night taken violently ill, and am unable to wait on your lordship, to beg what this most earnestly does for your lordship's most devoted servant,

BRILLIARD.

This billet, though it signified nothing to *Octavio*, it served *Sylvia* afterwards to very good use and purpose, as a little time shall make appear. And *Octavio* received these two notes from *Brilliard* and *Sylvia* at the same time; the one he flung by regardless, the other he read with inifinite pain, scorn, hate, indignation, all at once stormed in his heart, he felt every passion there but that of love, which caused them all; if he thought her false and ungrateful before, he now thinks her fallen to the lowest degree of lewdness, to own her crime with such impudence; he fancies now he is cured of love, and hates her absolutely, thinks her below even his scorn, and puts himself to bed, believing he shall sleep as well as before he saw the light, the foolish *Sylvia*: but oh he boasts in vain, the light, the foolish *Sylvia* was charming still; still all the beauty appeared; even in his slumbers the angel dawned about him, and all the fiend was laid: he sees her lovely face, but the false heart is hid; he hears her charming wit, but all the cunning is hushed: he views the motions of her delicate body, without regard to those of her mind; he thinks of all the tender words she has given him, in which the jilting part is lost, and all forgotten; or, if by chance it crossed his happier thought, he rolls and tumbles in his bed, he raves and calls upon her charming name, till he have quite forgot it, and takes all the pains he can to deceive his own heart: oh it is a tender part, and can endure no hurt; he soothes it therefore, and at the worst resolves, since the vast blessing may be purchased, to revel in delight, and cure himself that way: these flattering thoughts kept him all night waking, and in the morning he resolves his visit; but taking up her letter, which lay on the table, he read it over again, and, by degrees, wrought himself up to madness at the thought that *Sylvia* was possessed: *Philander* he could bear with little patience, but that, because before he loved or knew her, he could allow; but this —— this wrecks his very soul; and in his height of fury, he writes this letter without consideration.

OCTAVIO *to* SYLVIA.

Since you profess yourself a common mistress, and set up for the glorious trade of sin, send me your price, and I perhaps may purchase damnation at your rate. May be you have a method in your dealing, and I have mistook you all this while, and dealt not your way; instruct my youth, great mistress of the art, and I shall be obedient; tell me which way I may be happy too, and put in for an adventurer; I have a stock of ready youth and money; pray, name your time and sum for hours, or nights, or months; I will be in at all, or any, as you shall find leisure to receive the impatient *Octavio*.

This in a mad moment he writ, and sent it ere he had considered farther; and *Sylvia*, who expected not so coarse and rough a return, grew as mad as he in reading it; and she had much ado to hold her hands off from beating the innocent page that brought it: to whom she turned with fire in her eyes, flames in her cheeks, and thunder on her tongue, and cried, 'Go tell your master that he is a villain; and if you dare approach me any more from him, I'll have my footmen whip you:' and with a scorn, that discovered all the indignation in the world, she turned from him, and, tearing his note, threw it from her, and walked her way: and the page, thunder-struck, returned to his lord, who by this time was repenting he had managed his passion no better, and at what the boy told him was wholly convinced of his error; he now considered her character and quality, and accused himself of great indiscretion; and as he was sitting the most dejected melancholy man on earth, reflecting on his misfortune, the post arrived with letters from *Philander*, which he opened, and laying by that which was enclosed for *Sylvia*, he read that from *Philander* to himself.

PHILANDER *to* OCTAVIO.

There is no pain, my dear *Octavio*, either in love or friendship, like that of doubt; and I confess myself guilty of giving it you, in a great measure, by my silence the last post; but having business of so much greater concern to my heart than even writing to *Octavio*, I found myself unable to pursue any other; and I believe you could too with the less impatience bear with my neglect, having affairs of the same nature there; our circumstances and the business of our hearts then being so resembling, methinks I have as great an impatience to be recounting to you the story of my love and fortune, as I am to receive that of yours, and to know what advances you have made in the heart of the still charming *Sylvia*! Though there will be this difference in the relations; mine, whenever I recount it, will give you a double satisfaction; first from the share your friendship makes you have in all the pleasures of *Philander*; and next that it excuses *Sylvia*, if she can be false to me for *Octavio*; and still advances his design on her heart: but yours, whenever I receive it, will give me a thousand pains, which it is however but just I should feel, since I was the first breaker of the solemn league and covenant made between us; which yet I do, by all that is sacred, with a regret that makes me reflect with some repentance in all those moments, wherein I do not wholly give my soul up to love, and the more beautiful *Calista*; yes more, because new.

In my last, my dear *Octavio*, you left me pursuing, like a knight-errant, a beauty enchanted within some invisible tree, or castle, or lake, or any thing inaccessible, or rather wandering in a dream after some glorious disappearing phantom: and for some time indeed I knew not whether I slept or waked. I saw daily the good old Count of *Clarinau*, of whom I durst not so much as ask a civil question towards the satisfaction of my soul; the page was sent into *Holland* (with some express to a brother-in-law of the Count's) of whom before I had the intelligence of a fair young wife to the old lord his master; and for the rest of the servants they spoke all *Spanish*, and the devil a word we understood each other; so that it was impossible to learn any thing farther from them; and I found I was to owe all my good fortune to my own industry, but how to set it a-working I could not devise; at last it happened, that being walking in the garden which had very high walls on three sides, and a fine large apartment on the other, I concluded that it was in that part of the house my fair new conqueress resided, but how to be resolved I could not tell, nor which way the windows looked that were to give the light, towards that part of the garden there was none; at last I saw the good old gentleman come trudging through the garden, fumbling out of his pocket a key; I stepped into an arbour to observe him, and saw him open a little door, that led him into another garden, and locking the door after him vanished; and observing how that side of the apartment lay, I went into the street, and after a large compass found that which faced the garden, which made the fore-part of the apartment. I made a story of some occasion I had for some upper rooms, and went into many houses to find which fronted best the apartment, and still disliked something, till I met with one so directly to it, that I could, when I got a story higher, look into the very rooms, which only a delicate garden parted from this by-street; there it was I fixed, and learned from a young *Dutch* woman that spoke good *French*, that this was the very place I looked for: the apartment of Madam, the Countess of *Clarinau*; she told me too, that every day after dinner the old gentleman came thither, and sometimes a-nights; and bewailed the young beauty, who had no better entertainment than what an old withered *Spaniard* of threescore and ten could give her. I found this young woman apt for my purpose, and having very well pleased her with my conversation, and some little presents I made her, I left her in good humour, and resolved to serve me on any design; and returning to my lodging, I found old *Clarinau* returned, as brisk and gay, as if he had been caressed by so fair and young a lady; which very thought made me rave, and I had abundance of pain to with-hold my rage from breaking out upon him, so jealous and envious was I of what now I loved and desired a thousand times more than ever; since the relation my new, young, female friend had given me, who had wit and beauty sufficient to make her judgement impartial: however, I contained my jealousy with the hopes of a sudden revenge; for I fancied the business half accomplished in my knowledge of her residence. I feigned some business to the old gentleman, that would call me out of town for a week to consult with some of our party; and taking my leave of him, he offered me the compliment of money, or what else I should need in my affair, which at that time was not unwelcome to I me; and being well furnished for my enterprise, I took horse without a page or footman to attend me; because I pretended my business was a secret, and taking a turn about the town in the evening, I left my horse without the gates, and went to my secret new quarters, where my young friend received me with the joy of a mistress, and with whom indeed I could not forbear entertaining myself very well, which engaged her more to my service, with the aid of my liberality; but all this did not allay one spark of the fire kindled in my soul for the lovely *Calista*; and I was impatient for night, against which time I was preparing an engine to mount the battlement, for so it was that divided the garden from the street, rather than a wall: all things fitted to my purpose, I fixed myself at the window that looked directly towards her sashes, and had the satisfaction to see her leaning there, and looking on a fountain, that stood in the midst of the garden, and cast a thousand little streams into the air, that made a melancholy noise in falling into a large alabaster cistern beneath: oh how my heart danced at the dear sight to all the tunes of love! I had not power to stir or speak, or to remove my eyes, but languished on the window where I leant half dead with joy and transport; for she appeared more charming to my view;

undressed and fit for love; oh, my *Octavio*, such are the pangs which I believe thou feelest at the approach of *Sylvia*, so beats thy heart, so rise thy sighs and wishes, so trembling and so pale at every view, as I was in this lucky amorous moment! And thus I fed my soul till night came on, and left my eyes no object but my heart —— a thousand dear ideas. And now I sallied out, and with good success; for with a long engine which reached the top of the wall, I fixed the end of my ladder there, and mounted it, and sitting on the top brought my ladder easily up to me, and turned over to the other side, and with abundance of ease descended into the garden, which was the finest I had ever seen; for now, as good luck would have it, who was designed to favour me, the moon began to shine so bright, as even to make me distinguish the colours of the flowers that dressed all the banks in ravishing order; but these were not the beauty I came to possess, and my new thoughts of disposing myself, and managing my matters, now took off all that admiration that was justly due to so delightful a place, which art and nature had agreed to render charming to every sense; thus much I considered it, that there was nothing that did not invite to love; a thousand pretty recesses of arbours, grotts and little artificial groves; fountains, environed with beds of flowers, and little rivulets, to whose dear fragrant banks a wishing amorous god would make his soft retreat. After having ranged about, rather to seek a covert on occasion, and to know the passes of the garden, which might serve me in any extremity of surprise that might happen, I returned to the fountain that faced *Calista*'s window, and leaning upon its brink, viewed the whole apartment, which appeared very magnificent: just against me I perceived a door that went into it, which while I was considering how to get open I heard it unlock, and skulking behind the large basin of the fountain (yet so as to mark who came out) I saw to my unspeakable transport, the fair, the charming *Calista* dressed just as she was at the window, a loose gown of silver stuff lapped about her delicate body, her head in fine night-clothes, and all careless as my soul could wish; she came, and with her the old dragon; and I heard her say in coming out —'This is too fine a night to sleep in: prithee, *Dormina*, do not grudge me the pleasure of it, since there are so very few that entertain *Calista*.' This last she spoke with a sigh, and a languishment in her voice, that shot new flames of love into my panting heart, and trilled through all my veins, while she pursued her walk with the old gentlewoman; and still I kept myself at such a distance to have them in my sight, but slid along the shady side of the walk, where I could not be easily seen, while they kept still on the shiny part: she led me thus through all the walks, through all the maze of love; and all the way I fed my greedy eyes upon the melancholy object of my raving desire; her shape, her gait, her motion, every step, and every movement of her hand and head, had a peculiar grace; a thousand times I was tempted to approach her, and discover myself, but I dreaded the fatal consequence, the old woman being by; nor knew I whether they did not expect the husband there; I therefore waited with impatience when she would speak, that by that I might make some discovery of my destiny that night; and after having tired herself a little with walking, she sat down on a fine seat of white marble, that was placed at the end of a grassy walk, and only shadowed with some tall trees that ranked themselves behind it, against one of which I leaned: there, for a quarter of an hour, they sat as silent as the night, where only soft-breathed winds were heard amongst the boughs, and softer sighs from fair *Calista*; at last the old thing broke silence, who was almost asleep while she spoke. 'Madam, if you are weary, let us retire to bed, and not sit gazing here at the moon.' 'To bed,' replied *Calista*, 'What should I do there?' 'Marry sleep,' quoth the old gentlewoman; 'What should you do?' 'Ah, *Dormina*,' (sighed *Calista*,) 'would age would seize me too; for then perhaps I should find at least the pleasure of the old; be dull and lazy, love to eat and sleep, not have my slumbers disturbed with dreams more insupportable than my waking wishes; for reason then suppresses rising thoughts, and the impossibility of obtaining keeps the fond soul in order; but sleep —— gives an unguarded loose to soft desire, it brings the lovely phantom to my view, and tempts me with a thousand charms to love; I see a face, a mien, a shape, a look! Such as heaven never made, or any thing but fond imagination! Oh, it was a wondrous vision!' 'For my part,' replied the old one, 'I am such a heathen Christian, madam, as I do not believe there are any such things as visions, or ghosts, or phantoms: but your head runs of a young man, because you are married to an old one; such an idea as you framed in your wishes possessed your fancy, which was so strong (as indeed fancy will be sometimes) that it persuaded you it was a very phantom or vision.' 'Let it be fancy or vision, or whatever else you can give a name to,' replied *Calista*, 'still it is that, that never ceased since to torture me with a thousand pains; and prithee why, *Dormina*, is not fancy since as powerful in me as it was before? Fancy has not been since so kind; yet I have given it room for thought, which before I never did; I sat whole hours and days, and fixed my soul upon the lovely figure; I know its stature to an inch, tall and divinely made; I saw his hair, long, black, and curling to his waist, all loose and flowing; I saw his eyes, where all the *Cupids* played, black, large, and sparkling, piercing, loving, languishing; I saw his lips sweet, dimpled, red, and soft; a youth complete in all, like early *May*, that looks, and smells, and cheers above the rest: in fine, I saw him such as nothing but the nicest fancy can imagine, and nothing can describe; I saw him such as robs me of my rest, as gives me all the raging pains of love (love I believe it is) without the joy of any single hope.' 'Oh, madam,' said *Dormina*, 'that love will quickly die, which is not nursed with hope, why that is its only food.' 'Pray heaven I find it so,' replied *Calista*. At that she sighed as if her heart had broken, and leaned her arm upon a rail of the end of the seat, and laid her lovely cheek upon her hand, and so continued without speaking; while I, who was not a little transported with what I heard, with infinite pain with-held myself from kneeling at her feet, and prostrating before her that happy phantom of which she had spoke so favourably; but still I feared my fate, and to give any offence. While I was amidst a thousand thoughts considering which to pursue, I could hear *Dormina* snoring as fast as could be, leaning at her ease on the other end of the seat, supported by a wide marble rail; which *Calista* hearing also, turned and looked on her, then softly rose and walked away to see how long she would sleep there, if not waked. Judge now, my dear *Octavio*, whether love and fortune were not absolutely subdued to my interest, and if all things did not favour my design: the very thought of being alone with *Calista*, of making myself known to her, of the opportunity she gave me by going from *Dormina* into a by-walk, the very joy of ten thousand hopes, that filled my soul in that happy moment, which I fancied the most blessed of my life, made me tremble all over; and with unassured steps I softly pursued the object of my new desire: sometimes I even overtook her, and fearing to fright her, and cause her to make some noise that might alarm the sleeping *Dormina*, I slackened my pace, till in a walk, at the end of which she was obliged to turn back, I remained, and suffered her to go on; it was a walk of grass, broad, and at the end of it a little arbour of greens, into which she went and sat down, looking towards me; and methought she looked full at me; so that finding she made no noise, I softly approached the door of the arbour at a convenient distance; she then stood up in great amaze, as she after said; and I kneeling down in an humble posture, cried —'Wonder not, oh sacred charmer of my soul, to see me at your feet at this late hour, and in a place so inaccessible; for what attempt is there so hazardous despairing lovers dare not undertake, and what impossibility almost can they not overcome? Remove your fears, oh conqueress of my soul; for I am an humble mortal that adores you; I have a thousand wounds, a thousand pains that prove me flesh and blood, if you would hear my story: oh give me leave to approach you with that awe you do the sacred altars; for my devotion is as pure as that which from your charming lips ascends the heavens ——' With such cant and stuff as this, which lovers serve themselves with on occasion, I lessened the terrors of the frighted beauty, and she soon saw, with joy in her eyes, that I both was a mortal, and the same she had before seen in the outward garden: I rose from my knees then, and with a joy that wandered all over my body, trembling and panting I approached her, and took her hand and kissed it with a transport that was almost ready to lay me fainting at her feet, nor did she answer any thing to what I had said, but with sighs suffered her hand to remain in mine; her eyes she cast to earth, her breast heaved with nimble motions, and we both, unable to support ourselves, sat down together on a green bank in the arbour, where by the light we had, we gazed at each other, unable to utter a syllable on either side. I confess, my dear *Octavio*, I have felt love before, but do not know that ever I was possessed with such pleasing pain, such agreeable languishment in all my life, as in those happy moments with the fair *Calista*: and on the other, I dare answer for the soft fair one; she felt a passion as tender as mine; which, when she could recover her first transport, she expressed in such a manner as has wholly charmed me: for with all the eloquence of young angels, and all their innocence too, she said, she whispered, she sighed the softest things that ever lover heard. I told you before she had from her infancy been bred in a monastery, kept from the sight of men, and knew no one art or subtlety of her sex; but in the very purity of her innocence she appeared like the first-born maid in Paradise, generously giving her soul away to the great lord of all, the new-formed man, and nothing of her heart's dear thoughts she did reserve, (but such as modest nature should conceal;) yet, if I touched but on that tender part where honour dwelt, she had a sense too nice, as it was a wonder to find so vast a store of that mixed with so soft a passion. Oh what an excellent thing a perfect woman is, ere man has taught her arts to keep her empire, by being himself inconstant! All I could ask of love she freely gave, and told me every sentiment of her heart, but it was in such a way, so innocently she confessed her passion, that every word added new flames to mine, and made me raging mad: at last, she suffered me to kiss with caution; but one begat another —— that a number —— and every one was an advance to happiness; and I who knew my advantage, lost no time, but put each minute to the properest use; now I embrace, clasp her fair lovely body close to mine, which nothing parted but her shift and gown; my busy hands find passage to her breasts, and give and take a thousand nameless joys; all but the last I reaped; that heaven was still denied; though she were fainting in my trembling arms, still she had watching sense to guard that treasure: yet, in spite of all, a thousand times I brought her to the very point of yielding; but oh she begs and pleads with all the eloquence of love! tells me, that what she had to give me she gave, but would not violate her marriage-vow; no, not to save that life she found in danger with too much love, and too extreme desire: she told me, that I had undone her quite; she sighed, and wished that she had seen me sooner, ere fate had rendered her a sacrifice to the embraces of old *Clarinau*; she wept with love, and answered with a sob to every vow I made: thus by degrees she wrought me to undoing, and made me mad in love. It was thus we passed the night; we told the hasty hours, and cursed their coming: we told from ten to three, and all that time seemed but a little minute: nor would I let her go, who was as loath to part, till she had given me leave to see her often there; I told her all my story of her conquest, and how I came into the garden: she asked me pleasantly, if I were not afraid of old *Clarinau*; I told her no, of nothing but of his being happy with her, which thought I could not bear: she assured me I had so little reason to envy him, that he rather deserved my compassion; for that, her aversion was so extreme to him; his person, years, his temper, and his diseases were so disagreeable to her, that she could not dissemble her disgust, but gave him most evident proofs of it too frequently ever since she had the misfortune of being his wife; but that since she had seen the charming *Philander*, (for so we must let her call him too) his company and conversation was wholly insupportable to her; and but that he had ever used to let her have four nights in the week her own, wherein he never disturbed her repose, she should have been dead with his nasty entertainment: she vowed she never knew a soft desire but for *Philander*, she never had the least concern for any of his sex besides, and till she felt his touches —— took in his kisses, and suffered his dear embraces, she never knew that woman was ordained for any joy with man, but fancied it designed in its creation for a poor slave to be oppressed at pleasure by the husband, dully to yield obedience and no more: but I had taught her now, she said, to her eternal ruin, that there was more in nature than she knew, or ever should, had she not seen *Philander*; she knew not what dear name to call it by, but something in her blood, something that panted in her heart, glowed in her cheeks, and languished in her looks, told her she was not born for *Clarinau*, or love would do her wrong: I soothed the thought, and urged the laws of nature, the power of love, necessity of youth —— and the wonder that was yet behind, that ravishing something, which not love or kisses could make her guess at; so beyond all soft imagination, that nothing but a trial could convince her; but she resisted still, and still I pleaded with all the subtlest arguments of love, words mixed with kisses, sighing mixed with vows, but all in vain; religion was my foe, and tyrant honour guarded all her charms: thus did we pass the night, till the young morn advancing in the East forced us to bid adieu: which oft we did, and oft we sighed and kissed, oft parted and returned, and sighed again, and as she went away, she weeping, cried — wringing my hand in hers, 'Pray heaven, *Philander*, this dear interview do not prove fatal to me; for oh, I find frail nature weak about me, and one dear minute more would forfeit all my honour.' At this she started from my trembling hand, and swept the walk like wind so swift and sudden, and left me panting, sighing, wishing, dying, with mighty love and hope: and after a little time I scaled my wall, and returned unseen to my new lodging. It was four days after before I could get any other happiness, but that of seeing her at her window, which was just against mine, from which I never stirred, hardly to eat or sleep, and that she saw with joy; for every morning I had a billet from her, which we contrived that happy night should be conveyed me thus — It was a by-street where I lodged, and the other side was only the dead wall of her garden, where early in the morning she used to walk; and having the billet ready, she put it with a stone into a little leathern-purse, and tossed it over the wall, where either myself from the window, or my young friend below waited for it, and that way every morning and every evening she received one from me; but 'tis impossible to tell you the innocent passion she expressed in them, innocent in that there was no art, no feigned nice folly to express a virtue that was not in the soul; but all she spoke confessed her heart's soft wishes. At last, (for I am tedious in a relation of what gave me so much pleasure in the entertainment) at last, I say, I received the happy invitation to come into the garden as before; and night advancing for my purpose, I need not say that I delivered myself upon the place appointed, which was by the fountain-side beneath her chamber-window; towards which I cast, you may believe, many a longing look: the clock struck ten, eleven, and then twelve, but no dear star appeared to conduct me to my happiness; at last I heard the little garden-door (against the fountain) open, and saw *Calista* there wrapped in her night-gown only: I ran like lightning to her arms, with all the transports of an eager lover, and almost smothered myself in her warm rising breast; for she taking me in her arms let go her gown, which falling open, left nothing but her shift between me and all her charming body. But she bid me hear what she had to say before I proceeded farther; she told me she was forced to wait till *Dormina* was asleep, who lay in her chamber, and then stealing the key, she came softly down to let me in. 'But,' said she, 'since I am all undressed, and cannot walk in the garden with you, will you promise me, on love and honour, to be obedient to all my commands, if I carry you to my chamber? for *Dormina*'s sleep is like death itself; however, lest she chance to awake, and should take an occasion to speak to me, it were absolutely necessary that I were there; for since I served her such a trick the other night, and let her sleep so long, she will not let me walk late.' A very little argument persuaded me to yield to any thing to be with *Calista* any where; so that both returning softly to her chamber, she put herself into bed, and left me kneeling on the carpet: but it was not long that I remained so; from the dear touches of her hands and breast we came to kisses, and so equally to a forgetfulness of all we had promised and agreed on before, and broke all rules and articles that were not in the favour of love; so that stripping myself by degrees, while she with an unwilling force made some feeble resistance, I got into the arms of the most charming woman that ever nature made; she was all over perfection; I dare not tell you more; let it suffice she was all that luxurious man could wish, and all that renders woman fine and ravishing. About two hours thus was my soul in rapture, while sometimes she reproached me, but so gently, that it was to bid me still be false and perjured, if these were the effects of it; 'If disobedience have such wondrous charms, may I,' said she, 'be still commanding thee, and thou still disobeying.' While thus we lay with equal ravishment, we heard a murmuring noise at a distance, which we knew not what to make of, but it grew still louder and louder, but still at a distance too; this first alarmed us, and I was no sooner persuaded to rise, but I heard a door unlock at the side of the bed, which was not that by which I entered; for that was at the other end of the chamber towards the window. 'Oh heavens,' said the fair frighted trembler, 'here is the Count of *Clarinau*.' For he always came up that way, and those stairs by which I ascended were the back-stairs; so that I had just time to grope my way towards the door, without so much as taking my clothes with me; never was any amorous adventurer in so lamentable a condition, I would fain have turned upon him, and at once have hindered him from entering with my sword in my hand, and secured him from ever disturbing my pleasure any more; but she implored I would not, and in this minute's dispute he came so near me, that he touched me as I glided from him; but not being acquainted very well with the chamber, having never seen my way, I lighted in my passage on *Dormina*'s pallet-bed, and threw myself quite over her to the chamber-door, which made a damnable clattering, and awaking *Dormina* with my catastrophe, she set up such a bawl, as frighted and alarmed the old Count, who was just taking in a candle from his footman, who had lighted it at his flambeau: So that hearing the noise, and knowing it must be some body in the chamber, he let fall his candle in the fright, and called his footman in with the flambeau, draws his Toledo, which he had in his hand, and wrapped in his night-gown, with three or four woollen caps one upon the top of another, tied under his tawny, leathern chops, he made a very pleasant figure, and such a one as had like to have betrayed me by laughing at it; he closely pursued me, though not so close as to see me before him; yet so as not to give me time to ascend the wall, or to make my escape up or down any walk, which were straight and long, and not able to conceal any body from pursuers, approached so near as the Count was to me: what should I do? I was naked, unarmed, and no defence against his jealous rage; and now in danger of my life, I knew not what to resolve on; yet I swear to you, *Octavio*, even in that minute (which I thought my last) I had no repentance of the dear sin, or any other fear, but that which possessed me for the fair *Calista*; and calling upon *Venus* and her son for my safety (for I had scarce a thought yet of any other deity) the sea-born queen lent me immediate aid, and ere I was aware of it, I touched the fountain, and in the same minute threw myself into the water, which a mighty large basin or cistern of white marble contained, of a compass that forty men might have hid themselves in it; they had pursued me so hard, they fancied they heard me press the gravel near the fountain, and with the torch they searched round about it, and beat the fringing flowers that grew pretty high about the bottom of it, while I sometimes dived, and sometimes peeped up to take a view of my busy coxcomb, who had like to have made me burst into laughter many times to see his figure; the dashing of the stream, which continually fell from the little pipes above in the basin, hindered him from hearing the noise I might possibly have made by my swimming in it: after he had surveyed it round without-side, he took the torch in his own hand, and surveyed the water itself, while I dived, and so long forced to remain so, that I believed I had escaped his sword to die that foolisher way; but just as I was like to expire, he departed muttering, that he was sure some body did go out before him; and now he searched every walk and arbour of the garden, while like a fish I lay basking in element still, not daring to adventure out, lest his hasty return should find me on the wall, or in my passage over: I thanked my stars he had not found the ladder, so that at last returning to *Calista*'s chamber, after finding no body, he desired (as I heard the next morning) to know what the matter was in her chamber: but *Calista*, who till now never knew an art, had before he came laid her bed in order, and taken up my clothes, and put them between her bed and quilt; not forgetting any one thing that belonged to me, she was laid as fast asleep as innocence itself; so that *Clarinau* awaking her, she seemed as surprised and ignorant of all, as if she had indeed been innocent; so that *Dormina* now remained the only suspected person; who being asked what she could say concerning that uproar she made, she only said, as she thought, that she dreamed His Honour fell out of the bed upon her, and awaking in a fright she found it was but a dream, and so she fell asleep again till he awaked her whom she wondered to see there at that hour; he told them that while they were securely sleeping he was like to have been burned in his bed, a piece of his apartment being burned down, which caused him to come thither; but he made them both swear that there was no body in the chamber of *Calista*, before he would be undeceived; for he vowed he saw something in the garden, which, to his thinking, was all white, and it vanished on the sudden behind the fountain, and we could see no more of it. *Calista* dissembled abundance of fear, and said she would never walk after candlelight for fear of that ghost; and so they passed the rest of the night, while I, all wet and cold, got me to my lodging unperceived, for my young friend had left the door open for me.

Thus, dear *Octavio*, I have sent you a novel, instead of a letter, of my first most happy adventure, of which I must repeat thus much again, that of all the enjoyments I ever had, I was never so perfectly well entertained for two hours, and I am waiting with infinite patience for a second encounter. I shall be extremely glad to hear what progress you have made in your amour; for I have lost all for *Sylvia*, but the affection of a brother, with that natural pity we have for those we have undone; for my heart, my soul and body are all *Calista*'s, the bright, the young, the witty, the gay, the fondly-loving *Calista*: only some reserve I have in all for *Octavio*. Pardon this long history, for it is a sort of acting all one's joys again, to be telling them to a friend so dear, as is the gallant *Octavio* to

PHILANDER.

POSTSCRIPT.

I should, for some reasons that concern my safety, have quitted Ms town before, but I am chained to it, and no sense of danger while Calista *compels my stay.*

If *Octavio*'s trouble was great before, from but his fear of *Calista*'s yielding, what must it be now, when he found all his fears confirmed? The pressures of his soul were too extreme before, and the concern he had for *Sylvia* had brought it to the highest tide of grief; so that this addition overwhelmed it quite, and left him no room for rage; no, it could not discharge itself so happily, but bowed and yielded to all the extremes of love, grief, and sense of honour; he threw himself upon his bed, and lay without sense or motion for a whole hour, confused with thought, and divided in his concern, half for a mistress false, and half for a sister loose and undone; by turns the sister and the mistress torture; by turns they break his heart: he had this comfort left before, that if *Calista* were undone, her ruin made way for his love and happiness with *Sylvia*, but now —— he had no prospect left that could afford any ease; he changes from one sad object to another, from *Sylvia* to *Calista*, then back to *Sylvia*; but like to feverish men that toss about here and there, remove for some relief, he shifts but to new pain, wherever he turns he finds the madman still: in this distraction of thought he remained till a page from *Sylvia* brought him this letter, which in midst of all, he started from his bed with excess of joy, and read.

SYLVIA *to* OCTAVIO.

My Lord,

After your last affront by your page, I believe it will surprise you to receive any thing from *Sylvia* but scorn and disdain: but, my lord, the interest you have by a thousand ways been so long making in my heart, cannot so soon be cancelled by a minute's offence; and every action of your life has been too generous to make me think you writ what I have received, at least you are not well in your senses: I have committed a fault against your love, I must confess, and am not ashamed of the little cheat I put upon you in bringing you to bed to *Antonet* instead of *Sylvia*: I was ashamed to be so easily won, and took it ill your passion was so mercenary to ask so coarsely for the possession of me; too great a pay I thought for so poor service, as rendering up a letter which in honour you ought before to have shewed me: I own I gave you hope, in that too I was criminal; but these are faults that sure deserved a kinder punishment than what I last received — a whore — a common mistress! Death, you are a coward —— and even to a woman dare not say it, when she confronts the scandaler —— Yet pardon me, I mean not to revile, but gently to reproach; it was unkind —— at least allow me that, and much unlike *Octavio*.

I think I had not troubled you, my lord, with the least confession of my resentment, but I could not leave the town, where for the honour of your conversation and friendship alone I have remained so long, without acquitting myself of those obligations I had to you; I send you therefore the key of my closet and cabinet, where you shall find not only your letters, but all those presents you have been pleased once to think me worthy of: but having taken back your friendship, I render you the less valuable trifles, and will retain no more of *Octavio*, than the dear memory of that part of his life that was so agreeable to the unfortunate

SYLVIA.

He reading this letter, finished with tears of tender love; but considering it all over, he fancied she had put great constraint upon her natural high spirit to write in this calm manner to him, and through all he found dissembled rage, which yet was visible in that one breaking out in the middle of the letter: he found she was not able to contain at the word, common mistress. In fine, however calm it was, and however designed, he found, and at least he thought he found the charming jilt all over; he fancies from the hint she gave him of the change of *Antonet* for herself in bed, that it was some new cheat that was to be put upon him, and to bring herself off with credit: yet, in spite of all this appearing reason, he wishes, and has a secret hope, that either she is not in fault, or that she will so cozen him into a belief she is not, that it may serve as well to soothe his willing heart; and now all he fears is, that she will not put so neat a cheat upon him, but that he shall be able to see through it, and still be obliged to retain his ill opinion of her: but love returned, she had roused the flame anew, and softened all his rougher thoughts with this dear letter; and now in haste he calls for his clothes, and suffering himself to be dressed with all the advantage of his sex, he throws himself into his coach, and goes to *Sylvia*, whom he finds just dressed *en chevalier*, (and setting her head and feather in good order before the glass) with a design to depart the town, at least so far as should have raised a concern in *Octavio*, if yet he had any for her, to have followed her; he ran up without asking leave into her chamber; and ere she was aware of him he threw himself at her feet, and clasping her knees, to which he fixed his mouth, he remained there for a little space without life or motion, and pressed her in his arms as fast as a dying man. She was not offended to see him there, and he appeared more lovely than ever he yet had been. His grief had added a languishment and paleness to his face, which sufficiently told her he had not been at ease while absent from her; and on the other side, *Sylvia* appeared ten thousand times more charming than ever, the dress of a boy adding extremely to her beauty: 'Oh you are a pretty lover,' said she, raising him from her knees to her arms, 'to treat a mistress so for a little innocent raillery. —— Come, sit and tell me how you came to discover the harmless cheat;' setting him down on the side of her bed. 'Oh name it no more,' cried he, 'let that damned night be blotted from the year, deceive me, flatter me, say you are innocent; tell me my senses rave, my eyes were false, deceitful, and my ears were deaf: say any thing that may convince my madness, and bring me back to tame adoring love.' 'What means *Octavio*,' replied *Sylvia*, 'sure he is not so nice and squeamish a lover, but a fair young maid might have been welcome to him coming so prepared for love; though it was not she whom he expected, it might have served as well in the dark at least?' 'Well said,' replied *Octavio*, forcing a smile '—— advance, pursue the dear design, and cheat me still, and to convince my soul, oh swear it too, for women want no weapons of defence, oaths, vows, and tears, sighs, imprecations, ravings, are all the tools to fashion mankind coxcombs: I am an easy fellow, fit for use, and long to be initiated fool; come, swear I was not here the other night.' 'It is granted, sir, you were: why all this passion?' This *Sylvia* spoke, and took him by the hand, which burnt with raging fire; and though he spoke with all the heat of love, his looks were soft the while as infant *Cupids*: still he proceeded; 'Oh charming *Sylvia*, since you are so unkind to tell me truth, cease, cease to speak at all, and let me only gaze upon those eyes that can so well deceive: their looks are innocent, at least they will flatter me, and tell mine they lost their faculties that other night.' 'No,' replied *Sylvia*, 'I am convinced they did not, you saw *Antonet*——' 'Conduct a happy man' (interrupted he) 'to *Sylvia*'s bed. Oh, why by your confession must my soul be tortured over anew!' At this he hung his head upon his bosom, and sighed as if each breath would be his last. 'Heavens!' cried *Sylvia*, 'what is it *Octavio* says! Conduct a happy lover to my bed! by all that is sacred I am abused, designed upon to be betrayed and lost; what said you, sir, a lover to my bed!' When he replied in a fainting tone, clasping her to his arms, 'Now, *Sylvia*, you are kind, be perfect woman, and keep to cozening still —— Now back it with a very little oath, and I am as well as before I saw your falsehood, and never will lose one thought upon it more.' 'Forbear,' said she, 'you will make me angry. In short, what is it you would say? Or swear, you rave, and then I will pity what I now despise, if you can think me false.' He only answered with a sigh, and she pursued, 'Am I not worth an answer? Tell me your soul and thoughts, as ever you hope for favour from my love, or to preserve my quiet.' 'If you will promise me to say it is false,' replied he softly, 'I will confess the errors of my senses. I came the other night at twelve, the door was open. ———' 'It is true,' said *Sylvia*——'At the stairs-foot I found a man, and saw him led to you into your chamber, sighing as he went, and panting with impatience: now, *Sylvia*, if you value my repose, my life, my reputation, or my services, turn it off handsomely, and I am happy.' At that, being wholly amazed, she told him the whole story, as you heard of her dressing *Antonet*, and bringing him to her; at which he smiled, and begged her to go on —— She fetched the pieces of *Brilliard*'s counterfeit letters, and shewed him; this brought him a little to his wits, and at first sight he was ready to fancy the letters came indeed from him; he found the character his, but not his business; and in great amaze replied, 'Ah, madam, did you know *Octavio*'s soul so well, and could you imagine it capable of a thought like this? A presumption so daring to the most awful of her sex; this was unkind indeed: and did you answer them?' 'Yes,' replied she, 'with all the kindness I could force my pen to express.' So that after canvassing the matter, and relating the whole story again with his being taken ill, they concluded from every circumstance *Brilliard* was the man; for *Antonet* was called to council; who now recollecting all things in her mind, and knowing *Brilliard* but too well, she confessed she verily believed it was he, especially when she told how she stole a letter of *Octavio*'s for him that day, and how he was ill of the same disease still. *Octavio* then called his page, and sent him home for the note *Brilliard* had sent him, and all appeared as clear as day: but *Antonet* met with a great many reproaches for shewing her lady's letters, which she excused as well as she could: but never was man so ravished with joy as *Octavio* was at the knowledge of *Sylvia*'s innocence; a thousand times he kneeled and begged her pardon; and her figure encouraging his caresses, a thousand times he embraced her, he smiled, and blushed, and sighed with love and joy, and knew not how to express it most effectually: and *Sylvia*, who had other business than love in her heart and head, suffered all the marks of his eager passion and transport out of design, for she had a farther use to make of *Octavio*; though when she surveyed his person handsome, young, and adorned with all the graces and beauties of the sex, not at all inferior to *Philander*, if not exceeding in every judgement but that of *Sylvia*; when she considered his soul, where wit, love, and honour equally reigned, when she consults the excellence of his nature, his generosity, courage, friendship, and softness, she sighed and cried, it was pity to impose upon him; and make his love for which she should esteem him, a property to draw him to his ruin; for so she fancied it must be if ever he encountered *Philander*; and though good nature was the least ingredient that formed the soul of this fair charmer, yet now she found she had a mixture of it, from her concern for *Octavio*; and that generous lover made her so many soft vows, and tender protestations of the respect and awfulness of his passion, that she was wholly convinced he was her slave; nor could she see the constant languisher pouring out his soul and fortune at her feet, without suffering some warmth about her heart, which she had never felt but for *Philander*; and this day she expressed herself more obligingly than ever she had done, and allows him little freedoms of approaching her with more softness than hitherto she had; and, absolutely charmed, he promises, lavishly and without reserve, all she would ask of him; and in requital she assured him all he could wish or hope, if he would serve her in her revenge against *Philander*: she recounts to him at large the story of her undoing, her quality, her fortune, her nice education, the care and tenderness of her noble parents, and charges all her fate to the evil conduct of her heedless youth: sometimes the reflection on her ruin, she looking back upon her former innocence and tranquillity, forces the tears to flow from her fair eyes, and makes *Octavio* sigh, and weep by sympathy: sometimes (arrived at the amorous part of her relation) she would sigh and languish with the remembrance of past joys in their beginning love; and sometimes smile at the little unlucky adventures they met with, and their escapes; so that different passions seized her soul while she spoke, while that of all love filled *Octavio*'s: he dotes, he burns, and every word she utters enflames him still the more; he fixes his very soul upon her tongue, and darts his very eyes into her face, and every thing she says raises his vast esteem and passion higher. In fine, having with the eloquence of sacred wit, and all the charms of every differing passion, finished her moving tale, they both declined their eyes, whose falling showers kept equal time and pace, and for a little time were still as thought: when *Octavio*, oppressed with mighty love, broke the soft silence, and burst into extravagance of passion, says all that men (grown mad with love and wishing) could utter to the idol of his heart; and to oblige her more, recounts his life in short; wherein, in spite of all his modesty, she found all that was great and brave; all that was noble, fortunate and honest: and having now confirmed her, he deserved her, kneeling implored she would accept of him, not as a lover for a term of passion, for dates of months or years, but for a long eternity; not as a rifler of her sacred honour, but to defend it from the censuring world; he vowed he would forget that ever any part of it was lost, nor by a look or action ever upbraid her with a misfortune past, but still look forward on nobler joys to come: and now implores that he may bring a priest to tie the solemn knot. In spite of all her love for *Philander*, she could not choose but take this offer kindly; and indeed, it made a very great impression on her heart; she knew nothing but the height of love could oblige a man of his quality and vast fortune, with all the advantages of youth and beauty, to marry her in so ill circumstances; and paying him first those acknowledgements that were due on so great an occasion, with all the tenderness in her voice and eyes that she could put on, she excused herself from receiving the favour, by telling him she was so unfortunate as to be with child by the ungrateful man; and falling at that thought into new tears, she moved him to infinite love, and infinite compassion; insomuch that, wholly abandoning himself to softness, he assured her, if she would secure him all his happiness by marrying him now, that he would wait till she were brought to bed, before he would demand the glorious recompense he aspired to; so that *Sylvia*, being oppressed with obligation, finding yet in her soul a violent passion for *Philander*, she knew not how to take, or how to refuse the blessing offered, since *Octavio* was a man whom, in her height of innocence and youth, she might have been vain and proud of engaging to this degree. He saw her pain and irresolution, and being absolutely undone with love, delivers her *Philander*'s last letter to him, with what he had sent her enclosed; the sight of the very outside of it made her grow pale as death, and a feebleness seized her all over, that made her unable for a moment to open it; all which confusion *Octavio* saw with pain, which she perceiving recollected her thoughts as well as she could, and opened it, and read it; that to *Octavio* first, as being fondest of the continuation of the history of his falsehood, she read, and often paused to recover her spirits that were fainting at every period; and having finished it, she fell down on the bed where they sat. *Octavio* caught her in her fall in his arms, where she remained dead some moments; whilst he, just on the point of being so himself, ravingly called for help; and *Antonet* being in the dressing-room ran to them, and by degrees *Sylvia* recovered, and asked *Octavio* a thousand pardons for exposing a weakness to him, which was but the effects of the last blaze of love: and taking a cordial which *Antonet* brought her, she roused, resolved, and took *Octavio* by the hand: 'Now,' said she, 'shew yourself that generous lover you have professed, and give me your vows of revenge on *Philander*; and after that, by all that is holy,' kneeling as she spoke, and holding him fast, 'by all my injured innocence, by all my noble father's wrongs, and my dear mother's grief; by all my sister's sufferings, I swear, I will marry you, love you, and give you all!' This she spoke without considering *Antonet* was by, and spoke it with all the rage, and blushes in her face, that injured love and revenge could inspire: and on the other side, the sense of his sister's honour lost, and that of the tender passion he had for *Sylvia*, made him swear by all that was sacred, and by all the vows of eternal love and honour he had made to *Sylvia*, to go and revenge himself and her on the false friend and lover, and confessed the second motive, which was his sister's fame, 'For,' cried he, 'that foul adulteress, that false *Calista*, is so allied to me.' But still he urged that would add to the justness of his cause, if he might depart her husband as well as lover, and revenge an injured wife as well as sister; and now he could ask nothing she did not easily grant; and because it was late in the day, they concluded that the morning shall consummate all his desires: and now she gives him her letter to read; 'For,' said she, 'I shall esteem myself henceforth so absolutely *Octavio*'s, that I will not so much as read a line from that perjured ruiner of my honour;' he took the letter with smiles and bows of gratitude, and read it.

PHILANDER *to* SYLVIA.

There are a thousand reasons, dearest *Sylvia*, at this time that prevent my writing to you, reasons that will be convincing enough to oblige my pardon, and plead my cause with her that loves me: all which I will lay before you when I have the happiness to see you; I have met with some affairs since my arrival to this place, that wholly take up my time; affairs of State, whose fatigues have put my heart extremely out of tune, and if not carefully managed may turn to my perpetual ruin, so that I have not an hour in a day to spare for *Sylvia*; which, believe me, is the greatest affliction of my life; and I have no prospect of ease in the endless toils of life, but that of reposing in the arms of *Sylvia*: some short intervals: pardon my haste, for you cannot guess the weighty business that at present robs you of

Your PHILANDER.

'You lie, false villain ———' replied *Sylvia* in mighty rage, 'I can guess your business, and can revenge it too; curse on thee, slave, to think me grown as poor in sense as honour: to be cajoled with this — stuff that would never sham a chambermaid: death! am I so forlorn, so despicable, I am not worth the pains of being well dissembled with? Confusion overtake him, misery seize him; may I become his plague while life remains, or public tortures end him!' This, with all the madness that ever inspired a lunatic, she uttered with tears and violent actions: when *Octavio* besought her not to afflict herself, and almost wished he did not love a temper so contrary to his own: he told her he was sorry, extremely sorry, to find she still retained so violent a passion for a man unworthy of her least concern; when she replied —'Do not mistake my soul, by heaven it is pride, disdain, despite and hate — to think he should believe this dull excuse could pass upon my judgement; had the false traitor told me that he hated me, or that his faithless date of love was out, I had been tame with all my injuries; but poorly thus to impose upon my wit — By heaven he shall not bear the affront to hell in triumph! No more — I have vowed he shall not — my soul has fixed, and now will be at ease — Forgive me, oh *Octavio*;' and letting herself fall into his arms, she soon obtained what she asked for; one touch of the fair charmer could calm him into love and softness.

Thus, after a thousand transports of passion on his side, and all the seeming tenderness on hers, the night being far advanced, and new confirmations given and taken on either side of pursuing the happy agreement in the morning, which they had again resolved, they appointed that *Sylvia* and *Antonet* should go three miles out of town to a little village, where there was a church, and that *Octavio* should meet them there to be confirmed and secured of all the happiness he proposed to himself in this world —*Sylvia* being so wholly bent upon revenge (for the accomplishment of which alone she accepted of *Octavio*) that she had lost all remembrance of her former marriage with *Brilliard*: or if it ever entered into her thought, it was only considered as a sham, nothing designed but to secure her from being taken from *Philander* by her parents; and, without any respect to the sacred tie, to be regarded no more; nor did she design this with *Octavio* from any respect she had to the holy state of matrimony, but from a lust of vengeance which she would buy at any price, and which she found no man so well able to satisfy as *Octavio*.

But what wretched changes of fortune she met with after this, and what miserable portion of fate was destined to this unhappy wanderer, the last part of *Philander*'s life, and the third and last part of this history, shall most faithfully relate.

The End of the Second Part.

Chapter 3

The Amours of Philander and Sylvia

Octavio, the brave, the generous, and the amorous, having left *Sylvia* absolutely resolved to give herself to that doting fond lover, or rather to sacrifice herself to her revenge, that unconsidering unfortunate, whose passion had exposed him to all the unreasonable effects of it, returned to his own house, wholly transported with his happy success. He thinks on nothing but vast coming joys: nor did one kind thought direct him back to the evil consequences of what he so hastily pursued; he reflects not on her circumstances but her charms, not on the infamy he should espouse with *Sylvia*, but on those ravishing pleasures she was capable of giving him: he regards not the reproaches of his friends; but wholly abandoned to love and youthful imaginations, gives a loose to young desire and fancy that deludes him with a thousand soft ideas: he reflects not, that his gentle and easy temper was most unfit to join with that of *Sylvia*, which was the most haughty and humorous in nature; for though she had all the charms of youth and beauty that are conquering in her sex, all the wit and insinuation that even surpasses youth and beauty; yet to render her character impartially, she had also abundance of disagreeing qualities mixed with her perfections. She was imperious and proud even to insolence; vain and conceited even to folly; she knew her virtues and her graces too well, and her vices too little; she was very opinionated and obstinate, hard to be convinced of the falsest argument, but very positive in her fancied judgement: abounding in her own sense, and very critical on that of others: censorious, and too apt to charge others with those crimes to which she was herself addicted, or had been guilty of: amorously inclined, and indiscreet in the management of her amours, and constant rather from pride and shame than inclination; fond of catching at every trifling conquest, and loving the triumph, though she hated the slave. Yet she had virtues too that balanced her vices, among which we must allow her to have loved *Philander* with a passion, that nothing but his ingratitude could have decayed in her heart, nor was it lessened but by a force that gave her a thousand tortures, racks and pangs, which had almost cost her her less valued life; for being of a temper nice in love, and very fiery, apt to fly into rages at every accident that did but touch that tenderest part, her heart, she suffered a world of violence, and extremity of rage and grief by turns, at this affront and inconstancy of *Philander*. Nevertheless she was now so discreet, or rather cunning, to dissemble her resentment the best she could to her generous lover, for whom she had more inclination than she yet had leisure to perceive, and which she now attributes wholly to her revenge; and considering *Octavio* as the most proper instrument for that, she fancies what was indeed a growing tenderness from the sense of his merit, to be the effects of that revenge she so much thirsted after; and though without she dissembled a calm, within she was all fury and disorder, all storm and distraction: she went to bed racked with a thousand thoughts of despairing love: sometimes all the softness of *Philander* in their happy enjoyments came in view, and made her sometimes weep, and sometimes faint with the dear loved remembrance; sometimes his late enjoyments with *Calista*, and then she raved and burnt with frantic rage: but oh! at last she found her hope was gone, and wisely fell to argue with her soul. She knew love would not long subsist on the thin diet of despair, and resolving he was never to be retrieved who once had ceased to love, she strove to bend her soul to useful reason, and thinks on all *Octavio*'s obligations, his vows, his assiduity, his beauty, his youth, his fortune, and his generous offer, and with the aid of pride resolves to unfix her heart, and give it better treatment in his bosom: to cease at least to love the false *Philander*, if she could never force her soul to hate him: and though this was not so soon done as thought on, in a heart so prepossesed as that of *Sylvia*'s, yet there is some hope of a recovery, when a woman in that extremity will but think of listening to love from any new adorer, and having once resolved to pursue the fugitive no more with the natural artillery of their sighs and tears, reproaches and complaints, they have recourse to every thing that may soonest chase from the heart those thoughts that oppress it: for nature is not inclined to hurt itself; and there are but very few who find it necessary to die of the disease of love. Of this sort was our *Sylvia*, though to give her her due, never any person who did not indeed die, ever languished under the torments of love, as did that charming and afflicted maid.

While *Sylvia* remained in these eternal inquietudes, *Antonet*, having quitted her chamber, takes this opportunity to go to that of *Brilliard*, whom she had not visited in two days before, being extremely troubled at his design, which she now found he had on her lady; she had a mind to vent her spleen, and as the proverb says, 'Call Whore first'. *Brilliard* longed as much to see her to rail at her for being privy to *Octavio*'s approach to *Sylvia*'s bed (as he thought she imagined) and not giving him an account of it, as she used to do of all the secrets of her lady. She finds him alone in her chamber, recovered from all but the torments of his unhappy disappointment. She approached him with all the anger her sort of passion could inspire (for love in a mean unthinking soul, is not that glorious thing it is in the brave;) however she had enough to serve her pleasure; for *Brilliard* was young and handsome, and both being bent on railing without knowing each other's intentions, they both equally flew into high words, he upbraiding her with her infidelity, and she him with his. 'Are not you,' said he (growing more calm) 'the falsest of your tribe, to keep a secret from me that so much concerned me? Is it for this I have refused the addresses of burgomasters' wives and daughters, where I could have made my fortune and my satisfaction, to keep myself entirely for a thing that betrays me, and keeps every secret of her heart from me? False and forsworn, I will be fool no more.' 'It is well, sir,' (replied *Antonet*) 'that you having been the most perfidious man alive, should accuse me who am innocent: come, come sir, you have not carried matters so swimmingly, but I could easily dive into the other night's intrigue and secret.' 'What secret thou false one? Thou art all over secret; a very hopeful bawd at eighteen —— go, I hate ye ——' At this she wept, and he pursued his railing to out-noise her, 'You thought, because your deed were done in darkness, they were concealed from a lover's eye; no, thou young viper, I saw, I heard, and felt, and satisfied every sense of this thy falsehood, when *Octavio* was conducted to *Sylvia*'s bed by thee.' 'But what,' said she, 'if instead of *Octavio* I conducted the perfidious traitor to love, *Brilliard*? Who then was false and perjured?' At this he blushed extremely, which was too visible on his fair face. She being now confirmed she had the better of him, continued —'Let thy confusion,' said she with scorn, 'witness the truth of what I say, and I have been but too well acquainted with that body of yours,' weeping as she spoke, 'to mistake it for that of *Octavio*.' 'Softly, dear *Antonet*,' replied he ——'nay, now your tears have calmed me'; and taking her in his arms, sought to appease her by all the arguments of seeming love and tenderness; while she, yet wholly unsatisfied in that cheat of his of going to Sylvia's bed, remained still pouting and very frumpish. But he that had but one argument left, that on all occasions served to convince her, had at last recourse to that, which put her in good humour, and hanging on his neck, she kindly chid him for putting such a trick upon her lady. He told her, and confirmed it with an oath, that he did it but to try how far she was just to his friend and lord, and not any desire he had for a beauty that was too much of his own complexion to charm him; it was only the brunette and the black, such as herself, that could move him to desire; thus he shams her into perfect peace. 'And why,' said she, 'were you not satisfied that she was false, as well from the assignation, as the trial?' 'Oh no,' said he, 'you women have a thousand arts of gibing, and no man ought to believe you, but put you to the trial.' 'Well,' said she, 'when I had brought you to the bed, when you found her arms stretched out to receive you, why did you not retire like an honest man, and leave her to herself?' 'Oh fie,' said he, 'that had not been to have acted *Octavio* to the life, but would have made a discovery.' 'Ah,' said she, 'that was your aim to have acted *Octavio* to the life, I believe, and not to discover my lady's constancy to your lord; but I suppose you have been sworn at the Butt of *Heidleburgh*, never to kiss the maid, when you can kiss the mistress.' But he renewing his caresses and asseverations of love to her, she suffered herself to be convinced of all he had a mind to have her believe. After this she could not contain any secret from him, but told him she had something to say to him, which if he knew, would convince him she had all the passion in the world for him: he presses eagerly to know, and she pursues to tell him, it is as much as her life is worth to discover it, and that she lies under the obligation of an oath not to tell it; but kisses and rhetoric prevail, and she cries —'What will you say now, if my lady may marry one of the greatest and most considerable persons in all this country?' 'I should not wonder at her conquest,' (replied *Brilliard*) 'but I should wonder if she should marry.' 'Then cease your wonder,' replied she, 'for she is to-morrow to be married to Count *Octavio*, whom she is to meet at nine in the morning to that end, at a little village a league from this place.' She spoke, and he believes; and finds it true by the raging of his blood, which he could not conceal from *Antonet*, and for which he feigns a thousand excuses to the amorous maid, and charges his concern on that for his lord: at last (after some more discourse on that subject) he pretends to grow sleepy, and hastens her to her chamber; and locking the door after her, he began to reflect on what she had said, and grew to all the torment of rage and jealousy, and all the despairs of a passionate lover: and though this hope was not extreme before, yet as lovers do, he found, or fancied a probability (from his lord's inconstancy, and his own right of marriage) that the necessity she might chance to be in of his friendship and assistance in a strange country, might some happy moment or other render him the blessing he so long had waited for from *Sylvia*; for he ever designed, when either his lord left her, grew cold, or should happen to die, to put in his claim of husband. And the soft familiar way, with which she eternally lived with him, encouraged this hope and design; nay, she had often made him advances to that happy expectation. But this fatal blow had driven him from all his fancied joys, to the most wretched estate of a desperate lover. He traverses his chamber, wounded with a thousand different thoughts, mixed with those of preventing this union the next morning. Sometimes he resolves to fight *Octavio*, for his birth might pretend to it, and he wanted no courage; but he is afraid of being overcome by that gallant man, and either losing his hopes with his life, or if he killed *Octavio*, to be forced from his happiness, or die an ignominious death: sometimes he resolves to own *Sylvia* for his wife, but then he fears the rage of that dear object of his soul, which he dreads more than death itself: so that tossed from one extreme to another, from one resolution to a hundred, he was not able to fix upon any thing. In this perplexity he remained till day appeared, that day must advance with his undoing, while *Sylvia* and *Antonet* were preparing for the design concluded on the last night. This he heard, and every minute that approached gave him new torments, so that now he would have given himself to the Prince of Darkness for a kind disappointment: he was often ready to go and throw himself at her feet, and plead against her enterprise in hand, and to urge the unlawfulness of a double marriage, ready to make vows for the fidelity of *Philander*, though before so much against his own interest, and to tell her all those letters from him were forged: he thought on all things, but nothing remained with him, but despair of every thing. At last the devil and his own subtlety put him upon a prevention, though base, yet the most likely to succeed, in his opinion.

He knew there were many factions in *Holland*, and that the *States* themselves were divided in their interests, and a thousand jealousies and fears were eternally spread amongst the rabble; there were cabals for every interest, that of the *French* so prevailing, that of the *English*, and that of the illustrious *Orange*, and others for the *States*; so that it was not a difficulty to move any mischief, and pass it off among the crowd for dangerous consequences. *Brilliard* knew each division, and which way they were inclined; he knew *Octavio* was not so well with the *States* as not to be easily rendered worse; for he was so entirely a creature and favourite of the Prince, that they conceived abundance of jealousies of him which they durst not own. *Brilliard* besides knew a great man, who having a pique to *Octavio*, might the sooner be brought to receive any ill character of him: to this sullen magistrate he applies himself, and deluding the credulous busy old man with a thousand circumstantial lies, he discovers to him, that *Octavio* held a correspondence with the *French* King to betray the State; and that he caballed to that end with some who were looked upon as *French* rebels, but indeed were no other than spies to *France*. This coming from a man of that party, and whose lord was a

French rebel, gained a perfect credit with the old Sir *Politic*; so that immediately hasting to the state-house, he lays this weighty affair before them, who soon found it reasonable, if not true, at least they feared, and sent out a warrant for the speedy apprehending him; but coming to his house, though early, they found him gone, and being informed which way he took, the messenger pursued him, and found his coach at the door of a *cabaret*, too obscure for his quality, which made them apprehend this was some place of rendezvous where he possibly met with his traitorous associates: they send in, and cunningly inquire who he waited for, or who was with him, and they understood he stayed for some gentleman of the *French* nation; for he had ordered *Sylvia* to come in man's clothes that she might not be known; and had given order below, that if two *French* gentlemen came they should be brought to him. This information made the scandal as clear as day, and the messenger no longer doubted of the reasonableness of his warrant, though he was loath to serve it on a person whose father he had served so many years. He waits at some distance from the house unseen, though he could take a view of all; he saw *Octavio* come often out into the balcony, and look with longing eyes towards the road that leads to the town; he saw him all rich and gay as a young bridegroom, lovely and young as the morning that flattered him with so fair and happy a day; at last he saw two gentlemen alight at the door, and giving their horses to a page to walk the while, they ran up into the chamber where *Octavio* was waiting, who had already sent his page to prepare the priest in the village-church to marry them. You may imagine, with what love and joy the ravished youth approached the idol of his soul, and she, who beholds him in more beauty than ever yet she thought he had appeared, pleased with all things he had on, with the gay morning, the flowery field, the air, the little journey, and a thousand diverting things, made no resistance to those fond embraces that pressed her a thousand times with silent transport, and falling tears of eager love and pleasure; but even in that moment of content, she forgot *Philander*, and received all the satisfaction so soft a lover could dispense: while they were mutually thus exchanging looks, and almost hearts, the messenger came into the room, and as civilly as possible told *Octavio* he had a warrant for him, to secure him as a traitor to the State, and a spy for *France*. You need not be told the surprise and astonishment he was in; however he obeyed. The messenger turning to *Sylvia*, cried, 'Sir, though I can hardly credit this crime that is charged to my lord, yet the finding him here with two *French* gentlemen, gives me some more fears that there may be something in it; and it would do well if you would deliver yourselves into my hands for the farther clearing this gentleman.' This foolish grave speech of the messenger had like to have put *Octavio* into a loud laughter, he addressing himself to two women for two men: but *Sylvia* replied, 'Sir, I hope you do not take us for so little friends to the gallant *Octavio*, to abandon him in this misfortune; no, we will share it with him, be it what it will.' To this the generous lover blushing with kind surprise, bowed, and kissing her hand with transport, called her his charming friend; and so all three being guarded back in *Octavio*'s coach they return to the town, and to the house of the messenger, which made a great noise all over, that *Octavio* was taken with two *French* Jesuits plotting to fire *Amsterdam*, and a thousand things equally ridiculous. They were all three lodged together in one house, that of the messenger, which was very fine, and fit to entertain any persons of quality; while *Brilliard*, who did not like that part of the project, bethought him of a thousand ways how to free her from thence; for he designed, as soon as *Octavio* should be taken, to have got her to have quitted the town under pretence of being taken upon suspicion of holding correspondence with him, because they were *French*; but her delivering herself up had not only undone all his design, but had made it unsafe for him to stay. While he was thus bethinking himself what he should do, *Octavio*'s uncle, who was one of the *States*, extremely affronted at the indignity put upon his nephew and his sole heir, the darling of his heart and eyes, commands that this informer may be secured; and accordingly *Brilliard* was taken into custody, who giving himself over for a lost man, resolves to put himself upon *Octavio*'s mercy, by telling him the motives that induced him to this violent and ungenerous course. It was some days before the Council thought fit to call for *Octavio*, to hear what he had to say for himself; in the mean time, he having not had permission yet to see *Sylvia*; and being extremely desirous of that happiness, he bethought himself that the messenger, having been in his father's service, might have so much respect for the son, as to allow him to speak to that fair charmer, provided he might be a witness to what he should say: he sends for him, and demanded of him where those two fair prisoners were lodged who came with him in the morning; he told him, in a very good apartment on the same floor, and that they were very well accommodated, and seemed to have no other trouble but what they suffered for him. 'I hope, my Lord,' added he —'your confinement will not be long; for I hear there is a person taken up, who has confessed he did it for a revenge on you.' At this *Octavio* was very well pleased, and asked him who it was? And he told him a *French* gentleman belonging to the Count *Philander*, who about six months ago was obliged to quit the town as an enemy to *France*. He soon knew it to be *Brilliard*, and comparing this action with some others of his lately committed, he no longer doubts it the effects of his jealousy. He asked the messenger, if it were impossible to gain so much favour of him, as to let him visit those two *French* gentlemen, he being by while he was with them: the keeper soon granted his request, and replied — There was no hazard he would not run to serve him; and immediately putting back the hangings, with one of those keys he had in his hand, he opened a door in his chamber that led into a gallery of fine pictures, and from thence they passed into the apartment of *Sylvia*: as soon as he came in he threw himself at her feet, and she received him, and took him up into her arms with all the transports of joy a soul (more than ever possessed with love for him) could conceive; and though they all appeared of the masculine sex, the messenger soon perceived his error, and begged a thousand pardons. *Octavio* makes haste to tell her his opinion of the cause of all this trouble to both; and she easily believed, when she heard *Brilliard* was taken, that it was as he imagined; for he had been found too often faulty not to be suspected now. This thought brought a great calm to both their spirits, and almost reduced them to the first soft tranquillity, with which they began the day: for he protested his innocence a thousand times, which was wholly needless, for the generous maid believed, before he spoke, he could not be guilty of the sin of treachery. He renews his vows to her of eternal love, and that he would perform what they were so unluckily prevented from doing this morning; and that though possibly by this unhappy adventure, his design might have taken air, and have arrived to the knowledge of his uncle, yet in spite of all opposition of friends, or the malice of *Brilliard*, he would pursue his glorious design of marrying her, though he were forced for it to wander in the farthest parts of the earth with his lovely prize. He begs she will not disesteem him for this scandal on his fame; for he was all love, all soft desire, and had no other design, than that of making himself master of that greatest treasure in the world; that of the possessing, the most charming, the all-ravishing *Sylvia*: in return, she paid him all the vows that could secure an infidel in love, she made him all the endearing advances a heart could wish, wholly given up to tender passion, insomuch that he believes, and is the gayest man that ever was blest by love. And the messenger, who was present all this while, found that this caballing with the *French* spies, was only an innocent design to give himself away to a fine young lady: and therefore gave them all the freedom they desired, and which they made use of to the most advantage love could direct or youth inspire.

This suffering with *Octavio* begot a pity and compassion in the heart of *Sylvia*, and that grew up to love; for he had all the charms that could inspire, and every hour was adding new fire to her heart, which at last burnt into a flame; such power has mighty obligation on a heart that has any grateful sentiments! and yet, when she was absent a-nights from *Octavio*, and thought on *Philander*'s, passion for *Calista*, she would rage and rave, and find the effects of wondrous love, and wondrous pride, and be even ready to make vows against *Octavio*: but those were fits that seldomer seized her now, and every fit was like a departing ague, still weaker than the former, and at the sight of *Octavio* all would vanish, her blushes would rise and discover the soft thoughts her heart conceived for the approaching lover; and she soon found that vulgar error, of the impossibility of loving more than once. It was four days they thus remained without being called to the Council, and every day brought its new joys along with it. They were never asunder, never interrupted with any visit, but one for a few moments in a day by *Octavio*'s uncle, and then he would go into his own apartment to receive him: he offered to bail him out; but *Octavio*, who had found more real joy there, than in any part of the earth besides, evaded the obligation, by telling his uncle, he would be obliged to nothing but his innocence for his liberty: so would get rid of the fond old gentleman, who never knew a passion but for his darling nephew, and returned with as much joy to the lodgings of *Sylvia*, as if he had been absent a week, which is an age to a lover; there they sometimes would play at cards, where he would lose considerable sums to her, or at hazard, or be studying what they should do next to pass the hours most to her content; not but he had rather have lain eternally at her feet, gazing, doting, and saying a thousand fond things, which at every view he took were conceived in his soul: and though but this last minute he had finished, saying all that love could dictate, he found his heart oppressed with a vast store of new softness, which he languished to unload in her ravishing bosom. But she, who was not arrived to his pitch of loving, diverts his softer hours with play sometimes, and otherwhile with making him follow her into the gallery, which was adorned with pleasant pictures, all of *Hempskerk*'s hand, which afforded great variety of objects very droll and antique, *Octavio* finding something to say of every one that might be of advantage to his own heart; for whatever argument was in dispute, he would be sure to bring it home to the passion he had for *Sylvia*; it should end in love, however remotely begun: so strange an art has love to turn all things to the advantage of a lover!

It was thus they passed their time, and nothing was wanting that lavish experience could procure, and every minute he advances to new freedoms, and unspeakable delights, but still such as might hitherto be allowed with honour; he sighs and wishes, he languishes and dies for more, but dares not utter the meaning of one motion of breath; for he loved so very much, that every look from those fair eyes charmed him, awed him to a respect that robbed him of many happy moments, a bolder lover would have turned to his advantage, and he treated her as if she had been an unspotted maid; with caution of offending, he had forgot that general rule, that where the sacred laws of honour are once invaded, love makes the easier conquest.

All this while you may imagine *Brilliard* endured no little torment; he could not on the one side, determine what the *States* would do with him, when once they should find him a false accuser of so great a man; and on the other side, he suffered a thousand pains and jealousies from love; he knew too well the charms and power of *Octavio*, and what effects importunity and opportunity have on the temper of feeble woman: he found the *States* did not make so considerable a matter of his being impeached, as to confine him strictly, and he dies with the fears of those happy moments he might possibly enjoy with *Sylvia*, where there might be no spies about her to give him any kind intelligence; and all that could afford him any glimpse of consolation, was, that while they were thus confined, he was out of fear of their being married. *Octavio*'s uncle this while was not idle, but taking it for a high indignity his nephew should remain so long without being heard, he moved it to the Council, and accordingly they sent for him to the state-house the next morning, where *Brilliard* was brought to confront him; whom, as soon as *Octavio* saw, with a scornful smile, he cried — 'It is well, *Brilliard*, that you, who durst not fight me fairly, should find out this nobler way of ridding yourself of a rival: I am glad at least that I have no more honourable a witness against me.' *Brilliard*, who never before wanted assurance, at this reproach was wholly confounded; for it was not from any villainy in his nature, but the absolute effects of mad and desperate passion, which put him on the only remedy that could relieve him; and looking on *Octavio* with modest blushes, that half pleaded for him, he cried —'Yes, my lord, I am your accuser, and come to charge your innocence with the greatest of crimes, and you ought to thank me for my accusation; when you shall know it is regard to my own honour, violent love for *Sylvia*, and extreme respect to your lordship, has made me thus saucy with your unspotted fame.' 'How,' replied *Octavio*, 'shall I thank you for accusing me with a plot upon the State?' 'Yes, my lord,' replied *Brilliard*; 'and yet you had a plot to betray the State, and by so new a way, as could be found out by none but so great and brave a man'—'Heavens,' replied *Octavio*, enraged, 'this is an impudence, that nothing but a traitor to his own king, and one bred up in plots and mischiefs, could have invented: I betray my own country?'—'Yes, my lord,' cried he (more briskly than before, seeing *Octavio* colour so at him) 'to all the looseness of unthinking youth, to all the breach of laws both human and divine; if all the youth should follow your example, you would betray posterity itself, and only mad confusion would abound. In short, my lord, that lady who was taken with you by the messenger, was my wife.' And going towards *Sylvia*, who was struck as with a thunder-bolt, he seized her hand, and cried — while all stood gazing on — This lady, sir, I mean —— she is my wife, my lawful married wife.' At this *Sylvia* could no longer hold her patience within its bounds, but with that other hand he had left her, she struck him a box on the ear, that almost staggered him, coming unawares; and as she struck, she cried aloud, 'Thou liest, base villain —— and I will be revenged;' and flinging herself out of his hand, she got on the other side of *Octavio*, while the whole company remained confounded at what they saw and heard. 'How,' cried out old *Sebastian*, uncle to *Octavio*, 'a woman, this? By my troth, sweet lady, (if you be one) methought you were a very pretty fellow.' And turning to *Brilliard*, he cried — 'Why, what sir, then it seems all this noise of betraying the State was but a cuckold's dream. Hah! and this wonderful and dangerous plot, was but one upon your wife, sir; hah —— was it so? Marry, sir, at this rate, I rather think it is you have a design of betraying the State —— you cuckoldy knaves, that bring your handsome wives to seduce our young senators from their sobriety and wits.' 'Are these the recompenses,' replied *Brilliard*, 'you give the injured, and in lieu of restoring me my right, am I reproached with the most scandalous infamy that can befall a man?' 'Well, sir,' replied *Sebastian*, 'is this all you have to charge this gentleman with?' At which he bowed, and was silent —— and *Sebastian* continued —'If your wife, sir, have a mind to my nephew, or he to her, it should have been your care to have forbid it, or prevented it, by keeping her under lock and key, if no other way to be secured; and, sir, we do not sit here to relieve fools and cuckolds; if your lady will be civil to my nephew, what is that to us: let her speak for herself: what say you, madam?'—'I say,' replied *Sylvia*, 'that this fellow is mad and raves, that he is my vassal, my servant, my

slave; but, after this, unworthy of the meanest of these titles.' This
she spoke with a disdain that sufficiently shewed the pride and anger
of her soul ——'La you, sir,' replied *Sebastian*, 'you are discharged
your lady's service; it is a plain case she has more mind to the young
Count than the husband, and we cannot compel people to be honest
against their inclinations.' And coming down from the seat where he
sat, he embraced *Octavio* a hundred times, and told the board, he
was extremely glad they found the mighty plot, but a vagary of youth,
and the spleen of a jealous husband or lover, or whatsoever other
malicious thing; and desired the angry man might be discharged,
since he had so just a provocation as the loss of a mistress. So all
laughing at the jest, that had made so great a noise among the grave
and wise, they freed them all: and *Sebastian* advised his nephew,
that the next cuckold he made, he would make a friend of him first,
that he might hear of no more complaints against him. But *Octavio*
very gravely replied; 'Sir, you have infinitely mistaken the character
of this lady, she is a person of too great quality for this raillery; at
more leisure you shall have her story.' While he was speaking this,
and their discharges were making, *Sylvia* confounded with shame,
indignation, and anger, goes out, and taking *Octavio*'s coach that
stood at the gate, went directly to his house; for she resolved to go
no more where *Brilliard* was. After this, *Sebastian* fell seriously to
good advice, and earnestly besought his darling to leave off those
wild extravagancies that had so long made so great a discourse all
the province over, where nothing but his splendid amours, treats,
balls, and magnificences of love, was the business of the town, and
that he had forborne to tell him of it, and had hitherto justified his
actions, though they had not deserved it; and he doubted this was
the lady to whom for these six or eight months he heard he had
so entirely dedicated himself. He desires him to quit this lady, or if
he will pursue his love, to do it discreetly, to love some unmarried
woman, and not injure his neighbours; to all which he blushed and
bowed, and silently seemed to thank him for his grave counsel. And
Brilliard having received his discharge, and advice how he provoked
the displeasure of the *States* any more, by accusing of great persons,
he was ordered to ask *Octavio*'s pardon; but, in lieu of that, he came

up to him, and challenged him to fight him for the injustice he had done him, in taking from him his wife; for he was sure he was undone in her favour, and that thought made him mad enough to put himself on this second extravagancy: however, this was not so silently managed but *Sebastian* perceived it, and was so enraged at the young fellow for his second insolence, that he was again confined, and sent back to prison, where he swore he should suffer the utmost of the law; and the Council breaking up, every one departed to his own home. But never was man ravished with excess of joy as *Octavio* was, to find *Sylvia* meet him with extended arms on the stair-case, whom he did not imagine to have found there, nor knew he how he stood in the heart of the charmer of his own, since the affront she had received in the court from those that however did not know her; for they did not imagine this was that lady, sister to *Philander*, of whose beauty they had heard so much, and her face being turned from the light, the old gentleman did not so much consider or see it. *Sylvia* came into his house the back way, through the stables and garden, and had the good fortune to be seen by none of his family but the coachman, who brought her home, whom she conjured not to speak of it to the rest of his servants: and unseen of any body she got into his apartment, for often she had been there at treats and balls with *Philander*. She was alone; for *Antonet* stayed to see what became of her false lover, and, after he was seized again, retired to her lodging the most disconsolate woman in the world, for having lost her hopes of *Brilliard*, to whom she had engaged all that honour she had. But when she missed her lady there, she accused herself with all the falsehood in the world, and fell to repent her treachery. She sends the page to inquire at *Ocatvio*'s house, but no body there could give him any intelligence; so that the poor amorous youth returning without hope, endured all the pain of a hopeless lover; for *Octavio* had anew charmed his coachman: and calling up an ancient woman who was his house-keeper, who had been his nurse, he acquainted her with the short history of his passion for *Sylvia*, and ordered her to give her attendance on the treasure of his life; he bid her prepare all things as magnificent as she could in that apartment he designed her, which was very rich and gay, and towards a fine garden. The hangings and beds all glorious, and fitter for a monarch than a subject; the finest pictures the world afforded, flowers in-laid with silver and ivory, gilded roofs, carved wainscot, tables of plate, with all the rest of the movables in the chambers of the same, all of great value, and all was perfumed like an altar, or the marriage bed of some young king. Here *Sylvia* was designed to lodge, and hither *Octavio* conducted her; and setting her on a couch while the supper was getting ready, he sits himself down by her, and his heart being ready to burst with grief, at the thought of the claim which was laid to her by *Brilliard*, he silently views her, while tears were ready to break from his fixed eyes, and sighs stopped what he would fain have spoke; while she (wholly confounded with shame, guilt, and disappointment, for she could not imagine that *Brilliard* could have had the impudence to have claimed her for a wife) fixed her fair eyes to the earth, and durst not behold the languishing *Octavio*. They remained thus a long time silent, she not daring to defend herself from a crime, of which she knew too well she was guilty, nor he daring to ask her a question to which the answer might prove so fatal; he fears to know what he dies to be satisfied in, and she fears to discover too late a secret, which was the only one she had concealed from him. *Octavio* runs over in his mind a thousand thoughts that perplex him, of the probability of her being married; he considers how often he had found her with that happy young man, who more freely entertained her than servants use to do. He now considers how he had seen them once on a bed together, when *Sylvia* was in the disorder of a yielding mistress, and *Brilliard* of a ravished lover; he considers how he has found them alone at cards and dice, and often entertaining her with freedoms of a husband, and how he wholly managed her affairs, commanded her servants like their proper master, and was in full authority of all. These, and a thousand more circumstances, confirm *Octavio* in all his fears: a thousand times she is about to speak, but either fear to lose *Octavio* by clear confession, or to run herself into farther error by denying the matter of fact, stops her words, and she only blushes and sighs at what she dares not tell; and if by chance their speaking eyes meet, they would both decline them hastily again, as afraid to find there what their language could not confess. Sometimes he would press her hand and sigh. —'Ah, *Sylvia*, you have undone my quiet'; to which she would return no answer, but sigh, and now rising from the couch, she walked about the chamber as sad and silent as death, attending when he should have advanced in speaking to her, though she dreads the voice she wishes to hear, and he waits for her reply, though the mouth that he adores should deliver poison and daggers to his heart. While thus they remained in the most silent and sad entertainment (that ever was between lovers that had so much to say) the page, which *Octavio* only trusts to wait, brought him this letter.

BRILLIARD *to* OCTAVIO.

My Lord,

I am too sensible of my many high offences to your lordship, and have as much penitence for my sin committed towards you as it is possible to conceive; but when I implore a pardon from a lover, who by his own passion may guess at the violent effects of my despairing flame, I am yet so vain to hope it. *Antonet* gave me the intelligence of your design, and raised me up to a madness that hurried me to that barbarity against your unspotted honour. I own the baseness of the fact, but lovers are not, my lord, always guided by rules of justice and reason; or, if I had, I should have killed the fair adulteress that drew you to your undoing, and who merits more your hate than your regard; and who having first violated her marriage-vow to me with *Philander*, would sacrifice us both to you, and at the same time betray you to a marriage that cannot but prove fatal to you, as it is most unlawful in her; so that, my lord, if I have injured you, I have at the same time saved you from a sin and ruin, and humbly implore that you will suffer the good I have rendered you in the last, to atone for the ill I did you in the first. If I have accused you of a design against the State, it was to save you from that of the too subtle and too charming *Sylvia*, which none but myself could have snatched you from. It is true, I might have acted something more worthy of my birth and education; but, my lord, I knew the power of *Sylvia*; and if I should have sent you the knowledge of this, when I sent the warrant for the security of your person, the haughty creature would have prevailed above all my truths with the eloquence of love, and you had yielded and been betrayed worse by her, than by the most ungenerous measures I took to prevent it. Suffer this reason, my lord, to plead for me in that heart where *Sylvia* reigns, and shews how powerful she is every where. Pardon all the faults of a most unfortunate man undone by love, and by your own, guess what his passion would put him on, who aims or wishes at least for the entire possession of *Sylvia*, though it was never absolutely hoped by the most unfortunate

BRILLIARD.

At the beginning of this letter *Octavio* hoped it contained the confession of his fault in claiming *Sylvia*; he hoped he would have owned it done in order to his service to his lord, or his love to *Sylvia*, or any thing but what it really was; but when he read on — and found that he yet confirmed his claim, he yielded to all the grief that could sink a heart over-burdened with violent love; he fell down on the couch where he was sat, and only calling *Sylvia* with a dying groan, he held out his hand, in which the letter remained, and looked on her with eyes that languished with death, love, and despair; while she, who already feared from whom it came, received it with disdain, shame, and confusion: and *Octavio* recovering a little — cried in a faint voice —'See charming, cruel fair — see how much my soul adores you, when even this — cannot extinguish one spark of the flame you have kindled in my soul.' At this she blushed, and bowed with a graceful modesty that was like to have given the lie to all the accusations against her: she reads the letter, while he greedily fixes his eyes upon her face as she reads, observing with curious search every motion there, all killing and adorable. He saw her blushes sometimes rise, then sink again to their proper fountain, her heart; there swell and rise, and beat against her breast that had no other covering than a thin shirt, for all her bosom was open, and betrayed the nimble motion of her heart. Her eyes sometimes would sparkle with disdain, and glow upon the fatal tell-tale lines, and sometimes languish with excess of grief: but having concluded the letter, she laid it on the table, and began again to traverse the room, her head declined, and her arms a-cross her bosom, *Octavio* made too true an interpretation of this silence and calm in *Sylvia*, and no longer doubted his fate. He fixes his eyes eternally upon her, while she considers what she shall say to that afflicted lover; she considers *Philander* lost, or if he ever returns, it is not to love; to that he was for ever gone; for too well she knew no arts, obligations, or industry, could retrieve a flying *Cupid*: she found, if even that could return, his whole fortune was so exhausted he could not support her; and that she was of a nature so haughty and impatient of injuries, that she could never forgive him those affronts he had done her honour first, and now her love; she resolves no law or force shall submit her to *Brilliard*; she finds this fallacy she had put on *Octavio*, has ruined her credit in his esteem, at least she justly fears it; so that believing herself abandoned by all in a strange country, she fell to weeping her fate, and the tears wet the floor as she walked: at which sight so melting *Octavio* starts from the couch, and catching her in his trembling arms, he cried, 'Be false, be cruel, and deceitful; yet still I must, I am compelled to adore you ——' This being spoken in so hearty and resolved a tone, from a man of whose heart she was so sure, and knew to be generous, gave her a little courage — and like sinking men she catches at all that presents her any hope of escaping. She resolves by discovering the whole truth to save that last stake, his heart, though she could pretend to no more; and taking the fainting lover by the hand, she leads him to the couch: 'Well,' said she, '*Octavio*, you are too generous to be imposed on in any thing, and therefore I will tell you my heart without reserve as absolutely as to heaven itself, if I were interceding my last peace there.' She begged a thousand pardons of him for having concealed any part of her story from him, but she could no longer be guilty of that crime, to a man for whom she had so perfect a passion; and as she spoke she embraced him with an irresistible softness that wholly charmed him: she reconciles him with every touch, and sighs on his bosom a thousand grateful vows and excuses for her fault, while he weeps his love, and almost expires in her arms; she is not able to see his passion and his grief, and tells him she will do all things for his repose. 'Ah, *Sylvia*' sighed he, 'talk not of my repose, when you confess yourself wife to one and mistress to another, in either of which I have alas no part: ah, what is reserved for the unfortunate *Octavio*, when two happy lovers divide the treasure of his soul? Yet tell me truth, because it will look like love; shew me that excellent virtue so rarely found in all your fickle sex. O! tell me truth, and let me know how much my heart can bear before it break with love; and yet, perhaps, to hear thee speak to me, with that insinuating dear voice of thine, may save me from the terror of thy words; and though each make a wound, their very accents have a balm to heal! O quickly pour it then into my listening soul, and I will be silent as over-ravished lovers, whom joys have charmed to tender sighs and pantings.' At this, embracing her anew, he let fall a shower of tears upon her bosom, and sighing, cried —'Now I attend thy story': she then began anew the repetition of the loves between herself and *Philander*, which she slightly ran over, because he had already heard every circumstance of it, both from herself and *Philander*; till she arrived to that part of it where she left *Bellfont*, her father's house: 'Thus far,' said she, 'you have had a faithful relation; and I was no sooner missed by my parents, but you may imagine the diligent search that would be made, both by *Foscario*, whom I was to have married the next day, and my tender parents; but all search, all *hue-and-cries* were vain; at last, they put me into the weekly *Gazette*, describing me to the very features of my face, my hair, my breast, my stature, youth, and beauty, omitting nothing that might render me apparent to all that should see me, offering vast sums to any that should give intelligence of such a lost maid of quality. *Philander*, who understood too well the nature of the common people, and that they would betray their very fathers for such a proffered sum, durst trust me no longer to their mercy: his affairs were so involved with those of *Cesario*, he could not leave *Paris*; for they every moment expected the people should rise against their king, and those glorious chiefs of the faction were obliged to wait and watch the motions of the dirty crowd. Nor durst he trust me in any place from him; for he could not live a day without me'; (at that thought she sighed, and then went on); 'so that I was obliged to remain obscurely lodged in *Paris*, where now I durst no longer trust myself, though disguised in as many shapes as I was obliged to have lodgings. At last we were betrayed, and had only the short notice given us to yield, or secure ourselves from the hand of justice by the next morning, when they designed to surprise us. To escape we found almost impossible, and very hazardous to attempt it; so that *Philander*, who was raving with fears, called myself and this young gentleman, *Brilliard* (then Master of his Horse) and one that had served us faithfully through the whole course of our lives, to council: many things were in vain debated, but at last this hard shift was found out of marrying me to *Brilliard*, for to *Philander* it was impossible; so that no authority of a father could take me from the husband. I was at first extremely unwilling, but when *Philander* told me it was to be only a mock-marriage, to secure me to himself, I was reconciled to it, and more when I found the infinite submission of the young man, who vowed he would never look up to me with the eyes of a lover or husband, but in obedience to his lord did it to preserve me entirely for him; nay farther, to secure my future fear, he confessed to me he was already married to a gentlewoman by whom he had two children.' 'Oh! —— tell me true, my *Sylvia*, was he married to another!' cried out the overjoyed lover. 'Yes, on my life,' replied *Sylvia*; 'for when it was proved in court that I was married to *Brilliard* (as at last I was, and innocently bedded) this lady came and brought her children to me, and falling at my feet, wept and implored I would not own her husband, for only she had right to him; we all were forced to discover to her the truth of the matter, and that he had only married me to secure me from the rage of my parents, that if he were her husband she was still as entirely possessed of him as ever, and that he had advanced her fortune in what he had done, for she should have him restored with those advantages that should make her life, and that of her children more comfortable; and *Philander* making both her and the children considerable presents, sent her away very well satisfied. After this, before people, we used him to a thousand freedoms, but when alone, he retained his respect entire; however, this used him to something more familiarity than formerly, and he grew to be more a companion than a servant, as indeed we desired he should, and of late have found him more presumptuous than usual. And thus much more, I must confess, I have reason to believe him a most passionate lover, and have lately found he had designs upon me, as you well know.

'Judge now, oh dear *Octavio*, how unfortunate I am; yet judge too, whether I ought to esteem this a marriage, or him a husband?' 'No,' replied *Octavio*, more briskly than before, 'nor can he by the laws of God or man pretend to such a blessing, and you may be divorced.' Pleased with this thought, he soon assumed his native temper of joy and softness, and making a thousand new vows that he would perform all he had sworn on his part, and imploring and pressing her to renew those she had made to him, she obeys him; she makes a thousand grateful returns, and they pass the evening the most happily that ever lovers did. By this time supper was served up, noble and handsome, and after supper, he led her to his closet, where he presented her with jewels and other rarities of great value, and omitted nothing that might oblige an avaricious designing woman, if *Sylvia* had been such; nor any thing that might beget love and gratitude in the most insensible heart: and all he did, and all he gave, was with a peculiar grace, in which there lies as great an obligation as in the gift itself: the handsome way of giving being an art so rarely known, even to the most generous. In these happy and glorious moments of love, wherein the lover omitted nothing that could please, *Philander* was almost forgotten; for it is natural for love to beget love, and inconstancy its likeness or disdain: and we must conclude *Sylvia* a maid wholly insensible, if she had not been touched with tenderness, and even love itself, at all these extravagant marks of passion in *Octavio*; and it must be confessed she was of a nature soft and apt for impression; she was, in a word, a woman. She had her vanities and her little foiblesses, and loved to see adorers at her feet, especially those in whom all things, all graces, charms of youth, wit and fortune agreed to form for love and conquest: she naturally loved power and dominion, and it was her maxim, that never any woman was displeased to find she could beget desire.

It was thus they lived with uninterrupted joys, no spies to pry upon their actions, no false friends to censure their real pleasures, no rivals to poison their true content, no parents to give bounds or grave rules to the destruction of nobler lavish love; but all the day was passed in new delights, and every day produced a thousand pleasures; and even the thoughts of revenge were no more remembered on either side; it lessened in *Sylvia*'s heart as love advanced there, and her resentment against *Philander* was lost in her growing passion for *Octavio*: and sure if any woman had excuses for loving and inconstancy, the most wise and prudent must allow them now to *Sylvia*; and if she had reason for loving it was now, for what she paid the most deserving of his sex, and whom she managed with that art of loving (if there be art in love) that she gained every minute upon his heart, and he became more and more her slave, the more he found he was beloved: in spite of all *Brilliard*'s pretension he would have married her, but durst not do it while he remained in *Holland*, because of the noise *Brilliard*'s claim had made, and he feared the displeasure of his uncle; but waited for a more happy time, when he could settle his affairs so as to remove her into *Flanders*, though he could not tell how to accomplish that without ruining his interest: these thoughts alone took up his time whenever he was absent from *Sylvia*, and would often give him abundance of trouble; for he was given over to his wish of possessing of *Sylvia*, and could not live without her; he loved too much, and thought and considered too little. These were his eternal entertainments when from the lovely object of his desire, which was as seldom as possible; for they were both unwilling to part, though decency and rest required it, a thousand soft things would hinder him, and make her willing to retain him, and though they were to meet again next morning, they grudge themselves the parting hours, and the repose of nature. He longs and languishes for the blessed moment that shall give him to the arms of the ravishing *Sylvia*, and she finds but too much yielding on her part in some of those silent lone hours, when love was most prevailing, and feeble mortals most apt to be overcome by that insinuating god; so that though *Octavio* could not ask what he sighed and died for, though for the safety of his life, for any favours; and though, on the other side, *Sylvia* resolved she would not grant, no, though mutual vows had passed, though love within pleaded, and almost irresistible beauties and inducements without, though all the powers of love, of silence, night and opportunity, though on the very point a thousand times of yielding, she had resisted all: but oh! one night; let it not rise up in judgement against her, ye bashful modest maids, who never yet tried any powerful minute; nor ye chaste wives, who give no opportunities; one night —— they lost themselves in dalliance, forgot how very near they were to yielding, and with imperfect transports found themselves half dead with love, clasped in each other's arms, betrayed by soft degrees of joy to all they wished. It would be too amorous to tell you more; to tell you all that night, that happy night produced; let it suffice that *Sylvia* yielded all, and made *Octavio* happier than a god. At first, he found her weeping in his arms, raving on what she had inconsiderately done, and with her soft reproaches chiding her ravished lover, who lay sighing by; unable to reply any other way, he held her fast in those arms that trembled yet, with love and new-past joy; he found a pleasure even in her railing, with a tenderness that spoke more love than any other language love could speak. Betwixt his sighs he pleads his right of love, and the authority of his solemn vows; he tells her that the marriage-ceremony was but contrived to satisfy the ignorant, and to proclaim his title to the crowd, but vows and contracts were the same to heaven: he speaks —— and she believes; and well she might; for all he spoke was honourable truth. He knew no guile, but uttered all his soul, and all that soul was honest, just and brave; thus by degrees he brought her to a calm.

In this soft rencounter, he had discovered a thousand new charms in *Sylvia*, and contrary to those men whose end of love is lust (which extinguish together) *Octavio* found increase of tenderness from every bliss she gave; and grew at last so fond — so doting on the still more charming maid, that he neglected all his interest, his business in the State, and what he owed his uncle, and his friends, and became the common theme over all the United Provinces, for his wantonness and luxury, as they were pleased to call it, and living so contrary to the humour of those more sordid and slovenly men of quality, which make up the nobility of that parcel of the world. For while thus he lived retired, scarce visiting any one, or permitting any one to visit him, they charge him with a thousand crimes of having given himself over to effeminacy; as indeed he grew too lazy in her arms; neglecting glory, arms, and power, for the more real joys of life; while she even rifles him with extravagancy; and grows so bold and hardy, that regarding not the humours of the stingy censorious nation, his interest, or her own fame, she is seen every day in his coaches, going to take the air out of town; puts him upon balls, and vast expensive treats; devises new projects and ways of diversion, till some of the more busy impertinents of the town made a public complaint to his uncle, and the rest of the *States*, urging he was a scandal to the reverend and honourable society. On which it was decreed, that he should either lose that honour, or take up, and live more according to the gravity and authority of a senator: this incensed *Sebastian*, both against the *States* and his nephew; for though he had often reproved and counselled him; yet he scorned his darling should be schooled by his equals in power. So that resolving either to discard him, or draw him from the love of this woman; he one morning goes to his nephew's house, and sending him up word by his page he would speak to him, he was conducted to his chamber, where he found him in his night-gown: he began to upbraid him, first, with his want of respect and duty to him, and next, of his affairs, neglecting to give his attendance on the public: he tells him he is become a scandal to the commonwealth, and that he lived a lewd life with another man's wife: he tells him he has all her story, and she was not only a wife, but a scandalous mistress too to *Philander*. 'She boasts,' says he, 'of honourable birth; but what is that, when her conduct is infamous? In short, sir,' continued he, 'your life is obnoxious to the whole province: why what, sir —— cannot honest men's daughters' (cried he more angrily) 'serve your turn, but you must crack a Commandment? Why, this is flat adultery: a little fornication in a civil way might have been allowed, but this is stark naught. In fine, sir, quit me this woman, and quit her presently; or, in the first place, I renounce thee, cast thee from me as a stranger, and will leave thee to ruin, and the incensed *States*. A little pleasure — a little recreation, I can allow: a layer of love, and a layer of business — But to neglect the nation for a wench, is flat treason against the State; and I wish there were a law against all such unreasonable whore-masters — that are statesmen — for the rest it is no great matter. Therefore, in a word, sir, leave me off this mistress of yours, or we will secure her yet for a *French* spy, that comes to debauch our commonwealth's men —— The *States* can do it, sir, they can ——' Hitherto *Octavio* received all with a blush and bow, in sign of obedience; but when his uncle told him the *States* would send away his mistress; no longer able to contain his rage, he broke out into all the violence imaginable against them, and swore he would not now forgo *Sylvia* to be monarch over all the nasty provinces, and it was a greater glory to be a slave at her feet. 'Go, tell your *States*,' cried he — 'they are a company of cynical fops, born to moil on in sordid business, who never were worthy to understand so great a happiness of life as that of nobler love. Tell them, I scorn the dull gravity of those asses of the commonwealth, fit only to bear the dirty load of State-affairs, and die old busy fools.' The uncle, who little expected such a return from him who used to be all obedience, began more gently to persuade him with more solid reason, but could get no other answer from him, than that what he commanded he should find it difficult to disobey; and so for that time they parted. Some days after (he never coming so much as near their Councils) they sent for him to answer the contempt: he came, and received abundance of hard reproaches, and finding they were resolved to degrade him, he presently rallied them in answer to all they said; nor could all the cautions of his friends persuade him to any submission, after receiving so rough and ill-bred a treatment as they gave him: and impatient to return to *Sylvia*, where all his joys were centred, he was with much ado persuaded to stay and hear the resolution of the Council, which was to take from him those honours he held amongst them; at which he cocked and smiled, and told them he received what he was much more proud of, than of those useless trifles they called honours, and wishes they might treat all that served them at that ungrateful rate: for he that had received a hundred wounds, and lost a stream of blood for their security, shall, if he kiss their wives against their wills, be banished like a coward: so hasting from the Council, he got into his coach and went to *Sylvia*.

This incensed the old gentlemen to a high degree, and they carried it against the younger party (because more in number) that this *French* lady, who was for high-treason, as they called it, forced to fly *France*, should be no longer protected in *Holland*. And in order to her removal, or rather their revenge on *Octavio*, they sent out their

warrant to apprehend her; and either to send her as an enemy to
France, or force her to some other part of the world. For a day or two
Sebastian's interest prevailed for the stopping the warrant, believing
he should be able to bring his nephew to some submission; which
when he found in vain, he betook himself to his chamber, and refused
any visits or diversions: by this time, *Octavio*'s rallying the *States* was
become the jest of the town, and all the sparks laughed at them as
they passed, and lampooned them to damnable *Dutch* tunes, which
so highly incensed them, that they sent immediately, and served the
warrant on *Sylvia*, whom they surprised in *Octavio*'s coach as she
was coming from taking the air. You may imagine what an agony of
trouble and grief our generous and surprised lover was in: it was in
vain to make resistance, and he who before would not have submitted
to have saved his life, to the *States*, now for the preservation of one
moment's content to *Sylvia*, was ready to go and fall at their feet,
kiss their shoes, and implore their pity. He first accompanies her to
the house of the messenger, where he only is permitted to behold
her with eyes of dying love, and unable to say any thing to her, left
her with such gifts, and charge to the messenger's care, as might
oblige him to treat her well; while *Sylvia* less surprised, bid him, at
going from her, not to afflict himself for any thing she suffered; she
found it was the malice of the peevish old magistrates, and that the
most they could do to her, was to send her from him. This last she
spoke with a sigh, that pierced his heart more sensibly than ever any
thing yet had done; and he only replied (with a sigh) 'No, *Sylvia*,
no rigid power on earth shall ever be able to deprive you of my
eternal adoration, or to separate me one moment from *Sylvia*, after
she is compelled to leave this ungrateful place; and whose departure
I will hasten all that I can, since the land is not worthy of so great
a blessing.' So leaving her for a little space, he hasted to his uncle,
whom he found very much discontented: he throws himself at his
feet, and assails him with all the moving eloquence of sighs and
tears; in vain was all, in vain alas he pleads. From this he flies to
rage — and says all a distracted lover could pour forth to ease a
tortured heart; what divinity did he not provoke? Wholly regardless
even of heaven and man, he made a public confession of his passion,

denied her being married to *Brilliard*, and weeps as he protests her innocence: he kneels again, implores and begs anew, and made the movingest moan that ever touched a heart, but could receive no other return but threats and frowns: the old gentleman had never been in love since he was born, no not enough to marry, but bore an unaccountable hate to the whole sex, and therefore was pitiless to all he could say on the score of love; though he endeavours to soften him by a thousand things more dear to him. 'For my sake, sir,' said he, 'if ever my lost plea were grateful to you, when all your joy was in the young *Octavio*; release, release the charming *Sylvia*; regard her tender youth, her blooming beauty, her timorous helpless sex, her noble quality, and save her from rude assaults of power —— Oh save the lovely maid!' Thus he uttered with interrupting sighs and tears, which fell upon the floor as he pursued the obdurate on his knees: at last pity touched his heart, and he said —'Spare, sir, the character of your enchanting *Circe*; for I have heard too much of her, and what mischief she has bred in *France*, abandoning her honour, betraying a virtuous sister, defaming her noble parents, and ruining an illustrious young nobleman, who was both her brother and her lover. This, sir, in short, is the character of your beauteous innocent.' 'Alas, sir,' replied *Octavio*, 'you never saw this maid; or if you had, you would not be so cruel.' 'Go to, sir,' replied the old gentleman, 'I am not so soon softened at the sight of beauty.' 'But do but see her, sir,' replied *Octavio*, 'and then perhaps you will be charmed like me ——' 'You are a fop, sir,' replied *Sebastian*, 'and if you would have me allow any favour to your enchanting lady, you must promise me first to abandon her, and marry the widow of Monsieur —— who is vastly rich, and whom I have so often recommended to you; she loves you too, and though she be not fair, she has the best fortune of any lady in the *Netherlands*. On these terms, sir, I am for a reconciliation with you, and will immediately go and deliver the fair prisoner; and she shall have her liberty to go or stay, or do what she please — and now, sir, you know my will and pleasure'— *Octavio* found it in vain to pursue him any farther with his petitions; only replied, it was wondrous hard and cruel. To which the old one replied; 'It is what must be done; I have resolved it, or my estate, in value above two hundred thousand pounds, shall be disposed of to your sister, the Countess of *Clarinau:*' and this he ended with an execration on himself if he did not do; and he was a man that always was just to his word.

Much more to this ungrateful effect he spoke, and *Octavio* had recourse to all the dissimulation his generous soul was capable of; and it was the first base thing, and sure the last that ever he was guilty of. He promises his uncle to obey all his commands and injunctions, since he would have it so; and only begged he might be permitted but one visit, to take his last leave of her. This was at first refused, but at last, provided he might hear what he said to her, he would suffer him to go: 'For,' said the crafty old man, (who knew too well the cunning of youth,) 'I will have no tricks put upon me; I will not be outwitted by a young knave:' this was the worst part of all; he knew, if he alone could speak with her, they might have contrived, by handsome agreeing flattery, to have accomplished their design; which was, first, by the authority of the old gentleman to have freed her from confinement; and next, to have settled his affairs in the best posture he could, and without valuing his uncle's fortune, his own being greater, he resolved to go with her into *Flanders* or *Italy*; but his going with him to visit her would prevent whatever they might resolve: but since the liberty of *Sylvia* was first to be considered, he resolves, since it must be so and leaves the rest to time and his good fortune. 'Well then, sir,' said *Octavio*, 'since you have resolved yourself, to be a witness of those melancholy things, I shall possibly say to her, let us haste to end the great affair'—'Hang it,' cried *Sebastian*, 'if I go I shall abuse the young hussy, or commit some indecency that will not be suitable to good manners ——' 'I hope you will, sir'—— replied *Octavio*——'Whip them, whip them,' replied the uncle, 'I hate the young cozening baggages, that wander about the world undoing young and extravagant coxcombs; gots so they are naught, stark naught —— Be sure dispatch as soon as you can; and — do you hear — let's have no whining.' *Octavio*, overjoyed he should have her released to-night, promised lavishly all he was urged to: and his coach being at the gate, they both went immediately to the house of the messenger; all the way the old gentleman did nothing but rail against the vices of the age, and the sins of villainous youth; the snares of beauty, and the danger of witty women; and of how ill consequences these were to a commonwealth. He said, if he were to make laws he would confine all young women to monasteries, where they should never see man till forty, and then come out and marry for generation-sake, no more: for his part, he had never seen the beauty that yet could inspire him with that silly thing called love; and wondered what the devil ailed all the young fellows of this age, that they talked of nothing else. At this rate they discoursed till they arrived at the prison, and calling for the messenger, he conducted them both to the chamber of the fair prisoner, who was laid on a couch, near which stood a table with two candles, which gave a great light to that part of the room, and made *Sylvia* appear more fair than ever, if possible. She had not that day been dressed but in a rich night-gown, and cornets of the most advantageous fashion. At his approach she blushed (with a secret joy, which never had possessed her soul for him before) and spread a thousand beauties round her fair face. She was leaping with a transported pleasure to his arms, when she perceived an old grave person follow him into the room; at which she reassumed a strangeness, a melancholy languishment, which charmed no less than her gaiety. She approaches them with a modest grace in her beautiful eyes; and by the reception *Octavio* gave her, she found that reverend person was his uncle, or at least somebody of authority; and therefore assuming a gravity unusual, she received them with all the ceremony due to their quality: and first, she addressed herself to the old gentleman, who stood gazing at her, without motion; at which she was a little out of countenance. When *Octavio* perceiving it, approached his uncle and cried, 'Sir, this is the lady ——' *Sebastian*, starting as from a dream, cried —'Pardon me, madam, I am a fellow whom age hath rendered less ceremonious than youth: I have never yet been so happy as to have been used to a fair lady. Women never took up one minute of my more precious time, but I have been a satyr upon the whole sex; and, if my treatment of you be rougher than your birth and beauty merits, I beseech you —— fair creature, pardon it, since I come in order to do you service.' 'Sir,' replied *Sylvia*, (blushing with anger at the presence of a man who had contributed to the having brought her to that place) 'I cannot but wonder at this sudden change of goodness, in a person to whom I am indebted for part of my misfortune, and which I shall no longer esteem as such, since it has occasioned me a happiness, and an honour, to which I could no other way have arrived.' This last she spoke with her usual insinuating charms; the little affectation of the voice sweetened to all the tenderness it was possible to put on, and so easy and natural to *Sylvia*: and if before the old gentleman were seized with some unusual pleasure, which before he never felt about his icy and insensible heart, and which now began to thaw at the fire of her eyes —— l say, if before he were surprised with looking, what was he when she spoke — with a voice so soft, and an air so bewitching? He was all eyes and ears, and had use of no other sense but what informed those. He gazes upon her, as if he waited and listened what she would farther say, and she stood waiting for his reply, till ashamed, she turned her eyes into her bosom, and knew not how to proceed. *Octavio* views both by turns, and knows not how to begin the discourse again, it being his uncle's cue to speak: but finding him altogether mute — he steps to him, and gently pulled him by the sleeve — but finds no motion in him; he speaks to him, but in vain; for he could hear nothing but *Sylvia*'s charming voice, nor saw nothing but her lovely face, nor attended any thing but when she would speak again, and look that way. At this *Octavio* smiled, and taking his adorable by the hand, he led her nearer her admiring adversary; whom she approached with modesty and sweetness in her eyes, that the old fellow, having never before beheld the like vision, was wholly vanquished, and his old heart burnt in the socket, which being his last blaze made the greater fire. 'Fine lady,' cried he —'or rather fine angel, how is it I shall expiate for a barbarity that nothing could be guilty of but the brute, who had not learned humanity from your eyes: what atonement can I make for my sin; and how shall I be punished?' 'Sir,' replied *Sylvia*, 'if I can merit your esteem and assistance, to deliver me from this cruel confinement, I shall think of what is past as a joy, since it renders me worthy of your pity and compassion.' 'To answer you, madam, were to hold you under this unworthy roof too long; therefore let me convince you of my service, by leading you to a place more fit for so fair a person.' And calling for the messenger, he asked him if he would take his bail for his fair prisoner? Who replied, 'Your lordship may command all things:' so throwing him a little purse, about thirty pounds in gold, he bid him drink the lady's health; and without more ceremony or talk, led her to the coach; and never so much as asking her whether she would go, insensibly carries her, where he had a mind to have her, to his own house. This was a little affliction to *Octavio*, who nevertheless durst not say any thing to his uncle, nor so much as ask him the reason why: but being arrived all thither, he conducts her to a very fair apartment, and bid her there command that world he could command for her: he gave her there a very magnificent supper, and all three supped together. *Octavio* could not imagine that his uncle, who was a single man, and a grave senator, one famed for a womanhater, a great railer at the vices of young men, should keep a fair, young, single woman in his house: but it growing late, and no preparation for her departing, she took the courage to say —'Sir, I am so extremely obliged to you, and have received so great a favour from you, that I cannot flatter myself it is for any virtue in me, or merely out of compassion to my sex, that you have done this; but for some body's sake, to whom I am more engaged than I am aware of; and when you passed your parole for my liberty, I am not so vain to think it was for my sake; therefore pray inform me, sir, how I can pay this debt, and to whom; and who it is you require should be bound for me, to save you harmless.' 'Madam,' cried *Sebastian*, 'though there need no greater security than your own innocence, yet lest that innocence should not be sufficient to guard you from the outrage of a people approaching to savages, I beg, for your own security, not mine, that you will make this house your sanctuary; my power can save you from impending harms; and all that I call mine, you shall command.' At this she blushing bowed, but durst not make reply to contradict him: she knew, at least, that there she was safe and well, from fear of the tyranny of the rest, or any other apprehension. It is true, she found, by the shyness of *Octavio* towards her before his uncle, that she was to manage her amour with him by stealth, till they could contrive matters more to their advantage: she therefore finding she should want nothing, but as much of *Octavio*'s conversation as she desired, she begged he would give her leave to write a note to her page, who was a faithful, sober youth, to bring her jewels and what things she had of value to her, which he did, and received those and her servants together; but *Antonet* had like to have lost her place, but that *Octavio* pleaded for her, and she herself confessing it was love to the false *Brilliard* that made her do that foolish thing (in which she vowed she thought no harm, though it was like to have cost her so dear) she was again received into favour: so that for some days *Sylvia* found herself very much at her ease with the old gentleman, and had no want of any thing but *Octavio*'s company: but she had the pleasure to find, by his eyes and sighs, he wanted hers more: he died every day, and his fair face faded like falling roses: still she was gay; for if she had it not about her, she assumed it to keep him in heart: she was not displeased to see the old man on fire too, and fancied some diversion from the intrigue. But he concealed his passion all he could, both to hide it from his nephew, and because he knew not what he ailed. A strange change he found, a wondrous disorder in nature, but could not give a name to it, nor sigh aloud for fear he should be heard, and lose his reputation; especially for this woman, on whom he had railed so lavishly. One day therefore, after a night of torment, very incommode to his age, he takes *Octavio* into the garden alone, telling him he had a great secret to impart to him. *Octavio* guessing what it might be, put his heart in as good order as he could to receive it. He at least knew the worst was but for him at last to steal *Sylvia* from him, if he should be weak enough to dote on the young charmer, and therefore resolved to hear with patience. But if he were prepared to attend, the other was not prepared to begin, and so both walked many silent turns about the garden. *Sebastian* had a mind to ask a thousand questions of his nephew, who he found, maugre all his vows of deserting *Sylvia*, had no power of doing it: he had a mind to urge him to marry the widow, but durst not now press it, though he used to do so, lest he should take it for jealousy in him; nor durst he now forbid him seeing her, lest he should betray the secrets of his soul: he began every moment to love him less, as he loved *Sylvia* more, and beholds him as an enemy to his repose, nay his very life. At last the old man (who thought if he brought his nephew forth under pretence of a secret, and said nothing to him, it would have looked ill) began to speak. '*Octavio*,' said he, 'I have hitherto found you so just in all you have said, that it were a sin to doubt you in what relates to *Sylvia*. You have told me she is nobly born; and you have with infinite imprecations convinced me she is virtuous; and lastly, you have sworn she was not married'—— At this he sighed and paused, and left *Octavio* trembling with fear of the result: a thousand times he was like to have denied all, but durst not defame the most sacred idol of his soul: sometimes he thought his uncle would be generous, and think it fit to give him *Sylvia*; but that thought was too seraphic to remain a moment in his heart. 'Sir,' replied *Octavio*, 'I own I said so of *Sylvia*, and hope no action she has committed since she had a protection under your roof has contradicted any thing I said. 'No,' said *Sebastian*, sighing — and pausing, as loath to speak more: 'Sir,' said *Octavio*, 'I suppose this is not the secret you had to impart to me, for which you separate me to this lonely walk; fear not to trust me with it, whatever it be; for I am so entirely your own, that I will grant, submit, prostrate myself, and give up all my will, power, and faculties to your interest or designs.' This encouraged the old lover, who replied —'Tell me one truth, *Octavio*, which I require of you, and I will desire no more —— have not you had the possession of this fair maid? You apprehend me.' Now it was that he feared what design the amorous old gentleman had in his head and heart; and was at a loss what to say, whether to give him some jealousy that he had known and possessed her, and so prevent his designs on her; or by saying he had not, to leave her defenceless to his love. But on second thoughts, he could not resolve to say any thing to the disadvantage of *Sylvia*, though to save his own life; and therefore assured his uncle, he never durst assume the boldness to ask so rude a question of a woman of quality: and much more he spoke to that purpose to convince him: that it is true, he would have married her, if he could have gained his consent; maugre all the scandal that the malicious world had thrown upon her. But since he was positive in his command for the widow, he would bend his mind to obedience. 'In that,' replied *Sebastian*, 'you are wise, and

I am glad all your youthful fires are blown over; and having once fixed you in the world as I design, I have resolved on an affair ——' At this again he paused ——'I am,' says he, 'in love — I think it is love, or that which you call so: I cannot eat, nor sleep, nor even pray, but this fair stranger interposes; or, if by chance I slumber, all my dreams are of her, I see her, I touch her, I embrace her, and find a pleasure, even then, that all my waking thoughts could never procure me. If I go to the state-house, I mind nothing there, my heart's at home with the young gentlewoman; or the change, or wheresoever I go, my restless thoughts present her still before me: and prithee tell me, is not this love, *Octavio*? 'It may arrive to love,' replied the blushing youth, 'if you would fondly give way to it: but you are wise and grave, should hate all women, sir, till about forty, and then for generation only: you are above the follies of vain youth. And let me tell you, sir, without offending, already you are charged with a thousand little vanities, unsuitable to your years, and the character you have had, and the figure you have made in the world. I heard a lampoon on you the other day — (Pardon my freedom, sir,) for keeping a beauty in your house, who they are pleased to say was my mistress before.' And pulling out a lampoon, which his page had before given him, he gave it his uncle. But instead of making him resolve to quit *Sylvia*, it only served to incense him against *Octavio*; he railed at all wits, and swore there was not a more dangerous enemy to a civil, sober commonwealth: that a poet was to be banished as a spy, or hanged as a traitor: that it ought to be as much against the law to let them live, as to shoot with white powder; and that to write lampoons should be put into the statute against stabbing. And could he find the rogue that had the wit to write that, he would make him a warning to all the race of that damnable vermin; what! to abuse a magistrate, one of the *States*, a very monarch of the commonwealth! — It was abominable, and not to be borne — and looking on his nephew — and considering his face a while, he cried —'I fancy, sir, by your physiognomy, that you yourself have a hand in this libel:' at which Octavio blushed, which he taking for guilt, flew out into terrible anger against him, not suffering him to speak for himself, or clear his innocence. And as he was going in this rage from him, having forbidden him ever to set his foot within his doors, he told him — 'If,' said he, 'the scandalous town, from your instructions, have such thoughts of me, I will convince it by marrying this fair stranger the first thing I do: I cannot doubt but to find a welcome, since she is a banished woman, without friends or protection; and especially, when she shall see how civilly you have handled her here, in your doggerel ballad: I will teach you to be a wit, sir; and so your humble servant.'— And leaving him almost wild with his fears, he went directly to *Sylvia*, where he told her his nephew was going to make up the match between himself and madam the widow of —— and that he had made a scandalous lampoon on her fair self. He forgot nothing that might make her hate the amiable young nobleman, whom she knew too well to believe that any thing of this was other than the effects of his own growing passion for her. For though she saw *Octavio* every day, in this time she had remained at his uncle's, yet the old lover so watched their very looks, that it was impossible almost to tell one another's heart by the glance there. But *Octavio* had once in this time conveyed a letter to her, which having opportunity to do, he put it into her comb-box, when he was with his uncle one day in her dressing-room; for she durst not trust her page, and less *Antonet*, who had before betrayed them: and having for *Sylvia*'s release so solemnly sworn to his uncle, (to which vows he took religious care to keep him,) he had so perfect an awe upon his spirits from every look and command of his uncle's, he took infinite heed how he gave him any umbrage by any action of his; and the rather, because he hoped when time should serve, to bring about his business of stealing *Sylvia* from him; for she was kept and guarded like a mighty heiress; so that by this prudent management on both sides, they heightened the growing love in every heart. In that billet, which he dropped in her comb-box, he did not only make ten thousand vows of eternal passion and faith, and beg the same assurance of her again; but told her he was secured (so well he thought of her) from fears of his uncle's addresses to her, and begged she would not let them perplex her, but rather serve her for her diversion; that she should from time to time write him all he said to her, and how he treated her when alone; and that since the old lover was so watchful, she should not trust her letters with any body;

but as she walked into the garden, she should in passing through the hall, put her letter in at the broken glass of an old sedan that stood there, and had stood for several years; and that his own page, whom he could trust, should, when he came with him to his uncle's, take it from thence. Thus every day they writ, and received the dearest returns in the world; where all the satisfaction that vows oft repeated could give, was rendered each other; with an account from *Sylvia* that was very pleasant, of all the passion of the doting old *Sebastian*, the presents he made her, the fantastic youth he would assume, and unusual manner of his love, which was a great diversion to both; and this difficulty of speaking to *Sylvia*, and entertaining her with love, though it had its pains, had its infinite pleasure too; it increased their love on both sides, and all their wishes. But now by this last banishment from the house where she was, to lose that only pleasure of beholding the adorable maid, gave him all the pains, without the hope of one pleasure; and he began to fear he should have a world of difficulty to secure the dear object of his continual thoughts: he found no way to send to her, and dreads all his malicious uncle and rival may say to his disadvantage: he dreads even that infinite tenderness and esteem he had for the good old man, who had been so fond a parent to him; lest even that should make him unwilling to use that extremity against him in regaining *Sylvia*, which he could use to any other man. Oh, how he curses the fatal hour that ever he implored his aid for her release; and having overcome all difficulties, even that of his fears of *Philander*, (from whom they had received no letter in two months) and that of *Sylvia's* disdain, and had established himself in her soul and her arms; he should, by employing his uncle's authority for *Sylvia's* service, be so unfortunate to involve them into new dangers and difficulties, of which he could foresee no other end, than that which must be fatal to some of them. But he believed half his torture would be eased, could he but write to *Sylvia*, for see her he could not hope: he bethought himself of a way at last.

His uncle had belonging to his house the most fine garden of any in that province, where those things are not much esteemed; in which the old gentleman took wonderful delight, and kept a gardener and his family in a little house at the farther end of the garden, on purpose to look to it and dress it. This man had a very great veneration for *Octavio*, whom he called his young lord. Sure of the fidelity of this gardener, when it was dark enough to conceal him, he wrapped himself in his cloak, and got him thither by a back way, where with presents, he soon won those to his interest, who would before have been commanded by him in any service. He had a little clean room, and some little *French* novels which he brought; and there he was as well concealed as if he had been in the *Indies*; he left word at home, that he was gone out of the town. He knew well enough that *Sylvia*'s, lodgings looked that way; and when it was dark enough, he walked under her window, till he saw a candle lighted in *Sylvia*'s bed-chamber, which was as great a joy to him as the star that guides the traveller, or wandering seaman, or the lamp at *Sestos*, that guided the ravished lover over the *Hellespont*. And by that time he could imagine all in bed, he made a little noise with a key on the pummel of his sword; but whether *Sylvia* heard it or not, I cannot tell, but she anon came to the window, and putting up the sash, leaned on her arms and looked into the garden. Oh! Who but he himself that loved so well as *Octavio*, can express the transports he was in, at the sight? Which, more from the sight within than that without, he saw was the lovely *Sylvia*; whom calling softly by her name, answered him, as if she knew the welcome voice, and cried —'Who is there, *Octavio*? She was soon answered you may imagine. And they began the most endearing conversation that ever love could dictate. He complains on his fate that sets them at that distance, and she pities him. He makes a thousand doubts, and she undeceives them all. He fears, and she convinces his error, and is impatient at his suspicions. She will not endure him to question a heart that has given him so many proofs of its tenderness and gratitude; she tells him her own wishes, how soft and fervent they are; and assures him, he is extremely obliged to her ——'Since for you — my charming friend,' said she to *Octavio*, 'I have refused this night to marry your uncle; have a care,' said she, smiling, 'how you treat me, lest I revenge myself on you; become your aunt, and bring heirs to the estate you have a right to: the writings of all which I have now in my chamber, and which were but just now laid at my feet, and which I cannot yet get him to receive back. And to oblige me to a compliance, has told me how you have deceived me, by giving yourself to another, and exposing me in lampoons.'— To this *Octavio* would have replied, but she assured him she needed no argument to convince her of the falsehood of all. He sighs, and told her, all she said, though dear and charming, was not sufficient to ease his heart; for he foresaw a world of hazard to get her from thence, and mischiefs if she remained; insomuch that he caused the tears to flow from the fair eyes of *Sylvia*, with her reflections on her rigid fortune. And she cried, 'Oh, my *Octavio*! What strange fate or stars ruled my birth, that I should be born to the ruin of what I love, or those that love me!' At this rate they passed the night, sometimes more soft, sometimes encouraging one another; but the last result was to contrive the means of escaping. He fancied she might easily do it by the garden from the window: but that he was not sure he could trust the gardener so far, who in all things would serve him, in which his lord and master was not injured; and he, amongst the rest of the servants, had orders not to suffer *Sylvia* out of the garden, for which reason he kept a guard on that back-door. Some way must be found out which yet was not, and was left to time. He told her whence he was, and that he would not stir from thence, till he was secured of her flight: and day coming on, though loath, yet for fear of eyes and ears that might spy upon them, he retired to his little lodging, and *Sylvia* to bed; after giving and receiving a thousand vows and farewells. The next night he came to the same place, but instead of entertaining her — he only saw her softly put up the sash a little, and throw something white out of the window and retire. He was wondering at the meaning, but taking up what was thrown down, he found and smelt it was *Sylvia*'s handkerchief, in which was tied up a billet: he went to his little lodging, and read it.

SYLVIA *to* OCTAVIO.

Go from my window, my adorable friend, and be not afflicted that I do not entertain you as I had the joy to do last night; for both our voices were heard by some one that lodges below; and though your uncle could not tell me any part of our conversation, yet he heard I talked to some body: I have persuaded him the fellow dreamed who gave him this intelligence, and he is almost satisfied he did so; however, hazard not thy dear-self any more so, but let me lose for a while the greatest happiness this earth can afford me, (in the circumstances of our fortunes) rather than expose what is dearer to me than life or honour: pity the fate I was born to, and expect all things from

Your SYLVIA.

I will wait at the window for your answer, and let you down a ribband, by which I will draw it up: but as you love me do not speak.

He had no sooner read this, but he went to write an answer, which was this.

OCTAVIO *to* SYLVIA.

Complain not, thou goddess of my vows, on the fate thou wert born to procure to all mankind; but thank heaven for having received ten thousand charms that can recompense all the injuries you so unwillingly do us: and who would not implore his ruin from all the angry powers, if in return they would give him so glorious a reward? Who would not be undone to all the trifling honours of the mistaken world, to find himself, in lieu of all, possessed of the ravishing *Sylvia*? But oh! Where is that presumptuous man, that can at the price of all lay claim to so vast a blessing? Alas, my *Sylvia*, even while I dare call you mine, I am not that hoping slave; no, not after all the valued dear things you have said and vowed to me last night in the garden, welcome to my soul as life after a sentence of death, or heaven after life is ended. But, oh *Sylvia*! all this, even all you uttered from your dear mouth is not sufficient to support me: alas, I die for *Sylvia*! I am not able to bear the cruel absence longer, therefore without delay assist me to contrive your escape, or I shall die, and leave you to the ravage of his love who holds thee from me; the very thoughts of that is worse than death. I die, alas, I die, for an entire possession of thee: oh let me grasp my treasure, let me engross it all, here in my longing arms. I can no longer languish at this distance from my cruel joy, my life, my soul! But oh I rave, and while I should be speaking a thousand useful things, I am telling you my pain, a pain that you may guess; and confounding myself between those and their remedies, am able to fix on nothing. Help me to think, oh my dear charming creature, help me to think how I shall bear thee off! Take your own measures, flatter him with love, soothe him to faith and confidence, and then — oh pardon me, if there be baseness in the action — then — cozen him — deceive him — any thing — for he deserves it all, that thinks that lovely body was formed for his embraces, whom age has rendered fitter for a grave. Form any plots, use every stratagem to save the life of

> *Your* OCTAVIO.

....

He wrote this in haste and disorder, as you may plainly see by the style, and went to the window with it, where he found *Sylvia* leaning expecting him: the sashes were up, and he tossed it in the handkerchief into her window: she read it, and wrote an answer back as soft as love could form, to send him pleased to bed; wherein she commanded him to hope all things from her wit and industrious love.

This had partly the effects she wished, and after kissing his hand, and throwing it up towards *Sylvia*, they parted as silent as the night from day, which was now just dividing — so long they stayed, though but to look at each other; so that all the morning was passed in bed to make the day seem shorter, which was too tedious to both: this pleasure he had after noon, towards the evening, that when *Sylvia* walked, as she always did in the garden, he could see her through the glass of his window, but durst not open it; for the old gentleman was ever with her. In this time *Octavio* failed not however to essay the good nature of the gardener in order to *Sylvia*'s flight, but found there was no dealing with him in this affair; and therefore durst not come right down to the point: the next night he came under the beloved window again, and found the sacred object of his wishes leaning in the window expecting him: to whom, as soon as she heard his tread on the gravel, she threw down a handkerchief again, which he took up, and tossed his own with a soft complaining letter to entertain her till his return; for he hasted to read hers, and swept the garden as he passed as swift as wind; so impatient he was to see the inside — which he found thus:

SYLVIA *to* OCTAVIO.

I beg, my charming friend, you will be assured of all I have promised you; and to believe that but for the pleasure of those dear billets I receive from you, I could as little support this cruel confinement as you my absence. I have but one game to play, and I beseech you not to be surprised at it, it is to promise to marry *Sebastian*: he is eternally at my feet, and either I must give him my vow to become his wife, or give him hope of other favours. I am so entirely yours, that I will be guided by you, which I shall flatter him in to gain my liberty; for if I grant either, he has proposed to carry me to his country-house, two leagues from the town, and there consummate whatever I design to bless him with; and this is it that has wrought my consent, that we being to go alone, only my own servants, you may easily take me thence by force upon the road, or after our arrival, where he will not guard me perhaps so strictly as he does here: for that, I leave it to your conduct, and expect your answer to your impatient

SYLVIA.

· · · · · · · · · · · · · · · · · · ·

He immediately sat down, and wrote this:

· · · · · · · · · · · · · · · · · · ·

OCTAVIO *to* SYLVIA.

Have a care, my charming fair, how you play with vows; and however you are forced, for that religious end of saving your honour, to deceive the poor old lover, whom, by heaven I pity; yet rather let me die than know you can be guilty of vow-breach, though made in jest. I am well pleased at the glimpse of hope you give me, that I shall see you at his *villa*; and doubt not but to find a way to secure you to myself: say any thing, promise to sacrifice all to his desire; but oh, do not give away thy dear, thy precious self by vow, to any but the languishing

OCTAVIO.

....

After he had wrote this, he hasted, and throws it into her window, and returned to bed without seeing her, which was no small affliction to his soul: he had an ill night of it, and fancied a thousand tormenting things; that the old gentleman might then be with her; and if alone, what might he not persuade, by force of rich presents, of which his uncle was well stored; and so he guessed, and as he guessed it proved, as by his next night's letter he was informed, that the old lover no sooner saw *Sylvia* retire, but having in mind to try his fortune in some critical minute — for such a minute he had heard there was that favoured lovers; but he goes to his closet, and taking out some jewels of great value, to make himself the more welcome, he goes directly to *Sylvia*'s chamber, and entered just as she had taken up *Octavio*'s letter, and clapped it in her bosom as she heard some body at the door; but was not in a little confusion, when she saw who it was, which she excused, by telling him she was surprised to find herself with a man in her chamber. That there he fell to pleading his cause of love, and offered her again to settle his estate upon her, and implored she would be his wife. After a thousand faint denials, she told him she could not possibly receive that honour, but if she could, she would have looked upon it as a great favour from heaven; at that he was thunder-struck, and looked as ghastly as if his mother's ghost had frightened him; and after much debate, love and grief on his side, design and dissimulation on hers, she gave him hopes that atoned for all she had before said; insomuch that, before they parted, an absolute bargain was struck up, and he was to settle part of his estate upon her, as also that *villa*, to which he had resolved in two days to carry her; in earnest of this, he presents her with a necklace of pearl of good value, and other jewels, which was the best rhetoric he had yet spoke to her; and now she had appeared the most complaisant lady in the world, she suffers him to talk wantonly to her, nay, even to kiss her, and rub his grizzly beard on her divine face, grasp her hands, and touch her breast; a blessing he had never before arrived to, above the quality of his own servant-maid. To all which she makes the best resistance she can, under the circumstances of one who was to deceive well; and while she loathes, she seems well pleased, while the gay jewels sparkled in her eyes, and *Octavio* in her heart; so fond is youth of vanities, and to purchase an addition of beauty at any price. Thus with her pretty flatteries she wrought upon his soul, and smiled and looked him into faith; loath to depart, she sends him pleased away, and having her heart the more inclined to *Octavio*, by being persecuted with his uncle's love, (for by comparison she finds the mighty difference) she sets herself to write him the account of what I have related; this night's adventure, and agreement between his uncle and herself. She tells him that to-morrow, (for now it was almost day,) she had promised him to go to his *villa*: she tells him at what rate she has purchased the blessing expected; and lastly, leaves the management of the rest to him, who needs not to be instructed. This letter he received the next night at the old place, and *Sylvia* with it lets down a velvet night-bag, which contained all the jewels and things of value she had received of himself, his uncle, or any other: after which he retired, and was pretty well at ease, with the imagination he should 'ere long be made happy in the possession of *Sylvia*: in order to it, the next morning he was early up, and dressing himself in a great coarse campaign-coat of the gardener's, putting up his hair as well as he could, under a country hat, he got on a horse that suited his habit, and rides to the *villa*, whither they were to come, and which he knew perfectly well every room of; for there our hero was born. He went to a little *cabaret* in the village, from whence he could survey all the great house, and see every body that passed in and out: he remained fixed at the window, filled with a thousand agitations; this he had resolved, not to set upon the old man as a thief, or robber; nor could he find in his heart or nature, to injure him, though but in a little affrighting him, who had given him so many anxious hours, and who had been so unjust to desire that blessing himself he would not allow him; and to believe that virtue in himself, which he exclaims against as so great a vice in his nephew; nevertheless he resolved to deceive him, to save his own life. And he wanted that nice part of generosity, as to satisfy a little unnecessary lust in an old man, to ruin the eternal content of a young one, so nearly allied to his soul, as was his own dear proper person.

While he was thus considering, he saw his uncle's coach coming, and *Sylvia* with that doting lover in it, who was that day dressed in all the fopperies of youth, and every thing was young and gay about him but his person; that was winter itself, disguised in artificial spring; and he was altogether a mere contradiction: but who can guess the disorders and pantings of *Octavio*'s heart at the sight? And though he had resolved before, he would not to save his life, lay violent hands upon his old parent; yet at their approach, at their presenting themselves together before his eyes as two lovers, going to betray him to all the miseries, pangs and confusions of love; going to possess — her, the dear object and certain life of his soul, and he the parent of him, to whom she had disposed of herself, so entirely already, he was provoked to break from all his resolutions, and with one of those pistols he had in his pockets, to have sent unerring death to his old amorous heart; but that thought was no sooner born than stifled in his soul, where it met with all the sense of gratitude, that ever could present the tender love and dear care of a parent there; and the coach passing into the gate put him upon new designs, and before they were finished he saw *Sylvia*'s page coming from the house, after seeing his lady to her apartment, and being shewed his own, where he laid his valise and riding things, and was now come out to look about a country, where he had never been before. *Octavio* goes down and meets him, and ventures to make himself known to him: and so infinitely glad was the youth to have an opportunity to serve him, that he vowed he would not only do it with his life, on occasion, but believed he could do it effectually, since the old gentleman had no sort of jealousy now; especially, since they had so prudently managed matters in this time of his lady's remaining at *Sebastian*'s house. 'So that, sir, it will not be difficult,' says the generous boy, 'for me to convey you to my lodging, when it is dark.' He told him his lady cast many a longing look out towards the road, as she passed, 'for you, I am sure, my lord; — for she had told both myself and *Antonet* of her design before, lest our surprise or resistance should prevent any force you might use on the road, to take her from my lord *Sebastian*: she sighed, and looked on me as she alighted, with eyes, my lord, that told me her grief, for your disappointment.'

You may easily imagine how transported the poor *Octavio* was; he kissed and embraced the amiable boy a thousand times; and taking a ring from his finger of considerable value, gave it the dear reviver of his hopes. *Octavio* already knew the strength of the house, which consisted but of a gardener, whose wife was house-keeper, and their son who was his father's servant in the garden, and their daughter, who was a sort of maid-servant: and they had brought only the coachman, and one footman, who were likely to be merrily employed in the kitchen at night when all got to supper together. I say, *Octavio* already knew this, and there was now nothing that opposed his wishes: so that dismissing the dear boy, he remained the rest of the tedious day at the *cabaret*, the most impatient of night of any man on earth; and when the boy appeared, it was like the approach of an angel. He told him, his lady was the most melancholy creature that ever eyes beheld, and that to conceal the cause, she had feigned herself ill, and had not stirred from her chamber all the day: that the old lover was perpetually with her, and the most concerned dotard that ever *Cupid* enslaved: that he had so wholly taken up his lady with his disagreeable entertainment, that it was impossible either by a look or note to inform her of his being so near her, whom she considered as her present defender, and her future happiness. 'But this evening,' continued the youth, 'as I was waiting on her at supper, she spied the ring on my finger, which, my lord, your bounty made me master of this morning. She blushed a thousand times, and fixed her eyes upon it for she knew it, and was impatient to have asked me some questions, but contained her words: and after that, I saw a joy dance in her lovely eyes, that told me she divined you were not far from thence. Therefore I beseech your lordship let us haste.' So both went out together, and the page conducted him into a chamber he better knew than the boy, while every moment he receives intelligence, how affairs went in that of *Sylvia*'s by the page, who leaving *Octavio* there went out as a spy for him. In fine, with much ado, *Sylvia* persuaded her old lover to urge her for no favours that night, for she was indisposed and unfit for love; yet she persuades with such an air, so smiling, and insinuating, that she increases the fire, she endeavoured to allay: but he, who was all obedience, as well as new desire, resolves to humour her, and shew the perfect gallantry of his love; he promises her she shall command: and after that never was the old gentleman seen in so excellent a humour before in the whole course of his life; a certain lightning against a storm that must be fatal to him.

He was no sooner gone from her, with a promise to go to bed and sleep, that he might be the earlier up to shew her the fine gardens, which she loved, but she sends *Antonet* to call the page, from whom she longed to know something of *Octavio*, and was sure he could inform her. But she was undressing while she spoke, and got into her bed before she left her: but *Antonet*, instead of bringing the sighing youth, brought the transported and ravished *Octavio*, who had by this time pulled his coarse campaign, and put down his hair. He fell breathless with joy on her bed-side; when *Antonet*, who knew that love desired no lookers-on, retired, and left *Octavio* almost dead with joy, in the clasping arms of the trembling maid, the lovely *Sylvia*. Oh, who can guess their satisfaction? Who can guess their sighs and love, their tender words, half stifled in kisses? Lovers! fond lovers! only can imagine; to all besides, this tale will be insipid. He now forgets where he is, that not far off lay his amorous uncle, that to be found there was death, and something worse; but wholly ravished with the languishing beauty, taking his pistols out of either pocket, he lays them on a dressing-table, near the bed-side, and in a moment throws off his clothes, and gives himself up to all the heaven of love, that lay ready to receive him there, without thinking of any thing, but the vast power of either's charms. They lay and forgot the hasty hours, but old *Sebastian* did not. They were all counted by him with the impatience of a lover: he burnt, he raged with fierce desire, and tossed from side to side, and found no ease; *Sylvia* was present in imagination, and he like *Tantalus* reaches at the food, which, though in view, is not within his reach: he would have prayed, but he had no devotion for any deity but *Sylvia*; he rose and walked and went to bed again, and found himself uneasy every way. A thousand times he was about to go, and try what opportunity would do, in the dark silent night — but fears her rage — he fears she will chide at least; then he resolves, and unresolves as fast: unhappy lover — thus to blow the fire when there was no materials to supply it; at last, overcome with fierce desire too violent to be withstood, or rather fate would have it so ordained, he ventures all, and steals to *Sylvia*'s chamber, believing, when she found him in her arms, she could not be displeased; or if she were, that was the surest place of reconciliation: so that only putting his night-gown about him, he went softly to her chamber for fear of waking her: the unthinking lovers had left open the door, so that it was hardly put to; and the first alarm was *Octavio*'s hand being seized, which was clasping his treasure. He starts from the frighted arms of *Sylvia*, and leaping from the bed would have escaped; for he knew too well the touch of that old hand; but *Sebastian*, wholly surprised at so robust a repulse, took most unfortunately a stronger hold, and laying both his hands roughly upon him, with a resolution to know who he was, for he felt his hair; and *Octavio* struggling at the same minute to get from him, they both fell against the dressing-table, and threw down the pistols; in their fall, one of which going off, shot the unfortunate old lover into the head, so that he never spoke word more: at the going off of the pistol, *Sylvia*, who had not minded those *Octavio* laid on the table, cried out —'Oh my *Octavio*!' 'My dearest charmer,' replied he, 'I am well ——'and feeling on the dead body, which he wondered had no longer motion, he felt blood flowing round it, and sighing cried —'Ah *Sylvia*! I am undone — my uncle — oh my parent —— speak, dear sir! what unlucky accident has done this fatal deed?' *Sylvia*, who was very soft by nature, was extremely surprised, and frightened at the news of a dead man in her chamber, so that she was ready to run mad with the apprehension of it: she raved and tore herself, and expressed her fright in cries and distraction; so that *Octavio* was compelled from one charitable grief to another. He goes to her and comforts her, and tells, since it is by no design of either of them, their innocence will be their guardian angel. He tells her, all their fault was love, which made him so heedlessly fond of joys with her, he stayed to reap those when he should have secured them by flight. He tells her this is now no place to stay in, and that he would put on her clothes, and fly with her to some secure part of the world; 'For who,' said he, 'that finds this poor unfortunate here, will not charge his death on me, or thee?

—— Haste then, my dearest maid, haste, haste, and let us fly ——'
So dressing her, he led her into *Antonet's* chamber, while he went
to see which way they could get out. So locking the chamber-door
where the dead body lay, which by this time was stiff and cold, he
locked that also of his uncle's chamber, and calling the page, they
all got themselves ready; and putting two horses in the coach, they
unseen and unperceived got themselves all out: the servants having
drank hard at their meeting in the country last night, were all too
sound asleep to understand any thing of what passed. It being now
about the break of day, *Octavio* was the coachman, and the page
riding by the coach-side, while *Sylvia* and *Antonet* were in it, they
in an hour's time reached the town, where *Octavio* packed up all
that was carriageable; took his own coach and six horses; left his
affairs to the management of a kinsman, that dwelt with him, took
bills to the value of two thousand pounds, and immediately left the
town, after receiving some letters that came last night by the post,
one of which was from *Philander*; and indeed, this new grief upon
Octavio's soul, made him the most dejected and melancholy man
in the world, insomuch that he, who never wept for any thing but
for love, was often found with tears rolling down his cheeks, at the
remembrance of an accident so deplorable, and of which, he and his
unhappy passion was the cause, though innocently: yet could not
the dire reflection of that, nor the loss of so tender a parent as was
Sebastian, lessen one spark of that fire for *Sylvia*, whose unfortunate
flame had been so fatal. While they were safe out of danger, the
servants of *Sebastian* admired when ten, eleven and twelve o'clock
was come, they saw neither the old lord, nor any of the new guests.
But when the coachman missed his coach and horses, he was in a
greater maze, and thought some body had stolen them, and accusing
himself of sluggishness and debauchery, that made him not able to
hear, when the coach went out, he forswore all drinking: but when
the house-keeper and he met, and discoursed about the lady and the
rest, they concluded, that the old gentleman and she were agreed
upon the matter; and being got to bed together had quite forgot
themselves; and made a thousand roguish remarks upon them. They
believed the maid and the page too, were as well employed, since they

saw neither. But when dinner was ready, she went up to the maid's chamber and found it empty, as also that of the page; her heart then presaging something, she ventures to knock at her lord's chamber-door, but finding it locked, and none answer, they broke it open; and after doing the same by that of *Sylvia*, they found the poor *Sebastian* stretched on the floor, and shot in the head, the toilet pulled almost down, and the lock of the pistol hanging in the point of the toilet entangled, and the muzzle of it just against the wound. At first, when they saw him, they fancied *Sylvia* might kill him, for either offering to come to bed to her in the night, or some other malicious end. But when they saw how the pistol lay, they fancied it accident in the dark; 'For,' said the woman —'I and my daughter have been up ever since day-break, and I am sure no such thing happened then, nor could they since escape:' and it being natural in *Holland* to cry, 'Loop Schellum', that is, 'Run rogue', to him that is alive, and who has killed another; and for every man to set a helping hand to bear him out of danger, thinking it too much that one is already dead: I say, this being the nature of the people, they never pursued the murderers, or fled persons, but suffered *Sebastian* to lie till the coroner sat upon him, who found it, or at least thought it accident; and there was all for that time. But this, with all the reasonable circumstances, did not satisfy the *States*. Here is one of their high and mighties killed, a fair lady fled, and upon inquiry a fine young fellow too, the nephew: all knew they were rivals in this fair lady; all knew there were animosities between them; all knew *Octavio* was absconded some days before; so that, upon consideration, they concluded he was murdered by compact; and the rather, because they wished it so in spite of *Octavio*; and because both he and *Sylvia* were fled like guilty persons. Upon this they made a seizure of both his, and his uncle's estate, to the use of the *States*. Thus the best and most glorious man, that ever graced that part of the world, was undone by love. While *Sylvia* with sighs and tears would often say that sure she was born the fate of all that adored her, and no man ever thrived that had a design upon her, or a pretension to her.

Thus between excess of grief and excess of love, which indeed lay veiled in the first, they arrived at *Brussels*; where *Octavio*, having news of the proceedings of the *States* against him, resolving rather to lose his life, than tamely to surrender his right, he went forth in order to take some care about it: and in these extremes of a troubled mind, he had forgot to read *Philander*'s letters, but gave them to *Sylvia* to peruse, till he returned, beseeching and conjuring her, by all the charms of love, not to suffer herself to be afflicted, but now to consider she was wholly his; and she could not, and ought not to rob him of a sigh, or tear for any other man. For they had concluded to marry, as soon as *Sylvia* should be delivered from that part of *Philander*, of which she was possessed. Therefore beholding her entirely his own, of whom he was so fondly tender, he could not endure the wind should blow on her, and kiss her lovely face: jealous of even the air she breathed, he was ever putting her in mind, of whose and what she was; and she ever giving him new assurances, that she was only *Octavio*'s. The last part of his ill news he concealed from her; that of the usage of the *States*. He was so entirely careful of her fame, that he had two lodgings, one most magnificent for her, another for himself; and only visited her all the live-long day. And being now retired from her, she whose love and curiosity grew less every day, for the false *Philander*, opened his letter with a sigh of departed love, and read this.

Philander *to* Octavio.

Sure of your friendship, my dear *Octavio*, I venture to lay before you the history of my misfortunes, as well as those of my joys, equally extreme.

In my last, I gave you an account how triumphing a lover I was, in the possession of the adorable *Calista*; and how very near I was being surprised in the fountain, where I had hid myself from the rage of old *Clarinau*; and escaped wet and cold to my lodging: and though indeed I escaped, it was not without giving the old husband a jealousy, which put him upon inquiry, after a stricter manner, as I heard the next day from *Calista*; but with as ill success as the night before; notwithstanding it appears, by what after happened, that he still retained his jealousy, and that of me, from a thousand little inquiries I had from time to time made, from my being now absent, and most of all from my being, (as now he fancied) that vision,

which *Calista* saw in the garden. All these circumstances wrought a
thousand *conundrums*, in his *Spanish* politic noddle: and he resolves
that *Calista*'s actions should be more narrowly watched. This I can
only guess from what ensued. I am not able to say, by what good
fortune, I escaped several happy nights after the first, but it is certain
I did so; for the old man carrying all things fair to the lovely Countess,
she thought herself secure in her joys hitherto, as to any discovery:
however, I never went on this dear adventure but I was well armed
against any mishaps, of poniard, sword, and pistol, that garb of a
right *Spaniard*. *Calista* had been married above two years, before I
beheld her, and had never been with child: but it so chanced, that
she conceived the very first night of our happiness; since which time,
not all her flatteries and charms, could prevail for one night with
the old Count: for, whether from her seeming fondness he imagined
the cause, or what other reason he had to withstand her desire and
caresses, I know not: but still he found, or feigned some excuses
to put her off: so that *Calista*'s pleas and love increased with her
growing belly. And though almost every night I had the fair, young
charmer in bed with me, (without the least suspicion on *Dormina*'s
side) or, else in the arbours, or on flowery banks in the garden; till
I am confident there was not a walk, a grove, an arbour, or bed of
sweets, that was not conscious of our stolen delights; nay, we grew so
very bold in love, that we often suffered the day to break upon us; and
still escaped his spies, who by either watching at the wrong door, or
part of the vast garden, or by sleepiness, or carelessness, still let us
pass their view. Four happy months, thus blessed, and thus secured,
we lived, when *Calista* could no longer conceal her growing shame,
from the jealous *Clarinau*, or *Dormina*. She feared, with too much
reason, that it was jealousy, which made him refrain her bed, though
he dissembled well all day; and one night, weeping in my bosom, with
all the tenderness of love, she said, that if I loved her, as she hoped
I did, I should be shortly very miserable: 'For oh,' cries she, 'I can
no longer hide this —— dear effect of my stolen happiness —— and
Clarinau will no sooner perceive my condition, but he will use his
utmost rigour against me; I know his jealous nature, and find I am
undone ——' With that she told me how he had killed his first wife;

for which he was obliged to fly from the Court, and country of *Spain*: and that she found from all his severity, he was not changed from his nature. In fine, she said and loved so much, that I was wholly charmed, and vowed myself her slave, or sacrifice, either to follow what she could propose, or fall a victim with her to my love. After which it was concluded, (neither having a mind to leave the world, when we both knew so well how to make ourselves happy in it) that the next night I should bring her a suit of men's clothes; and she would in that disguise fly with me to any part of the world. For she vowed, if this unlucky force of flying had not happened to her, she had not been longer able to endure his tyranny and slavery; but had resolved to break her chain, and put herself upon any fortune. So that after the usual endearments on both sides, I left her, resolved to follow my fortune, and she me, to sacrifice all to her repose. That night, and all next day, she was not idle; but put up all her jewels, of which she had the richest of any lady in all those parts; for in that the old Count was over-lavish: and the next night I brought her a suit, which I had made that day on purpose, as gay as could be made in so short a time; and scaling my wall, well armed, I found her ready at the door to receive me; and going into an arbour, by the aid of a dark-lanthorn I carried, she dressed her in a laced shirt of mine, and this suit I had brought her, of blue velvet, trimmed with rich loops and buttons of gold; a white hat, and white feather; a fair peruke, and scarlet breeches, the rest suitable. And I must confess to you, my dear *Octavio*, that never any thing appeared so ravishing, and yet I have seen *Sylvia*! But even she a baby to this more noble figure. *Calista* is tall, and fashioned the most divinely — the most proper for that dress of any of her sex: and I own I never saw any thing so beautiful all over, from head to foot: and viewing her thus, (carrying my lanthorn all about her) but more especially her face, her wondrous, charming face —(pardon me, if I say, what does but look like flattery)— I never saw any thing more resembling my dear *Octavio*, than the lovely *Calista*, Your very feature, your very smile and air; so that, if possible, that increased my adoration and esteem for her: thus completed, I armed her, and buckled on her sword, and she would needs have one of my pistols too, that stuck in my belt; and now she appeared all lovely man. It was so late by that time we had done, that the moon, which began to shine very bright, gave us a thousand little fears, and disposing her jewels all about us safe, we began our adventure, with a thousand dreadful apprehensions on *Calista*'s side. And going up the walk, towards the place where we were to mount the wall, just at the end of it, turning a corner, we encountered two men, who were too near us to be prevented. 'Oh,' cried *Calista* to me, who saw them first — 'My dear *Philander*, we are undone!' I looked and saw them, and replied, 'My charmer, do not fear, they are but two to two, whoever they be; for love and I shall be of force enough to encounter them.' 'No, my *Philander*,' replied she briskly, 'it is I will be your second in this rencounter.' At this approaching them more near, (for they hasted to us, nor could we fly from them,) we soon found by his hobbling, that old *Clarinau* was one, and the other a tall *Spaniard*, his nephew. I clapped my hair under my hat, and both of us making a stand, we resolved, if they durst not venture on us, to let them pass —— but *Clarinau*, who was on that side which faced *Calista*, cried, 'Ah villain, have I caught thee!' and at the same instant with a poniard stabbed her into the arm; for with a sudden turn she evaded it from her heart, to which it was designed. At which, repaying his compliment, she shot off her pistol, and down he fell, crying out for a priest; while I, at the same time, laid my tall boy at his feet. I caught my dear *virago* in my arms, and hasted through the garden with her, and was very hasty in mounting the ladder, putting my fair second before me, without so much as daring yet to ask her, if she were wounded, lest it should have hindered our flight, if I had found her hurt: nor knew I she was so, till I felt her warm precious blood, streaming on my face, as I lifted her over the wall; but I soon conveyed her into my new lodgings, yet not soon enough to secure her from those that pursued us. For with their bawling they alarmed some of the servants, who looking narrowly for the murderers, tracked us by *Calista*'s, blood, which they saw with their flambeaus, from the place where *Clarinau*, and his nephew lay, to the very wall; and thinking from our wounds we could not escape far, they searching the houses, found me dressing *Calista*'s wound, which I kissed a thousand times. But the matchless courage of the fair *virago*! the magnanimity of *Calista*'s soul! Nothing of foolish woman harboured there, nothing but softest love; for whilst I was raving mad, tearing my hair and cursing my fate in vain, she had no concern but for me; no pain but that of her fear of being taken from me, and being delivered to old *Clarinau*, whom I feared was not dead; nor could the very seizing her, daunt her spirits, but with an unmatched fortitude she bore it all; she only wished she could have escaped without bloodshed. We were both led to prison, but none knew who we were; for those that seized us, had by chance never seen me, and *Calista*'s habit secured the discovery. While we both remained there, we had this comfort of being well lodged together; for they did not go about to part us, being in for one crime. And all the satisfaction she had, was, that she should, she hoped, die concealed, if she must die for the crime; and that was much a greater joy, than to think she should be rendered back to *Clarinau*, who in a few days we heard was upon his recovery. This gave her new fears; but I confess to you, I was not afflicted at it; nor did I think it hard for me to bribe *Calista* off; for the master of the prison was very civil and poor, so that with the help of some few of *Calista*'s, jewels, he was wrought upon to let her escape, I offering to remain, and bear all the brunt of the business, and to pay whatever he could be fined for it. These reasons, with the ready jewels, mollified the needy rascal; and though loath she were to leave me, yet she being assured that all they could do was but to fine me, and her stay she knew was her inevitable ruin, at last submitted, leaving me sufficient in jewels to satisfy for all that could happen, which were the value of a hundred thousand crowns. She is fled to *Brussels*, to a nunnery of *Augustines*, where the Lady Abbess is her aunt, and where for a little time she is secure, till I can follow her.

I beg of you my dear *Octavio*, write to me, and write me a letter of recommendation to the magistrates here, who all being concerned when any one of them is a cuckold, are very severe upon criminals in those cases. I tire you with my melancholy adventure — but it is some ease in the extremes of grief, to receive the tender pity of a friend, and that I am sure *Octavio* will afford his unhappy

PHILANDER.

As cold and as unconcerned as *Sylvia* imagined she had found her heart to *Philander*'s, memory, at the reading of this letter, in spite of all the tenderness she had for *Octavio*, she was possessed with all those pains of love and jealousy, which heretofore tormented her, when love was young, and *Philander* appeared with all those charms, with which he first conquered; she found the fire was but hid under those embers, which every little blast blows off, and makes it flame anew. It was now that she, forgetting all the past obligations of *Octavio*, all his vast presents, his vows, his sufferings, his passion and his youth, abandoned herself wholly to her tenderness for *Philander*, and drowns her fair cheeks in a shower of tears: and having eased her heart a little by this natural relief of her sex, she opened the letter that was designed for herself, and read this.

To SYLVIA.

I know, my lovely *Sylvia*, I am accused of a thousand barbarities for unkindly detaining your lover, who long ere this ought to have thrown himself at your feet, imploring a thousand pardons for his tedious six months' absence, though the affliction of it, is all my own, and I am afraid all the punishment; but when, my dearest *Sylvia*, I reflect again, it is in order to our future tranquillity, I depend on your love and reason for my excuse. I know my absence has procured me a thousand rivals, and you as many adorers, and fear *Philander* appears grown old in love, and worn out with sorrow and care, unfit for the soft play of the young and delicate *Sylvia*; new lovers have new vows and new presents, and your fickle sex stoop to the lavish prostrate. Ill luck — unkind fate has rifled me, and of a shining fortune left me even to the charity of a stingy world; and I have now no compliment to maintain the esteem in so great a soul as that of *Sylvia*, but that old repeated one, of telling her my dull, my trifling heart is still her own: but, oh! I want the presenting eloquence that so persuades and charms the fair, and am reduced to that fatal torment of a generous mind, rather to ask and take, than to bestow. Yet out of my contemptible stock, I have sent my *Sylvia* something towards that dangerous, unavoidable hour, which will declare me, however, a happy father of what my *Sylvia* bears about her; it is a bill for a thousand pattacoons. I am at present under an easy restraint about a little dispute between a man of quality here and myself; I had also been at *Brussels* to have provided all things for your coming illness, but every day expect my liberty, and then without delay I will take post, and bring *Philander* to your arms. I have news that *Cesario* is arrived at *Brussels*. I am at present a stranger to all that passes, and having a double obligation to haste, you need not fear but I shall do so.

This letter raised in her a different sentiment, from that of the story of his misfortune; and that taught her to know, that this he had writ to her was all false, and dissembled; which made her, in concluding the letter, cry out with a vehement scorn and indignation. —'Oh how I hate thee, traitor! who hast the impudence to continue thus to impose upon me, as if I wanted common sense to see thy baseness: for what can be more base and cowardly than lies, that poor plebeian shift, condemned by men of honour or of wit.'

Thus she spoke, without reminding that this most contemptible quality she herself was equally guilty of, though infinitely more excusable in her sex, there being a thousand little actions of their lives, liable to censure and reproach, which they would willingly excuse and colour over with little falsities; but in a man, whose most inconstant actions pass oftentimes for innocent gallantries, and to whom it is no infamy to own a thousand amours, but rather a glory to his fame and merit; I say, in him, (whom custom has favoured with an allowance to commit any vices and boast it) it is not so brave. And this fault of *Philander*'s cured *Sylvia* of her disease of love, and chased from her heart all that softness, which once had so much favoured him. Nevertheless she was filled with thoughts that failed not to make her extremely melancholy: and it was in this humour *Octavio* found her; who, forgetting all his own griefs to lessen hers, (for his love was arrived to a degree of madness) he caresses her with all the eloquence his passion could pour out; he falls at her feet, and pleads with such a look and voice as could not be resisted; nor ceased he till he had talked her into ease, till he had looked and loved her into a perfect calm: it was then he urged her to a new confirmation of her heart to him, and took hold of every yielding softness in her to improve his advantage. He pressed her to all he wished, but by such tender degrees, by arts so fond and endearing, that she could deny nothing. In this humour, she makes a thousand vows against *Philander*, to hate him as a man, that had first ruined her honour, and then abandoned her to all the ills that attend ungovern'd youth, and unguarded beauty: she makes *Octavio* swear as often to be revenged on him for the dishonour of his sister: which being performed, they re-assumed all the satisfaction which had seemed almost destroyed by adverse fate, and for a little space lived in great tranquillity; or if *Octavio* had sentiments that represented past unhappinesses, and a future prospect of ill consequences, he strove with all the power of love to hide them from *Sylvia*. In this time, they often sent to the nunnery of the *Augustines*, to inquire of the Countess of *Clarinau*; and at last, hearing she was arrived, no force of persuasion or reason could hinder *Sylvia* from going to make her a visit. *Octavio* pleads in vain the overthrow of all his revenge, by his sister's knowledge that her intrigue was found out: but in an undress — for her condition permitted no other, she is carried to the monastery, and asks for the Mother Prioress, who came to the grate; where, after the first compliments over, she tells her she is a relation to that lady, who such a day came to the house. *Sylvia*, by her habit and equipage, appearing of quality, was answered, that though the lady were very much indisposed, and unfit to appear at the grate, she would nevertheless endeavour to serve her, since she was so earnest; and commanding one of the nuns to call down Madam the Countess, she immediately came; but though in a dress all negligent, and a face where languishment appeared, she at first sight surprised our fair one, with a certain majesty in her mien and motion, and an air of greatness in her face, which resembled that of *Octavio*: so that not being able to sustain herself on her trembling supporters, she was ready to faint at a sight so charming, and a form so angelic. She saw her all that *Philander* had described; nor could the partiality of his passion render her more lovely than she appeared this instant to *Sylvia*. She came to reproach her —— but she found a majesty in her looks above all censure, that awed the jealous upbraider, and almost put her out of countenance; and with a rising blush she seemed ashamed of her errand. At this silence the lovely *Calista*, a little surprised, demanded of an attending nun if that lady would speak with her? This awaked *Sylvia* into an address, and she replied, 'Yes, madam, I am the unfortunate, who am compelled by my hard fate to complain of the most charming woman that ever nature made: I thought, in my coming hither, I should have had no other business but to have told you how false, how perjured a lover I had had; but at a sight so wondrous, I blame him no more, (whom I find now compelled to love) but you, who have taken from me, by your charms, the only blessing heaven had lent me.' This she ended with a sigh; and Madam the Countess, who from the beginning of her speaking, guessed, from a certain trembling at her heart, who it was she spoke of, resolved to shew no signs of a womanish fear or jealousy, but with an unalterable air and courage, replied, 'Madam, if my charms were so powerful, as you are pleased to tell me they are, they sure have attracted too many lovers for me to understand which it is I have been so unhappy to rob you of. If he be a gallant man, I shall neither deny him, nor repent my loving him the more for his having been a lover before.' To which *Sylvia*, who expected not so brisk an answer, replied; 'She makes such a confession with so much generosity, I know she cannot be insensible of the injuries she does, but will have a consideration and pity for those wretches at least, who are undone to establish her satisfaction.' 'Madam,' replied the Countess, (a little touched with the tenderness and sadness with which she spoke) 'you have so just a character of my soul, that I assure you I would not for any pleasure in the world do an action should render it less worthy of your good thoughts. Name me the man — and if I find him such as I may return you with honour, he shall find my friendship no more.' 'Ah, madam, it is impossible,' cried *Sylvia*, 'that he can ever be mine, that has once had the glory of being conquered by you; and what is yet more, of having conquered you.' 'Nay, madam,' replied *Calista*, 'if your loss be irrecoverable, I have no more to do but to sigh with you, and join our hard fates; but I am not so vain of my own beauty, nor have so little admiration for that of yours, to imagine I can retain any thing you have a claim to; for me, I am not fond of admirers, if heaven be pleased to give me one, I ask no more. I will leave the world to you, so it allow me my *Philander*.' This she spoke with a little malice, which called up all the blushes in the fair face of *Sylvia*; who a little nettled at the word *Philander*, replied; 'Go, take the perjured man, and see how long you can maintain your empire over his fickle heart, who has already betrayed you to all the reproach an incensed rival and an injured brother can load you with: see where he has exposed you to *Octavio*; and after that tell me what you can hope from such a perjured villain ——' At these words, she gave her the letter *Philander* had writ to *Octavio*, with that he had writ to herself — and without taking leave, or speaking any more, she left her thoughtful rival: who after pausing a moment on what should be writ there, and what the angry lady meant, she silently passed on to her chamber. But if she were surprised with her visitor, she was much more, when opening the letters she found one to her brother, filled with the history of her infamy, and what pressed her soul more sensibly, the other filled with passion and softness to a mistress. She had scarcely read them out, but a young nun, her kinswoman, came into her chamber; whom I have since heard protest, she scarce saw in that moment any alteration in her, but that she rose and received her, with her wonted grace and sweetness; and but for some answers that she made *mal à propos*, and sighs, that against her will broke from her heart, she should not have found an alteration; but this being unusual, made her inquisitive; and the faint denial she met with made her importune, and that so earnestly, and with so many vows of fidelity and secrecy, that *Calista*'s heart, even breaking within, poured itself for ease, into the faithful bosom of this young devotee; and having told her all the story of her misfortune, she began with so much courage and bravery of mind, to make vows against the charming betrayer of her fame, and with him all mankind, and this with such consideration and repentance, as left no room for reproach, or persuasion; and from this moment resolved never to quit the solitude of the cloisters. She had all her life, before her marriage, lived in one, and wished now, she had never seen the world, or departed from a life so pure and innocent. She looked upon this fatal accident, now a blessing, to bring her back to a life of devotion and tranquillity: and indeed is a miracle of piety. Some time after this, she was brought to bed, but commanded the child should be removed, where she might never see it, which accordingly was done; after which, in due time, she took the habit, and remains a rare example of repentance and holy-living. This new penitent became the news of the whole town; and it was not without some pleasure, that *Octavio* heard it, as the only action she could do, that could reconcile him to her; the knowledge of which, and some few soft days with *Sylvia*, made him chase away all those shiverings, that had seized him upon several occasions: but *Sylvia* was all sweetness, all love and good humour, and made his days easy, and his nights entirely happy. While, on the other side, there was no satisfaction, no pleasure, that the fond lavish lover did not, at any price, purchase for her repose; for it was the whole business of his life, to study what would charm and please her: and being assured by so many vows of her heart, there was nothing rested, to make him perfectly happy, but her being delivered of what belonged to his rival, and in which he had no part, he was at perfect ease. This she wishes with an impatience equal to his; whose love and fondness for *Octavio* appeared to be arrived to the highest degree, and she every minute expected to be free from the only thing, that hindered her from giving herself entirely to her impatient love.

In the midst of this serenity of affairs, *Sylvia*'s page one day brings them news his lord was arrived, and that he saw him in the park walking with some *French* gentlemen, and undiscovered to him came to give her notice, that she might take her measures accordingly. In spite of all her love to *Octavio*, her blushes flew to her cheeks at the news, and her heart panted with unusual motion; she wonders at herself, and fears and doubts her own resolution; she till now believed him wholly indifferent to her, but she knows not what construction this new disorder will bear; and what confounded and perplexed her more, was, that *Octavio* beheld all these emotions, with unconceivable resentment; he swells with pride and anger, and even bursts with grief, and not able longer to contain his complaint, he reproaches her in the softest language that ever love and grief invented; while she weeps with shame and divided love, and demands of him a thousand pardons; she deals thus kindly at least with him, to confess this truth; that it was impossible, but at the approach of a man, who taught her first to love, and for which knowledge she had paid so infinitely dear, she could not but feel unusual motions; that that tenderness and infant flame, he once inspired, could not but have left some warmth about her heart, and that *Philander*, the once charming dear *Philander*, could never be absolutely to her as a common man, and begged that he would give some grains of allowance to a maid, so soft by nature, and who had once loved so well, to be undone by the dear object; and though every kind word she gave his rival was a dagger at his heart, nevertheless, he found, or would think he found, some reason in what she said; at least he seemed more appeased, while she, on the other side, dissembled all the ease, and repose of mind, that could flatter him to calmness.

You must know, that for *Sylvia*'s, honour, she had lodgings by herself, and *Octavio* had his in another house, at an aunt's of his, a widow, and a woman of great quality; and *Sylvia* being near her lying-in, had provided all things, with the greatest magnificence imaginable, and passed for a young widow, whose husband died, at the Siege of ——*Octavio* only visited her daily, and all the nights she had to herself. For he treated her as one whom he designed to make his wife, and one whose honour was his own; but that night the news of *Philander*'s, arrival was told her, she was more than ordinary impatient to have him gone, pretending illness, and yet seemed loath to let him go, and lovers (the greatest cullies in nature, and the aptest to be deceived, though the most quick-sighted)— do the soonest believe; and finding it the more necessary he should depart, the more ill she feigned to be, he took his leave, and left her to repose, after taking all care necessary, for one in her circumstances. But she, to make his absence more sure, and fearing lest he should suspect something of her design, being herself guilty, she orders him to be called back, and caresses him anew, tells him she was never more unwilling to part with him, and all the while is complaining and wishing to be in bed; and says he must not stir till he sees her laid. This obliges and cajoles him anew, and he will not suffer her women to undress her, but does the grateful business himself, and reaps some dear recompense by every service, and pleases his eyes and lips, with the ravishing beauties, of the loose unguarded, suffering fair one. She permits him any thing to have him gone, which was not till he saw her laid, as if to her rest: but he was no sooner got into his coach, but she rose, and slipped on her night-gown, and some other loose thingss and got into a chair, commanding her page to conduct the chairmen to all the great *cabarets*, where she believed it most likely to find *Philander*; which was accordingly done; and the page entering, inquires for such a *cavalier*, describing his person, his fine remarkable black hair of his own: but the first he entered into, he saw *Brilliard* bespeaking supper: for you must know that, that husband-lover being left, as I have said, in prison in *Holland*, for the accusation of *Octavio*; the unhappy young nobleman was no sooner fled upon the unlucky death of his uncle, but the *States* set *Brilliard* at liberty; who took his journey immediately to *Philander*, whom he found just released from his troublesome affair, and designed for *Brussels*, where they arrived that very morning: where the first thing he did, was to go to the nunnery of St *Austin*, to inquire for the fair *Calista*; but instead of encountering the kind, the impatient, the brave *Calista*, he was addressed to, by the old Lady Abbess, in so rough a manner, that he no longer doubted, upon what terms he stood there, though he wondered how they should know his story with *Calista*: when to put him out of doubt, she assured him, he should never more behold the face of her injured niece; for whose revenge she left him to heaven. It was in vain he kneeled and implored; he was confirmed again and again, she should never come from out the confines of those walls; and that her whole remaining life spent in penitence, was too little to wash away her sins with him: and giving him the letter he sent to *Octavio*, (which *Sylvia* had given *Calista*, and she the Lady Abbess, with a full confession of her fault) she cried; 'See there, sir, the treachery you have committed against a woman of quality — whom your criminal love has rendered the most miserable of her sex.' At the ending of which, she drew the curtain over the grate, and left him, wholly amazed and confounded, finding it to be the same he had writ to *Octavio*, and in it, that he had writ to *Sylvia*: by the sight of which, he no longer doubted, but that confidante had betrayed him every way. He rails on his false friendship, curses the Lady Abbess, himself, his fortune, and his birth; but finds it all in vain: nor was he so infinitely afflicted with the thought of the eternal loss of *Calista*, (because he had possessed her) as he was to find himself betrayed to her, and doubtless to *Sylvia*, by *Octavio*; and nothing but *Calista*'s being confined from him, (though she were very dear and charming to his thought) could have made him rave so extremely for a sight of her: he loves her the more, by how much the more it was impossible for him to see her; and that difficulty and his despair increased his flame. In this humour he went to his lodging, the most undone extravagant that ever raged with love. He considers her in a place, where no art, or force of love, or human wit, can retrieve her; no nor so much as send her a letter. This added to his fury, and in his first wild imaginations, he resolves nothing less than firing the monastery, that in that confusion he might seize his right of love, and do a deed, that would render his name famous as the *Athenian* youth, who to get a fame, though an inglorious one, fired the temple of their gods. But his rage abating by consideration, that impiety dwelt not long with him: and he ran over a number more, till from one to another, he reduced himself, to a degree of moderation, which presenting him with some flattering hope, that give him a little ease: it was then that *Chevalier Tomaso*, and another *French* gentleman of *Cesario*'s faction, (who were newly arrived at *Brussels*) came to pay him their respects: and after a while carried him into the park to walk, where *Sylvia*'s page had seen him; and from whence they sent *Brilliard* to bespeak supper at this *cabaret*, where *Sylvia*'s chair and herself waited, and where the page found *Brilliard*, of whom he asked for his lord; but understanding he could not possibly come in some hours, being designed for Court that evening, whither he was obliged to go and kiss the Governor's hands, he went to the lady, who was almost dead with impatience, and told her, what he had learned: upon which she ordered her chairmen to carry her back to her lodgings, for she would not be persuaded to ask any questions of *Brilliard*, for whom she had a mortal hate: however, she resolved to send her page back with a billet, to wait *Philander*'s coming, which was not long; for having sooner dispatched their compliment at Court than they believed they should, they went all to supper together, where *Brilliard* had bespoke it; where being impatient to learn all the adventures of *Cesario*, since his departure from him, and of which no person could give so good an account as *Chevalier Tomaso*, *Philander* gave order that no body whomsoever should disturb them, and sat himself down to listen to the fortune of the Prince.

'You know, my lord,' said *Tomaso*, 'the state of things at your departure; and that all our glorious designs, for the liberty of all *France* were discovered, and betrayed by some of those little rascals, that great men are obliged to make use of in the greatest designs: upon whose confession you were proscribed, myself, this gentleman, and several others: it was our good fortunes to escape untaken, and yours to fall first in the messenger's hands, and carried to the *Bastille*, even from whence you had the luck to escape: but it was not so with *Cesario*.' 'Heavens,' cried *Philander*, 'the Prince, I hope is not taken.' 'Not so neither,' replied *Tomaso*, 'nor should you wonder you have received no news of him, in a long time, since forty thousand crowns being offered for his head, or to any thing that could discover him, it would have exposed him to have written to any body, he being beset on all sides with spies from the King; so that it was impossible to venture a letter, without very great hazard of his life. Besides all these hindrances, *Cesario*, who, you know, was ever a great admirer of the fair sex, happened in this his retreat to fall most desperately in love: nor could the fears of death, which alarmed him on all sides, deter him from his new amour: which, because it has relation to some part of his adventures, I cannot omit, especially to your lordship, his friend, to whom every circumstance of that Prince's fate and fortune will be of concern.

'You must imagine, my lord, that your seizure and escape was enough to alarm the whole party; and there was not a man of the League who did not think it high time to look about him, when one, so considerable as your lordship, was surprised. Nor did the Prince himself any longer believe himself safe, but retired himself under the darkness of the following night: he went only accompanied with his page to a lady's house, a widow of quality at *Paris*, that populous city being, as he conceived, the securest place to conceal himself in.

This lady was Madam the Countess of —— who had, as you know, my lord, one only daughter, *Mademoiselle Hermione*, the heiress of her family. The Prince knew this young lady had a tenderness for him ever since they were both very young, which first took beginning in a masque at Court, where she then acted *Mercury*, and danced so exceedingly finely, that she gave our young hero new desire, if not absolute love, and charmed him at least into wishes. She was not then old enough to perceive she conquered, as well as to make a conquest: and she was capable of receiving impressions as well as to give them: and it was believed by some who were very near the Prince, and knew all his secrets then, that this young lady pitied the sighs of the royal lover, and even then rewarded them: and though this were most credibly whispered, yet methinks it seems impossible he should then have been happy; and after so many years, after the possession of so many other beauties, should return to her again, and find all the passions and pains of a beginning flame. But there is nothing to be wondered at in the contradictions and humours of human nature. But however inconstant and wavering he had been, *Hermione* retained her first passion for him; and that I less wonder at, since you know the Prince has the most charming person in the world, and is the most perfectly beautiful of all his sex: to this his youth and quality add no little lustre; and I should not wonder, if all the softer sex should languish for him, nor that any one should love on — who hath once been touched with love for him.

'It was his last assurance the Prince so absolutely depended on, that (notwithstanding she was far from the opinion of his party) made him resolve to take sanctuary in those arms he was sure would receive him in any condition and circumstances. But now he makes her new vows, which possibly at first his safety obliged him to, while she returned them with all the passion of love. He made a thousand submissions to Madam the Countess, who he knew was fond of her daughter to that degree, that for her repose she was even willing to behold the sacrifice of her honour to this Prince, whom she knew *Hermione* loved even to death; so fond, so blindly fond is nature: and indeed after a little time that he lay there concealed, he reaped all the satisfaction that love could give him, or his youth could wish, with all the freedom imaginable. He only made vows of renouncing all other women, what ties or obligations soever he had upon him, and to resign himself entirely up to *Hermione*. I know not what new charms he had found by frequent conversation with her, and being uninterrupted by the sight of any other ladies; but it is most certain, my lord, that he grew to that excess of love, or rather dotage, (if love in one so young can be called so) that he languished for her, even while he possessed her all: he died, if obliged by company to retire from her an hour, at the end of which, being again brought to her, he would fall at her feet, and sigh, and weep, and make the most piteous moan that ever love inspired. He would complain upon the cruelty of a moment's absence, and vow he would not live where she was not. All that disturbed his happiness he reproached as enemies to his repose, and at last made her feign an illness, that no visits might be made her, and that he might possess all her hours. Nor did *Hermione* perceive all this without making her advantages of so glorious an opportunity; but, with the usual cunning of her sex, improved every minute she gave him: she now found herself sure of the heart of the finest man in the world; and of one she believed would prove the greatest, being the head of a most powerful faction, who were resolved, the first opportunity, to order affairs so as to come to an open rebellion, and to make him a king. All these things, how unlikely soever in reason, her love and ambition suggested to her; so that she believed she had but one game more to play, to establish herself the greatest and most happy woman in the world. She consults in this weighty affair, with her mother, who had a share of cunning that could carry on a design as well as any of her sex. They found but one obstacle to all *Hermione*'s rising greatness; and that was the Prince's being married; and that to a lady of so considerable birth and fortune, so eminent for her virtue, and all perfections of womankind, and withal so excellent for wit and beauty, that it was impossible to find any cause of a separation between them. So that finding it improbable to remove that let to her glories, she grew very melancholy, which was soon perceived by the too amorous Prince, who pleads, and sighs, and weeps on her bosom day and night to find the cause: but she, who found she had a difficult game to play, and that she had need of all her little aids, pretends a thousand little frivolous reasons before she discovers the true one; which served but to oblige him to ask anew, as she designed he should —— At last, one morning, finding him in the softest fit in the world, and ready to give her whatever she could ask in return for the secret of her disquiet, she told him with a sigh, how unhappy she was in loving so violently a man who could never be any thing to her more than the robber of her honour: and at last, with abundance of sighs and tears, bewailed his marriage —— He taking her with all the joy imaginable in his arms, thanked her for speaking of the only thing he had a thousand times been going to offer to her, but durst not for fear she should reproach him. He told her he looked upon himself as married to no woman but herself, to whom by a thousand solemn vows he had contracted himself, and that he would never own any other while he lived, let fortune do what she pleased with him. *Hermione*, thriving hitherto so well, urged his easy heart yet farther, and told him, though she had left no doubt remaining in her of his love and virtue, no suspicion of his vows, yet the world would still esteem the Princess his wife, and herself only as a prostitute to his youthful pleasure; and as she conceived her birth and fortune not to be much inferior to that of the Princess, she should die with indignation and shame, to bear all the reproach of his wantonness, while his now wife would live esteemed and pitied as an injured innocent. To all which he replied, as mad in love, that the Princess, he confessed, was a lady to whom he had obligations, but that he esteemed her no more his wife, since he was married to her at the age of twelve years; an age, wherein he was not capacitated to choose good or evil, or to answer for himself, or his inclinations: and though she were a lady of absolute virtue, of youth, wit and beauty; yet fate had so ordained it, that he had reserved his heart to this moment entirely for herself; and that he renounced all pretenders to him except herself; that he had now possessed the Princess for the space of twenty years; that youth had a long race to run, and could not take up at those years with one single beauty: that hitherto ravage and destruction of hearts had been his province and glory, and that he thought he never lost time but when he was a little while constant: but now he was fixed to all he would ever possess whilst he had breath; and that she was both his mistress and his wife; his eternal happiness, and the end of all his loving. It is there he said he would remain as in his first state of innocence: that hitherto his ambition had been above his passion, but that now his heart was so entirely subdued to this fair charmer (for so he call'd and thought her) that he could be content to live and die in the glory of being hers alone, without wishing for liberty or empire, but to render her more glorious. A thousand things tender and fond he said to this purpose, and the result of all ended in most solemn vows, that if ever fortune favoured him with a crown, he would fix it on her head, and make her in spite of all former ties and obligations, Queen of *France*. This was sufficient to appease her sighs and tears, and she remained entirely satisfied of his vows, which were exchanged before Madam the Countess, and confirmed by all the binding obligations, love on his side could invent, and ambition and subtlety on hers. When I came at any time to visit him, which by stealth a-nights sometimes I did, to take orders from him how I should act in all things, (though I lay concealed like himself) he would tell me all that had passed between him and *Hermione*. I suppose, not so much for the reposing the secret in my breast, as out of a fond pleasure to be repeating passages of his dotage, and repeating her name, which was ever in his mouth: I saw she had reduced him to a great degree of slavery, and could not look tamely on, while a hero so young, so gay, so great, and so hopeful, lay idling away his precious time, without doing any thing, either in order for his own safety or ambition. It was, my lord, a great pity to see how his noble resolution was changed, and how he was perfectly effeminated into soft woman. I endeavoured at first to rouse him from this lethargy of love; and argued with him the little reason, that in my opinion he had to be so charmed. I told him, *Hermione*, of all the beauties of *France*, was esteemed one of the meanest, and that if ever she had gained a conquest (as many she was infamously famed for) it was purely the force of her youth and quality; but that now that bloom was past, and she was one of those, which in less quality we called old. At these reproaches of his judgement, I often perceived him to blush, but more with anger than shame. Yet because, according to the vogue of the town, he found there was reason in what I said, and which he could only contradict by saying, however she was, she appeared all otherwise to him: he blamed me a little kindly for my hard words against her, and began to swear to me, that he thought her all over charm. He vowed there was absolute fascination in her eyes and tongue. "It is confessed," said he, "she has not much of youth, nor of that which we agree to call beauty: but she has a grace so masculine, an air so ravishing, a wit and humour so absolutely made to charm, that they all together sufficiently recompense for her want of delicacy in complexion and feature: and in a word, my *Tomaso*," cries he, embracing me, "she is, though I know not what, or how, a maid that compels me to adore her; she has a natural power to please above the rest of her dull sex; and I can abate her a face and shape, and yet vie her for beauty, with any of the celebrated ones of *France*."

'I found, by the manner of his saying this, that he was really charmed, and past all retrieve, bewitched to this lady. I found it vain therefore to press him to a separation, or to lessen his passion, but on the contrary told him, there was a time for all things; if fate had so ordained it that he must love. But I besought him, with all the eloquence of perfect duty and friendship, not to suffer his passion to surmount his ambition and his reason, so far as to neglect his interest and safety; and for a little pleasure with a woman, suffer all his friends to perish, that had woven their fortunes with his, and must stand or fall, as he thrived: I implored him not to cast away the *good cause*, which was so far advanced, and that yet, notwithstanding this discourse, might all be retrieved by his conduct, and good management, that I knew however the King appeared in outward shew to be offended, that it was yet in his power to calm the greatest tempest this discovery had raised: that it was but casting himself at His Majesty's feet, and begging his mercy, by a confession of the truth of some part of the matter; and that it was impossible he could fail of a pardon, from so indulgent a monarch, as he had offended: that there was no action could wholly rase out of the King's heart, that tenderness and passion he had ever expressed towards him; and his peace might be made with all the facility imaginable. To this he urged a very great reluctancy, and cried, he would sooner die, than by a confession expose the lives of his friends, and let the world see their whole design before they had power to effect it: and not only so, but put it past all their industry, ever to bring so hopeful a plot about again. At this I smiled, and asked His Highness's pardon, told him I was of another opinion, as most of the heads of the *Huguenots* were, that what he said to His Majesty in private could never possibly be made public: that His Majesty would content himself with the knowledge of the truth, without caring to satisfy the world, so greatly to the prejudice of a prince of the blood, and a man so very dear to him as himself. He urged the fears this would give those of the Reformed Religion, and alarm them with a thousand apprehensions, that it would discover every man of them, by unravelling the intrigue. To this I replied, that their fears would be very short-lived; for as soon as he had, by his submission and confession, gained his pardon, he had no more to do, but to renounce all he had said, leave the Court, and put himself into the protection of his friends, who were ready to receive him. That he need but appear abroad a little time, and he would see himself addressed to again, by all the *Huguenot* party, who would quickly put him into a condition of fearing nothing.

'My counsel, with the same persuasion from all of quality of the party, who came to see him, was at last approved of by him, and he began to say a thousand things to assure me of his fidelity to his friends, and the faction, which he vowed never to forsake, for any other interest, but to stand or fall in its defence, and that he was resolved to be a king, or nothing; and that he would put in practice all the arts and stratagems of cunning, as well as force, to attain to this glorious end, however crooked and indirect they might appear to fools. However, he conceived the first necessary step to this, was the getting his pardon, to gain a little time, to manage things anew to the best advantage: that at present all things were at a stand without life or motion, wanting the sight of himself, who was the very life and soul of motion, the axle-tree that could turn the wheel of fortune round about again.

'And now he had talked himself in to sense again; he cried —"Oh my *Tomaso*! I long to be in action, my soul is on the wing, and ready to take its flight through any hazard ——" but sighing on a sudden, again he cried: "But oh, my friend, my wings are impt by love, I cannot mount the regions of the air, and thence survey the world; but still, as I would rise to mightier glory, they flag to humble love, and fix me there. Here I am charmed to lazy, soft repose, here it is I smile and play, and love away my hours: but I will rouse, I will, my dear *Tomaso*; nor shall the winged boy hold me enslaved: believe me, friend, he shall not." He sent me away pleased with this, and I left him to his repose.'

Supper being ready to come upon the table; though *Philander* were impatient to hear the story out, yet he would not press *Tomaso*, till after supper; in which time, they discoursed of nothing but of the miracles of *Cesario*'s love to *Hermione*. He could not but wonder a prince so young, so amorous, and so gay, should return again, after almost fifteen years, to an old mistress, and who had never been in her youth a celebrated beauty: one, whom it was imagined the King, and several after him at Court, had made a gallantry with —— On this he paused for some time, and reflected on his passion for *Sylvia*; and this fantastic intrigue of the Prince's inspired him with a kind of curiosity to try, whether fleeting love, would carry him back again to this abandoned maid. In these thoughts, and such discourse, they passed away the time during supper; which ended, and a fresh bottle brought to the table, with a new command that none should interrupt them, the impatient *Philander* obliged *Tomaso* to give him a farther account of the Prince's proceedings; which he did in this manner.

'My lord, having left the Prince, as I imagined very well resolved, I spoke of it to as many of our party, as I could conveniently meet with, to prepare them for the discovery, I believed the Prince would pretend to make, that they should not by being alarmed at the first news of it, put themselves into fears, that might indeed discover them: nor would I suffer *Cesario* to rest, but daily saw him, or rather nightly stole to him, to keep up his resolution: and indeed, in spite of love, to which he had made himself so entire a slave, I brought him to his own house, to visit Madam his wife, who was very well at Court, maugre her husband's ill conduct, as they called it; the King being, as you know, my lord, extremely kind to that deserving lady, often made her visits, and would without very great impatiency hear her plead for her husband, the Prince; and possibly it was not ungrateful to him: all this we daily learned from a page, who secretly brought intelligence from Madam the Princess: so that we conceived it wholly necessary for the interest of the Prince, that he should live in a good understanding with this prudent lady. To this end, he feigned more respect than usual to her, and as soon as it was dark, every evening made her his visits. One evening, amongst the rest, he happened to be there, just as the proclamation came forth, of four thousand crowns to any that could discover him; and within half an hour after came the King, to visit the Princess, as every night he did; her lodging being in the Court: the King came without giving any notice, and with a very slender train that night; so that he was almost in the Princess's bed-chamber before any body informed her he was there; so that the Prince had no time to retire but into Madam the Princess's cabaret, the door of which she immediately locking, made such a noise and bustle, that it was heard by His Majesty, who nevertheless had passed it by, if her confusion and blushes had not farther betrayed her, with the unusual address she made to the King: who therefore asked her, who she had concealed in her closet. She endeavoured to put him off with some feigned replies, but it would not do; the more her confusion, the more the King was inquisitive, and urged her to give him the key of her *cabaret*: but she, who knew the life of the Prince would be in very great danger, should he be taken so, and knew on the other side, that to deny it, would betray the truth as much as his discovery would, and cause him either to force the key, or the door, fell down at his feet, and wetting his shoes with her tears, and grasping his knees with her trembling arms, implored that mercy and pity, for the Prince her husband, whom her virtue had rendered dear to her, however criminal he appeared to His Majesty: she told him, His Majesty had more peculiarly the attributes of a god, than any other monarch upon earth, and never heard the wretched or the innocent plead in vain. She told him, that herself, and her children, who were dearer to her than life, should all be as hostages for the good conduct and duty of the Prince's future life and actions: and they would all be obliged to suffer any death, though ever so ignominious, upon the

least breaking out of her lord: that he should utterly abandon those
of the Reformed Religion, and yield to what articles His Majesty
would graciously be pleased to impose, quitting all his false and
unreasonable pretensions to the crown, which was only the effects
of the flattery of the *Huguenot* party, and the *malcontents*. Thus
with the virtue and goodness of an angel, she pleaded with such
moving eloquence, mixed with tears from beautiful eyes, that she
failed not to soften the royal heart, who knew not how to be deaf
when beauty pleaded: yet he would not seem to yield so suddenly,
lest it should be imagined he had too light a sense of his treasons,
which, in any other great man, would have been punished with no
less than death: yet, as she pleaded, he grew calmer, and suffered
it without interruption, till she waited for his reply; and obliged
him by her silence to speak. He numbers up the obligations he had
heaped on her husband; how he had, by putting all places of great
command and interest into his hands, made him the greatest prince,
and favourite of a subject, in the world; and infinitely happier than
a monarch: that he had all the glory and power of one, and wanted
but the care: all the sweets of empire, while all that was disagreeable
and toilsome, remained with the title alone. He therefore upbraided
him with infinite ingratitude, and want of honour; with all the folly
of ambitious youth: and left nothing unsaid that might make the
Princess sensible it was too late to hide any of his treasons from him,
since they were all but too apparent to His Majesty. It was therefore
that she urged nothing but his royal mercy, and forgiveness, without
endeavouring to lessen his guilt, or enlarge on his innocency. In fine,
my lord, so well she spoke, that at last, she had the joy to perceive
the happy effects of her wit and goodness, which had moved tears of
pity and compassion from His Majesty's eyes; which was *Cesario*'s
cue to come forth, as immediately he did, (having heard all that had
passed) and threw himself at His Majesty's feet: and this was the
critical minute he was to snatch for the gaining of his point, and of
which he made a most admirable use. He called up all the force of
necessary dissimulation, tenderness to his voice, tears to his eyes,
and trembling to his hands, that stayed the too willing and melting
monarch by his robe, till he had heard him implore, and granted

him his pity: nor did he quit his hold, till the King cried, with a soft voice —"Rise"— at which he was assured of what he asked. He refused however to rise, till the pardon was pronounced. He owned himself the greatest criminal in nature; that he was drawn from his allegiance by the most subtle artifices of his enemies, who under false friendships had allured his hopes with gilded promises; and which he now too plainly saw were designed to propagate their own private interests, and not his glory. He humbly besought His Majesty to make some gracious allowances for his vanities of youth, and to believe now he had so dearly bought discretion, at almost the price of His Majesty's eternal displeasure, that he would reform, and lead so good a life, so absolutely free from any appearance of ambition, that His Majesty should see he had not a more faithful subject than himself. In fine, he found himself, by this acknowledgement he had begun with, to advance yet further: nor would His Majesty be satisfied without the whole scene of the matter; and how they were to have surprised and seized him; where, and by what numbers. All which he was forced to give an account of; since now to have fallen back, when he was in their hands, had been his infallible ruin. All which he performed with as much tenderness and respect to his friends concerned, as if his own life had been depending: and though he were extremely pressed to discover some of the great ones of the party, he would never give his consent to an action so mean, as to be an evidence. All that could be got from him farther, was to promise His Majesty, to give under his hand, what he had in private confessed to him; with which the King remained very well satisfied, and ordered him to come to Court the next day. Thus for that night they parted with infinite caresses on the King's part, and no little joy on his. His Majesty was no sooner gone, but he gave immediate order to the Secretaries of State, to draw up his pardon, which was done with so good speed, that he had it in his hands the next day. When he came to Court, it is not to be imagined the surprise it was to all, to behold the man, in the greatest state imaginable, who but yesterday was to have been crucified at any price: and those who most exclaimed against him, were the first that paid him homage, and caressed him at the highest rate; only the most wise and judicious prophesied his glories were not of long continuation. The King made no visits where the Prince did not publicly appear: he told all the people, with infinite joy, that the Prince had confessed the whole plot, and that he would give it, under his hand and seal, in order to have it published throughout all *France*, for the satisfaction of all those who had been deluded and deceived by our specious pretences; and for the terror of those, who had any ways adhered to so pernicious a villainy: so that he met with nothing but reproaches from those of our own party at Court: for there were many, who hitherto were unsuspected, and who now, out of fear of being betrayed by the Prince, were ready to fall at the King's feet and confess all: others there were, that left the Court and town upon it. In fine, the face of things seemed extremely altered, while the Prince bore himself like a person who had the misfortune justly to lie beneath the exclamations of a disobliged multitude, as they at least imagined and bore all, as if their fears had been true, without so much as offering at his justification, to confirm His Majesty's good opinion of him: he added to his pardon, a present of twenty thousand crowns, half of it being paid the next day after his coming to Court. And in short, my lord, His Majesty grew so fond of the Prince, he could not endure to suffer him out of his presence, and was never satisfied with seeing him: he carried him the next day to the public *theatre* with him, to shew the world he was reconciled. But by this time he had all confirmed, and grew impatient to declare himself to his friends, whom he would not have remain long in their ill opinion of him. It happened the third day of his coming to Court, (in returning some of those visits he had received from all the great persons) he went to wait upon the Duchess of —— a lady, who had ever had a tender respect for the Prince: in the time of this visit, a young lady of quality happened to come in; one whom your lordship knows, a great wit, and much esteemed at Court, *Mademoiselle Mariana*: by this lady he found himself welcomed to Court, with all the demonstrations of joy; as also by the old Duchess, who had divers times heretofore persuaded the Prince to leave the *Huguenots*, and return to the King and Court: she used to tell him he was a handsome youth, and she loved his mother well; that he danced finely, and she had rather see him in a ball at Court, than in rebellion in the field; and often to this purpose her love would rally him; and now shewed no less concern of joy for his reconciliation; and looking on him as a true convert, fell a railing, with all the malice and wit she could invent, at those public-spirited knaves who had seduced him. She railed on, and cursed those politics which had betrayed him to almost ruin itself.

'The Prince heard her with all the patience he could for some time, but when he found her touch him so tenderly, and name his friends as if he had owned any such ill counsellors, his colour came in his face, and he could not forbear defending us with all the force of friendship. He told her, he knew of no such seducers, no villains of the party, nor of any traitorous design, that either himself, or any man in *France*, had ever harboured: at which, she going to upbraid him in a manner too passionate, he thought it decent to end his visit, and left her very abruptly. At his going out, he met with the Duke of —— brother to the Duchess, going to visit her: *en passant*, a very indifferent ceremony passed on both sides, for this Duke never had entertained a friendship, or scarce a respect for *Cesario*; but going into his sister's the Duchess, her chamber, he found her all in a rage at the Prince's so public defence of the *Huguenots* and their allies; and the Duke entering, they told him what had passed. This was a very great pleasure to him, who had a mortal hate at this time to the Prince. He made his visit very short, hastens to Court, and went directly to the King, and told him how infinitely he found His Majesty mistaken in the imagined penitence of the Prince; and then told him what he had said at the Duchess of —— lodgings, and had disowned, he ever confessed any treasonable design against His Majesty, and gave them the lie, who durst charge him with any such villainy. The King, who was unwilling to credit what he wished not true, plainly told the Duke he could not believe it, but that it was the malice of his enemies, who had forged this: the Duke replied, he would bring those to His Majesty that heard the words: immediately thereupon dispatched away his page to beg the Duchess would come to Court, with *Mademoiselle Mariana*. The Duchess suspecting the truth of the business, and unwilling to do the Prince an ill office, excused herself by sending word she was ill of the colic. But *Mariana*, who loved the King's interest, and found the ingratitude, as she called it, of the Prince, hastened in her chair to Court, and justified all the Duke had said; who being a woman of great wit and honour, found that credit which the Duke failed of, as an open enemy to the Prince. About an hour after, the Prince appeared at Court, and found the face of things changed extremely; and those, who before had kissed his hand, and were proud of every smile from him, now beheld him with coldness, and scarce made way as he passed. However, he went to the Presence, and found the King, whose looks were also very much changed; who taking him into the bed-chamber, shewed him his whole confession, drawn up ready for him to sign, as he had promised, though he never intended any such thing; and now resolved to die rather than do it, he took it in his hand, while the King cried —"Here keep your word, and sign your narrative —" "Stay, sir," replied the Prince, "I have the counsel of my friends to ask in so weighty an affair." The King, confirmed in all he had heard, no longer doubted but he had been too cunning for him; and going out in a very great discontent, he only cried —"Sir, if you have any better friends than myself, I leave you to them; ——" and with this left him. The Prince was very glad he had got the confession-paper, hoping it would never come to light again; the King was the only person to whom he had made the confession, and he was but one accuser; and him he thought the party could at any time be too powerful to oppose, all being easily believed on their side, and nothing on that of the Court. After this, in the evening, the King going to visit Madam the Duchess of —— for whom he had a very great esteem, and whither every day the whole Court followed him; the Prince, with all the assurance imaginable, made his Court there also; but he was no sooner come into the Presence, but he perceived anger in the eyes of that monarch, who had indeed a peculiar greatness and fierceness there, when angry: a minute after, he sent Monsieur —— to the Prince, with a command to leave the Court; and without much ceremony he accordingly departed, and went directly to *Hermione*, who with all the impatience of love expected him; nor was much surprised to find him banished the Court: for he made her acquainted with his most secret designs; who having made all his interests her own, espoused whatever related to him, and was capable of retaining all with great fidelity: nor had he quitted her one night, since his coming to Court; and he hath often with rapture told me, *Hermione* was a friend, as well as a mistress, and one with whom, when the first play was ended, he could discourse with of useful things of State as well as love; and improve in both the noble mysteries by her charming conversation. The night of this second disgrace I went to *Hermione*'s to visit him, where we discoursed what was next to be done. He did not think his pardon was sufficient to secure him, and he was not willing to trust a King who might be convinced, that that tenderness he had for him, was absolutely against the peace and quiet of all *France*. I was of this opinion, so that upon farther debate, we thought it absolutely necessary to quit *France*, till the Court's heat should be a little abated; and that the King might imagine himself by his absence, in more tranquillity than he really is. In order to this, he made me take my flight into *Flanders*, here to provide all things necessary against his coming, and I received his command to seek you out, and beg you would attend his coming hither. I expect him every day. He told me at parting, he longed to consult with you, how next to play this mighty game, on which so many kingdoms are staked, and which he is resolved to win, or be nothing.' 'An imperfect relation,' replied *Philander*, 'we had of this affair, but I never could learn by what artifice the Prince brought about his good fortune at Court; but of your own escape I have heard nothing, pray oblige me with the relation of it.' 'Sir,' said *Tomaso*, 'there is so little worthy the trouble you will take in hearing it, that you may spare yourself the curiosity.' 'Sir,' replied Philander, 'I always had too great a share in what concerned you, not to be curious of the story.' 'In which,' replied *Tomaso*, 'though there be nothing novel, I will satisfy you.'

'Be pleased to know, my lord, that about a week before our design was fully discovered by some of our own under-rogues, I had taken a great house in *Faubourg St Germain*, for my mistress, whom you know, my lord, I had lived with the space of a year. She was gone to drink the waters of *Bourbon*, for some indisposition, and I had promised her all things should be fitted against her return, agreeable to her humour and desire; and indeed, I spared no cost to make her apartment magnificent: and I believe few women of quality could purchase one so rich; for I loved the young woman, who had beauty and discretion enough to charm, though the *Parisians* of the royal party called her *Nicky Nacky*, which was given her in derision to me, not to her, for whom every body, for her own sake, had a considerable esteem. Besides, my lord, I had taken up money out of the Orphans' and Widows' Bank, from the Chamber of *Paris*, and could very well afford to be lavish, when I spent upon the public stock. While I was thus ordering all things, my valet came running out of breath, to tell me, that being at the *Louvre*, he saw several persons carried to the secretary's office, with messengers; and that inquiring who they might be, he found they were two *Parisians*, who had offered themselves to the messengers to be carried to be examined about a plot, the Prince *Cesario* and those of the Reformed Religion, had to surprise His Majesty, kill Monsieur his brother, and set all *Paris* in a flame: and as to what particularly related to myself, he said, that I was named as the person designed to seize upon the King's guards, and dispatch Monsieur. This my own conscience told me was too true, for me to make any doubt but I was discovered: I therefore left a servant in the house, and in a hackney-coach took my flight. I drove a little out of *Paris* till night, and then returned again, as the surest part of the world where I could conceal myself: I was not long in studying who I should trust with my life and safety, but went directly to the palace of Madam, the Countess of —— who you know, my lord, was a widow, and a woman who had, for a year past, a most violent passion for me; but she being a lady, who had made many such gallantries, and past her youth, I had only a very great respect and acknowledgement for her, and her quality, and being obliged to her, for the effects of her tenderness, shewn upon several occasions, I could not but acquit myself like a *cavalier* to her, whenever I could possibly; and which, though I have a thousand times feigned great business to prevent, yet I could not always be ungrateful; and when I paid her my services, it was ever extremely well received, and because of her quality, and setting up for a second marriage, she always took care to make my approaches to her, in as concealed a manner as possible; and only her porter, one page, and one woman, knew this secret amour; and for the better carrying it on, I ever went in a hackney-coach, lest my livery should be seen at her gate: and as it was my custom at other times, so I now sent the porter, (who, by my bounty, and his lady's, was entirely my own creature) for the page to come to me, who immediately did, and I desired him to let his lady know, I waited her commands; that was the word: he immediately brought me answer, that by good fortune his lady was all alone, and infinitely wishing she knew where to send him for me: and I immediately, at that good news, ran up to her chamber; where I was no sooner come, but desiring me to sit, she ordered her porter to be called, and gave orders, upon pain of life, not to tell of my being in the house, whatever inquiry should be made after me; and having given the same command to her page, she dismissed them, and came to me with all the fear and trembling imaginable. "Ah Monsieur," cried she, falling on my neck, "we are undone —" I, not imagining she had heard the news already, cried, "Why, is my passion discovered?" "Ah," replied she in tears, "I would to heaven it were no worse! would all the earth had discovered that, which I should esteem my glory — But it is, my charming monsieur," continued she, "your treasons and not amour, whose discovery will be so fatal to me." At this I seemed amazed, and begged her, to let me understand her: she told me what I have said before; and moreover, that the Council had that very evening issued out warrants for me, and she admired how I escaped. After a little discourse of this kind, I asked her, what she would advise me to do? for I was very well assured, the violent hate the King had particularly for me, would make him never consent I should live on any terms: and therefore it was determined I should not surrender myself; and she resolved to run the risk of concealing me; which, in fine, she did three days, furnishing me with money and necessaries for my flight. In this time a proclamation came forth, and offered five hundred crowns for my head, or to seize me alive, or dead. This sum so wrought with the slavish minds of men, that no art was left unassayed to take me: they searched all houses, all hackney-coaches that passed by night; and did all that avarice could inspire to take me, but all in vain: at last, this glorious sum so dazzled the mind of Madam the Countess's porter, that he went to a captain of the Musketeers, and assured him, if the King would give him the aforesaid sum, he would betray me, and bring him the following night to surprise me, without any resistance: the captain, who thought, if the porter should have all the sum, he should get none; and every one hoping to be the happy man, that should take me, and win the prize, could not endure another should have the glory of both, and so never told the King of the offer the porter had made. But however secret, one may imagine an amour to be kept, yet in so busy a place as *Paris* and the apartments of the Court-coquets, this of ours had been discoursed, and the intrigue more than suspected: whether this, or the captain, before named, imagined to find me at the house of the Countess, because the porter had made such an offer; I say, however it was, the next morning, upon a *Sunday*, the guards broke into several chambers, and missing me, had the insolence to come to the door of that of the Countess; and she had only time to slip on her night-gown, and running to the door besought them to have respect to her sex and quality, while I started from my bed, which was the same from whence the Countess rose; and not knowing where to hide, or what to do, concealing my clothes between the sheets, I mounted from the table to a great silver sconce that was fastened to the wall by the bed-side, and from thence made but one spring up to the tester of the bed; which being one of those raised with strong wood-work and japan, I could easily do; or, rather it was by miracle I did it; and laid myself along the top, while my back touched the ceiling of the chamber; by this time, when no entreaties could prevail, they had burst open the chamber-door, and running directly to the bed, they could not believe their eyes: they saw no person there, but the plain print of two, with the pillows for two persons. This gave them the curiosity to search farther, which they did, with their swords, under the bed, in every corner, behind every curtain, up the chimney, felt all about the wainscot and hangings for false doors or closets; surveyed the floor for a trap-door: at last they found my fringed gloves at the window, and the sash a little up, and then they concluded I had made my escape out at that window: this thought they seemed confirmed in, and therefore ran to the garden, where they thought I had descended, and with my gloves, which they bore away as the trophies of their almost gained victory, they searched every hedge and bush, arbour, grotto, and tree; but not being able to find what they sought, they concluded me gone, and told all the town, how very near they were to seizing me. After this, the very porter and page believed me escaped out of that window, and there was no farther search made after me: but the Countess was amazed, as much as any of the soldiers, to find which way I had conveyed myself, when I came down and undeceived her; but when she saw from whence I came, she wondered more than before how I could get up so high; when trying the trick again, I could not do it, if I might have won never so considerable a wager upon it, without pulling down the sconce, and the tester also.

'After this, I remained there undiscovered the whole time the Prince was at *Hermione*'s, till his coming to Court, when I verily believed he would have gained me my pardon, with his own; but the King had sworn my final destruction, if he ever got me in his power; and proclaiming me a traitor, seized all they could find of mine. It was then that I believed it high time to take my flight; which, as soon as I heard the Prince again in disgrace, I did, and got safely into *Holland*, where I remained about six weeks. But, oh! what is woman! The first news I heard, and that was while I remained at the Countess's that my mistress, for whom I had taken such cares and who had professed to love me above all things, no sooner heard I was fled and proscribed, but retiring to a friend's house, (for her own was seized for mine) and the officers imagining me there too, they came to search; and a young *cavalier*, of a noble aspect, great wit and courage, and indeed a very fine gentleman, was the officer that entered her chamber, to search for me; who, being at first sight surprised with her beauty, and melting with her tears, fell most desperately in love with her, and after hearing how she had lost all her money, plate, and jewels, and rich furniture, offered her his service to retrieve them, and did do it; and from one favour to another, continued so to oblige the fair fickle creature, that he won, with that and his handsome mien, a possession of her heart, and she yielded in a week's time to my most mortal enemy. And the Countess, who at my going from her, swooned, and bathed me all in tears, making a thousand vows of fidelity, and never to favour mankind more: this very woman, sir, as soon as my back was turned, made new advances to a young lord, who, believing her to be none of the most faithful, would not trust her under matrimony: he being a man of no great fortune, and she a mistress of a very considerable one, his standing off on these terms inflames her the more; and I have advice, that she is very much in love with him, and it is believed will do what he desires of her: so that I was no sooner abandoned by fortune, but fickle woman followed her example, and fled me too. Thus, my lord, you have the history of my double unhappiness: and I am waiting here a fate which no human wit can guess at: the arrival of the Prince will give a little life to our affair; and I yet have hope to see him in *Paris*, at the head of forty thousand *Huguenots*, to revenge all the insolences we have suffered.'

After discoursing of several things, and of the fate of several persons, it was bed-time; and they taking leave, each man departed to his chamber.

Philander, while he was undressing, being alone with *Brilliard*, began to discourse of *Sylvia*, and to take some care of letting her know, he was arrived at *Brussels*; and for her convoy thither. *Brilliard*, who even yet retained some unaccountable hope, as lovers do, of one day being happy with that fair one; and believing he could not be so, with so much felicity, while she was in the hands of *Octavio* as those of *Philander*, would never tell his lord his sentiments of her conduct, nor of her love to *Octavio*, and those other passages that had occurred in *Holland*: he only cried, he believed she might be overcome, being left to herself and by the merits and good fashion of *Octavio*; but would not give his master an absolute fear, or any account of truth, that he might live with her again, if possible, as before; and that she might hold herself so obliged to him for silence in these affairs, as might one day render him happy. These were the unweighed reasons he gave for deluding his lord into a kind opinion to the fickle maid: but ever when he named *Sylvia*, *Philander* could perceive his blushes rise, and from them believed there was something behind in his thought, which he had a mind to know: he therefore pressed him to the last degree — and cried —'Come —

confess to me, *Brilliard*, the reason of your blushes: I know you are a lover, and I was content to suffer you my rival, knowing your respect to me.' This, though he spoke smiling, raised a greater confusion in *Brilliard*'s heart. 'I own, my lord,' said he, 'that I have, in spite of that respect, and all the force of my soul, had the daring to love her whom you loved; but still the consideration of my obligations to your lordship surmounted that saucy flame, notwithstanding all the encouragement of your inconstancy, and the advantage of the rage it put Sylvia in against you.' 'How,' cried *Philander*, 'does *Sylvia* know then of my falseness, and is it certain that *Octavio* has betrayed me to her?' With that *Brilliard* was forced to advance, and with a design of some revenge upon *Octavio*, (who, he hoped, would be challenged by his lord, where one, or both might fall in the rencounter, and leave him master of his hopes) he told him all that had passed between them, all but real possession, which he only imagined, but laid the whole weight on *Octavio*, making *Sylvia* act but as an incensed woman, purely out of high revenge and resentment of so great an injury as was done her love. He farther told him, how, in the extravagancy of her rage, she had resolved to marry *Octavio*, and how he prevented it by making a public declaration she was his wife already; and for which *Octavio* procured the *States* to put him in prison; but by an accident that happened to the uncle of *Octavio*, for which he was forced to fly, the *States* released him, when he came to his lord: 'How,' cried *Philander*, 'and is the traitor *Octavio* fled from *Holland*, and from the reach of my chastisement?' 'Yes,' replied *Brilliard*; 'and not to hold you longer from the truth, has forced *Sylvia* away with him.' At this *Philander* grew into a violent rage, sometimes against *Octavio* for his treasons against friendship; sometimes he felt the old flame revive, raised and blown jealousy, and was raving to imagine any other should possess the lovely *Sylvia*. He now beholds her with all those charms that first fired him, and thinks, if she be criminal, it was only the effects of the greatest love, which always hurries women on to the highest revenges. In vain he seeks to extinguish his returning flame by the thought of *Calista*; yet, at that thought, he starts like one awakened from a dream of honour, to fall asleep again, and dream of love. Before it was rage and pride, but now it was tenderness and grief, softer passions, and more insupportable. New wounds smart most, but old ones are most dangerous. While he was thus raging, walking, pausing, and loving, one knocked at his chamber-door. It was *Sylvia*'s page, who had waited all the evening to speak to him, and could not till now be admitted. *Brilliard* was just going to tell him he was there before, when he arrived now again: *Philander* was all unbuttoned, his stockings down, and his hair under his cap, when the page, being let in by *Brilliard*, ran to his lord, who knew him and embraced him: and it was a pretty while they thus caressed each other, without the power of speaking; he of asking a question, and the boy of delivering his message; at last, he gave him *Sylvia*'s billet, which was thus —

To PHILANDER.

False and perjured as you are, I languish for a sight of you, and conjure you to give it me, as soon as this comes to your hands. Imagine not, that I have prepared those instruments of revenge that are so justly due to your perfidy; but rather, that I have yet too tender sentiments for you, in spite of the outrage you have done my heart; and that for all the ruin you have made, I still adore you: and though I know you now another's slave, yet I beg you would vouchsafe to behold the spoils you have made, and allow me this recompense for all, to say — Here was the beauty I once esteemed, though now she is no more *Philander*'s

SYLVIA.

'How,' cried he out, 'No more *Philander*'s *Sylvia*! By heaven, I had rather be no more *Philander*!' And at that word, without considering whether he were in order for a visit or not, he advancing his joyful voice, cried out to the page, 'Lead on, my faithful boy, lead on to *Sylvia*.' In vain *Brilliard* beseeches him to put himself into a better equipage; in vain he urges to him, the indecency of making a visit in that posture; he thought of nothing but *Sylvia*; however he ran after him with his hat, cloak, and comb, and as he was in the chair dressed his hair, and suffered the page to conduct him where he pleased: which being to *Sylvia*'s, lodgings, he ran up stairs, and into her chamber, as by instinct of love, and found her laid on her bed, to which he made but one step from the door; and catching her in his arms, as he kneeled upon the carpet, they both remained unable to utter any thing but sighs: and surely *Sylvia* never appeared more charming; she had for a month or two lived at her ease, and had besides all the advantage of fine dressing which she had purposely put on, in the most tempting fashion, on purpose to engage him, or rather to make him see how fine a creature his perfidy had lost him: she first broke silence, and with a thousand violent reproaches, seemed as if she would fain break from those arms, which she wished might be too strong for her force; while he endeavours to appease her as lovers do, protesting a thousand times that there was nothing in that history of his amour with *Calista*, but revenge on *Octavio*, who he knew was making an interest in her heart, contrary to all the laws of honour and friendship, (for he had learned, by the reproaches of the Lady Abbess, that *Calista* was sister to *Octavio*). 'He has had the daring to confess to me his passion,' said he, 'for you, and could I do less in revenge, than to tell him I had one for his sister? I knew by the violent reproaches I ever met with in your letters, though they were not plainly confessed, that he had played me foul, and discovered my feigned intrigue to you; and even this I suffered, to see how far you could be prevailed with against me. I knew *Octavio* had charms of youth and wit, and that you had too much the ascendant over him, to be denied any secret you had a mind to draw from him; I knew your nature too curious, and your love too inquisitive, not to press him to a sight of my letters, which seen must incense you; and this trial I designedly made of your faith, and as a return to *Octavio*.' Thus he flatters, and she believes, because she has a mind to believe; and thus by degrees he softens the listening *Sylvia*; swears his faith with sighs, and confirms it with his tears, which bedewed her fair bosom, as they fell from his bright dissembling eyes; and yet so well he dissembled, that he scarce knew himself that he did so: and such effects it wrought on *Sylvia*, that in spite of all her honour and vows engaged to *Octavio*, and horrid protestations never to receive again the fugitive to her arms, she suffers all he asks, gives herself up again to love, and is a second time undone. She regards him as one to whom she had a peculiar right as the first lover: she was married to his love, to his heart; and *Octavio* appeared the intruding gallant, that would, and ought to be content with the gleanings of the harvest, *Philander* should give him the opportunity to take up: and though, if she had at this very time been put to her sober choice, which she would have abandoned, it would have been *Philander*, as not in so good circumstances at that time to gratify all her extravagances of expense; but she would not endure to think of losing either: she was for two reasons covetous of both, and swore fidelity to both, protesting each the only man; and she was now contriving in her thoughts, how to play the jilt most artificially; a help-meet, though natural enough to her sex, she had not yet much essayed, and never to this purpose: she knew well she should have need of all her cunning in this affair; for she had to do with men of quality and honour, and too much wit to be grossly imposed upon. She knew *Octavio* loved so well, it would either make her lose him by death, or resenting pride, if she should ever be discovered to him to be untrue; and she knew she should lose *Philander* to some new mistress, if he once perceived her false. He asked her a thousand questions concerning *Octavio*, and she seemed to lavish every secret of her soul to her lover; but like a right woman, so ordered her discourse, as all that made for her advantage she declared, and all the rest she concealed. She told him, that those hopes which her revenge had made her give *Octavio*, had obliged him to present her with such and such fine jewels, such plate, such sums; and in fine, made him understand that all her trophies from the believing lover should be laid at his feet, who had conquered her heart: and that now, having enriched herself, she would abandon him wholly to despair. This did not so well satisfy Philander, but that he needed some greater proofs of her fidelity, fearing all these rich presents were not for a little hope alone; and she failed not giving what protestations he desired.

Thus the night passed away, and in the morning, she knowing he was not very well furnished with money, gave him the key of her cabinet, where she bid him furnish himself with all he wanted; which he did, and left her, to go take orders about his horses, and other affairs, not so absolutely satisfied of her virtue, but he feared himself put upon, which the advantage he was likely to reap by the deceit, made him less consider, than he would perhaps otherwise have done.

He had all the night a full possession of *Sylvia*, and found in the morning he was not so violently concerned as he was over night: it was but a repetition of what he had been feasted with before; it was no new treat, but, like matrimony, went dully down: and now he found his heart warm a little more for *Calista*, with which little impatience he left *Sylvia*.

That morning a lady having sent to *Octavio*, to give her an assignation in the park; though he were not curious after beauty, yet believing there might be something more in it than merely a lady, he dressed himself and went, which was the reason he made not his visit that morning, as he used to do, to *Sylvia*, and so was yet ignorant of her ingratitude; while she, on the other side, finding herself more possessed with vanity than love; for having gained her end, as she imagined, and a second victory over his heart, in spite of all *Calista*'s charms, she did not so much consider him as before; nor was he so dear to her as she fancied he would have been, before she believed it possible to get him any more to her arms; and she found it was pride and revenge to *Calista*, that made her so fond of endearing him, and that she should thereby triumph over that haughty rival, who pretended to be so sure of the heart of her hero: and having satisfied her ambition in that point, she was more pleased than she imagined she should be, and could now turn her thoughts again to *Octavio*, whose charms, whose endearments, and lavish obligations, came anew to her memory, and made him appear the most agreeable to her genius and humour, which now leaned to interest more than love; and now she fancies she found *Philander* duller in her arms than *Octavio*; that he tasted of *Calista*, while *Octavio* was all her own entirely, adoring and ever presenting; two excellencies, of which *Philander* now had but part of one. She found *Philander* now in a condition to be ever taking from her, while *Octavio*'s was still to be giving; which was a great weight in the scale of love, when a fair woman guides the balance: and now she begins to distrust all that *Philander* had said of his innocence, from what she now remembers she heard from *Calista* herself, and reproaches her own weakness for believing: while her penitent thoughts were thus wandering in favour of *Octavio*, that lover arrived, and approached her with all the joy in his soul and eyes that either could express. 'It is now, my fair charmer,' said he, 'that I am come to offer you what alone can make me more worthy of you ——' And pulling from his pocket the writings and inventories of all his own and his uncle's estate —'See here,' said he, 'what those mighty powers that favour love have done for *Sylvia*. It is not,' continued he, 'the trifle of a million of money, (which these amount to) that has pleased me, but because I am now able to lay it without control at your feet.' If she were before inclined to receive him well, what was she now, when a million of money rendered him so charming? She embraced his neck with her snowy arms, laid her cheeks to his ravished face, and kissed him a thousand welcomes; so well she knew how to make herself mistress of all this vast fortune. And I suppose he never appeared so fine, as at this moment. While she thus caressed him, he could not forbear sighing, as if there were yet something behind to complete his happiness: for though Octavio were extremely blinded with love, he had abundance of wit, and a great many doubts, (which were augmented by the arrival of *Philander*) and he was, too wise and too haughty, to be imposed upon, at least as he believed: and yet he had so very good an opinion of *Sylvia*'s honour and vows, which she had engaged to him, that he durst hardly name his fears, when by his sighs she found them: and willing to leave no obstacle unremoved, that might hinder her possessing this fortune, she told him; 'My dear *Octavio*— I am sensible these sighs proceed from some fears you have of *Philander*'s being in *Brussels*, and consequently that I will see him, as heretofore; but be assured, that that false man shall no more dare to pretend to me; but, on the contrary, I will behold him as my mortal enemy, the murderer of my fame and innocence, and as the most ungrateful and perfidious man that ever lived.' This she confirmed with oaths and tears, and a thousand endearing expressions. So that establishing his heart in a perfect tranquillity, and he leaving his writings and accounts with her, he told her he was obliged to dine with the advocates, who had acted for him in *Holland*, and could not stay to dine with her.

You must know, that as soon as the noise of old *Sebastian*, *Octavio*'s uncle's death was noised about, and that he was thereupon fled, they seized all the estates, both that of the uncle, and that of *Octavio*, as belonging to him by right of law; but looking upon him as his uncle's murderer, they were forfeited to the *States*. This part of ill news *Octavio* kept from *Sylvia*, but took order, that such a process might be begun in his name with the *States* that might retrieve it; and sent word, if it could not be carried on by attornies (for he was not, he said, in health) that nevertheless he would come into *Holland* himself. But they being not able to prove, by the witness of any of *Octavio*'s or *Sebastian*'s servants, that *Octavio* had any hand in his death; but, on the contrary all circumstances, and the coroner's verdict, brought it in as a thing done by accident, and through his own fault, they were obliged to release to *Octavio* all his fortune, with that of his uncle, which was this day brought to him, by those he was obliged to dine, and make up some accounts withal: he therefore told her, he feared he should be absent all that afternoon; which she was the more pleased at, because if *Philander* should return before she had ordered the method of their visit, so as not to meet with each other (which was her only contrivance now) she should be sure he would not see or be seen by *Octavio*; who had no sooner taken his leave, but *Philander* returns; who being now fully bent upon some adventure to see *Calista*, if possible, and which intrigue would take up his whole time; to excuse his absence to the jealous *Sylvia*, he feigned that he was sent to by *Cesario*, to meet him upon the frontiers of *France*, and conduct him into *Flanders*, and that he should be absent some days. This was as *Sylvia* could have wished; and after forcing herself to take as kind a leave of him as she could, whose head was wholly possessed with a million of gold, she sent him away, both parties being very well pleased with the artifices with which they jilted each other. At *Philander*'s, going into his chair, he was seen by the old Count of *Clarinau*, who, cured perfectly of his wound, was come thither to seek *Philander*, in order to take the revenge of a man of honour, as he called it; which in *Spanish* is the private stab, for private injuries; and indeed more reasonable than base *French* duelling, where the injured is as likely to suffer as the injurer: but *Clarinau* durst not attack him by daylight in the open street, nor durst he indeed appear in his own figure in the King of *Spain*'s dominions, standing already there convicted of the murder of his first wife; but in a disguise came to *Brussels*. The chair with *Philander* was no sooner gone from the lodgings, but he inquired of some of the house, who lodged there that that gentleman came to visit? And they told him a great-bellied woman, who was a woman of quality, and a stranger: this was sufficient, you may believe, for him to think it Madam the Countess of *Clarinau*. With this assurance he repairs to his lodging, which was but hard by, and sets a footman that attended him to watch the return of *Philander* to those lodgings, which he believed would not be long: the footman, who had not seen *Philander*, only asked a description of him; he told him, he was a pretty tall man, in black clothes (for the Court was then in mourning) with long black hair, fine black eyes, very handsome, and well made; this was enough for the lad; he thought he should know him from a thousand by these marks and tokens. Away goes the footman, and waited till the shutting in of the evening, and then, running to his lord, told him, that *Philander* was come to those lodgings; that he saw him alight out of the chair, and took perfect notice of him; that he was sure it was that *Philander* he looked for: *Clarinau*, overjoyed that his revenge was at hand, took his dagger, sword and pistol, and hasted to *Sylvia*'s lodgings, where he found the chair still waiting, and the doors all open; he made no more ado, but goes in and ascends the stairs, and passes on, without opposition, to the very chamber where they sat, *Sylvia* in the arms of her lover, not *Philander*, but *Octavio*, who being also in black, tall, long, brown hair, and handsome, and by a sight that might very well deceive; he made no more to do, not doubting but it was *Philander* and *Calista*, but steps to him, and offering to stab him, was prevented by his starting at the suddenness of his approach; however, the dagger did not absolutely miss him, but wounded him in the left arm; but *Octavio*'s youth, too nimble for *Clarinau*'s age, snatching at the dagger as it wounded him, at once prevented the hurt being much, and returned a home blow at *Clarinau*, so that he fell at *Sylvia*'s feet, whose shrieks alarmed the house to their aid, where they found by the light of the candle that was brought, that the man was not dead, but lay gazing on *Octavio*, who said to him, 'Tell me, thou unfortunate wretch, what miserable fate brought thee to this place, to disturb the repose of those who neither know thee, nor had done thee injury?' 'Ah, sir,' replied *Clarinau*, 'you have reason for what you say, and I ask heaven, that unknown lady, and yourself, a thousand pardons for my mistake and crime: too late I see my error, pity and forgive me; and let me have a priest, for I believe I am a dead man.' *Octavio* was extremely moved with compassion at these words, and immediately sent his page, who was alarmed up in the crowd, for a Father and a surgeon; and he declared before the rest, that he forgave that stranger, meaning *Octavio*, since he had, by a mistake of his footman, pulled on his own death, and had deserved it: and thereupon, as well as he could, he told them for whom he had mistaken *Octavio*, who, having injured his honour, he had vowed revenge upon; and that he took the fair lady, meaning *Sylvia*, for a faithless wife of his, who had been the authoress of all this. *Octavio* soon divined this to be his brother-in-law, *Clarinau*, whom yet he had never seen; and stooping down to him, he cried, 'It is I, sir, that ought to demand a thousand pardons of you, for letting the revenge of *Calista*'s honour alone so long.' *Clarinau* wondered who he should be that named *Calista*, and asking him his name, he told him he was the unhappy brother to that fair wanton, whose story was but too well known to him. Thus while *Clarinau* viewing his face, found him the very picture of that false charmer; while *Octavio* went on and assured him, if it were his unhappiness to die, that he would revenge the honour of him and his sister, on the betrayer of both. By this time the surgeon came who found not his wound to be mortal, as was feared, and ventured to remove him to his own lodgings, whither *Octavio* would accompany him; and leaving *Sylvia* inclined, after her fright, to be reposed, he took his leave of her for that evening, not daring, out of respect to her, to visit her any more that night: he was no sooner gone, but *Philander*, who never used to go without two very good pocket-pistols about him, having left them under his pillow last night at *Sylvia*'s lodgings; and being upon love-adventures, he knew not what occasion he might have for them, returned back to her lodgings: when he came, she was a little surprised at first to see him, but after reflecting on what revenge was threatened him, she exposed

Octavio's secret to him, and told him the whole adventure, and how she had got his writings, which would be all her own, if she might be suffered to manage the fond believer. But he, whose thought ran on the revenge was threatened him, cried out —'He has kindly awakened me to my duty by what he threatens; it is I that ought to be revenged on his perfidy, of shewing you my letters; and to that end, by heaven, I will defer all the business in the world to meet him, and pay his courtesy — If I had enjoyed his sister, he might suppose I knew her not to be so; and what man of wit or youth, would refuse a lovely woman, that presents a heart laden with love, and a person all over charms, to his bosom? I were to be esteemed unworthy the friendship of a man of honour, if I should: but he has basely betrayed me every way, makes love to my celebrated mistress, whom he knows I love, and getting secrets, unravels them to make his court and his access the easier.'

She foresaw the dangerous consequence of a quarrel of this nature, and had no sooner blown the fire, (which she did, to the end that *Philander* should avoid her lodgings, and all places where he might meet *Octavio*) but she hinders all her designs; and fixing him there, he was resolved to expect him at the first place he thought most likely to find him in: she endeavoured, by a thousand entreaties, to get him gone, urging it all for his safety; but that made him the more resolved; and all she could do, could not hinder him from staying supper, and after that, from going to bed: so that she was forced to hide a thousand terrors and fears by feigned caresses, the sooner to get him to meet *Cesario* in the morning, as he said he was to do; and though she could not help flattering both, while by; yet she ever loved the absent best; and now repented a thousand times that she had told him any thing.

Early the next morning, as was his custom, *Octavio* came to inquire of *Sylvia*'s health; and though he had oftentimes only inquired and no more, (taking excuse of ill nights, or commands that none should come to her till she called) and had departed satisfied, and came again: yet now, when he went into *Antonet*'s chamber, he found she was in a great consternation, and her looks and flattering excuses made him know, there was more than usual in his being to-day denied; he therefore pressed it the more, and she grew to greater confusion by his pressing her. At last he demanded the key of her lady's chamber, he having, he said, business of great importance to communicate to her; she told him she had as great reason not to deliver it — 'That is,' said she, (fearing she had said too much) 'my lady's commands'; and finding no persuasion would prevail, and rather venturing *Sylvia*'s eternal displeasure, than not to be satisfied in the jealousies she had raised; especially reflecting on *Philander*'s being in town, he took *Antonet* in his arms, and forced the key from her; who was willing to be forced; for she admired *Octavio*'s bounty, and cared not for *Philander*. *Octavio* being master of the key, flies to *Sylvia*'s door like lightning, or a jealous lover, mad to discover what seen would kill him: he opens the chamber-door, and goes softly to the bed-side, as if he now feared to find what he sought, and wished to heaven he might be mistaken; he opened the curtains, and found *Sylvia* sleeping with *Philander* in her arms. I need make no description of his confusion and surprise; the character I have given of that gallant honest, generous lover, is sufficient to make you imagine his heart, when indeed he could believe his eyes: before he thought — he was about to draw his sword, and run them both through, and revenge at once his injured honour, his love, and that of his sister; but that little reason he had left checked that barbarity, and he was readier, from his own natural sweetness of disposition, to run himself upon his own sword: and there the Christian pleaded —— and yet found his heart breaking, his whole body trembling, his mind all agony, his cheeks cold and pale, his eyes languishing, his tongue refusing to give utterance to his pressure, and his legs to support his body; and much ado he had to reel into *Antonet*'s, chamber, where he found the maid dying with grief for her concern for him. He was no sooner got to her bed-side, but he fell dead upon it; while she, who was afraid to alarm her lady and *Philander*, lest *Octavio*, being found there, had accused her with betraying them; but shutting the door close, (for yet no body had seen him but herself) she endeavoured all she could to bring him to life again, and it was a great while before she could do so: as soon as he was recovered, he lay a good while without speaking, reflecting on his fate; but after appearing as if he had assumed all his manly spirits together, he rose up, and conjured *Antonet* to say nothing of what had happened, and that she should not repent the service she would do him by it. *Antonet*, who was his absolute, devoted slave, promised him all he desired; and he had the courage to go once again, to confirm himself in the lewdness of this undone fair one, whose perjuries had rendered her even odious now to him, and he beheld her with scorn and disdain: and that she might know how indifferently he did so, (when she should come to know it) he took *Philander*'s sword that lay on her *toilet*, and left his own in the place, and went out pleased; at least in this, that he had commanded his passion in the midst of the most powerful occasion for madness and revenge that ever was.

They lay thus secured in each other's arms till nine o'clock in the morning, when *Philander* received a note from *Brilliard*, who was managing his lord's design of getting a billet delivered to *Calista* by the way of a nun, whom *Brilliard* had made some address to, to that end, and sent to beg his lord would come to the grate, and speak to the young nun, who had undertaken for any innocent message. This note made him rise and haste to go out, when he received another from an unknown hand; which was thus:

....

To Philander.

My Lord, I have important business with you, and beg I may speak with you at three of the clock; I will wait for you by the fountain in the park: Yours.

....

Sylvia, who was impatient to have him gone, never asked to see either of these notes, lest it should have deterred him; and she knew *Octavio* would visit her early though she knew withal she could refuse him entrance with any slight excuse, so good an opinion he had of her virtue, and so absolute an ascendant she had over him. — She had given orders, if he came, to be refused her chamber; and she was glad to know he had not yet been at her lodgings. A hundred times she was about to make use of the lessened love *Philander* had for her, and to have proposed to him the suffering *Octavio* to share her embraces, for so good an interest, since no returns could be had from *France*, nor any signs of amendment of their fortunes any other way: but still she feared he had too much honour to permit such a cheat in love, to be put even upon an enemy. This fear deferred her speaking of it, or offering to sacrifice *Octavio* as a cully to their interest, though she wished it; nor knew she long how to deceive both; the business was to put *Philander* off handsomely, if possible, since she failed of all other hopes. These were her thoughts while *Philander* was dressing, and raised by his asking for some more pistoles from her cabinet, which she found would quickly be at an end, if one lover diminished daily, and the other was hindered from increasing: but *Philander* was no sooner dressed but he left her to her repose; and *Octavio* (who had a *Grison* attending the motions of *Philander*, all that morning, and had brought him word he was gone from *Sylvia*) went to visit her, and entering her chamber, all changed from what he was before, and death sat in his face and eyes, maugre all his resolves and art of dissembling. She, not perceiving it as she lay, stretched out her arms to receive him with her wonted caresses; but he gently put her off, and sighing, cried —'No, *Sylvia*, I leave those joys to happier lovers.' She was a little surprised at that — but not imagining he had known her guilt, replied: 'Then those caresses were only meant for him; for if *Sylvia* could make him happy, he was sure of being the man;' and by force compelled him to suffer her kisses and embraces, while his heart was bursting, without any sense of the pleasure of her touches. 'Ah, *Sylvia*,' says he, 'I can never think myself secure, or happy, while *Philander* is so near you; every absent moment alarms me with ten thousand fears; in sleep I dream thou art false, and givest thy honour up all my absent nights, and all day thy vows:' and that he was sure, should she again suffer herself to see *Philander*, he should be abandoned; and she again undone. 'For since I parted with you,' continued he, 'I heard from *Clarinau*, that he saw *Philander* yesterday come out of your lodgings. How can I bear this, when you have vowed not to see him, with imprecations that must damn thee, *Sylvia*, without severe repentance?'—— At this she offered to swear again — but he stopped her, and begged her not to swear till she had well considered; then she confessed he made her a visit, but that she used him with that pride and scorn, that if he were a man of honour he could never bear; and she was sure he would trouble her no more: in fine, she flattered, fawned, and jilted so, as no woman, common in the trade of sinful love, could be so great a mistress of the art. He suffered her to go on, in all that could confirm him she thought him an errant coxcomb; and all that could render her the most contemptible of her sex. He was pleased, because it made him despise her; and that was easier than adoring her; yet, though he heard her with scorn, he heard her with too much love. When she was even breathless with eager prostitution — he cried, 'Ah, indiscreet and unadvised *Sylvia*, how I pity thee!' 'Ah,' said she — observing him speak this with a scornful smile —'Is it possible, you should indeed be offended for a simple visit! which neither was by my invitation or wish: can you be angry, if I treat *Philander* with the civility of a brother? Or rather, that I suffer him to see me, to receive my reproaches?'—'Stop here,' said he, 'thou fair deluding flatterer, or thou art for ever ruined. Do not charge thy soul yet farther; — do not delude me on — all yet I can forgive as I am dying, but should I live, I could not promise thee. Add not new crimes by cozening me anew; for I shall find out truth, though it lie hid even in the bottom of *Philander*'s, heart.' This he spoke with an air of fierceness — which seeing her grow pale upon, he sunk again to compassion, and in a soft voice cried —'Whatever injuries thou hast done my honour, thy word, and faith to me, and my poor heart, I can perhaps forgive when you dare utter truth: there is some honesty in that'— She once more embracing him, fell anew to protesting her ill treatment of *Philander*, how she gave him back his vows, and assured him she would never be reconciled to him. 'And did you part so, *Sylvia*?' replied the dying *Octavio*. 'Upon my honour,' said she, 'just so.'—'Did you not kiss at parting?' said he faintly. —'Just kissed, as friends, no more, by all thy love.' At this he bursts into tears, and cried —'Oh! why, when I reposed my heart with thee, and lavished out my very soul in love, could I not merit

this poor recompense of being fairly dealt with? Behold this sword
— I took it from your *toilet*; view it, it is *Philander*'s; myself this
morning took it from your table: no more — since you may guess
the fatal rest: I am undone, and I am satisfied — I had a thousand
warnings of my fate, but still the beauty charmed, and my too good
nature yielded: oft you have cozened me, and oft I saw it, and still
love made me willing to forgive; the foolish passion hung upon my
soul, and soothed me into peace.' *Sylvia*, quite confounded, (not so
much with the knowledge he had of the unlucky adventure, as at her
so earnestly denying and forswearing any love had passed between
them) lay still to consider how to retrieve this lost game, and gave
him leisure to go on —'Now,' said he, 'thou art silent —— would thou
hadst still been so: ah, hapless maid, who hast this fate attending
thee, to ruin all that love thee! Be dumb, be dumb for ever; let the
false charm that dwells upon thy tongue, be ended with my life: let
it no more undo believing man, lest amongst the number some one
may conquer thee, and deaf to all thy wit, and blind to beauty, in
some mad passion think of all thy cozenings, should fall upon thee,
and forget thy sex, and by thy death revenge the lost *Octavio*.' At
these words he would have rose from her arms, but she detained him,
and with a piteous voice implored his pardon; but he calmly replied,
'Yes, *Sylvia*, I will pardon thee, and wish that heaven may do so; to
whom apply thy early rhetoric and penitence; for it can never, never
charm me more: my fortune, if thou ever wanted support to keep thee
chaste and virtuous, shall still be commanded by thee, with that usual
frankness it has hitherto served thee; but for *Octavio*, he is resolved
to go where he will never more be seen by woman — or hear the name
of love to ought but heaven — Farewell — one parting kiss, and then
a long farewell —' As he bowed to kiss her, she caught him fast in
her arms, while a flood of tears bathed his face, nor could he prevent
his from mixing with hers: while thus they lay, *Philander* came into
the room, and finding them so closely entwined, he was as much
surprised almost as *Octavio* was before; and, drawing his sword, was
about to have killed him; but his honour overcame his passion; and
he would not take him at such disadvantage, but with the flat of his
sword striking him on the back as he lay, he cried, 'Rise, traitor, and

turn to thy mortal enemy.' *Octavio*, not at all surprised, turned his head and his eyes bedewed in tears towards his rival. 'If thou be'est an enemy,' said he, 'though never couldst have taken me in a better humour of dying. Finish, *Philander*, that life then, which if you spare, it will possibly never leave thine in repose; the injuries you have done me being too great to be forgiven.' 'And is it thus,' replied *Philander* — 'thus with my mistress, that you would revenge them? Is it in the arms of *Sylvia*, that you would repay me the favours I did your sister *Calista*?' 'You have by that word,' said *Octavio*, 'handsomely reproached my sloth.' And leaping briskly from the bed, he took out his sword, and cried: 'Come then — — let us go where we may repair both our losses, since ladies' chambers are not fit places to adjust debts of this nature in.' At these words they both went down stairs; and it was in vain *Sylvia* called and cried out to conjure them to come back; her power of commanding she had in one unlucky day lost over both those gallant lovers. And both left her with pity; to say no worse of the effect of her ill conduct.

Octavio went directly to the park, to the place whither he before had challenged *Philander*, who lost no time but followed him: as soon as he was come to the fountain he drew, and told *Philander* that was the place whither he invited him in his billet that morning; however, if he liked not the ground, he was ready to remove to any other: *Philander* was a little surprised to find that invitation was a challenge; and that *Octavio* should be beforehand with him upon the score of revenge; and replied, 'Sir, if the billet came from you, it was a favour I thank you for; since it kindly put me in mind of that revenge I ought so justly to take of you, for betraying the secrets of friendship I reposed in you, and making base advantages of them, to recommend yourself to a woman you knew I loved, and who hates you, in spite of all the ungenerous ways you have taken to gain her.' 'Sir,' replied *Octavio*, 'I confess with a blush and infinite shame, the error with which you accuse me, and have nothing to defend so great a perfidy. To tell you, I was wrought out of it by the greatest cunning imaginable, and that I must have seen *Sylvia* die at my feet if I had refused them, is not excuse enough for the breach of that friendship. No, though I were exasperated with the relation there of my sister's dishonour: I must therefore adjust that debt with you as well as I can; and if I die in the juster quarrel of my sister's honour, I shall believe it the vengeance of heaven upon me for that one breach of friendship.' 'Sir,' replied *Philander*, 'you have given me so great a satisfaction in this confession, and have made so good and gallant an atonement by this acknowledgement, that it is with reluntancy I go to punish you for other injuries, of which I am assured you cannot so well acquit yourself.' 'Though I would not justify a baseness,' replied *Octavio*, 'for which there ought to be no excuse; yet I will not accuse myself, or acknowledge other injuries, but leave you something to maintain the quarrel on — and render it a little just on your side; nor go to wipe off the outrage you pretend I have done your love, by adoring the fair person who at least has been dear to you, by the wrongs you have done my sister.' 'Come, sir, we shall not by disputing quit scores,' cried *Philander*, a little impatiently; 'what I have lately seen, has made my rage too brisk for long parly.' At that they both advanced, and made about twenty passes before either received any wound; the first that bled was *Octavio*, who received a wound in his breast, which he returned on *Philander*, and after that many were given and taken; so that the track their feet made, in following and advancing as they fought, was marked out by their blood: in this condition, (still fighting) *Sylvia*, (who had called them back in vain, and only in her night-gown in a chair pursued them that minute they quitted her chamber) found them thus employed, and without any fear she threw herself between them: *Octavio*, out of respect to her, ceased; but *Philander*, as if he had not regarded her, would still have been striving for victory, when she stayed his hand, and begged him to hear her; he then set the point of his sword to the ground, and breathless and fainting almost, attended what she had to say: she conjured him to cease the quarrel, and told him if *Octavio* had injured him in her heart, he ought to remember he had injured *Octavio* as much in that of his sister: she conjured him by all the friendship both she and himself had received at *Octavio*'s hands; and concluded with saying so many fine things of that cavalier, that in lieu of appeasing, it but the more exasperated the jealous *Philander*, who took new courage with new breath, and passed at *Octavio*. She then addressed to *Octavio*, and cried: 'Hold, oh hold, or make your way through me; for here I will defend virtue and honour!' and put herself before *Octavio*: she spoke with so piteous a voice, and pleaded with so much tenderness, that *Octavio*, laying his sword at her feet, bid her dispose — false as she was, of his honour: 'For oh,' said he, 'my life is already fallen a victim to your perjuries!' He could say no more, but falling where he had laid his sword, left *Philander* master of the field. By this time some gentlemen that had been walking came up to them, and found a man lie dead, and a lady imploring another to fly: they looked on *Oclavio*, and found he had yet life; and immediately sent for surgeons, who carried him to his lodgings with very little hope: *Philander*, as well as his wounds would give him leave, got into a chair, telling the gentlemen that looked on him, he would be responsible for *Octavio*'s life, if he had had the ill fortune to take it; that his quarrel was too just to suffer him to fly. — So being carried to the *cabaret*, with an absolute command to *Sylvia* not to follow him, or visit him: for fear of hurting him by disobeying, she suffered herself to be carried to her lodgings, where she threw herself on her bed, and drowned her fair eyes in a shower of tears: she advises with *Antonet* and her page what to do in this extremity; she fears she has, by her ill management, lost both her lovers, and she was in a condition of needing every aid. They, who knew the excellent temper of *Octavio*, and knew him to be the most considerable lover of the two, besought her, as the best expedient she could have recourse to, to visit *Octavio*, who could not but take it kindly; and they did not doubt but she had so absolute a power over him, that with a very little complaisance towards him, she would retrieve that heart her ill luck had this morning forfeited; and which, they protested, they knew nothing of, nor how he got into her chamber. This advice she took; but, because *Octavio* was carried away dead, she feared, (and swooned with the fear) that he was no longer in the world, or, at least, that he would not long be so: however, she assumed her courage again at the thought, that, if he did die, she had an absolute possession of all his fortune, which was to her the most considerable part of the man, or at least, what rendered him so very agreeable to her: however, she thought fit to send her page, which she did in an hour after he was carried home, to see how he did; who brought her word that he was revived to life, and had commanded his gentleman to receive no messages from her. This was all she could learn, and what put her into the greatest extremity of grief. She after sent to *Philander*, and found him much the better of the two, but most infinitely incensed against *Sylvia*: this also added to her despair; yet since she found she had not a heart that any love, or loss of honour, or fortune could break; but, on the contrary, a rest of youth and beauty, that might oblige her, with some reason, to look forward on new lovers, if the old must depart: the next thing she resolved was, to do her utmost endeavour to retrieve *Octavio*, which, if unattainable, she would make the best of her youth. She sent therefore (notwithstanding his commands to suffer none of her people to come and see him) to inquire of his health; and in four days (finding he received other visits) she dressed herself, with all the advantages of her sex, and in a chair was carried to his aunt's, where he lay. The good lady, not knowing but she might be that person of quality whom she knew to be extremely in love with her nephew, and who lived at the Court of *Brussels*, and was niece to the Governor, carried her to his chamber, where she left her, as not willing to be a witness of a visit she knew must be supposed *incognito*: it was evening, and *Octavio* was in bed, and, at the first sight of her his blood grew disordered in his veins, flushed in his pale face, and burnt all over his body, and he was near to swooning as he lay: she approached his bed with a face all set for languishment, love, and shame in her eyes, and sighs, that, without speaking, seemed to tell her grief at his disaster; she sat, or rather fell, on his bed, as unable to support the sight of him in that condition; she in a soft manner, seized his burning hand, grasped it and sighed, then put it to her mouth, and suffered a tear or two to fall upon it; and when she would have spoke, she made her sobs resist her words; and left nothing unacted, that might move the tender-hearted *Octavio* to that degree of passion she wished. A hundred times fain he would have spoke, but still his rising passion choked his words; and still he feared they would prove either too soft and kind for the injuries he had received, or too rough and cold for so delicate and charming a creature, and one, whom, in spite of all those injuries, he still adored: she appeared before him with those attractions that never failed to conquer him, with that submission and pleading in her modest bashful eyes, that even gave his the lie, who had seen her perfidy. Oh! what should he do to keep that fire from breaking forth with violence, which she had so thoroughly kindled in his heart? How should that excellent good nature assume an unwonted sullenness, only to appear what it could not by nature be? He was all soft and sweet, and if he had pride, he knew also how to make his pleasure; and his youth loved love above all the other little vanities that attend it, and was the most proper to it. Fain he would palliate her crime, and considers, in the condition she was, she could not but have some tenderness for *Philander*; that it was no more than what before passed; it was no new lover that came to kindle new passions, or approach her with a new flame; but a decliner, who came, and was received with the dregs of love, with all the cold indifference imaginable: this he would have persuaded himself, but dares not till he hears her speak; and yet fears she should not speak his sense; and this fear makes him sighing break silence, and he cried in a soft tone: 'Ah! why, too lovely fair, why do you come to trouble the repose of my dying hours? Will you, cruel maid, pursue me to my grave? Shall I not have one lone hour to ask forgiveness of heaven for my sin of loving thee? The greatest that ever loaded my youth — and yet, alas! — the least repented yet. Be kind, and trouble not my solitude, depart with all the trophies of my ruin, and if they can add any glory to thy future life, boast them all over the universe, and tell what a deluded youth thou hast undone. Take, take, fair deceiver, all my industry, my right of my birth, my thriving parents have been so long a-getting to make me happy with; take the useless trifle, and lavish it on pleasure to make thee gay, and fit for luckier lovers: take that best part of me, and let this worst alone; it was that first won the dear confession from thee that drew my ruin on — for which I hate it — and wish myself born a poor cottage boor, where I might never have seen thy tempting beauty, but lived for ever blessed in ignorance.' At this the tears ran from his eyes, with which the softened *Sylvia* mixed her welcome stream, and as soon as she could speak, she replied (with half cunning and half love, for still there was too much of the first mingled with the last), 'Oh, my *Octavio*, to what extremities are you resolved to drive a poor unfortunate, who, even in the height of youth, and some small stock of beauty, am reduced to all the miseries of the wretched? Far from my noble noble parents, lost to honour, and abandoned by my friends; a helpless wanderer in a strange land, exposed to want, and perishing, and had no sanctuary but thyself, thy dear, thy precious self, whom heaven had sent, in mercy, to my aid; and thou, at last, by a mistaken turn of miserable fate, hast taken that dear aid away.' At this she fell weeping on his panting bosom; nevertheless he got the courage to reply once again, before he yielded himself a shameful victim to her flattery, and said; 'Ah cruel *Sylvia*, is it possible that you can charge the levity on me? Is it I have taken this poor aid, as you are pleased to call it, from you? Oh! rather blame your own unhappy easiness, that after having sworn me faith and love, could violate them both, both where there was no need. It would have better become thy pride and quality, to have resented injuries received, than brought again that scorned, abandoned person (fine as it was and shining still with youth) to his forgetful arms.' 'Alas,' said she, 'I will not justify my hateful crime: a crime I loathe to think of, it was a fault beyond a prostitution; there might have possibly been new joy in such a sin, but here it was palled and gone — fled to eternity away:— And but for the dear cause I did commit it, there were no expiation for my fault; no penitent tears could wash away my crime.' 'Alas,' said he —'if there were any cause, if there be any possible excuse for such a breach of love, give it my heart; make me believe it, and I may yet live; and though I cannot think thee innocent, to be compelled by any frivolous reason, it would greatly satisfy my longing soul. But, have a care, do not delude me on — for if thou durst persuade me into pardon, and to return to all my native fondness, and then again shouldst play me fast and loose; by heaven — by all my sacred passion to thee, by all that men call holy, I will pursue thee with my utmost hate; forsake thee with my fortune and my heart; and leave thee wretched to the scorning crowd. Pardon these rude expressions of a love that can hardly forgive the words it utters: I blush with shame while I pronounce them true.' When she replied, 'May all you have pronounced, and all your injured love can invent, fall on me when I ever more deceive you; believe me now, and but forgive what is past, and trust my love and honour for the future.' At this she told him, that in the first visit *Philander* made her, she, using him so reproachfully, and upbraiding him with his inconstancy, made him understand, that he was betrayed by *Octavio*, and that the whole intrigue with *Calista*, confessed by him, was discovered to *Sylvia*; which, he said, put him into so violent a rage against *Octavio*, that he vowed that minute to find him out and kill him. Nor could all the persuasions of reason serve to hinder him; so that she who (as she said) loved *Octavio* to death, finding so powerful an enemy, as her fears made her fancy *Philander* was, ready to have snatched from her, in one furious moment, all she adored; she had recourse to all the flattery of love to with-hold him from an attempt so dangerous: and it was with much ado, with all those aids, that he was obliged to stay, which she had forced him to do, to get time to give him notice in the morning for his approaching danger: not that she feared *Octavio*'s life, had *Philander* attacked it fairly; but he looked on himself as a person injured by close private ways, and would take a like revenge, and have hurt him when he as little dreamed of it, as *Philander* did of the discovery he made of his letter to her. To this she swore, she wept, she embraced, and still protested it true; adding withal a thousand protestations of her future detestation of him; and that since the worst was past, and that they had fought, and he was come off, though with so many wounds, yet with life, she was resolved utterly to defy *Philander*, as the most perfidious of his sex; and assured him, that nothing in the world was so indifferent as she in his arms. In fine, after having omitted nothing that might gain a credit, and assure him of her love and heart, and possess him with a belief, for the future, of her lasting vows: he, wholly convinced and overcome, snatches her in his arms, and bursting into a shower of tears, cried —'Take — take all my soul, thou lovely charmer of it, and dispose of the destiny of *Octavio*.' And smothering her with kisses and embraces made a perfect reconciliation. When the surgeons, who came to visit him, finding him in the disorder of a fever, though more joy was triumphing in his face than before, they imagined this lady the fair person for whom this quarrel was; for it had made a great noise you may believe; and finding it hurtful for his wounds, either to be transported with too much rage, grief, or love, besought him he would not talk too much, or suffer any visits that might prejudice his health: and indeed, with what had been past, he found himself after his transport very ill and feverish, so that *Sylvia* promised the doctors she would visit him no more in a day or two, though she knew not well how to be from him so long; but would content herself with sending her page to inquire of his health. To this *Octavio* made very great opposition, but his aunt, and the rest of the learned, were of opinion it ought for his health to be so, and he was obliged to be satisfied with her absence: at parting she came to him, and again besought him to believe her vows to be well, and that she would depart somewhere with him far from *Philander*, who she knew was obliged to attend the motions of *Cesario* at *Brussels*, whom again she imprecated never to see more. This satisfied our impatient lover, and he suffered her to go, and leave him to that rest he could get. She was no sooner got home, and retired to her chamber, but, finding herself alone, which now she did not care to be, and being assured she should not see *Octavio*, instead of triumphing for her new-gained victory, she sent her page to inquire again of *Philander*'s health, and to entreat that she might visit him: at first before she sent, she checked this thought as base, as against all honour, and all her vows and promises to the brave *Octavio*; but finding an inclination to it, and proposing a pleasure and satisfaction in it, she was of a nature not to lose a pleasure for a little punctilio of honour; and without considering what would be the event of such a folly, she sent her page, though he had been repulsed before, and forbid coming with any messages from his lady. The page found no better success than hitherto he had done: but being with much entreaty brought to *Philander*'s chamber, he found him sitting in his night-gown, to whom addressing himself — he had no sooner named his lady — but *Philander* bid him be gone, for he would hear nothing from that false woman: the boy would have replied, but he grew more enraged; and reviling her with all the railings of incensed lovers, he puts himself into his closet without speaking any more, or suffering any answer. This message being delivered to the expecting lady, put her into a very great rage — which ended in as deep a concern: her great pride, fortified by her looking-glass, made her highly resent the affront; and she believed it more to the glory of her beauty to have quitted a hundred lovers, than to be abandoned by one. It was this that made her rave and tear, and talk high; and after all, to use her cunning to retrieve what it had been most happy for her should have been for ever lost; and she ought to have blessed the occasion. But her malicious star had designed other fortune for her: she wrote to him several letters, that were sent back sealed: she railed, she upbraided, and then fell to submission. At last, he was persuaded to open one, but returned such answers as gave her no satisfaction, but encouraged her with a little hope that she should draw him on to a reconciliation: between whiles she failed not to send *Octavio* the kindest, impatient letters in the world, and received the softest replies that the tongue of man could utter, for he could not write yet. At last, *Philander* having reduced *Sylvia* to the very brink of despair, and finding, by her passionate importunity, that he could make his peace with her on any terms of advantage to himself, resolved to draw such articles of agreement as should wholly subdue her to him, or to stand it out to the last: the conditions were, that he being a person by no means of a humour to be imposed upon; if he were dear to her, she should give herself entirely to his possession, and quit the very conversation of all those he had but an apprehension would disturb his repose: that she should remove out of the way of his troublesome rivals, and suffer herself to be conducted whither he thought good to carry her. These conditions she liked, all but the going away; she could not tell to what sort of confinement that might amount. He flies off wholly, and denies all treaty upon her least scruple, and will not be asked the explanation of what he has proposed: so that she bends like a slave for a little empire over him; and to purchase the vanity of retaining him, suffers herself to be absolutely undone. She submits; and that very day she had leave from the doctors to visit *Octavio*, and that all-ravished lover lay panting in expectation of the blessed sight, believing every minute an age, his apartment dressed and perfumed, and all things ready to receive the darling of his soul, *Philander* came in a coach and six horses (and making her pack up all her jewels and fine things, and what they could not carry in the coach, put up to come after them) and hurries her to a little town in *Luke–Land*, a place between Flanders and Germany, without giving her time to write, or letting her know whither she was going. While she was putting up her things (I know she has since confessed) her heart trembled, and foreboded the ill that was to come; that is, that she was hastening to ruin: but she had chanced to say so much to him of her passion to retrieve him, that she was ashamed to own the contrary so soon; but suffered that force upon her inclinations to do the most dishonourable and disinterested thing in the world. She had not been there a week, and her trunks of plate and fine things were arrived, but she fell in labour, and was brought to bed, though she shewed very little of her condition all the time she went. This great affair being well over, she considers herself a new woman, and began, or rather continued, to consider the advantage she had lost in *Octavio*: she regrets extremely her conduct, and from one degree to another she looks on herself as lost to him; she every day saw what she had decayed, her jewels sold one by one, and at last her necessaries. *Philander*, whose head was running on *Calista*, grudged every moment he was not about that affair, and grew as peevish as she; she recovers to new beauty, but he grows colder and colder by possession; love decayed, and ill humour increased: they grew uneasy on both sides, and not a day passed wherein they did not break into open and violent quarrels, upbraiding each other with those faults, which both wished that either would again commit, that they might be fairly rid of one another: it grew at last to that height, that they were never well but when they were absent from one another; he making a hundred little intrigues and gallantries with all the pretty women, and those of any quality in the town or neighbouring *villas*. She saw this with grief, shame, and disdain, and could not tell which way to relieve herself: she was not permitted the privilege of visits, unless to some grave ladies, or to monasteries; a man was a rarity she had hardly seen in two months, which was the time she had been there; so that she had leisure to think of her folly, bemoan the effects of her injustice, and contrive, if she could, to remedy her disagreeable life, which now was reduced, not only to scurrilous quarrels, and hard words; but, often in her fury, she flying upon him, and with the courage or indiscretion of her sex, would provoke him to indecencies that render life insupportable on both sides. While they lived at this rate, both contriving how handsomely to get quit of each other, *Brilliard*, who was left in *Brussels*, to take care of his lord's affairs there, and that as soon as he had heard of *Cesario*'s arrival he should come with all speed and give him notice, thought every minute an hour till he could see again the charmer of his soul, for whom he suffered continual fevers of love. He studies nothing but how first to get her pardon, and then to compass his designs of possessing her: he had not seen her, nor durst pretend to it, since she left *Holland*. He believed she would have the discretion to conceal some of his faults, lest he should discover in revenge some of hers; and fancied she would imagine so of his conduct: he had met with no reproaches yet from his lord, and believed himself safe. With this imagination, he omitted nothing that might render him acceptable to her, nor to gain any secrets he believed might be of use to him: knowing therefore she had not dealt very generously with *Octavio*, by this flight with *Philander*, and believing that that exasperated lover, would in revenge declare any thing to the prejudice of the fair fugitive, he (under pretence of throwing himself at his feet, and asking his pardon for his ill treating him in *Holland*) designed before he went into *Luke–Land* to pay *Octavio* a visit, and accordingly went; he met first with his page, who being very well acquainted with *Brilliard*, discoursed with him before he carried him to his lord: he told him that his lord that day that *Sylvia* departed, being in impatient expectation of her, and that she came not according to appointment, sent him to her lodgings, to know if any accident had prevented her coming; but that when he came, though he had been with her but an hour before, she was gone away with *Philander*, never more to return. The youth, not being able to carry this sad news to his lord, when he came home offered at a hundred things to conceal the right; but the impatient lover would not be answered, but, all enraged, commanded him to tell that truth, which he found already but too apparently in his eyes. The lad so commanded, could no longer defer telling him *Sylvia* was gone; and being asked, again and again, what he meant, with a face and voice that every moment altered to dying; the page assured him she was gone out of *Brussels* with *Philander*, never more to return; which was no sooner told him, but he sunk on the couch where he lay, and fainted: he farther told him how long it was, and with what difficulty he was recovered to life; and that after he was so, he refused to speak or see any visitors; could for a long time be neither persuaded to eat nor sleep, but that he had spoken to no body ever since, and did now believe he could not procure him the favour he begged: that nevertheless he would go, and see what the very name of any that had but a relation to the family of *Sylvia* would produce in him, whether a storm of passion, or a calm of grief: either would be better than a dullness, all silent and sad, in which there was no understanding what he meant by it: whoever spoke, he only made a short sign, and turned away, as much as to say, speak no more to me: but now resolved to try his temper, he hastened to his lord, and told him that *Brilliard*, full of penitence for his past fault, and grief for the ill condition he heard he was in, was come to pay his humble respects to him, and gain his pardon before he went to his lord and *Sylvia*; without which he had not, nor could have, any peace of mind, he being too sensible of the baseness of the injury he had done him. At the name of *Philander* and *Sylvia*, *Octavio* shewed some signs of listening, but to the rest no regard; and starting from the bed where he was laid: 'Ah! what hast thou said?' cried he. The page then repeated the message, and was commanded to bring him up; who, accordingly, with all the signs of submission, cast himself at his feet and mercy; and, though he were an enemy, the very thought that he belonged to *Sylvia* made *Octavio* to caress him as the dearest of friends: he kept him with him two or three days, and would not suffer him to stir from him; but all their discourse was of the faithless *Sylvia*; of whom, the deceived lover spoke the softest, unheard, tender things, that ever passion uttered: he made the amorous *Brilliard* weep a hundred times a day; and ever when he would have soothed his heart with hopes of seeing her, and one day enjoying her entirely to himself, he would with so much peace of mind renounce her, as Brilliard no longer doubted but he would indeed no more trust her fickle sex. At last, the news arrived that Cesario was in Brussels, and Brilliard was obliged the next morning to take horse, and go to his lord: and to make himself the more acceptable to Sylvia, he humbly besought Octavio to write some part of his resentments to her, that he might oblige her to a reason for what she had so inhumanly done: this flattered him a little, and he was not long before he was overcome by Brilliard's entreaties; who, having his ends in every thing, believed this letter might contain at least something to assist in his design, by giving him authority over her by so great a secret: the next morning, before he took horse he waited on Octavio for his letter, and promised him an answer at his return, which would be in a few days. This letter was open, and Octavio suffered Brilliard to read it, making him an absolute confidant in his amour; which having done, he besought him to add one thing more to it; and that was, to beg her to forgive Brilliard, which for his sake he knew she would do: he told him, he was obliged as a good Christian, and a dying man, one resolved for heaven to do that good office; and accordingly did. Brilliard taking post immediately, arrived to Philander, where he found every thing as he wished, all out of humour, still on the fret, and ever peevish. He had not seen Sylvia, as I said, since she went from Holland, and now knew not which way to approach her; Philander was abroad on some of his usual gallantries when Brilliard arrived; and having discoursed a while of the affairs of his lord and Sylvia, he told Antonet he had a great desire to speak with that dissatisfied fair one, assuring her, he believed his visit would be welcome, from what he had to say to her concerning Octavio: she told him (with infinite joy) that she did not doubt of his pardon from her lady, if he brought any news from that gallant injured man; and in all haste, though her lady saw no body, but refused to rise from her couch, she ran to her, and besought her to see Brilliard; for he came with a message from Octavio, the person, who was the subject of their discourse night and day, when alone. She immediately sent for Brilliard, who approached his goddess with a trembling devotion; he knelt before her, and humbly besought her pardon for all that was past: but she, who with the very thought that he had something to say from Octavio, forgot all but that, hastily bid him rise, and take all he asked, and hoped for what he wished:

in this transport she embraced his head, and kissed his cheek, and took him up. 'That, madam,' said *Brilliard*, 'which your divine bounty alone has given me, without any merit in me, I durst not have had the confidence to have hoped without my credential from a nobler hand — this, madam,' said he — and gave her a letter from *Octavio*: the dear hand she knew, and kissed a hundred times as she opened it; and having entreated *Brilliard* to withdraw for a moment, that he might not see her concern at the reading it, she sat her down, and found it thus.

OCTAVIO *to* SYLVIA.

I confess, oh faithless *Sylvia*! that I shall appear in writing to you, to shew a weakness even below that of your infidelity; nor durst I have trusted myself to have spoken so many sad soft things, as I shall do in this letter, had I not tried the strength of my heart, and found I could upbraid you without talking myself out of that resolution I have taken — but, because I would die in perfect charity with thee, as with all the world, I should be glad to know I could forgive thee; for yet thy sins appear too black for mercy. Ah! why, charming ingrate, have you left me no one excuse for all your ills to me? Why have you injured me to that degree, that I, with all the mighty stock of love I had hoarded up together in my heart, must die reproaching thee to my last gasp of life? which hadst thou been so merciful to have ended, by all the love that's breaking of my heart, that yet, even yet, is soft and charming to me, I swear with my last breath, I had blessed thee, *Sylvia*: but thus to use me; thus to leave my love, distracted, raving love, and no one hope or prospect of relief, either from reason, time, or faithless *Sylvia*, was but to stretch the wretch upon the rack, and screw him up to all degrees of pain; yet such, as do not end in kinder death. Oh thou unhappy miner of my repose! Oh fair unfortunate! if yet my agony would give me leave to argue, I am so miserably lost, to ask thee yet this woeful satisfaction; to tell me why thou hast undone me thus? Why thou shouldst choose me out from all the crowd of fond admiring fools, to make the world's reproach, and turn to ridicule? How couldst thou use that soft good nature so, that had not one ungrateful sullen humour in it, for thy revenge and pride to work upon? No baseness in my love, no dull severity for malice to be busy with; but all was gay and kind, all lavish fondness, and all that woman, vain with youth and beauty, could wish in her adorer: what couldst thou ask, but empire, which I gave not? My love, my soul, my life, my very honour, all was resigned to thee; that youth that might have gained me fame abroad was dedicated to thy service, laid at thy feet, and idly passed in love. Oh charming maid, whom heaven has formed for the punishment of all, whose flames are criminal! Why couldst not thou have made some kind distinction between those common passions and my flame? I gave thee all my vows, my honest vows, before I asked a recompense for love. I made thee mine before the sacred powers, that witness every sacred solemn vow, and fix them in the eternal book of fate; if thou hadst given thy faith to any other, as, oh! too sure thou hadst, what fault was this in me, who knew it not? Why should I bear that sin? I took thee to me as a virgin treasure, sent from the gods to charm the ills of life, to make the tedious journey short and joyful; I came to make atonement for thy sin, and to redeem thy fame; not add to the detested number. I came to gild thy stains of honour over; and set so high a price upon thy name, that all reproaches for thy past offences should have been lost in future crowds of glory: I came to lead thee from a world of shame, approaching ills and future miseries; from noisy flatterers that would sacrifice thee, first to dull lust, and more unthinking wit; possess thee, then traduce thee. By heaven, I swear it was not for myself alone I took such pains to gain thee, and set thee free from all those circumstances, that might perhaps debauch thy worthier nature, and I believed it was with pain you yielded to every buying lover: no, it was for thy sake, in pity to thy youth, heaven had inspired me with religious flame; and when I aimed at *Sylvia* it was alone I might attain to heaven the surest way, by such a pious conquest; why hast thou ruined a design so glorious, as saving both our souls? Perhaps thou vainly thinkest that while I am pleading thus — I am arguing still for love; or think this way to move thee into pity; no, by my hopes of death to ease my pain, love is a passion not to be compelled by any force of reason's arguments: it is an unthinking motion of the soul, that comes and goes as unaccountably as changing moons, or ebbs and flows of rivers, only with far less certainty. It is not that my soul is all over love, that can beget its likeness in your heart: had heaven and nature added to that love all the perfections that adorn our sex, it had availed me nothing in your soul: there is a chance in love as well as life, and often the most unworthy are preferred; and from a lottery I might win the prize from all the venturing throng with as much reason, as think my chance should favour me with *Sylvia*; it might perhaps have been, but it was a wondrous odds against me. Beauty is more uncertain than the dice; and though I ventured like a forward gamester, I was not yet so vain to hope to win, nor had I once complained upon my fate, if I had never hoped: but when I had fairly won, to have it basely snatched from my possession, and like a baffled cully see it seized by a false gamester, and look tamely on, has given me such *ideas* of the fool, I scorn to look into my easy heart, and loathe the figure you made me there. Oh *Sylvia*! what an angel hadst thou been, hadst thou not soothed me thus to my undoing! Alas, it had been no crime in thee to hate me; it was not thy fault I was not amiable; if thy soft eyes could meet no charms to please them, those soft, those charming eyes were not in fault; nor that thy sense, too delicate and nice, could meet no proper subject for thy wit, thy heart, thy tender heart was not in fault, because it took not in my tale of love, and sent soft wishes back: oh! no, my *Sylvia*, this, though I had died, had caused you no reproach; but first to fan my fire by all the arts that ever subtle beauty could invent; to give me hope; nay, to dissemble love; yes, and so very well dissemble too, that not one tender sigh was breathed in vain: all that my love-sick soul was panting for, the subtle charmer gave; so well, so very well, she could dissemble! Oh, what more proofs could I expect from love, what greater earnest of eternal victory? Oh! thou hadst raised me to the height of heaven, to make my fall to hell the more precipitate. Like a fallen angel now I howl and roar, and curse that pride that taught me first ambition; it is a poor satisfaction now, to know (if thou couldst yet tell truth) what motive first seduced thee to my ruin? Had it been interest — by heaven, I would have bought my wanton pleasures at as high rates as I would gratify my real passions; at least when *Sylvia* set a price on pleasure: nay, higher yet, for love when it is repaid with equal love, it saves the chafferer a great expense:

or were it wantonness of youth in thee, alas, you might have made me understood it, and I had met you with an equal ardour, and never thought of loving, but quenched the short-lived blaze as soon as kindled; and hoping for no more, had never let my hasty flame arrive any higher than that powerful minute's cure. But oh! in vain I seek for reasons from thee; perhaps thy own fantastic fickle humour cannot inform thee why thou hast betrayed me; but thou hast done it, *Sylvia*, and may it never rise in judgement on thee, nor fix a brand upon thy name for ever, greater than all thy other guilts can load thee with: live, fair deceiver, live, and charm *Philander* to all the heights of his beginning flame; mayst thou be gaining power upon his heart, and bring it repentance for inconstancy; may all thy beauty still maintain its lustre, and all thy charms of wit be new and gay; mayst thou be chaste and true; and since it was thy fate to be undone, let this at least excuse the hapless maid; it was love alone betrayed her to that ruin, and it was *Philander* only had that power. If thou hast sinned with me, as heaven is my witness, after I had plighted thee my sacred vows, I do not think thou didst: may all the powers above forgive thee, *Sylvia*; and those thou hast committed since those vows, will need a world of tears to wash away: it is I will weep for both; it is I will go and be a sacrifice to atone for all our sins: it is I will be the pressing penitent, and watch, and pray, and weep, until heaven have mercy; and may my penance be accepted for thee; — farewell — I have but one request to make thee, which is, that thou wilt, for *Octavio*'s sake, forgive the faithful slave that brings thee this from thy

OCTAVIO.

Sylvia, whose absence and ill treatment of *Octavio*, had but served to raise her flame to a much greater degree, had no sooner read this letter, but she suffered herself to be distracted with all the different passions that possess despairing lovers; sometimes raving, and sometimes sighing and weeping: it was a good while she continued in these disorders, still thinking on what she had to do next that might redeem all: being a little come to herself, she thought good to consult with *Brilliard* in this affair, between whom and *Octavio* she found there was a very good understanding: and resolving absolutely to quit *Philander*, she no longer had any scruples or doubt what course to take, nor cared she what price she paid for a reconciliation with *Octavio*, if any price would purchase it: in order to this resolve, fixed in her heart, she sends for *Brilliard*, whom she caresses anew, with all the fondness and familiarity of a woman, who was resolved to make him her confidant, or rather indeed her next gallant. I have already said he was very handsome, and very well made, and you may believe he took all the care he could in dressing, which he understood very well: he had a good deal of wit, and was very well fashioned and bred:— With all these accomplishments, and the addition of love and youth, he could not be imagined to appear wholly indifferent in the eyes of any body, though hitherto he had in those of *Sylvia*, whose heart was doting on *Philander*; but now, that that passion was wholly extinguished, and that their eternal quarrels had made almost a perpetual separation, she being alone, without the conversation of men, which she loved, and was used to, and in her inclination naturally addicted to love, she found *Brilliard* more agreeable than he used to be; which, together with the designs she had upon him, made her take such a freedom with him, as wholly transported this almost hopeless lover: she discourses with him concerning *Octavio* and his condition, and he failed not to answer, so as to please her, right or wrong; she tells him how uneasy she was with *Philander*, who every day grew more and more insupportable to her; she tells him she had a very great inclination for *Octavio*, and more for his fortune that was able to support her, than his person; she knew she had a great power over him, and however it might seem now to be diminished by her unlucky flight with *Philander*, she doubted not but to reduce him to all that love he once professed to her, by telling him she was forced away, and without her knowledge, being carried only to take the air was compelled to the fatal place where she now was. *Brilliard* soothes and flatters her in all her hope, and offers her his service in her flight, which he might easily assist, unknown to *Philander*. It was now about six o'clock at night, and she commanded a supper to be provided, and brought to her chamber, where *Brilliard* and she supped together, and talked of nothing but the new design; the hope of effecting which put her into so good a humour, that she frankly drank her bottle, and shewed more signs of mirth than she had done in many months before: in this good humour, *Brilliard* looked more amiable than ever; she smiles upon him, she caresses him with all the assurance of friendship imaginable; she tells him she shall behold him as her dearest friend, and speaks so many kind things, that he was emboldened, and approached her by degrees more near; he makes advances; and the greatest encouragement was, the secret he had of her intended flight: he tells her, he hoped she would be pleased to consider, that while he was serving her in a new amour, and assisting to render her into the arms of another, he was wounding his own heart, which languished for her; that he should not have taken the presumption to have told her this, at such a time as he offered his life to serve her, but that it was already no secret to her, and that a man who loved at his rate, and yet would contrive to make his mistress happy with another, ought in justice to receive some recompense of a flame so constant and submissive. While he spake, he found he was not regarded with the looks of scorn or disdain; he knew her haughty temper, and finding it calm, he pressed on to new submissions; he fell at her feet, and pleaded so well, where no opposers were, that *Sylvia* no longer resisted, or if she did, it was very feebly, and with a sort of a wish that he would pursue his boldness yet farther; which at last he did, from one degree of softness and gentle force to another, and made himself the happiest man in the world; though she was very much disordered at the apprehension of what she had suffered from a man of his character, as she imagined, so infinitely below her; but he redoubled his submission in so cunning a manner, that he soon brought her to her good humour; and after that, he used the kind authority of a husband whenever he had an opportunity, and found her not displeased at his services. She considered he had a secret from her, which, if revealed, would not only prevent her design, but ruin her for ever; she found too late she had discovered too much to him to keep him at the distance of a servant, and that she had no other way to attach him eternally to her interest, but by this means. He now every day appeared more fine, and well dressed, and omitted nothing that might make him, if possible, an absolute master of her heart, which he vowed he would defend with his life, from even *Philander* himself; and that he would pretend to no other empire over her, nor presume, or pretend to engross that fair and charming person, which ought to be universally adored. In fine, he failed not to please both her desire and her vanity, and every day she loved *Philander* less, who sometimes in two or three days together came not to visit her. At this time it so happened, he being in love with the young daughter of an advocate, about a league from his own lodgings, and he is always eager on the first address, till he has completed the conquest; so that she had not only time to please and revenge her with *Brilliard*, but fully to resolve their affairs, and to provide all things against their flight, which they had absolutely done before *Philander's* return; who, coming home, received *Brilliard* very kindly, and the news which he brought, and which made him understand he should not have any long time to finish his new amour in; but as he was very conquering both in wit and beauty, he left not the village without some ruins behind of beauty, which ever after bewailed his charms; and since his departure was so necessary, and that in four or five days he was obliged to go, they deferred their flight till he was gone; which time they had wholly to themselves, and made as good use of it as they could; at least, she thought so, and you may be sure, he also, whose love increased with his possession. But *Sylvia* longs for liberty, and those necessary gallantries, which every day diminished; she loved rich clothes, gay coaches, and to be lavish; and now she was stinted to good housewifery, a penury she hated.

The time of *Philander's*, departure being come, he took a very careless leave of *Sylvia*, telling her he would see what commands the Prince had for him, and return in ten or twelve days. *Brilliard* pretended some little indisposition, and begged he might be permitted to follow him, which was granted; and the next day, though Erilliard pleaded infinitely for a continuation of his happiness two or three days more, she would not grant it, but obliged him, by a thousand kind promises of it for the future, to get horses ready for her page, and woman, and her coach for herself; which accordingly was done, and they left the village, whose name I cannot now call to mind, taking with her what of value she had left. They were three days on their journey: *Brilliard*, under pretence of care of her health, the weather being hot, and for fear of overtaking *Philander* by some accident on the road, delayed the time as much as was possible, to be as happy as he could all the while; and indeed *Sylvia* was never seen in a humour more gay. She found this short time of hope and pleasure had brought all her banished beauties back, that care, sickness, and grief, had extremely tarnished; only her shape was a little more inclining to be fat, which did not at all however yet impair her fineness; and she was indeed too charming without, for the deformity of her indiscretion within; but she had broke the bounds of honour, and now stuck at nothing that might carry on an interest, which she resolved should be the business of her future life.

She at last arrived at *Brussels*, and caused a lodging to be taken for her in the remotest part of the town; as soon as she came she obliged *Brilliard* to visit *Octavio*; but going to his aunt's, to inquire for him, he was told that he was no longer in the world; he stood amazed a-while, believing he had been dead, when madam the aunt told him he was retired to the monastery of the Order of St *Bernard*, and would, in a day or two, without the probationary year, take Holy Orders. This did not so much surprise him as the other, knowing that he discoursed to him, when he saw him last, as if some such retirement he meant to resolve upon; with this news, which he was not altogether displeased at, *Brilliard* returned to *Sylvia*, which soon changed all her good humour to tears and melancholy: she inquired at what place he was, and believed she should have power to withdraw him from a resolution so fatal to her, and so contradictive to his youth and fortune; and having consulted the matter with *Brilliard*, he had promised her to go to him, and use all means possible to withdraw him. This resolved, she writ a most insinuating letter to him, wherein she excused her flight by a surprise of *Philander's*, and urged her condition, as it then was, for the excuse of her long silence; and that as soon as her health would give her leave, she came to put herself eternally into his arms, never to depart more from thence. These arguments and reasons, accompanied with all the endearing tenderness her artful fancy was capable of framing, she sent with a full assurance it would prevail to persuade him to the world, and her fair arms again. While she was preparing this to go, *Philander*, who had heard at his arrival, what made so much noise, that he had been the occasion of the world's loss of two of the finest persons in it, the sister *Calista* by debauching her, and the brother by ravishing his mistress from him, both which were entering, without all possibility of prevention, into Holy Orders; he took so great a melancholy at it, as made him keep his chamber for two days, maugre all the urgent affairs that ought to have invited him from thence; he was consulting by what power to prevent the misfortune; he now ran back to all the obligations he had to *Octavio*, and pardons him all the injuries he did him; he loves him more by loving *Sylvia* less, and remembered how that generous friend, after he knew he had dishonoured his sister, had notwithstanding sent him Letters of Credit to the magistrates of *Cologne*, and Bills of Exchange, to save him from the murder of his brother-in-law, as he was likely to have been. He now charges all his little faults to those of love, and hearing that old *Clarinau* was dead of the wound *Octavio* had given him by mistake, which increased in him new hope of *Calista*, could she be retrieved from the monastery, he resolved, in order to this, to make *Octavio* a visit, to beg his pardon, and beg his friendship, and his continuation in the world. He came accordingly to the monastery, and was extremely civilly received by *Octavio*, who yet had not the habit on. *Philander* told him, he heard he was leaving the world, and could not suffer him to do so, without endeavouring to gain his pardon of him, for all the injuries he had done him; that as to what related to his sister the Countess, he protested upon his honour, if he had but imagined she had been so, he would have suffered death sooner than his passion to have approached her indiscreetly; and that for *Sylvia*, if he were assured her possession would make him happy, and call him to the world again, he assured him he would quit her to him, were she ten times dearer to him than she was. This he confirmed with so many protestations of friendship, that *Octavio*, obliged to the last degree, believed and returned him this answer. 'Sir, I must confess you have found out the only way to disarm me of my resentment against you, if I were not obliged, by those vows I am going to take, to pardon and be at peace with all the world. However, these vows cannot hinder me from conserving entirely that friendship in my heart, which your good qualities and beauties at first sight engaged there, and from esteeming you more than perhaps I ought to do; the man whom I must yet own my rival, and the undoer of my sister's honour. But oh — no more of that; a friend is above a sister, or a mistress.' At this he hung down his eyes and sighed —*Philander* told him he was too much concerned in him, not to be extremely afflicted at the resolution he had taken, and besought him to quit a design so injurious to his youth, and the glorious things that heaven had destined him to; he urged all that could be said to dissuade him, and, after all, could not believe he would quit the world at this age, when it would be sufficient forty years hence so to do. *Octavio* only answered with a smile; but, when he saw *Philander* still persist, he endeavoured to convince him by speaking; and lifting up his eyes to heaven, he vowed, by all the holy powers there, he never would look down to earth again; nor more consider fickle, faithless, beauty: 'All the gay vanities of youth,' said he, 'for ever I renounce, and leave them all to those that find a pleasure, or a constancy in them; for the fair, faithless, maid, that has undone me, I leave to you the empire of her heart; but have a care,' said he (and sighing laid his arms about his neck) 'for even you, with all that stock of charms, she will at last betray: I wish her well — so well, as to repent of all her wrongs to me — It is all I have to say.' What *Philander* could urge, being impossible to prevail with him: and begging his pardon and friendship (which was granted by *Octavio*, and implored on his side from *Philander*) he took a ring of great value from his finger, and presented it to *Philander*, and begged him to keep it for his sake; and to remember him while he did so: they kissed, and sighing parted.

Philander was no sooner gone, but *Brilliard* came to wait on *Octavio*, whom he found at his devotion, and begged his pardon for disturbing him: he received him with a very good grace, and a cheerful countenance, embracing him; and after some discourse of the condition he was going to reduce himself to, and his admiration, that one so young should think of devoting himself so early to heaven, and things of that nature, as the time and occasion required, he told him the extreme affliction *Sylvia* was seized with, at the news of the resolution he had taken, and delivered him a letter, which he read without any emotions in his heart or face, as at other times used to be visible at the very mention of her name, or approach of her letters. At the finishing of which, he only smiling cried: 'Alas, I pity her,' and gave him back the letter. *Brilliard* asked, if he would not please to write her some answer, or condescend to see her; 'No,' replied *Octavio*, 'I have done with all the gilded vanities of life, now I shall think of *Sylvia* but as some heavenly thing, fit for diviner contemplations, but never with the youthful thoughts of love.' What he should send her now, he said, would have a different style to those she used to receive from him; it would be pious counsel, grave advice, unfit for ladies so young and gay as *Sylvia*, and would scarce find a welcome: he wished he could convert her from the world — and save her from the dangers that pursued her. To this purpose was all he said of her, and all that could be got from him by the earnest solicitor of love, who perhaps was glad his negotiation succeeded no better, and took his leave of him, with a promise to visit him often; which *Octavio* besought him to do, and told him he would take some care, that for the good of *Sylvia*'s better part, she should not be reduced by want of necessaries for her life, and little equipage, to prostitute herself to vile inconstant man; he yet had so much respect for her — and besought *Brilliard* to come and take care of it with him, and to entreat *Sylvia* to accept of it from him; and if it contributed to her future happiness, he should be more pleased than to have possessed her entirely.

You may imagine how this news pleased *Sylvia*; who trembling with fear every moment, had expected *Brilliard*'s coming, and found no other benefit by his negotiation, but she must bear what she cannot avoid; but it was rather with the fury of a bacchanal, than a woman of common sense and prudence; all about her pleaded some days in vain, and she hated *Brilliard* for not doing impossibilities; and it was some time before he could bring her to permit him to speak to her, or visit her.

Philander having left *Octavio*, went immediately to wait on *Cesario*, who was extremely pleased to meet him there, and they exchanged their souls to each other, and all the secrets of them. After they had discoursed of all that they had a mind to hear and know on both sides, *Cesario* inquired of him of *Sylvia*'s health; and *Philander* gave him an account of the uneasiness of her temper, and the occasions of their quarrels, in which *Octavio* had his part, as being the subject of some of them: from this he falls to give a character of that rival, and came to this part of it, where he had put himself into the Orders of the *Bernardines*, resolving to leave the world, and all its charms and temptations. As they were speaking, some gentlemen, who came to make their court to the Prince, finding them speak of *Octavio*, told them that to-morrow he was to be initiated, without the year's trial; the Prince would needs go and see the ceremony, having heard so much of the man; and accordingly next day, accompanied with the Governor, *Philander, Tomaso*, and abundance of persons of quality and officers, he went to the great church, where were present all the ladies of the Court, and all that were in the town. The noise of it was so great, that *Sylvia*, all languishing, and ill as she was, would not be persuaded from going, but so muffled in her hoods, as she was not to be known by any.

Never was any thing so magnificent as this ceremony, the church was on no occasion so richly adorned; *Sylvia* chanced to be seated near the Prince of *Mechlenburgh*, who was then in *Brussels*, and at the ceremony; sad as she was, while the soft music was playing, she discoursed to him, though she knew him not, of the business of the day: he told her, she was to see a sight, that ought to make her sex less cruel; a man extremely beautiful and young, whose fortune could command almost all the pleasures of the world; yet for the love of the most amiable creature in the world, who has treated him with rigour, he abandons this youth and beauty to all the severity of rigid devotion: this relation, with a great deal he said of *Octavio*'s virtues and bravery, had like to have discovered her by putting her into a swoon; and she had much ado to support herself in her seat. I myself went among the rest to this ceremony, having, in all the time I lived in *Flanders*, never been so curious to see any such thing. The Order of St *Bernard* is one of the neatest of them, and there is a monastery of that Order, which are obliged to be all noblemen's sons; of which I have seen fifteen hundred at a time in one house, all handsome, and most of them young; their habit adds a grace to their person, for of all the Religious, that is the most becoming: long white vests of fine cloth, tied about with white silk sashes, or a cord of white silk; over this a long cloak without a cape, of the same fine white broad cloth; their hair of a pretty length, as that of our persons in *England*, and a white beaver; they have very fine apartments, fit for their quality, and above all, every one their library; they have attendance and equipage according to their rank, and have nothing of the inconveniencies and slovenliness of some of the Religious, but served in as good order as can be, and they have nothing of the monastic — but the name, the vow of chastity, and the opportunity of gaining heaven, by the sweetest retreat in the world, fine house, excellent air, and delicate gardens, grottoes and groves. It was this Order that *Octavio* had chosen, as too delicate to undertake the austerity of any other; and in my opinion, it is here a man may hope to become a saint sooner than in any other, more perplexed with want, cold, and all the necessaries of life, which takes the thought too much from heaven, and afflicts it with the cares of this world, with pain and too much abstinence: and I rather think it is necessity than choice, that makes a man a *Cordelier*, that may be a *Jesuit*, or *Bernardine*, to the best of the *Holy Orders*. But, to return, it was upon a *Thursday* this ceremony began; and, as I said, there was never any thing beheld so fine as the church that day was, and all the Fathers that officiated at the high-altar; behind which a most magnificent scene of glory was opened, with clouds most rarely and artificially set off, behind which appeared new ones more bright and dazzling, till from one degree to another, their lustre was hardly able to be looked on; and in which sat an hundred little angels so rarely dressed, such shining robes, such charming faces, such flowing bright hair, crowned with roses of white and red, with such artificial wings, as one would have said they had borne the body up in the splendid sky; and these to soft music, turned their soft voices with such sweetness of harmony, that, for my part, I confess, I thought myself no longer on earth; and sure there is nothing gives an idea of real heaven, like a church all adorned with rare pictures, and the other ornaments of it, with whatever can charm the eyes; and music, and voices, to ravish the ear; both which inspire the soul with unresistible devotion; and I can swear for my own part, in those moments a thousand times I have wished to die; so absolutely had I forgot the world, and all its vanities, and fixed my thoughts on heaven. While this music continued, and the anthems were singing, fifty boys all in white, bearing silver censers, cast incense all round, and perfumed the place with the richest and most agreeable smells, while two hundred silver lamps were burning upon the altar, to give a greater glory to the opened scene, whilst other boys strewed flowers upon the inlaid pavement, where the gay victim was to tread; for no crowd of gazers filled the empty space, but those that were spectators, were so placed, as rather served to adorn than disorder the awful ceremony, where all were silent, and as still as death; as awful, as mourners that attend the hearse of some loved monarch: while we were thus listening, the soft music playing, and the angels singing, the whole fraternity of the Order of St *Bernard* came in, two by two, in a very graceful order; and going up to the shining altar, whose furniture that day was embroidered with diamonds, pearls, and stones of great value, they bowed and retired to their places, into little gilded stalls, like our Knights of the Garter at *Windsor*: after them, fifty boys that sang approached in order to the altar, bowed, and divided on each side; they were dressed in white cloth of silver, with golden wings and rosy chaplets: after these the Bishop, in his pontific robes set with diamonds of great price, and his mitre richly adorned, ascended the altar, where, after a short anthem, he turned to receive the young devotee, who was just entered the church, while all eyes were fixed on him: he was led, or rather, on each side attended with two young noblemen, his relations; and I never saw any thing more rich in dress, but that of *Octavio* exceeded all imagination, for the gaiety and fineness of the work: it was white cloth of silver embroidered with gold, and buttons of diamonds; lined with rich cloth of gold and silver flowers, his breeches of the same, trimmed with a pale pink garniture; rich linen, and a white plume in his white hat: his hair, which was long and black, was that day in the finest order that could be imagined; but, for his face and eyes, I am not able to describe the charms that adorned them; no fancy, no imagination, can paint the beauties there: he looked indeed, as if he were made for heaven; no mortal ever had such grace: he looked methought, as if the gods of love had met in council to dress him up that day for everlasting conquest; for to his usual beauties he seemed to have the addition of a thousand more; he bore new lustre in his face and eyes, smiles on his cheeks, and dimples on his lips: he moved, he trod with nobler motions, as if some supernatural influence had took a peculiar care of him: ten thousand sighs, from all sides, were sent him, as he passed along, which, mixed with the soft music, made such a murmuring, as gentle breezes moving yielding boughs: I am assured, he won that day more hearts, without design, than ever he had gained with all his toils of love and youth before, when industry assisted him to conquer. In his approach to the altar, he made three bows; where, at the foot of it on the lower step, he kneeled, and then High–Mass began; in which were all sorts of different music, and that so excellent, that wholly ravished with what I saw and heard, I fancied myself no longer on earth, but absolutely ascended up to the regions of the sky. All I could see around me, all I heard, was ravishing and heavenly; the scene of glory, and the dazzling altar; the noble paintings, and the numerous lamps; the awfulness, the music, and the order, made me conceive myself above the stars, and I had no part of mortal thought about me. After the holy ceremony was performed, the Bishop turned and blessed him; and while an anthem was singing, *Octavio*, who was still kneeling, submitted his head to the hands of a Father, who, with a pair of scissors, cut off his delicate hair; at which a soft murmur of pity and grief filled the place: those fine locks, with which *Sylvia* had a thousand times played, and wound the curls about her snowy fingers, she now had the dying grief, for her sake, for her infidelity, to behold sacrificed to her cruelty, and distributed among the ladies, who, at any price, would purchase a curl: after this they took off his linen, and his coat, under which he had a white satin waistcoat, and under his breeches drawers of the same. Then, the Bishop took his robes, which lay consecrated on the altar, and put them on, and invested him with the holy robe: the singing continuing to the end of the ceremony; where, after an anthem was sung (while he prostrated himself before the altar) he arose, and instead of the two noblemen that attended him to the altar, two *Bernardines* approached, and conducted him from it, to the seats of every one of the Order, whom he kissed and embraced, as they came forth to welcome him to the Society. It was with abundance of tears that every one beheld this transformation; but *Sylvia* swooned several times during the ceremony, yet would not suffer herself to be carried out; but *Antonet* and another young lady of the house where she lodged, that accompanied her, did what they could to conceal her from the public view. For my part, I swear I was never so affected in my life with any thing, as I was at this ceremony; nor ever found my heart so oppressed with tenderness; and was myself ready to sink where I sat, when he came near me, to be welcomed by a Father that sat next to me: after this, he was led by two of the eldest Fathers to his apartment, and left a thousand sighing hearts behind him. Had he died, there had not been half that lamentation; so foolish is the mistaken world to grieve at our happiest fortune; either when we go to heaven or retreat from this world, which has nothing in it that can really charm, without a thousand fatigues to attend it: and in this retreat, I am sure, he himself was the only person that was not infinitely concerned; who quitted the world with so modest a bravery, so entire a joy, as no young conqueror ever performed his triumphs with more.

The ceremony being ended, *Antonet* got *Sylvia* to her chair, concerned even to death; and she vowed afterwards she had much ado to with-hold herself from running and seizing him at the altar, and preventing his fortune and design, but that she believed *Philander* would have resented it to the last degree, and possibly have made it fatal to both herself and *Octavio*. It was a great while before she could recover from the indisposition to which this fatal and unexpected accident had reduced her: but, as I have said, she was not of a nature to die for love; and charming and brave as *Octavio* was, it was perhaps her interest, and the loss of his considerable fortune that gave her the greatest cause of grief. Sometimes she vainly fancied that yet her power was such, that with the expense of one visit, and some of her usual arts, which rarely fail, she had power to withdraw his thoughts from heaven, and fix them all on herself again, and to make him fly those enclosures to her more agreeable arms: but again she wisely considered, though he might be retrieved, his fortune was disposed of to holy uses, and could never be so. This last thought more prevailed upon her, and had more convincing reason in it, than all that could besides oppose her flame; for she had this wretched prudence, even in the highest flights and passions of her love, to have a wise regard to interest; insomuch, that it is most certain, she refused to give herself up entirely even to *Philander*; him, whom one would have thought nothing but perfect love, soft irresistible love, could have compelled her to have transgressed withal, when so many reasons contradicted her passion: how much more then ought we to believe, that interest was the greatest motive of all her after-passions? However, this powerful motive failed not to beget in her all the pains and melancholies that the most violent of passions could do: but *Brilliard*, who loved her to a greater degree than ever, strove all he could to divert the thoughts of a grief, for which there was no remedy; and believed, if he could get her out of *Brussels*, retired to the little town, or rather village, where he was first made happy, and where *Philander* still believed her to be, he should again re-assume that power over her heart he had before: in this melancholy fit of hers he proposed it, urging the danger he should be in for obeying her, should *Philander* once come to know that she was in *Brussels*; and that possibly she would not find so civil a treatment as he ought to pay her, if he should come to the knowledge of it: besides these reasons, he said, he had some of greater importance, which he must not discover till she were withdrawn from *Brussels*: but there needed not much to persuade her to retire, in the humour she then was; and with no opposition on her side, she told him, she was ready to go where he thought fit; and accordingly the next day they departed the town, and in three more arrived to the village. In all this journey *Brilliard* never approached her but with all the respect imaginable, but withal, with abundance of silent passion: which manner of carriage obliged *Sylvia* very often to take notice of it, with great satisfaction and signs of favour; and as he saw her melancholy abate, he increased in sighing and lover's boldnesses: yet with all this, he could not oblige her to those returns he wished: when, after ten days' stay, *Philander* writ to him to inquire of his health, and of *Sylvia*, to whom he sent a very kind good-natured letter, but no more of the lover, than if there had never been such a joy between them: he begged her to take care of herself, and told her, he would be with her in ten or fifteen days; and desired her to send him *Brilliard*, if he were not wholly necessary to her service; for he had urgent affairs to employ him in: so that *Brilliard*, not being able longer with any colour to defend his stay, writ him word he would wait on him in two days; which short time he wholly employed in the utmost endeavour to gain *Sylvia*'s favour; but she, whose thoughts were roving on new designs, which she thought fit to conceal from a lover, still put him off with pretended illness, and thoughtfulness on the late melancholy object and loss of *Octavio*: but assured him, as soon as she was recovered of that pressure, she would receive him with the same joy she had before, and which his person and his services merited from her; it was thus she soothed the hoping lover, who went away with all the satisfaction imaginable, bearing a letter from *Sylvia* to *Philander*, written with all the art of flattery. *Brilliard* was no sooner gone, but *Sylvia*, whose head ran on new adventures, resolved to try her chance; and being, whenever she pleased, of a humour very gay, she resolved upon a design, in which she could trust no body but her page, who loved his lady to the last degree of passion, though he never durst shew it even in his looks or sighs; and yet the cunning *Sylvia* had by chance found his flame, and would often take delight to torture the poor youth, to laugh at him: she knew he would die to serve her, and she durst trust him with the most important business of her life: she therefore the next morning sends for him to her chamber, which she often did, and told him her design; which was, in man's clothes to go back to *Brussels*, and see if they could find any adventures by the way that might be worth the journey, and divert them: she told him she would trust him with all her secrets; and he vowed fidelity. She bid him bring her a suit of those clothes she used to wear at her first arrival at *Holland*, and he looked out one very fine, and which she had worn that day she went to have been married to *Octavio*, when the *States'* messengers took her up for a *French* spy, a suit *Philander* had never seen: she equips herself, and leaving in charge with *Antonet* what to say in

her absence, and telling her she was going upon a frolic to divert
herself a day or two; she, accompanied by her page only, took horse
and made away towards *Brussels*: you must know, that the halfway stage is a very small village, in which there is most lamentable
accommodation, and may vie with any part of *Spain* for bad inns.
Sylvia, not used much to riding as a man, was pretty well tired by
that time she got to one of those *hotels*; and, as soon as she alighted,
she went to her chamber to refresh and cool herself; and while the
page was gone to the kitchen to see what there was to eat, she was
leaning out of the window, and looking on the passengers that rode
along, many of which took up in the same house. Among them that
alighted, there was a very handsome young gentleman, appearing
of quality, attended only by his page. She considered this person a
little more than the rest, and finding him so unaccompanied, had a
curiosity, natural to her, to know who he was: she ran to another
window that looked into the yard, a kind of balcony, and saw him
alight, and look at her; and saluted her in passing into the kitchen,
seeing her look like a youth of quality: coming in, he saw her page,
and asked if he belonged to that young cavalier in the gallery; the
page told him he did: and being asked who he was, he told him he
was a young nobleman of *France*; a stranger to all those parts, and
had made an escape from his tutors; and said he was of a humour
never to be out of his way; all places being alike to him in those little
adventures. So leaving him (with yet a greater curiosity) he ran to
Sylvia, and told her what had passed between the young stranger
and him: while she, who was possessed with the same inquisitive
humour, bid him inquire who he was; when the master of the *hotel*
coming in the interim up to usher in her supper, she inquired of him
who that young stranger was; he told her, one of the greatest persons
in *Flanders*; that he was nephew to the Governor, and who had a
very great equipage at other times; but that now he was *incognito*,
being on an intrigue: this intrigue gave *Sylvia* new curiosity; and
hoping the master would tell him again, she fell into great praises
of his beauty and his mien; which for several reasons pleased the
man of the inn, who departed with the good news, and told every
word of it to the young cavalier: the good man having, besides the

pleasing him with the grateful compliments, a farther design in the relation; for his house being very full of persons of all sorts, he had no lodgings for the Governor's nephew, unless he could recommend him to our young cavalier. The gay unknown, extremely pleased with the character he had given him by so beautiful a gentleman, and one who appeared of so much quality, being alone, and knowing he was so also, sent a *Spanish* page, that spoke very good *French*, and had a handsome address, and quick wit, to make his compliment to the young *Monsieur*; which was to beg to be admitted to sup with him; who readily accepted the honour, as she called it; and the young Governor, whom we must call *Alonzo*, for a reason or two, immediately after entered her chamber, with an admirable address, appearing much handsomer near, than at a distance, though even then he drew *Sylvia*'s eyes with admiration on him: there were a thousand young graces in his person, sweetnesses in his face, love and fire in his eyes, and wit on his tongue: his stature was neither tall nor low, very well made and fashioned; a light-brown hair, hazel eyes, and a very soft and amorous air; about twenty years of age: he spoke very good *French*; and after the first compliments on either side were over, as on such occasions are necessary; in which on both sides were nothing but great expressions of esteem, *Sylvia* began so very well to be pleased with the fair stranger, that she had like to have forgot the part she was to act, and have made discoveries of her sex, by addressing herself with the modesty and blushes of a woman: but *Alonzo*, who had no such apprehension, though she appeared with much more beauty than he fancied ever to have seen in a man, nevertheless admired, without suspecting, and took all those signs of effeminacy to unassured youth, and first address; and he was absolutely deceived in her. *Alonzo*'s supper being brought up, which was the best the bad inn afforded, they sat down, and all the supper time talked of a thousand pleasant things, and most of love and women, where both expressed abundance of gallantry for the fair sex. *Alonzo* related many short and pleasant accidents and amours he had had with women.

Though the stranger were by birth a *Spaniard*; yet, while they discoursed the glass was not idle, but went as briskly about, as if

Sylvia had been an absolute good fellow. *Alonzo* drinks his and his mistress's health, and *Sylvia* returned the civility, and so on, till three bottles were sacrificed to love and good humour; while she, at the expense of a little modesty, declared herself so much of the opinion of *Don Alonzo*, for gay inconstancy, and the blessing of variety, that he was wholly charmed with a conversation so agreeable to his own. I have heard her page say, from whom I have had a great part of the truths of her life, that he never saw *Sylvia* in so pleasant a humour all his life before, nor seemed so well pleased, which gave him, her lover, a jealousy that perplexed him above any thing he had ever felt from love; though he durst not own it. But *Alonzo* finding his young companion altogether so charming (and in his own way too) could not forbear very often from falling upon his neck, and kissing the fair disguised, with as hearty an ardour, as ever he did one of the other sex: he told her he adored her; she was directly of his principle, all gay, inconstant, galliard and roving, and with such a gusto, he commended the joys of fickle youth, that *Sylvia* would often say, she was then jealous of him, and envious of those who possessed him, though she knew not whom. The more she looked on him, and heard him speak, the more she fancied him: and wine that warmed her head, made her give him a thousand demonstrations of love, that warmed her heart; which he mistook for friendship, having mistaken her sex. In this fit of beginning love (which is always the best) and jealousy, she bethought her to ask him on what adventure he had now been; for he being without his equipage, she believed, she said, he was upon some affair of love: he told her there was a lady, within an hour's riding of that place, of quality, and handsome, very much courted: amongst those that were of the number of her adorers, he said, was a young man of quality of *France*, who called himself *Philander*: this *Philander* had been about eight days very happy in her favour, and had happened to boast his good fortune the next night at the Governor's table, where he dined with the Prince *Cesario*. 'I told him,' continued *Alonzo*, 'that the person he so boasted of, had so soon granted him the favour, that I believed she was of a humour to suffer none to die at her feet: but this,' said he, '*Philander* thought an indignity to his good parts, and told me, he believed he was the only man happy in her favour, and that could be so: on this I ventured a wager, at which he coloured extremely, and the company laughed, which incensed him more; the Prince urged the wager, which was a pair of *Spanish* horses, the best in the Court, on my side, against a discretion on his: this odds offered by me incensed him yet more; but urged to lay, we ended the dispute with the wager, the best conclusion of all controversies. He would have known what measures I would take; I refused to satisfy him in that; I only swore him upon honour, that he should not discover the wager, or the dispute to the lady. The next day I went to pay her a visit, from my aunt, the Governor's lady, and she received me with all the civility in the world. I seemed surprised at her beauty, and could talk of nothing but the adoration I had for her, and found her extremely pleased, and vain; of which feeble resistance I made so good advantage, that before we parted, being all alone, I received from her all the freedoms, that I could with any good manners be allowed the first time; she firing me with kisses, and suffering my closest embraces. Having prospered so well, I left her for that time, and two days after I made my visit again; she was a married lady, and her husband was a *Dutch* Count, and gone to a little government he held under my uncle, so that again I found a free admittance; I told her, it was my aunt's compliment I brought before, but that now it was my own I brought, which was that of an impatient heart, that burnt with a world of fire and flame, and nonsense. In fine, so eager I was, and so pressing for something more than dull kissing, that she began to retire as fast as she advanced before, and told me, after abundance of pressing her to it, that she had set a price upon her beauty, and unless I understood how to purchase her, it was not her fault if I were not happy. At first I so little expected it had been money, that I reiterated my vows, and fancied it was the assurance of my heart she meant; but she very frankly replied, "Sir, you may spare your pains, and five hundred pistoles will ease you of a great deal of trouble, and be the best argument of your love." This generous conscientious humour of hers, of suffering none to die that had five hundred pistoles to present for a cure, was very good news to me, and I found I was not at all obliged to my youth or beauty, but that a man with half a nose, or a single eye, or that stunk like an old *Spaniard* that had dined on rotten cheese and garlic, should have been equally as welcome for the aforesaid sum, to this charming insensible. I must confess, I do not love to chaffer for my pleasure, it takes off the best part of it; and were I left to my own judgement of its worth, I should hardly have offered so sneaking a sum; but that sort of bargaining, was her humour, and to enjoy her mind, though she had strangely palled me by this management of the matter: all I had now to do, was to appoint my night, and bring my money; now was a very proper time for it, her husband being absent: I took my leave of her, infinitely well pleased to have gained my point on any terms, with a promise to deliver myself there the next night: but she told me, she had a brother to come to-morrow, whom she would not have see me, and for that reason (being however not willing to delay the receiving her pistoles) she desired I would wait at this very house 'till a footman should give me notice when to come; accordingly I came, and sent her a billet, that I waited prepared at all points; and she returned me a billet to this purpose; that her brother with some relations being arrived, as she expected, she begged for her honour's sake, that I would wait till she sent, which should be as soon as they were gone to their chambers; and they, having rid a long journey, would early retire; that she was impatient of the blessing, and should be as well prepared as himself, and that she would leave her woman *Letitia* to give me admittance. —— This satisfied me very well; and as I attended her, some of my acquaintance chanced to arrive; with whom I supped, and took so many glasses to her health as it passed down, that I was arrived at a very handsome pitch, and to say truth, was as full of *Bacchus* as of *Venus*. However, as soon as her footman arrived, I stole away, and took horse, and by that time it was quite dark arrived at her house, where I was led in by a young maid, whose habit was very neat and clean, and she herself appeared to my eyes, then dazzling with wine, the most beautiful young creature I had ever seen, as in truth she was; she seemed all modesty, and blushing innocence; so that conducting me into a low parlour, while she went to tell her lady I was come, who lay ready dressed in all the magnificences of night-dress to receive me, I sat contemplating on this fair young maid, and no more thought of her lady than of *Bethlehem Gaber*. The maid soon returned, and curtseying, told me, with blushes on her face, that her lady expected me; the house was still as sleep, and no noise heard, but the little winds that rushed among the jessamine that grew at the window; now whether at that moment, the false light in the room, or the true wine deceived me, I know not; but I beheld this maid as an angel for beauty, and indeed I think she had all the temptations of nature. I began to kiss her, and she to tremble and blush; yet not so much out of fear, as surprise and shame at my address. I found her pleased with my vows, and melting at my kisses; I sighed in her bosom, which panted me a welcome there; that bosom whiter than snow, sweeter than the nosegay she had planted there. She urged me faintly to go to her lady, who expected me, and I swore it was for her sake I came (whom I never saw) and that I scorned all other beauties: she kindled at this, and her cheeks glowed with love. I pressed her to all I wished; but she replied, she was a maid, and should be undone. I told her, I would marry her, and swore it with a thousand oaths; she believed, and grew prettily fond —— In fine, at last she yielded to all I asked of her, which we had scarce recovered when her lady rung. I could not stir, but she who feared a surprise ran to her, and told her, I was gone into the garden, and would come immediately; she hastens down again to me, fires me anew, and pleased me anew; it was thus I taught a longing maid the first lesson of sin, at the price of fifty pistoles, which I presented her; nor could I yet part from this young charmer, but stayed so long, that her lady rung a silver bell again; but my new prize was so wholly taken up with the pleasure of this new amour, and the good fortune arrived to her, she heard not the bell, so that the fair deceived put on her night-gown and slippers, and came softly down stairs, and found my new love and I closely embracing, with all the passion and fondness imaginable. I know not what she saw in me in that kind moment to her woman, or whether the disappointment gave her a greater desire, but it is most certain she fell most desperately in love with me, and scorning to take notice of the indignity I put upon her, she unseen stole to her chamber; where, after a most afflicting night, she next morning called her woman to her (whom I left towards morning, better pleased with my fifty pistoles worth of beauty, than I should have been with that of five hundred): the maid, whose guilt made her very much unassured, approached her lady with such tremblings, as she no longer doubted but she was guilty, but durst not examine her about it, lest she, who had her honour in keeping, should, by the discovery she found she had made of her levity, expose that of her lady. She therefore dissembled as well as she could, and examined her about my stay; to which the maid answered, I had fallen asleep, and it was impossible to awake me 'till day appeared; when for fear of discovery I posted away. This, though the lady knew was false, she was forced to take for current excuse; and more raging with love than ever, she immediately dispatched away her footman with a letter to me, upbraiding me extremely; but, at the same time, inviting me with all the passion imaginable; and, because I should not again see my young mistress, who was dying in love with me, she appointed me to meet her at a little house she had, a bow-shot from her own, where was a fine decoy, and a great number of wild-fowl kept, which her husband took great delight in; there I was to wait her coming; where lived only a man and his old wife, her servants: I was very glad of this invitation, and went; she came adorned with all her charms.

I considered her a new woman, and one whom I had a wager to win upon, the conquest of one I had inclination to, till by the discovery of the jilt in her, I began to despise the beauty; however, as I said, she was new, and now perhaps easy to be brought to any terms, as indeed it happened; she caressed me with all imaginable fondness; was ready to eat my lips instead of kissing them, and much more forward than I wished, who do not love an over-easy conquest; however, she pleased me for three days together, in all which time she detained me there, coming to me early, and staying the latest hour; and I have no reason to repent my time; for besides that I have passed it very well, she at my coming away presented me this jewel in my hat, and this ring on my finger, and I have saved my five hundred pistoles, my heart, and my credit in the encounter, and am going to *Brussels* to triumph over the haughty conceited *Philander*, who set so great a value on his own beauty, and yet, for all his fine person, has paid the pistoles, before he could purchase the blessing, as she swore to me, who have made a convert of her, and reduced her to the thing she never yet was, a lover; insomuch, that she has promised me to renounce *Philander*: I have promised to visit her again; but if I do it will be more for the vanity to please, than to be pleased; for I never repeat any thing with pleasure.' All the while he spoke, *Sylvia* fixed her eyes, and all her soft desires upon him; she envies the happy Countess, but much more the happy maid, with whom his perfect liking made him happy; she fancies him in her arms, and wishes him there; she is ready a thousand times to tell him she is a woman, but, when she reflects on his inconstancy, she fears. When he had ended his story, she cried, sighing, 'And you are just come from this fair lady?' He answered her, he was sound and heart whole: she replied, 'It is very well you are so, but all the young do not thus escape from beauty, and you may, some time or other, be entrapped.' 'Oh,' cried he, 'I defy the power of one, while heaven has distributed variety to all.' 'Were you never in love?' replied Sylvia. 'Never,' said he, 'that they call love: I have burnt and raved an hour or two, or so; pursued, and gazed, and laid sieges, till I had overcome; but, what is this to love? Did I ever make a second visit, unless upon necessity, or gratitude? And yet ——' and there he sighed; 'and yet,' said he, 'I saw a beauty once upon the *Tour*, that has ever since given me torment.' 'At *Brussels*? said *Sylvia*. 'There,' replied he; 'she was the fairest creature heaven ever made, such white and red by nature, such hair, such eyes, and such a mouth! —— All youth and ravishing sweetness; — I pursued her to her lodgings, and all I could get, was, that she belonged to a young nobleman, who since has taken Orders. From the night I saw her, I never left her window, but had spies of all sorts, who brought me intelligence, and a little after, I found she had quitted the place with a new lover, which made me love and rave ten times more, when I knew assuredly she was a whore — and how fine a one I had missed.' This called all the blood to *Sylvia*'s face, and so confounded her she could not answer; she knew it was herself of whom he spoke; and that coarse word, though innocently spoken, or rather gaily expressed, put her quite out of countenance; however, she recovered again, when she considered they were not meant as rudenesses to her. She loved him, and was easy to pardon: with such discourse they passed the evening till towards bed-time, and the young *Spaniard*, who had taken little rest in three nights before, wanted some repose; and calling for his chamber, the host besought him, since they had the happiness (the young *French* gentleman and himself) to be so good friends, that they would share a bed together: 'For in truth,' said he, 'sir, you must sit up all night else;' he replied, with all his soul, it was the most grateful proposal had been ever made him; and addressing himself to *Sylvia*, asked him if he would allow him that blessing: she blushed extremely at the question, and hung down her eyes, and he laughed to see it: 'Sir,' said *Sylvia*, 'I will give you my bed, for it is all one to me to lie on a bed, or on the chairs.' 'Why, sir,' said *Alonzo*, 'I am too passionate an adorer of the female sex, to incommode any of my own with addresses; nor am I so nice, but I can suffer a man to lie by me, especially so dear a youth as yourself;' at which he embraced her in his arms, which did but the more raise *Sylvia*'s blushes, who wished for what she dreaded: 'With you, sir,' said she, 'I could methinks be content to do what I do not use to do;' and, fearing to betray her sex, forced a consent; for either one or the other she was compelled to do; and with the assurance that he thought her what she seemed, she chose to give her consent, and they both went to bed together: to add to her deceit (she being forced in her sickness to cut off her hair) when she put off her periwig she discovered nothing of the woman; nor feared she any thing but her breasts, which were the roundest and the whitest in the world; but she was long in undressing, which to colour the matter, she suffered her page to do; who, poor lad, was never in so trembling a condition, as in that manner to be obliged to serve her, where she discovered so many charms he never before had seen, but all such as might be seen with modesty: by that time she came to bed, *Alonzo* was fast asleep, being so long kept waking, and never so much as dreamt he had a woman with him; but she, whose fears kept her waking, had a thousand agitations and wishes; so natural it is, when virtue has broke the bounds of modesty, to plunge in past all retreat; and, I believe there are very few who retire after the first sin. She considers her condition in a strange country, her splendour declining, her love for *Philander* quite reduced to friendship, or hardly that; she was

young, and ate and drank well; had a world of vanity, that food
of desire, that fuel to vice: she saw this the beautifullest youth she
imagined ever to have seen, of quality and fortune able to serve her;
all these made her rave with a desire to gain him for a lover, and
she imagined as all the vain and young do, that though no charms
had yet been able to hold him, she alone had those that would; her
glass had a thousand times told her so; she compares him to *Octavio*,
and finds him, in her opinion, handsomer; she was possessed with
some love for *Philander*, when he first addressed to her, and *Octavio*
shared at best but half a heart; but now, that she had lost all for
Philander and *Octavio*, and had a heart to cast away, or give a new
lover; it was like her money, she hated to keep it, and lavished it on
any trifle, rather than hoard it, or let it lie by: it was a loss of time her
youth could not spare; she, after reflection, resolved, and when she
had resolved, she believed it done. By a candle she had by her, to read
a little novel she had brought, she surveyed him often, as curiously
as *Psyche* did her *Cupid*, and though he slept like a mere mortal, he
appeared as charming to her eyes as the winged god himself; and
it is believed she wished he would awake and find by her curiosity,
her sex: for this I know, she durst no longer trust herself a-bed with
him, but got up, and all the last part of the night walked about the
room: her page lay in the room with her, by her order, on the table,
with a little valise under his head, which he carried *Sylvia*'s linen
in; she awoke him, and told him all her fears, in a pleasant manner.
In the morning *Alonzo* awakes, and wonders to find her up so soon,
and reproached her for the unkindness; new protestations on both
sides passing of eternal friendship, they both resolved for *Brussels*;
but, lest she should encounter *Philander* on the way, who possibly
might be on visiting his *Dutch* countess, she desired him to ride on
before, and to suffer her to lose the happiness of his company, till
they met in *Brussels*: with much ado he consents, and taking the ring
the countess gave him, from off his finger, 'Sir,' said he, 'be pleased to
wear this, and if ever you need my fortune, or my sword, send it, and
in what part of the world soever I am, I will fly to your service.' *Sylvia*
returned him a little ring set round with diamonds, that Philander in
his wooing time had given her, amongst a thousand of finer value: his

name and hers were engraven instead of a posie in it; which was only *Philander* and *Sylvia*, and which he took no notice of, and parted from each other in the tenderest manner, that two young gentlemen could possibly be imagined to do, though it were more than so on her side; for she was madly in love with him.

As soon as *Sylvia* came to *Brussels*, she sent in the evening to search out *Brilliard*, for she had discovered, if he should come to the knowledge of her being in town, and she should not send to him, he would take it so very ill, that he might prevent all her designs and rambles, the now joy of her heart; she knew she could make him her slave, her pimp, her any thing, for love, and the hope of her favour, and his interest might defend her; and she should know all *Philander*'s, motions, whom now, though she loved no more, she feared. She found him, and he took her lodgings, infinitely pleased at the trust she reposed in him, the only means by which he could arrive to happiness. She continues her man's habit, and he supplied the place of *valet*, dressed her and undressed her, shifted her linen every day; nor did he take all these freedoms, without advancing a little farther upon occasion and opportunity, which was the hire she gave him, to serve her in more lucky amours; the fine she paid to live free, and at ease. She tells him her adventure, which, though it were daggers to his heart, was, however, the only way to keep her his own; for he knew her spirit was too violent to be restrained by any means. At last, she told him her design upon a certain young man of quality, who she told him, was the same she encountered. She assured him it was not love or liking, but perfectly interest that made her design upon him, and that if he would assist her, she would be very kind to him, as a man that had gained very greatly upon her heart. This flattery she urged with infinite fondness and art, and he, overjoyed, believed every word as gospel; so that he promised her the next day to carry a billet to the young *don*: in the mean time, she caused him to sup with her, purposely to give him an account of *Philander*, *Cesario* and *Hermione*, whom she heard was come to *Brussels*, and lived publicly with the Prince. He told her, it was very true, and that he saw them every day, nay, every moment together; for he verily believed they could not live asunder; that *Philander* was every evening caballing there, where all the malcontents of the Reformed Religion had taken sanctuary, and where the Grand Council was every night held; for some great things were in agitation, and debating how to trouble the repose of all *France* again with new broils; he told her, that all the world made their court to *Hermione*, that if any body had any petitions, or addresses to make to the Prince, it was by her sole interest; she sat in their closest councils, and heard their gravest debates; and she was the oracle of the board: the Prince paying her perfect adoration, while she, whose charms of youth were ended, being turned of thirty, fortified her decays with all the art her wit and sex were capable of, and kept her illustrious lover as perfectly her slave, as if she had engaged him by all those ties that fetter the most circumspect, and totally subdued him to her will, who was, without exception, the most lovely person upon earth; 'and though, madam, you know him so perfectly well, yet I must tell you my opinion of him: he is all the softer sex can wish, and ours admire; he is formed for love and war; and as he is the most amorous and wanton in courts, he is also the most fierce and brave in field; his birth the most elevated, his age arrived to full blown man, adorned with all the spreading glories that charm the fair, and engage the world; and I have often heard some of our party say, his person gained him more numbers to his side, than his cause or quality; for he understood all the useful arts of popularity, the gracious smile and bow, and all those cheap favours that so gain upon hearts; and without the expense of any thing but ceremony, has made the nation mad for his interest, who never otherwise obliged them; and sure nothing is more necessary in the great, than affability; nor shews greater marks of grandeur, or shall more eternize them, than bowing to the crowd. As the maiden queen I have read of in *England*, who made herself idolized by that sole piece of politic cunning, understanding well the stubborn, yet good nature of the people; and gained more upon them by those little arts, than if she had parted with all the prerogatives of her Crown. Ah! madam, you cannot imagine what little slights govern the whole universe, and how easy it is for monarchs to oblige. This *Cesario* was made to know, and there is no one so poor an object, who may not have access to him, and whom he does not send away well pleased, though he do not grant what they ask. He dispatches quickly, which is a grateful virtue in great men; and none ever espoused his interest, that did not find a reward and a protection; it is true, these are all the tools he is to work with, and he stops at nothing that leads to his ambition; nor has he done all that lies in the power of man only, to set all *France* yet in a flame, but he calls up the very devils from hell to his aid, and there is no man famed for necromancy, to whom he does not apply himself; which, indeed, is done by the advice of *Hermione*, who is very much affected with those sort of people, and puts a great trust and confidence in them. She sent at great expense, for a *German* conjurer, who arrived the other day, and who is perpetually consulting with another of the same sort, a *Scot* by birth, called *Fergusano*. He was once in Holy Orders, and still is so, but all his practice is the Black Art; and excellent in it he is reported to be. *Hermione* undertakes nothing without his advice; and as he is absolutely her creature, so his art governs her, and she the Prince: she holds her midnight conferences with him; and as she is very superstitious, so she is very learned, and studies this art, taught by this great master *Fergusano*; and so far is this glorious hero bewitched with these sorcerers, that he puts his whole trust in these conjurations and charms; and so far they have imposed on him, that with an enchanted ointment, which they had prepared for him, he shall be invulnerable, though he should face the mouth of a cannon: they have, at the earnest request of *Hermione*, calculated his nativity, and find him born to be a king; and, that before twenty moons expire, he shall be crowned in *France*: and flattering his easy youth with all the vanities of ambition, they have made themselves absolutely useful to him. This *Scot*, being a most inveterate enemy to *France*, lets the Prince rest neither night nor day, but is still inspiring him with new hopes of a crown, and laying him down all the false arguments imaginable, to spur the active spirit: my lord is not of the opinion, yet seems to comply with them in Council; he laughs at all the fopperies of charms and incantations; insomuch, that he many times angers the Prince, and is in eternal little feuds with *Hermione*. The *German* would often in these disputes say, he found by his art, that the stop to the Prince's glory would be his love. This so incensed *Hermione*, and consequently the Prince, that they had like to have broke with him, but durst not for fear; he knowing too much to be disobliged: on the other side, *Fergusano* is most wonderfully charmed with the wit and masculine spirit of *Hermione*, her courage, and the manliness of her mind; and understanding which way she would be served, resolved to obey her, finding she had an absolute ascendancy over the Prince, whom, by this means, he knew he should get into his sole management. *Hermione*, though she seemed to be possessed so entirely of *Cesario*'s heart, found she had great and powerful opposers, who believed the Prince lay idling in her arms, and that possibly she might eclipse his fame, by living at that rate with a woman he had no other pretensions to but love; and many other motives were urged daily to him by the admirers of his great actions: and she feared, with reason, that some time or other, ambition might get the ascendancy of love: she, therefore, in her midnight conferences with *Fergusano*, often urged him to shew her that piece of his art, to make a philtre to retain fleeting love; and not only keep a passion alive, but even revive it from the dead. She tells him of her contract with him; she urges his forced marriage, as she was pleased to call it, in his youth; and that he being so young, she believed he might find it lawful to marry himself a second time; that possibly his Princess was for the interest of the King; and men of his elevated fortune ought not to be tied to those strictnesses of common men, but for the good of the public, sometimes act beyond the musty rules of law and equity, those politic bands to confine the *mobile*. At this unreasonable rate she pleads her right to *Cesario*, and he hearkens with all attention, and approves so well all she says, that he resolves, not only to attach the Prince to her by all the force of the Black Art, but that of necessary marriage also: this pleased her to the last degree; and she left him, after he had promised her to bring her the philtre by the morning: for it was that she most urged, the other requiring time to argue with him, and work him by degrees to it. Accordingly, the next morning he brings her a tooth-pick-case of gold, of rare infernal workmanship, wrought with a thousand charms, of that force, that every time the Prince should touch it, and while he but wore it about him, his fondness should not only continue, but increase, and he should hate all womankind besides, at least in the way of love, and have no power to possess another woman, though she had all the attractions of nature. He tells her the Prince could never suspect so familiar a present, and for the fineness of the work, it was a present for a Prince; 'For,' said he, 'no human art could frame so rare a piece of workmanship; that nine nights the most delicate of the Infernals were mixing the metal with the most powerful of charms, and watched the critical minutes of the stars, in which to form the mystic figures, every one being a spell upon the heart, of that unerring magic, no mortal power could ever dissolve, undo, or conquer.' The only art now was in giving it, so as to oblige him never to part with it; and she, who had all the cunning of her sex, undertook for that part; she dismissed her infernal confidant, and went to her *toilet* to dress her, knowing well, that the Prince would not be long before that he came to her: she laid the tooth-pick-case down, so as he could not avoid seeing it: the Prince came immediately after in, as he ever used to do night and morning, to see her dress her; he saw this gay thing on the table, and took it in his hand, admiring the work of it, as he was the most curious person in the world: she told him, there was not a finer wrought thing in the world, and that she had a very great esteem for it, it being made by the *Sybils*; and bid him mind the antiqueness of the work: the more she commended it, the more he liked it, and told her, she must let him call it his: she told him, he would give it away to the next commender: he vowed he would not: she told him then he should not only call it his, but it should in reality be so; and he vowed it should be the last thing he would part with in the world. From that time forward she found, or thought she found, a more impatient fondness in him than she had seen before: however it was, she ruled and governed him as she pleased; and indeed never was so great a slave to beauty, as, in my opinion, he was to none at all; for she is far from having any natural charms; yet it was not long since it was absolutely believed by all, that he had been resolved to give himself wholly up to her arms; to have sought no other glory, than to have retired to a corner of the world with her, and changed all his crown of laurel for those of roses: but some stirring spirits have roused him anew, and awakened ambition in him, and they are on great designs, which possibly 'ere long may make all *France* to tremble; yet still *Hermione* is oppressed with love, and the effects of daily increasing passion. He has perpetual correspondence with the party in *Paris*, and advice of all things that pass; they let him know they are ready to receive him whenever he can bring a force into *France*; nor needs he any considerable number, he having already there, in every place through which he shall pass, all, or the most part of the hearts and hands at his devotion; and they want but arms, and they shall gather as they go: they desire he will land himself in some part of the kingdom, and it would be encouragement enough to all the joyful people, who will from all parts flock together. In fine, he is offered all assistance and money; and lest all the forces of *France* should be bent against him, he has friends, of great quality and interest, that are resolved to rise in several places of the kingdom, in *Languedoc* and *Guyenne*, whither the King must be obliged to send his forces, or a great part of them; so that all this side of *France* will be left defenceless. I myself, madam, have some share in this great design, and possibly you will one day see me a person of a quality sufficient to merit those favours I am now blessed with.' 'Pray,' replied *Sylvia*, smiling with a little scorn, 'what part are you to play to arrive at this good fortune?' 'I am,' said he, 'trusted to provide all the ammunition and arms, and to hire a vessel to transport them to some sea-port town in *France*, which the Council shall think most proper to receive us.' *Sylvia* laughed, and said, she prophesied another end of this high design than they imagined; but desperate fortunes must take their chance. 'What,' continued she, 'does not *Hermione* speak of me, and inquire of me?' 'Yes,' replied *Brilliard*; 'but in such a way, as if she looked on you as a lost creature, and one of such a reputation, she would not receive a visit from for all the world.' At this *Sylvia* laughed extremely, and cried, '*Hermione* would be very well content to be so mean a sinner as myself, to be so young and so handsome a one. However,' said she, 'to be serious, I would be glad to know what real probability there is in advancing and succeeding in this design, for I would take my measures accordingly, and keep *Philander*, whose wavering, or rather lost fortune, is the greatest motive of my resolves to part with him, and that have made me so uneasy to him.' *Brilliard* told her, he was very confident of the design, and that it was almost impossible to miscarry in the discontent all *France* was in at this juncture; and they feared nothing but the Prince's relapsing, who, now, most certainly preferred love to glory. He farther told her, that as they were in Council, one deputed from the *Parisians* arrived with new offers, and to know the last result of the Prince, whether he would espouse their interest or not, as they were with life and fortune ready to espouse his glory. 'They sent him word, it was from him they expected liberty, and him whom they looked upon as their tutelar deity. Old *Fergusano* was then in Council, that *Highland* wizard that manages all, and who is ever at hand to awaken mischief, alarmed the Prince to new glories, reproaching his scandalous life, withal telling him, there were measures to be taken to reconcile love and fame; and which he was to discourse to him about in his closet only; but as things were, he bid him look into the story of *Armida* and *Renaldo*, and compare his own with it, and he doubted not, but he would return blushing at his remissness and sloth: not that he would exempt his youth from the pleasures of love, but he would not have love hinder his glory: this bold speech before *Hermione* had like to have begot an ill understanding; but she was as much for the Prince's glory as *Fergusano*, and therefore could not be angry, when she considered the elevation of the Prince would be her own also: at this necessary reproach the Prince blushed; the board seconding the wizard, had this good effect to draw this assurance from him, that they should see he was not so attached to love, but he could for some time give a cessation to his heart, and that the envoy from the *Parisians* might return assured, that he would, as soon as he could put his affairs in good order, come to their relief, and bring arms for those that had none, with such friends as he could get together; he could not promise numbers, lest by leading so many here, their design should take air, but would wholly trust to fortune, and their good resolutions: he demanded a sum of money of them for the buying these arms, and they have promised him all aids. This is the last result of Council, which broke immediately up; and the Prince retired to his closet, where he was no sooner come, but reflecting on the necessity of leaving *Hermione*, he fell into the most profound melancholy and musing that could seize a man; while he sat thus, *Hermione* (who had schooled *Fergusano* for his rough speech in Council, and desired he would now take the opportunity to repair that want of respect, while the Prince was to be spoken to alone) sent him into the closet to him; where he found him walking with his arms a-cross, not minding the bard who stood gazing on him, and at last called to him; and finding no reply, he advanced, and pulling him gently by the arm, cried — "Awake royal young man, awake! and look up to coming greatness"—"I was reflecting," replied *Cesario*, "on all the various fortunes I have passed, from the time of my birth to this present hapless day, and would be glad to know if any supernatural means can tell me what future events will befall me? If I believed I should not gain a crown by this great enterprise I am undertaking, here I would lay me down in silent ease, give up my toils and restless soul to love, and never think on vain ambition more: ease thou my troubled mind, if thou hast any friend among the Infernals, and they dare utter truth." "My gracious Prince," replied the fawning wizard, "this night, if you dare loose yourself from love, and come unattended to my apartment, I will undertake to shew you all the future fortune you are to run, the hazards, dangers, and escapes that attend your mighty race of life; I will lay the adamantine Book before you, where all the destinies of princes are hieroglyphick'd. I will shew you more, if hell can furnish objects, and you dare stand untrembling at the terror of them." "Enough," replied *Cesario*, "name me the hour." "Betwixt twelve and one," said he; "for that is the sacred dismal time of night for fiends to come, tombs to open and let loose their dead. — We shall have use of both ——" "No more," replied *Cesario*, "I will attend them." The Prince was going out, when *Fergusano* recalled him, and cried, "One thing, sir, I must caution you, that from this minute to that, wherein I shall shew you your destiny, you commit nothing unlawful with women-kind." "Away," replied the Prince, smiling, "and leave your canting." The wizard, putting on a more grave countenance, replied —"By all the Infernals, sir, if you commit unlawful things I cannot serve you." "If your devils," replied the Prince, laughing, "be so nice, I doubt I shall find them too honest for my purpose." "Sir," said the subtle old fiend, "such conscientious devils Your Highness is to converse with to-night; and if you discover the secret, it will I not prove so lucky." "Since they are so humorous," cried *Cesario*, "I will give them way for once." And going out of the room, he went directly to *Hermione*'s apartment; where, it being late, she is preparing for bed, and with a thousand kisses, and hanging on his neck, she asked him why he is so slow, and why he suffers not himself to be undressed? He feigns a thousand excuses, at which she seems extremely amazed; she complains, reproaches, and commands —— He tells her, he was to wait on the Governor about his most urgent affairs, and was (late as it was) to consult with him: she asked him what affairs he was to negotiate, of which she was not to bear her part? He refuses to tell her, and she replied she had sense and courage for any enterprise, and should resent it very ill, if she were not made acquainted with it: but he swore I to her she should know all the truth, as soon as he returned.

'This pacified her in some measure, and at the hour appointed she suffered him to go; and in a chair was carried to a little house *Fergusano* had taken without the town, to which belonged a large garden, at the farther end of which was a thicket of unordered trees, that surrounded the grotto, which I passed a good way under the ground. It had had some rarities of water-work formerly belonging to it, but now they were decayed; only here and there a broken rock let out a little stream, that murmured and dashed upon the earth below, and ran away in a little rivulet, which served to add a melancholy to the dismal place: into this the Prince was conducted by the old *German*, who assisted in the charm; they had only one torch to light the way, which at the entrance of the cave they put out, and within was only one glimmering lamp, that rather served to add to the horror of the vault, discovering its hollowness and ruins. At his entrance, he was saluted with a noise like the rushing of wind, which whizzed and whistled in the mighty concave. Anon a more silent whispering surrounded him, without being able to behold any creature save the old *German*. Anon came in old *Fergusano*, who rolling a great stone, that lay at one corner of the cave, he desired the Prince to place himself on it, and not be surprised at any thing he should behold, nor to stir from that enchanted ground; he, nodding, assented to obey, while *Fergusano* and the *German*, with each a wand in their hands, struck against the unformed rocks that finished the end of the cave, muttering a thousand incantations, with voices dreadful, and motions antic; and, after a mighty stroke of thunder that shook the earth, the rude rock divided, and opened a space that discovered a most magnificent apartment; in which was presented a young hero, attended with military officers; his pages dressing him for the field all in gilded armour. The Prince began to doubt himself, and to swear in his thought, that the apparition was himself, so very like he was to himself, as if he had seen his proper figure in a glass. After this, several persons seemed to address to this great man, of all sorts and conditions, from the Prince to the peasant, with whom he seemed to discourse with great confidence and affability; they offered him the League, which he took and signed, and gave them back; they attend him to the door with great joy and respect; but as soon as he was gone, they laughed and pointed at him; at which the Prince infinitely incensed, rose, and cried out, "What means all this; s'death, am I become the scorn and mockery of the crowd?" *Fergusano* besought him to sit and have patience, and he obeyed, and checked himself. The scene of the apartment being changed to an arbour of flowers, and the prospect of a noble and ravishing garden, the hero is presented armed as he was, only without his plume head-piece, kneeling at the feet of a fair woman, in loose robes and hair, and attended with abundance of little Loves, who disarm him by degrees of those ornaments of war. While she caresses him with all the signs of love, the *Cupids* made garlands of flowers, and wreath round his arms and neck, crowning his head, and fettering him all over in these sweet soft chains. They curl his hair, and adorn him with all effeminacy while he lies smiling and pleased — the wanton boys disposing of his instruments of war as they think fit, putting them to ridiculous uses, and laughing at them. While thus he lay, there enter to him a great many statesmen, and politicians; grave men in furs and chains, attended by the common crowd; and opening a scene farther off in prospect, shew him crowns, sceptres, globes, ensigns, arms, and trophies, promiscuously shuffled together, with heaps of gold, jewels, parchments, records, charters and seals; at which sight, he starts from the arms of the fair *Medea*, and strove to have approached those who waited for him; but she held him fast, and with abundance of tears and sighs of moving flattery, brought him back to her arms again, and all dissatisfied the promiscuous crowd depart, some looking back with scorn, others with signs of rage: and all the scene of glory, of arms and crowns, disappeared with the crowd. *Cesario* wholly forgetting, cried out again, "Ha! lost all for a trifling woman! Lost all those trophies of thy conquest for a mistress! By heaven I will shake the charmer from my soul, if both I cannot have." When *Fergusano* advancing to him, cried —"See, sir, how supinely the young hero's laid upon her downy breast," and smiled as he spoke, which angered the Prince, who replied with scorn, "Now, by my life, a plot upon my love;" but they protested it was not so, and begged he would be silent. While thus the hero lay, regardless of his glory, all decked with flowers and bracelets, the drums beat, and the trumpets were heard, or seemed to be heard to sound, and a vast opening space was filled with armed warriors, who offer him their swords, and seem to point at crowns that were borne behind them; a while they plead in vain, and point to crowns in vain, at which he only casts a scornful smile, and lays him down in the soft arms of love. They urge again, but with one amorous look the *Circe* more prevails than all their reasonings. At last, by force they divested him of his rosy garlands, in which there lay a charm, and he assumes new life, while others bore the enchantress out of his sight; and then he suffered himself to be conducted where they pleased, who led him forth, shewing him all the way a prospect of crowns. At this *Cesario* sighed, and the ceremony continued.

'The scene changed, discovering a sea-shore, where the *hero* is represented landed, but with a very melancholy air, attended with several officers and gentlemen; the earth seems to ring with joy and loud acclamations at his approach; vast multitudes thronging to behold him, and striving who first should kiss his hand; and bearing him aloft in the air, carry him out of sight with peals of welcome and joy.

'He is represented next in Council and deep debate, and so disappears: then soft music is heard, and he enters in the royal robe, with a crown presented him on the knee, which he receives, and bows to all the rabble and the numbers to give them thanks: he having in his hand blue garters, with the order of St *Esprit*, which he distributes to several persons on either hand; throwing ducal crowns and coronets among the rabble, who scuffle and strive to catch at them: after a great shout of joy, thunder and lightning again shook the earth; at which they seemed all amazed, when a thick black cloud descended, and covered the whole scene, and the rock closed again, and *Fergusano* let fall his wand.

'The Prince, seeing the ceremony end here, rises in a rage, and cries out, "I charge you to go on —— remove the veil, and let the sun appear; advance your mystic wand, and shew what follows next." "I cannot, sir," replied the trembling wizard, "the Fates have closed the everlasting Book, forbidding farther search." "Then damn your scanted art," replied the Prince, "a petty juggler could have done as much." "Is it not enough," replied the *German* rabbi, "that we have shewed you crowned, and crowned in *France* itself? I find the Infernals themselves are bounded here, and can declare no more." "Oh, they are petty powers that can be bounded," replied the Prince with scorn. They strove with all their art to reconcile him, laying the fault on some mistake of theirs, in the ingredients of the charm, which at another time they would strive to prevent: they soothe him with all the hope in the world, that what was left unrevealed must needs be as glorious and fortunate to him, as what he had seen already, which was absolutely to be depended on: thus they brought him to the open garden again, where they continued their instructions to him, telling him, that now was the time to arrive at all the glories he had seen; they presented to him the state of affairs in *France*, and how much a greater interest he had in the hearts of the people than their proper monarch, arguing a thousand fallacies to the deluded hero, who blind and mad with his dreams of glory, his visions and prospects, listened with reverence and attention to all their false persuasions. I call them false, madam, for I never had faith in those sort of people, and am sorry so many great men and ladies of our time are so bewitched to their prophecies. They there presented him with a list of all the considerable of the Reformed Religion in *Paris*, who had assured him aids of men and money in this expedition; merchants, rich tradesmen, magistrates and gownmen of the Reformed Church and the law. Next to this, another of the contribution of pious ladies; all which sums being named, amounted to a considerable supply; so that they assured him hell itself could not with these aids obstruct his glory, but on the contrary, should be compelled to render him assistance, by the help of charms, to make him invincible; so that wholly overcome by them, he has given order that all preparations be forthwith made for the most secret and speedy conveyance of himself and friends to some sea-port in *France*; he has ordered abundance of letters to be writ to those of the *Huguenot* party in all parts of *France*; all which will be ready to assist him at his landing. *Fergusano* undertakes for the management of the whole affair, to write, to speak, and to persuade; and you know, madam, he is the most subtle and insinuating of all his non-conforming race, and the most malignant of all our party, and sainted by them for the most pious and industrious labourer in the *Cause*; all that he says is oracle to the crowd, and all he says authentic; and it is he alone is that great engine that sets the great work a turning.' 'Yes,' replied *Sylvia*, 'and makes the giddy world mad with his damnable notions.' 'Pernicious as he is,' replied *Brilliard*, 'he has the sole management of affairs under *Hermione*; he has power to treat, to advise, to raise money, to make and name officers, and lastly, to draw out a scene of fair pretences for *Cesario* to the Crown of *France*, and the lawfulness of his claim; for let the conquest be never so sure, the people require it, and the conqueror is obliged to give some better reason than that of the strength of his sword, for his dominion over them. This pretension is a declaration, or rather a most scandalous, pernicious and treasonable libel, if I may say so, who have so great an interest in it, penned with all the malice envy can invent; the most unbred, rude piece of stuff, as makes it apparent the author had neither wit nor common good manners; besides the hellish principles he has made evident there. My lord would have no hand in the approbation of this gross piece of villainous scandal, which has more unfastened him from their interest, than any other designs, and from which he daily more and more declines, or seems disgusted with, though he does not wholly intend to quit the interest; having no other probable means to make good that fortune, which has been so evidently and wholly destroyed by it.' 'I am extremely glad,' said *Sylvia*,'that *Philander's* sentiments are so generous, and am at nothing so much amazed, as to hear the Prince could suffer so gross a thing to pass in his name.' 'I must,' said *Brilliard*,'do the Prince right in this point, to assure you when the thing was first in the rough draught shewed him, he told *Fergusano*, that those accusations of a crowned head, were too villainous for the thoughts of a gentleman; and giving it him again — cried —"No — let it never be said, that the royal blood that runs in my veins, could dictate to me no more noble ways for its defence and pretensions, than the mean cowardice of lies; and that to attain to empire, I should have recourse to the most detestable of all shifts. No, no, my too zealous friend," continued he, "I will, with only my sword in my hand, at the head of my army proclaim my right, and demand a crown, which if I win is mine; if not, it is his whose sword is better or luckier; and though the future world may call this unjust, at least they will say it was brave." At this the wizard smiled, and replied, "Alas, sir, had we hitherto acted by rules of generosity only, we had not brought so great advantages to our interest. You tell me, sir, of a speech you will make, with your sword in your hand, that will do very well at the head of an army, and a handsome declaration would be proper for men of sense; but this is not to the wise, but to the fools, on whom nothing will pass, but what is penned to their capacity, and who will not be able to hear the speeches you shall make to an army: this is to rouse them, and find them wherever they are, how far remote soever from you, that at once they may be incited to assist you, and espouse your interest: this is the sort of gospel they believe; all other is too fine: believe me, sir, it is by these gross devices you are to persuade those sons of earth, whose spirits never mounted above the dunghill, whence they grew like over-ripe pumpkins. Lies are the spirit that inspires them, they are the very brandy that makes them valiant; and you may as soon beat sense into their brains, as the very appearance of truth; it is the very language of the scarlet beast to them. They understand no other than their own, and he that does, knows to what ends we aim. No matter, sir, what tools you work withal, so the finished piece be fine at last. Look forward to the goal, a crown attends it! and never mind the dirty road that leads to it." 'With such false arguments as these, he wrought upon the easy nature of the Prince, who ordered some thousands of them to be printed for their being dispersed all over France, as soon as they should be landed: especially among the *Parisians*, too apt to take any impressions that bore the stamp and pretence of religion and liberty.

'While these and all other things necessary were preparing, *Cesario*, wholly given over to love, being urged by *Hermione* to know the occasion of his last night's absence, unravels all the secret, and told my lord and her, one night at supper, the whole scene of the *grotto*; so that *Hermione*, more than ever being puffed up with ambitious thoughts, hastened to have the Prince pressed to marry her; and consulting with the counsellor of her closest secrets, sets him anew to work; swearing violently, that if he did not bring that design about, she should be able, by her ascendancy over *Cesario*, to ruin all those they had undertaken, and yet turn the Prince from the enterprise; and that it was more to satisfy her ambition (to which they were obliged for all the Prince had promised) that he had undertaken to head an army, and put himself again into the hands of the *Huguenots*, and forsake all the soft repose of love and life, than for any inclination or ambition of his own; and that she who had power to animate him one way, he might be assured had the same power another. This she ended in very high language, with a look too fierce and fiery to leave him any doubt of; and he promised all things should be done as she desired, and that he would overcome the Prince, and bring him absolutely under her power. "Not," said she, with a scornful look, "that I need your aid in this affair, or want of power of my own to command it; but I will not have him look upon it as my act alone, or a thing of my seeking, but by your advice shall be made to understand it is for the good of the public; that having to do with a sort of people of the Reformed Religion, whose pretences were more nice than wise, more seemingly zealous than reasonable or just, they might look upon the life she led the Prince as scandalous, that was not justified by form, though never so unlawful." A thousand things she urged to him, who needed no instruction how to make that appear authentic and just, however contrary to religion and sense: but, so informed, he parted from her, and told her the event should declare his zeal for her service, and so it did; for he no sooner spoke of it to the Prince, but he took the hint as a divine voice; his very soul flushed in his lovely cheeks, and all the fire of love was dancing in his eyes: yet, as if he had feared what he wished could not handsomely and lawfully be brought to pass, he asked a thousand questions concerning it, all which the subtle wizard so well resolved, at least in his judgement, who easily was convinced of what he wished, that he no longer deferred his happiness, but that very night, in the visit he made *Hermione*, fell at her feet, and implored her consent of what he told her *Fergusano* had fully convinced him was necessary for his interest and glory, neither of which he could enjoy or regard, if she was not the partner of them; and that when he should go to *France*, and put himself in the field to demand a crown, he should do it with absolute vigour and resolution, if she were to be seated as queen on the same throne with him, without whom a cottage would be more pleasant; and he could relish no joys that were not as entirely and immediately hers as his own: he pleaded impatiently for what she longed, and would have made her petition for, and all the while she makes a thousand doubts and scruples only to be convinced and confirmed by him; and after seeming fully satisfied, he led her into a chamber (where *Fergusano* waited, and only her woman, and his faithful confidant *Tomaso*) and married her: since which, she has wholly managed him with greater power than before; takes abundance of state, is extremely elevated, I will not say insolent; and though they do not make a public declaration of this, yet she owns it to all her intimates; and is ever reproaching my lord with his lewd course of life, wholly forgetting her own; crying out upon infamous women, as if she had been all the course of her life an innocent.'

By this time dinner was ended, and *Sylvia* urged *Brilliard* to depart with her letter; but he was extremely surprised to find it to be to the Governor's nephew *Don Alonzo*, who was his lord's friend, and who would doubtless give him an account of all, if he did not shew him the billet: all these reasons could not dissuade this fickle wanderer, whose heart was at that time set on this young inconstant, at least her inclinations: he tells her that her life would be really in danger, if *Philander* comes to the knowledge of such an intrigue, which could not possibly be carried on in that town without noise; she tells him she is resolved to quit that false injurer of her fame and beauty; who had basely abandoned her for other women of less merit, even since she had pardoned him the crimes of love he committed at *Cologne*; that while he was in the country with her during the time of her lying-in, he had given himself to all that would receive him there; that, since he came away, he had left no beauty unattempted; and could he possibly imagine her of a spirit to bow beneath such injuries? No, she would on to all the revenges her youth and beauty were capable of taking, and stick at nothing that led to that interest; and that if he did not join with her in her noble design she would abandon him, and put herself wholly out of his protection: this she spoke with a fierceness that made the lover tremble with fear of losing her: he therefore told her she had reason; and that since she was resolved, he would confess to her that *Philander* was the most perfidious creature in the world; and that *Hermione*, the haughty *Hermione*, who hated naughty women, invited and treated all the handsome ladies of the Court to balls, and to the Basset-table, and made very great entertainments, only to draw to her interest all the brave and the young men; and that she daily gained abundance by these arts to *Cesario*, and above all strove by these amusements to engage *Philander*, whom she perceived to grow cold in the great concern; daily treating him with variety of beauty; so that there was no gaiety, no gallantry, or play, but at *Hermione*'s, whither all the youth of both qualities repaired; and it was there the Governor's nephew was every evening to be found. 'Possibly, madam, I had not told you this, if the Prince's bounty had not taken me totally off from *Philander*; so that I have no other dependence on him, but that of my respect and duty, out of perfect gratitude.' After this, to gain *Brilliard* entirely, she assured him if his fortune were suitable to her

quality, and her way of life, she believed she should devote herself
to him; and though what she said were the least of her thoughts, it
failed not to flatter him agreeably, and he sighed with grief that he
could not engage her; all he could get was little enough to support
him fine, which he was always as any person of quality at Court,
and appeared as graceful, and might have had some happy minutes
with very fine ladies, who thought well of him. To salve this defect
of want of fortune, he told her he had received a command from
Octavio to come to him about settling of a very considerable pension
upon her, and that he had at his investing put money into his aunt's
hands, who was a woman of considerable quality, to be disposed of
to that charitable use; and that if she pleased to maintain her rest of
fame, and live without receiving love-visits from men, she might now
command that, which would be a much better and nobler support
than that from a lover, which would be transitory, and last but as
long as her beauty, or a less time, his love. To this she knew not
what to answer, but ready money being the joy of her heart, and
the support of her vanity, she seems to yield to this, having said so
much before; and she considered she wanted a thousand things to
adorn her beauty, being very expensive; she was impatient till this
was performed, and deferred the sending to *Don Alonzo*, though her
thoughts were perpetually on him. She, by the advice of *Brilliard*,
writes a letter to *Octavio*; which was not like those she had before
written, but as an humble penitent would write to a ghostly Father,
treating him with all the respect that was possible; and if ever she
mentioned love, it was as if her heart had violently, and against her
will, burst out into softness, as still she retained there; and then she
would take up again, and ask pardon for that transgression; she told
him it was a passion, which, though she could never extinguish for
him, yet that it should never warm her for another, but she would
leave *Philander* to the world, and retire where she was not known,
and try to make up her broken fortunes; with abundance of things
to this purpose, which he carried to *Octavio*: he said he could have
wished she would have retired to a monastery, as all the first part
of her letter had given him hope; and resolved, and retired as he
was, he could not read this without extreme confusion and change

of countenance. He asked *Brilliard* a thousand times whether he believed he might trust her, or if she would abandon those ways of shame, that at last lost all: he answered, he verily believed she would. 'However,' said *Octavio*, 'it is not my business to capitulate, but to believe and act all things, for the interest and satisfaction of her whom I yet adore;' and without further delay, writ to his aunt, to present *Sylvia* with those sums he had left for her; and which had been sufficient to have made her happy all the rest of her life, if her sins of love had not obstructed it. However, she no sooner found herself mistress of so considerable a sum, but in lieu of retiring, and ordering her affairs so as to render it for ever serviceable to her, the first thing she does, is to furnish herself with new coach and equipage, and to lavish out in clothes and jewels a great part of it immediately; and was impatient to be seen on the *Tour*, and in all public places; nor could *Brilliard* persuade the contrary, but against all good manners and reason, she flew into most violent passions with him, till he had resolved to give her her way; it happened that the first day she shewed on the *Tour*, neither *Philander*, *Cesario* nor *Hermione* chanced to be there; so that at supper it was all the news, how glorious a young creature was seen only with one lady, which was *Antonet*, very well dressed, in the coach with her: every body that made their court that night to *Hermione* spoke of this new vision, as the most extraordinary charmer that had ever been seen; all were that day undone with love, and none could learn who this fair destroyer was; for all the time of *Sylvia*'s being at *Brussels* before, her being big with child had kept her from appearing in all public places; so that she was wholly a new face to all that saw her; and it is easy to be imagined what charms that delicate person appeared with to all, when dressed to such advantage, who naturally was the most beautiful creature in the world, with all the bloom of youth that could add to beauty. Among the rest that day that lost their hearts, was the Governor's nephew, who came into the Presence that night wholly transported, and told *Hermione* he died for the lovely charmer he had that day seen; so that she, who was the most curious to gain all the beauties to her side, that the men might be so too, endeavoured all she could to find out where this beauty dwelt. *Philander*, now

grown the most amorous and gallant in the world, grew passionately
in love with the very description of her, not imagining it had been
Sylvia, because of her equipage: he knew she loved him, at least he
thought she loved him too well to conceal herself from him, or be
in *Brussels*, and not let him know it; so that wholly ravished with
the description of the imagined new fair one, he burnt with desire of
seeing her; and all this night was passed in discourse of this stranger
alone; the next day her livery being described to *Hermione*, she sent
two pages all about the town, to see if they could discover a livery
so remarkable; and that if they did, they should inquire of them who
they belonged to, and where that person's lodging was. This was
not a very difficult matter to perform: *Brussels* is not a large place,
and it was soon surveyed from one end to the other: at last they
met with two of her footmen, whom they saluted, and taking notice
of their livery, asked them who they belonged to? These lads were
strangers to the lady they served, and newly taken; and *Sylvia* at first
coming, resolved to change her name, and was called Madame de ——
a name very considerable in *France*, which they told the pages, and
that she lived in such a place: this news *Hermione* no sooner heard,
but she sends a gentleman in the name of the Prince and herself
to compliment her, and tell her she had the honour to know some
great persons of that name in *France*, and did not doubt but she was
related to them: she therefore sent to offer her her friendship, which
possibly in a strange place might not be unserviceable to her, and that
she should be extreme glad to see her at Court, that is, at *Cesario*'s
palace. The gentleman who delivered this message, being surprised
at the dazzling beauty of the fair stranger, was almost unassured in
his address, and the manner of it surprised *Sylvia* no less, to be
invited as a strange lady by one that hated her; she could not tell
whether it were real, or a plot upon her; however she made answer,
and bid him tell Madam the Princess, which title she gave her, that
she received her compliment as the greatest honour that could arrive
to her, and that she would wait upon Her Highness, and let her
know from her own mouth the sense she had of the obligation. The
gentleman returned and delivered his message to *Hermione*; but so
altered in his look, so sad and unusual, that she took notice of it,

and asked him how he liked the new beauty: he blushed and bowed, and told her she was a wonder —— This made *Hermione*'s colour rise, it being spoke before *Cesario*; for though she was assured of the hero's heart, she hated he should believe there was a greater beauty in the world, and one universally adored. She knew not how so great a miracle might work upon him, and began to repent she had invited her to Court.

In the mean time *Sylvia*, after debating what to do in this affair, whether to visit *Hermione* and discover herself, or to remove from *Brussels*, resolved rather upon the last; but she had fixed her design as to *Don Alonzo*, and would not depart the town. To her former beginning flame for him was added more fuel; she had seen him the day before on the *Tour*; she had seen him gaze at her with all the impatience of love, with madness of passion in his eyes, ready to fling himself out of the coach every time she passed by: and if he appeared beautiful before, when in his riding dress, and harassed for four nights together with love and want of sleep; what did he now appear to her amorous eyes and heart? She had wholly forgot *Octavio*, *Philander* and all, and made a sacrifice of both to this new young lover: she saw him with all the advantages of dress, magnificent as youth and fortune could invent; and above all, his beauty and his quality warmed her heart anew; and what advanced her flame yet farther, was a vanity she had of fixing the dear wanderer, and making him find there was a beauty yet in the world, that could put an end to his inconstancy, and make him languish at her feet as long as she pleased. Resolved on this new design, she defers it no longer; but as soon as the persons of quality, who used to walk every evening in the park, were got together, she accompanied with *Antonet*, and three or four strange pages and footmen, went into the park, and dressed in perfect glory. She had not walked long there before she saw *Don Alonzo*, richer than ever in his habit, and more beautiful to her eyes than any thing she had ever seen; he was gotten among the young and fair, caressing, laughing, playing, and acting all the little wantonnesses of youth. *Sylvia*'s blood grew disordered at this, and she found she loved by her jealousy, and longs more than ever to have the glory of vanquishing that heart, that so boasted of never having yet been conquered. She therefore uses all her art to get him to look at her; she passed by him often, and as often as she did so he viewed her with pleasure; her shape, her air, her mien, had something so charming, as, without the assistance of her face, she gained that evening a thousand conquests; but those were not the trophies she aimed at, it was *Alonzo* was the marked-out victim, that she destined for the sacrifice of love. She found him so engaged with women of great quality, she almost despaired to get to speak to him; her equipage which stood at the entrance of the park, not being by her, he did not imagine this fine lady to be her he saw on the *Tour* last night; yet he looked at her so much, as gave occasion to those he was with to rally him extremely, and tell him he was in love with what he had not seen, and who might, notwithstanding all that delicate appearance, be ugly when her mask was off. *Sylvia*, however, still passed on with abundance of sighing lovers after her, some daring to speak, others only languishing; to all she would vouchsafe no word, but made signs, as if she were a stranger, and understood them not; at last *Alonzo*, wholly impatient, breaks from these ralliers, and gets into the crowd that pursued this lovely unknown: her heart leaped when he approached her, and the first thing she did was to pull off her glove, and not only shew the fairest hand that ever nature made, but that ring on her finger *Alonzo* gave her when they parted at the village. The hand alone was enough to invite all eyes with pleasure to look that way; but *Alonzo* had a double motive, he saw the hand with love, and the ring with jealousy and surprise; and as it is natural in such cases, the very first thought that possessed him was, that the young *Bellumere* (for so *Sylvia* had called herself at the village) was a lover of this lady, and had presented her this ring. And after his sighings and little pantings, that seized him at this thought, would give him leave, he bowing and blushing cried —'Madam, the whole piece must be excellent, when the pattern is so very fine.' And humbly begging the favour of a nearer view, he took her hand and kissed it with a passionate eagerness, which possibly did not so well please *Sylvia*, because she did not think he took her for the same person, to whom he shewed such signs of love last night. In taking her hand he surveyed the ring, and cried — 'Madam, would to heaven I could lay so good a claim to this fair hand, as I think I once could to this ring, which this hand adorns and honours.' 'How, sir,' replied *Sylvia*, 'I hope you will not charge me with felony?' 'I am afraid I shall,' replied he sighing, 'for you have attacked me on the King's high-way, and have robbed me of a heart:' 'I could never have robbed a person,' said *Sylvia*, 'who could more easily have parted with that trifle; the next fair object will redeem it, and it will be very little the worse for my using.' 'Ah Madam,' replied he sighing, 'that will be according as you will treat it; for I find already you have done it more damage, than it ever sustained in all the rencounters it has had with love and beauty.' 'You complain too soon,' replied *Sylvia*, smiling, 'and you ought to make a trial of my good nature, before you reproach me with harming you.' 'I know not,' replied *Alonzo* sighing, 'what I may venture to hope from that; but I am afraid, from your inclinations, I ought to hope for nothing, since a thousand reasonable jealousies already possess me, from the sight of that ring; and I more than doubt I have a powerful rival, a youth of the most divine form, I ever met with of his sex; if from him you received it, I guess my fate.' 'I perceive, stranger,' said *Sylvia*, 'you begin to be inconstant already, and find excuses to complain on your fate before you have tried your fortune. I persuade myself that fine person you speak of, and to whom you gave this ring, has so great a value for you, that to leave you no excuse, I assure you, he will not be displeased to find you a rival, provided you prove a very constant lover.' 'I confess,' said *Alonzo*, 'constancy is an imposition I never yet had the confidence and ill nature to impose on the fair; and indeed I never found that woman yet, of youth and beauty, that ever set so small a value on her own charms, to be much in love with that dull virtue, and require it of my heart; but, upon occasion, madam, if such an unreasonable fair one be found'——'I am extremely sorry' (interrupted *Sylvia*) 'to find you have no better way of recommending yourself; this will be no great encouragement to a person of my humour to receive your address.' 'Madam, I do not tell you that I am not in my nature wondrous constant,' replied he; 'I tell you only what has hitherto happened to me, not what will; that I have yet never been so, is no fault of mine, but power or truth in those beauties, to whom I have given my heart; rather believe they wanted charms to hold me, than that I, (where wit and beauty engaged me) should prove so false to my own pleasure. I am very much afraid, madam, if I find my eyes as agreeably entertained when I shall have the honour to see your face, as my ears are with your excellent wit, I shall be reduced to that very whining, sighing coxcomb, you like so well in a lover, and be ever dying at your feet. I have but one hope left to preserve myself from this wretched thing you women love; that is, that I shall not find you so all over charming, as what I have hitherto found presents itself to be. You have already created love enough in me for any reasonable woman, but I find you are not to be approached with the common devotions we pay your sex; but, like your beauty, the passion too must be great, and you are not content unless you see your lovers die; this is that fatal proof alone that can satisfy you of their passion. And though you laugh to see a Sir *Courtly Nice*, a fop in fashion acted on the stage; in your hearts that foolish thing, that fine neat pasquil, is your darling, your fine gentleman, your well-bred person.'

Thus sometimes in jest, and sometimes in earnest, they recommended themselves to each other, and to so great a degree, that it was impossible for them to be more charmed on either side, which lasted 'till it was time to depart; but he besought her not to do so, 'till she had informed him where he might wait on her, and most passionately solicit, what she as passionately desired: 'To tell you truth,' said she, 'I cannot permit you that freedom without you ask it of *Bellumere*.' He replied, 'Next to waiting on her, he should be the most overjoyed in the world, to pay his respects to that young gentleman.' However, to name him, gave him a thousand fears; which when he would have urged, she bid him trust to the generosity of that man, who was of quality, and loved him; she then told him his lodgings (which were her own): *Alonzo*, infinitely overjoyed, resolved to lose no time, but promised that evening to visit him: and at their parting, he treated her with so much passionate respect, that she was vexed to see it paid to one he yet knew not. However, she verily believed her conquest was certain: he having seen her three times, and all those times for a several person, and yet was still in love with her; and she doubted not, when all three were joined in one, he would be much more in love than yet he had been; with this assurance they parted.

Sylvia was no sooner got home, but she resolved to receive *Alonzo*, who she was assured would come: she hasted to dress herself in a very rich suit of man's clothes, to receive him as the young *French* gentleman. She believed *Brilliard* would not come 'till late, as was his use, now being at play at *Hermione*'s. She looked extreme pretty when she was dressed, and had all the charms that heaven could adorn a face and shape withal: her apartment was very magnificent, and all looked very great. She was no sooner dressed, but the young lover came. *Sylvia* received him on the stair-case with open arms, and all the signs of joy that could be expressed, and led him to a rich drawing-room, where she began to entertain him with that happy night's adventure; when they both lay together at the village; while *Alonzo* makes imperfect replies, wholly charmed with the look of the young cavalier, which so resembled what he had seen the day before in another garb on the *Tour*. He is wholly ravished with his voice, it being absolutely the same, that had charmed him that day in the park; the more he gazed and listened, the more he was confirmed in his opinion, that he was the same, and he had the music of that dear accent still in his ears, and could not be deceived. A thousand times he is about to kneel before her, and ask her pardon, but still is checked by doubt: he sees, he hears, this is the same lovely youth, who lay in bed with him at the village *cabaret*; and then no longer thinks her woman: he hears and sees it is the same face, and voice, and hands he saw on the *Tour*, and in the park, and then believes her woman: while he is in these perplexities, *Sylvia*, who with vanity and pride perceived his disorder, taking him in her arms, cried, 'Come, my *Alonzo*, that you shall no longer doubt but I am perfectly your friend, I will shew you a sister of mine, whom you will say is a beauty, or I am too partial, and I will have your judgement of her.' With that she called to *Antonet* to beg her lady would permit her to bring a young stranger to kiss her hand. The maid, instructed, retires, and *Alonzo* stood gazing on *Sylvia* as one confounded and amazed, not knowing yet how to determine; he now begins to think himself mistaken in the fair youth, and is ready to ask his pardon for a fault but imagined, suffering by his silence the little prattler to discourse and laugh at him at his pleasure. 'Come,' said *Sylvia* smiling, 'I find the naming a beauty to you has made you melancholy; possibly when you see her she will not appear so to you; we do not always agree in one object.' 'Your judgement,' replied *Alonzo*, 'is too good to leave me any hope of liberty at the sight of a fine woman; if she be like yourself I read my destiny in your charming face.' *Sylvia* answered only with a smile — and calling again for *Antonet*, she asked if her sister were in a condition of being seen; she told her she was not, but all undressed and in her night-clothes; 'Nay then,' said *Sylvia*, 'I must use my authority with her:' and leaving *Alonzo* trembling with expectation, she ran to her dressing-room, where all things were ready, and slipping off her coat put on a rich night-gown, and instead of her peruke, fine night-clothes, and came forth to the charmed *Alonzo*, who was not able to approach her, she looked with such a majesty, and so much dazzling beauty; he knew her to be the same he had seen on the *Tour*. She, (seeing he only gazed without life or motion) approaching him, gave him her hand, and cried —'Sir, possibly this is a more old acquaintance of yours than my face.' At which he blushed and bowed, but could not speak: at last *Sylvia*, laughing out-right, cried —'Here, *Antonet*, bring me again my peruke, for I find I shall never be acquainted with *Don Alonzo* in petticoats.' At this he blushed a thousand times more than before, and no longer doubted but this charmer, and the lovely youth were one; he fell at her feet, and told her he was undone, for she had made him give her so indisputable proofs of his dullness, he could never hope she should allow him capable of eternally adoring her. 'Rise,' cried *Sylvia* smiling, 'and believe you have not committed so great an error, as you imagine; the mistake has been often made, and persons of a great deal of wit have been deceived.' 'You may say what you please,' replied *Alonzo*, 'to put me in countenance; but I shall never forgive myself the stupidity of that happy night, that laid me by the most glorious beauty of the world, and yet afforded me no kind instinct to inform my soul how much I was blest: oh pity a wretchedness, divine maid, that has no other excuse but that of infatuation; a thousand times my greedy ravished eyes wandered over the dazzling brightness of yours; a thousand times I wished that heaven had made you woman! and when I looked, I burnt; but, when I kissed those soft, those lovely lips, I durst not trust my heart; for every touch begot wild thoughts about it; which yet the course of all my fiery youth, through all the wild debauches I had wandered, had never yet betrayed me to; and going to bed with all this love and fear about me, I made a solemn oath not to approach you, lest so much beauty had overcome my virtue. But by this new discovery, you have given me a flame, I have no power nor virtue to oppose: it is just, it is natural to adore you; and not to do it, were a greater than my sin of dullness; and since you have made me lose a charming friend, it is but just I find a mistress; give me but your permission to love, and I will give you all my life in service, and wait the rest: I will watch and pray for coming happiness; which I will buy at any price of life or fortune.' 'Well, sir,' replied our easy fair one; 'if you believe me worth a conquest over you, convince me you can love; for I am no common beauty to be won with petty sudden services; and could you lay an empire at my feet, I should despise it where the heart were wanting.' You may believe the amorous youth left no argument to convince her in that point unsaid; and it is most certain they came to so good an understanding, that he was not seen in *Brussels* for eight days and nights after, nor this rare beauty, for so long a time, seen on the *Tour* or any public place. *Brilliard* came every day to visit her, and receive her commands, as he used to do, but was answered still that *Sylvia* was ill, and kept her chamber, not suffering even her domestics to approach her: this did not so well satisfy the jealous lover, but he soon imagined the cause, and was very much displeased at the ill treatment; if such a design had been carried on, he desired to have the management of it, and was angry that *Sylvia* had not only deceived him in the promise he had made for her to *Octavio*, but had done her own business without him: he spoke some hard words; so that to undeceive him she was forced to oblige *Alonzo* to appear at Court again; which she had much ado to incline him to, so absolutely she had charmed him; however he went, and she suffered *Brilliard* to visit her, persuading that easy lover (as all lovers are easy) that it was only indisposition, that hindered her of the happiness of seeing him; and after having perfectly reconciled herself to him, she asked him the news at *Hermione*'s, to whom, I had forgot to tell you, she sent every day a page with a compliment, and to let her know she was ill, or she should have waited on her: she every day received the compliment from her again, as an unknown lady. *Brilliard* told her that all things were now prepared, and in a very short time they should go for *France*; but that whatever the matter was, *Philander* almost publicly disowned the Prince's interest, and to some very considerable of the party has given out, he does not like the proceedings, and that he verily believed they would find themselves all mistaken; and that instead of a throne the Prince would meet a scaffold; 'so bold and open he has been. Something of it has arrived to the Prince's ear, who was so far from believing it, that he could hardly be persuaded to speak of it to him; and when he did, it was with an assurance before-hand, that he did not credit such reports. So that he gives him not the pain to deny them: for my part I am infinitely afraid he will disoblige the Prince one day; for last night, when the Prince desired him to get his equipage ready, and to make such provision for you as was necessary, he coldly told him he had a mind to go to *Vienna*, which at that time was besieged by *Solyman* the Magnificent, and that he had no inclination of returning to *France*. This surprised and angered the Prince; but they parted good friends at last, and he has promised him all things: so that I am very well assured he will send me where he supposes you still are; and how shall we manage that affair?'

Sylvia, who had more cunning and subtleness than all the rest of her sex, thought it best to see *Philander*, and part with him on as good terms as she could, and that it was better he should think he yet had the absolute possession of her, than that he should return to *France* with an ill opinion of her virtue; as yet he had known no guilt of that kind, nor did he ever more than fear it with *Octavio*; so that it would be easy for her to cajole him yet a little longer, and when he was gone, she should have the world to range in, and possess this new lover, to whom she had promised all things, and received from him all assurances imaginable of inviolable love: in order to this then she consulted with *Brilliard*; and they resolved she should for a few days leave *Antonet* with her equipage, at that house where she was, and retire herself to the village where *Philander* had left her, and where he still imagined she was: she desired *Brilliard* to give her a day's time for this preparation, and it should be so. He left her, and going to *Hermione*'s, meets *Philander*, who immediately gave him orders to go to *Sylvia* the next morning, and let her know how all things went, and tell her, he would be with her in two days. In the mean time *Sylvia* sent for *Alonzo*, who was but that evening gone from her. He flies on the wings of love, and she tells him, she is obliged to go to a place six or seven days' journey off, whither he could not conduct her, for reasons she would tell him at her return: whatever he could plead with all the force of love to the contrary, she gets his consent, with a promise wholly to devote herself to him at her return, and pleased she sent him from her, when *Brilliard* returning told her the commands he had; and it was concluded they should both depart next morning, accompanied only by her page. I am well assured she was very kind to *Brilliard* all that journey, and which was but too visible to the amorous youth who attended them; so absolutely had she depraved her reason, from one degree of sin and shame to another; and he was happy above any imagination, while even her heart was given to another, and when she could propose no other interest in this looseness, but security, that *Philander* should not know how ill she had treated him. In four days *Philander* came, and finding *Sylvia* more fair than ever, was anew pleased; for she pretended to receive him with all the joy imaginable, and the deceived lover believed, and expressed abundance of grief at the being obliged to part from her; a great many vows and tears were lost on both sides, and both believed true: but the grief of *Brilliard* was not to be conceived; he could not persuade himself he could live, when absent from her: some bills *Philander* left her, and was so plain with her, and open-hearted, he told her that he went indeed with *Cesario*, but it was in order to serve the King; that he was weary of their actions, and foresaw nothing but ruin would attend them; that he never repented him of any thing so much, as his being drawn in to that faction; in which he found himself so greatly involved, he could not retire with any credit; but since self-preservation was the first principle of nature, he had resolved to make that his aim, and rather prove false to a party, who had no justice and honour on their side, than to a King, whom all the laws of heaven and earth obliged him to serve; however, he was so far in the power of these people, that he could not disengage himself without utter ruin to himself; but that as soon as he was got into *France*, he would abandon their interest, let the censuring world say what it would, who never had right notions of things, or ever made true judgements of men's actions.

He lived five or six days with *Sylvia* there; in which time she failed not to assure him of her constant fidelity a thousand ways, especially by vows that left no doubt upon his heart; and it was now that they both indeed found there was a very great friendship still remaining at the bottom of their hearts for each other, nor did they part without manifold proofs of it. *Brilliard* took a sad and melancholy leave of her, and had not the freedom to tell her aloud, but obliged to depart with his lord, they left *Sylvia*, and posted to *Brussels*, where they found the Prince ready to depart, having left *Hermione* to her women more than half dead. I have heard there never was so sad a parting between two lovers; a hundred times they swooned with the apprehension of the separation in each other's arms, and at last the Prince was forced from her while he left her dead, and was little better himself: he would have returned, but the officers and people about him, who had espoused his quarrel, would by no means suffer him: and he has a thousand times told a person very near him, that he had rather have forfeited all his hoped-for glory, than have left that charmer of his soul. After he had taken all care imaginable for *Hermione*, for that name so dear to him was scarce ever out of his mouth, he suffered himself with a heavy heart and pace to be conducted to the vessel: and I have heard he was hardly seen to smile all the little voyage, or his whole life after, or do any thing but sigh, and sometimes weep, which was a very great discouragement to all that followed him; they were a great while at sea, tossed to and fro by stress of weather, and often driven back to the shore where they first took shipping; and not being able to land where they first designed, they got ashore in a little harbour, where no ship of any bigness could anchor; so that with much ado, getting all their arms and men on shore, they sunk the ship, both to secure any from flying, and that it might not fall into the hands of the *French*. *Cesario* was no sooner on the *French* shore, but numbers came to him of the *Huguenot* party, for whom he had arms, and who wanted them he furnished as far as he could, and immediately proclaimed himself King of *France* and *Navarre*, while the dirty crowd rang him peals of joy. But though the under world came in great crowds to his aid, he wanted still the main supporters of his cause, the men of substantial quality: if the ladies could have composed an army, he would not have wanted one, for his beauty had got them all on his side, and he charmed the fair wheresoever he rode.

He marched from town to town without any opposition, proclaiming himself king in all the places he came to; still gathering as he marched, till he had composed a very formidable army. He made officers of the kingdom —*Fergusano* was to have been a cardinal, and several lords and dukes were nominated; and he found no opposition in all his prosperous course. — In the mean time the royal army was not idle, which was composed of men very well disciplined, and conducted by several princes and men of great quality and conduct. But as it is not the business of this little history to treat of war, but altogether love; leaving those rougher relations to the chronicles and historiographers of those times, I will only hint on such things in this enterprise, as are most proper for my purpose, and tell you, that *Cesario* omitted nothing for the carrying on his great design; he dispersed his scandals all over *France*, though they met with an obstruction at *Paris*, and were immediately suppressed, it being proclaimed death for any person to keep one in their houses; and if any should by chance come to their hands, they were on this penalty to carry them to the Secretary of State; and after the punishment had passed on two or three offenders, it deterred the rest from meddling with those edge tools: I must tell you also, that the title of king, which *Cesario* had taken so early upon him, was much against his inclinations; and he desired to see himself at the head of a more satisfiable army, before he would take on him a title he found (in the condition he was in) he should not defend; but those about him insinuated to him, that it was the title that would not only make him more venerable, but would make his cause appear more just and lawful; and beget him a perfect adoration with those people who lived remote from Courts, and had never seen that glorious thing called a king. So that believing it would give nerves to the cause, he unhappily took upon him that which ruined him; for he had often sworn to the greatest part of those of any quality, of his interest, that his design was liberty only, and that his end was the public good, so infinitely above his own private interest, that he desired only the honour of being the champion for the oppressed *Parisians*, and people of *France*; that if they would allow him to lead their armies, to fight and spend his dearest blood for them, it was all the glory he aimed at: it was this pretended humility in a person of his high rank that cajoled the *mobile*, who looked on him as their god, their deliverer, and all that was sacred and dear to them; but the wiser sort regarded him only as one that had most power and pretension to turn the whole affairs of *France*, which they disliking, were willing at any price, to reduce to their own conditions, and to what they desired; not imagining he would have laid a claim to the Crown, which many of them fancied themselves as capable of as himself, rather that he would perhaps have set up the King of *Navarre*. This *Cesario* knew; and understanding their sentiments, was unwilling to hinder their joining with him, by such a declaration, which he knew would be a means to turn abundance of hearts against him, as indeed it fell out; and he found himself master of some few towns, only with an army of fifteen or sixteen thousand peasants, ill armed, unused to war, watchings, and very ill lodging in the field, very badly victualled, and worse paid. For, from *Paris* no aids of any kind could be brought him; the roads all along being so well guarded and secured by the royal forces, and wanting some great persons to espouse his quarrel, made him not only despair of success, but highly resent it of those, who had given him so large promises of aid. Many, as I said, and most were disgusted with his title of king; but some waited the success of his first battle; which was every day expected, though *Cesario* kept himself as clear of the royal army as he could a long time, marching away as soon as they drew near, hoping by these means, not only to tire them out, and watch an advantage when to engage, but gather still more numbers. So that the greatest mischief he did was teasing the royal army, who could never tell where to have him, so dexterous he was in marching off. They often came so near, as to have skirmishes with one another by small parties, where some few men would fall on both sides: and to say truth, *Cesario* in this expedition shewed much more of a soldier than the politician: his skill was great, his conduct good, expert in advantages, and indefatigable in toils. And I have heard it from the mouth of a gentleman, who in all that undertaking never was from him, that in seven or eight weeks that he was in arms, he never absolutely undressed himself, and hardly slept an hour in the four and twenty; and that sometimes he was on his horse's back, in a chariot, or on the ground, suffering even with the meanest of his soldiers all the fatigues of the enterprise: this gentleman told me he would, in those hours he should sleep, and wherein he was not taking measures and councils, (which were always held in the night) that he would be eternally speaking to him of *Hermione*; and that with the softest concern, it was possible for love and tenderest passion to express. That he being the only friend he could repose so great a weakness in, and who soothed him to the degree he wished, the Prince was so well pleased with him, as to establish him a colonel of horse, for no other merit than that of having once served *Hermione*, and now would flatter his disease agreeably: and though he did so, he protested he was ashamed to hear how this poor fond concern rendered this great man, and he has often pitied what should have been else admired; but who can tell the force of love, backed by charms supernatural? And who is it that will not sigh, at the fate of so illustrious a young man, whom love had rendered the most miserable of all those numbers he led?

But now the royal army, as if they had purposely suffered him to take his tour about the country, to ensnare him with the more facility, had at last, by new forces that came to their assistance daily, so encompassed him, that it was impossible for him to avoid any longer giving them battle; however, he had the benefit of posting himself the most advantageously that he could wish; he had the rising grounds to place his cannon, and all things concurred to give him success; his numbers exceeding those of the royal army: not but he would have avoided a set battle, if it had been possible, till he had made himself master of some places of stronger hold; for yet, as I said, he had only subdued some inconsiderable places which were not able to make defence; and which as soon as he was marched out, surrendered again to their lawful prince; and pulling down his proclamation, put up those of the King: but he was on all sides so embarrassed, he could not come even to parly with any town of note; so that, as I said, at last, being as it were blocked up, though the royal army did not offer him battle: three nights they lay thus in view of each other; the first night the Prince sent out his scouts, who brought him intelligence, that the enemy was not so well prepared for battle, as they feared they might be, if they imagined the Prince would engage them, but he had so often given them the slip, that they believed he had no mind to put the fortune of the day to the push; and they were glad of these delays, that new forces might advance. When the scouts returned with this news, the Prince was impatient to fall upon the enemy, but *Fergusano*, who was continually taking counsel of his charms, and looking into his black Book of Fate, for every sally and step they made, persuaded His Highness to have a little patience; positively assuring him his fortune depended on a critical minute, which was not yet come; and that if he offered to give battle before the change of the moon, he was inevitably lost, and that the attendance of that fortunate moment would be the beginning of those of his whole life: with such like positive persuasions he gained upon the Prince, and overcame his impatience of engaging for that night, all which he passed in counsel, without being persuaded to take any rest, often blaming the nicety of their art, and his stars; and often asking, if they lost that opportunity that fortune had now given them, whether all their arts, or stars, or devils, could retrieve it? And nothing would that night appease him, or dispossess the sorcerers of this opinion.

The next day they received certain intelligence, that a considerable supply would reinforce the royal army under the conduct of a Prince of the Blood; which were every moment expected: this news made the Prince rave, and he broke out into all the rage imaginable against the wizards, who defended themselves with all the reasons of their art, but it was all in vain, and he vowed he would that night engage the enemy, if he found but one faithful friend to second him, though he died in the attempt; that he was worn out with the toils he had undergone; harassed almost to death, and would wait no longer the approach of his lazy fate, but boldly advancing, meet it, what face so ever it bore. They besought him on their knees, he would not overthrow the glorious design, so long in bringing to perfection, just in the very minute of happy projection; but to wait those certain Fates, that would bring him glory and honour on their wings; and who, if slighted, would abandon him to destruction; it was but some few hours more, and then they were his own, to be commanded by him: it was thus they drilled and delayed him on till night; when again he sent out his scouts to discover the posture of the enemy; and himself in the mean time went to Council. *Philander* failed not to be sent for thither, who sometimes feigned excuses to keep away, and when he did come, he sat unconcerned, neither giving or receiving any advice. This was taken notice of by all, but *Cesario*, who looked upon it as being overwatched, and fatigued with the toils of the day; his sullenness did not pass so in the opinion of the rest; they saw, or at least thought they saw, some other marks of discontent in his fine eyes, which love so much better became. One of the Prince's officers, and Captain of his Guard, who was an old hereditary rogue, and whose father had suffered in rebellion before, a fellow rough and daring, comes boldly to the Prince when the Council rose, and asked him, if he were resolved to engage? He told him, he was. 'Then,' said he, 'give me leave to shoot *Philander* in the head.' This blunt proposition given, without any manner of reason or circumstance, made the Prince start back a step or two, and ask him his meaning of what he said. 'Sir,' replied the Captain, 'if you will be safe, *Philander* must die; for however it appear to Your Highness, to all the camp he shows the traitor, and it is more than doubted, he and the King of *France*, understand one another but too well: therefore, if you would be victor, let him be dispatched, and I myself will undertake it.' 'Hold,' said the Prince, 'if I could believe what you say to be true, I should not take so base a revenge; I would fight like a soldier, and he should be treated like a man of honour.' 'Sir,' said *Vaneur*, for that was the Captain's name; 'do not, in the circumstances we are now in, talk of treating (with those that would betray us) like men of honour; we cannot stand upon decency in killing, who have so many to dispatch; we came not into *France* to fight duels, and stand on nice punctilios: I say, we must make quick work, and I have a good pistol, charged with two handsome bullets, that shall, as soon as he appears amongst us on horseback, do his business as genteelly as can be, and rid you of one of the most powerful of your enemies.' To this the Prince would by no means agree; not believing one syllable of the accusation. *Vaneur* swore then that he would not draw a sword for his service, while *Philander* was suffered to live; and he was as good as his word. He said, in going out, that he would obey the Prince, but he begged his pardon, if he did not lift a hand on his side; and in an hour after sent him his commission, and waited on him, and was with him almost till the last, in all the danger, but would not fight, having made a solemn vow. Several others were of *Vaneur*'s opinion, but the Prince believed nothing of it; *Philander* being indeed, as he said, weary of the design and party, and regarded them as his ruiners, who with fair pretences drew him into a bad cause; which his youth had not then considered, and from which he could not untangle himself.

By this time, the scout was come back, who informed the Prince that now was the best time in the world to attack the enemy, who all lay supinely in their tents, and did not expect a surprise: that the very out-guards were slender, and that it would not be hard to put them to a great deal of confusion. The Prince, who was enough impatient before, now was all fire and spirit, and it was not in the power of magic to withhold him; but hasting immediately to horse, with as much speed as possible, he got at the head of his men; and marching on directly to the enemy, put them into so great a surprise, that it may be admired how they got themselves into a condition of defence; and, to make short of a business that was not long in acting, I may avow, nothing but the immediate hand of the Almighty, (who favours the juster side, and is always ready for the support of those, who approach so near his own divinity; sacred and anointed heads) could have turned the fortune of the battle to the royal side: it was prodigious to consider the unequal numbers, and the advantage all on the Prince's part; it was miraculous to behold the order on his side, and surprise on the other, which of itself had been sufficient to have confounded them; yet notwithstanding all this unpreparedness on this side, and the watchfulness and care on the other; so well the general and officers of the royal army managed their scanted time, so bravely disciplined and experienced the soldiers were, so resolute and brave, and all so well mounted and armed, that, as I said, to a miracle they fought, and it was a miracle they won the field: though that fatal night *Cesario* did in his own person wonders; and when his horse was killed under him, he took a partisan, and as a common soldier, at the head of his foot, acted the *hero* with as much courage and bravery, as ever *Caesar* himself could boast; yet all this availed him nothing: he saw himself abandoned on all sides, and then under the covert of the night, he retired from the battle, with his sword in his hand, with only one page, who fought by his side: a thousand times he was about to fall on his own sword, and like *Brutus* have finished a life he could no longer sustain with glory: but love, that coward of the mind, and the image of divine *Hermione*, as he esteemed her, still gave him love to life; and while he could remember she yet lived to charm him, he could even look with contempt on the loss of all his glory; at which, if he repined, it was for her sake, who expected to behold him return covered over with laurels. In these sad thoughts he wandered as long as his wearied legs would bear him, into a low forest, far from the camp; where, over-pressed with toil, all over pain, and a royal heart even breaking with anxiety, he laid him down under the shelter of a tree, and found but his length of earth left to support him now, who, not many hours before, beheld himself the greatest monarch, as he imagined, in the world. Oh who, that had seen him thus; which of his most mortal enemies, that had viewed the royal youth, adorned with all the charms of beauty, heaven ever distributed to man; born great, and but now adored by all the crowding world with hat and knee; now abandoned by all, but one kind trembling boy weeping by his side, while the illustrious *hero* lay gazing with melancholy weeping eyes, at those stars that had lately been so cruel to him; sighing out his great soul to the winds, that whistled round his uncovered head;

breathing his griefs as silently as the sad fatal night passed away; where nothing in nature seemed to pity him, but the poor wretched youth that kneeled by him, and the sighing air: I say, who that beheld this, would not have scorned the world, and all its fickle worshippers? Have cursed the flatteries of vain ambition, and prized a cottage far above a throne? A garland wreathed by some fair innocent hand, before the restless glories of a crown?

Some authors, in the relation of this battle, affirm, that *Philander* quitted his post as soon as the charge was given, and sheered off from that wing he commanded; but all historians agree in this point, that if he did, it was not for want of courage; for in a thousand encounters he has given sufficient proofs of as much bravery as a man can be capable of: but he disliked the cause, disapproved of all their pretensions, and looked upon the whole affair and proceeding to be most unjust and ungenerous; and all the fault his greatest enemies could charge him with was, that he did not deal so gratefully with a prince that loved him and trusted him; and that he ought frankly to have told him, he would not serve him in this design; and that it had been more gallant to have quitted him that way, than this; but there are so many reasons to be given for this more politic and safe deceit, than are needful in this place, and it is most certain, as it is the most justifiable to heaven and man, to one born a subject of *France*, and having sworn allegiance to his proper king, to abandon any other interest; so let the enemies of this great man say what they please, if a man be obliged to be false to this or that interest, I think no body of common honesty, sense and honour, will dispute which he ought to abandon; and this is most certain, that he did not forsake him because fortune did so, as this one instance may make appear. When *Cesario* was first proclaimed king, and had all the reason in the world to believe that fortune would have been wholly partial to him, he offered *Philander* his choice of any principality and government in *France*, and to have made him of the Order of *Saint Esprit*: all which he refused, though he knew his great fortune was lost, and already distributed to favourites at Court, and himself proscribed and convicted as a traitor to *France*. Yet all these refusals did not open the eyes of this credulous great young man, who still believed it the sullenness and generosity of his temper.

No sooner did the day discover to the world the horrid business of the preceding night, but a diligent search was made among the infinite number of dead that covered the face of the earth, for the body of the Prince, or new King, as they called him: but when they could not find him among the dead, they sent out parties all ways to search the woods, the forests and the plains; nor was it long they sought in vain; for he who had laid himself, as I said, under the shelter of a tree, had not for any consideration removed him; but finding himself seized by a common hand, suffered himself, without resistance, to be detained by one single man 'till more advanced, when he could as easily have killed the rustic as speak or move; an action so below the character of this truly brave man, that there is no reason to be given to excuse his easy submission but this, that he was stupefied with long watching, grief, and the fatigues of his daily toil for so many weeks before: for it is not to be imagined it was carelessness, or little regard for life; for if it had been so, he would doubtless have lost it nobly with the victory, and never have retreated while there had been one sword left advanced against him; or if he had disdained the enemy should have had the advantage and glory of so great a conquest, at least when his sword had been yet left him, he should have died like a *Roman*, and have scorned to have added to the triumph of the enemy. But love had unmanned his great soul, and *Hermione* pleaded within for life at any price, even that of all his glory; the thought of her alone blackened this last scene of his life, and for which all his past triumphs could never atone nor excuse.

Thus taken, he suffered himself to be led away tamely by common hands without resistance: a victim now even fallen to the pity of the *mobile* as he passed, and so little imagined by the better sort who saw him not, they would not give a credit to it, every one affirming and laying wagers he would die like a hero, and never surrender with life to the conqueror. But this submission was but too true for the repose of all his abettors; nor was his mean surrender all, but he shewed a dejection all the way they were bringing him to *Paris*, so extremely unworthy of his character, that it is hardly to be credited so great a change could have been possible. And to shew that he had lost all his spirit and courage with the victory, and that the great strings of his heart were broke, the Captain who had the charge of him, and commanded that little squadron that conducted him to *Paris*, related to me this remarkable passage in the journey; he said, that they lodged in an inn, where he believed both the master, and a great many strangers who that night lodged there, were *Huguenots*, and great lovers of the Prince, which the Captain did not know, till after the lodgings were taken: however, he ordered a file of Musketeers to guard the door; and himself only remaining in the chamber with the Prince, while supper was getting ready: the Captain being extremely weary with watching and toiling for a long time together, laid himself down on a bench behind a great long table, that was fastened to the floor, and had unadvisedly laid his pistols on the table; and though he durst not sleep, he thought there to stretch himself into a little ease, who had not quitted his horseback in a great while: the Prince, who was walking with his arms a-cross about the room, musing in a very dejected posture, often casting his eyes to the door, at last advances to the table, and takes up the Captain's pistols; the while he who saw him advance, feared in that moment, what the Prince was going to do; he thought, if he should rise and snatch at the pistols, and miss of them, it would express so great a distrust of the Prince, it might provoke him to do, what by his generous submitting of them, might make him escape; and therefore, since it was too late, he suffered the Prince to arm himself with two pistols, who before was disarmed of even his little penknife. He was, he said, a thousand times about to call out to the guards; but then he thought before they could enter to his relief, he was sure to be shot dead, and it was possible the Prince might make his party good with four or five common soldiers, who perhaps loved the Prince as well as any, and might rather assist than hinder his flight; all this he thought in an instant, and at the same time, seeing the Prince stand still, in a kind of consideration what to do, looking, turning, and viewing of the pistols, he doubted not but his thoughts would determine with his life, and though he had been in the heat of all the battle, and had looked death in the face, when it appeared most horrid, he protested he knew not how to fear till this moment, and that now he trembled with the apprehension of unavoidable ruin; he cursed a thousand times his unadvisedness, now it was too late; he saw the Prince, after he had viewed and reviewed the pistols, walk in a great thoughtfulness again about the chamber, and at last, as if he had determined what to do, came back and laid them again on the table; at which the Captain snatched them up, resolving never to commit so great an over-sight more. He did not doubt, he said, but the Prince, in taking them up, had some design of making his escape; and most certainly, if he had but had courage to have attempted it, it had not been hard to have been accomplished: at worst, he could but have died: but there is a fate, that over-rules the most lucky minutes of the greatest men in the world, and turns even all advantages offered to misfortunes, when it designs their ruin.

While they were on their way to *Paris*, he gave some more signs, that the misfortunes he had suffered, had lessened his heart and courage: he writ several the most submissive letters in the world to the King, and to the Queen–Mother of *France*; wherein he strove to mitigate his treason, with the poorest arguments imaginable, and, as if his good sense had declined with his fortune, his style was altered, and debased to that of a common man, or rather a schoolboy, filled with tautologies and stuff of no coherence; in which he neither shewed the majesty of a prince, nor sense of a gentleman; as I could make appear by exposing those copies, which I leave to history; all which must be imputed to the disorder his head and heart were in, for want of that natural rest, he never after found. When he came to *Paris*, he fell at the feet of His Majesty, to whom they brought him, and with a shower of tears bedewing his shoes, as he lay prostrate, besought his pardon, and asked his life; perhaps one of his greatest weaknesses, to imagine he could hope for mercy, after so many pardons for the same fault; and which, if he had had but one grain of that bravery left him, he was wont to be master of, he could not have expected, nor have had the confidence to have implored; and he was a poor spectacle of pity to all that once adored him, to see how he petitioned in vain for life; which if it had been granted, had been of no other use to him, but to have passed in some corner of the earth, with *Hermione*, despised by all the rest: and, though he fetched tears of pity from the eyes of the best and most merciful of kings, he could not gain on his first resolution; which was never to forgive him that scurrilous Declaration he had dispersed at his first landing in *France*; that he took upon him the title of king, he could forgive; that he had been the cause of so much bloodshed, he could forgive; but never that unworthy scandal on his unspotted fame, of which he was much more nice, than of his crown or life; and left him (as he told him this) prostrate on the earth, when the guards took him up, and conveyed him to the *Bastille*: as he came out of the *Louvre*, it is said, he looked with his wonted grace, only a languishment sat there in greater beauty, than possibly all his gayer looks ever put on, at least in his circumstances all that beheld him imagined so; all the *Parisians* were crowded in vast numbers to see him: and oh, see what fortune is! Those that had vowed him allegiance in their hearts, and were upon all occasions ready to rise in mutiny for his least interest, now saw him, and suffered him to be carried to the *Bastille* with a small company of guards, and never offered to rescue the royal unfortunate from the hands of justice, while he viewed them all around with scorning, dying eyes.

While he remained in the *Bastille*, he was visited by several of the ministers of State, and cardinals, and men of the Church, who urged him to some discoveries, but could not prevail with him: he spoke, he thought, he dreamed of nothing but *Hermione*; and when they talked of heaven, he ran on some discourse of that beauty, something of her praise; and so continued to his last moment, even on the scaffold, where, when he was urged to excuse, as a good Christian ought, his invasion, his bloodshed, and his unnatural war, he set himself to justify his passion to *Hermione*, endeavouring to render the life he had led with her, innocent and blameless in the sight of heaven; and all the churchmen could persuade could make him speak of very little else. Just before he laid himself down on the block, he called to one of the gentlemen of his chamber, and taking out the enchanted tooth-pick-case, he whispered him in the ear, and commanded him to bear it from him to *Hermione*; and laying himself down, suffered the justice of the law, and died more pitied than lamented; so that it became a proverb, 'If I have an enemy, I wish he may live like —— and die like *Cesario*': so ended the race of this glorious youth, who was in his time the greatest man of a subject in the world, and the greatest favourite of his prince, happy indeed above a monarch, if ambition and the inspiration of knaves and fools, had not led him to destruction, and from a glorious life, brought him to a shameful death.

This deplorable news was not long in coming to *Hermione*, who must receive this due, that when she heard her *hero* was dead, (and with him all her dearer greatness gone) she betook herself to her bed, and made a vow she would never rise nor eat more; and she was as good as her word, she lay in that melancholy estate about ten days, making the most piteous moan for her dead lover that ever was heard, drowning her pillow in tears, and sighing out her soul. She called on him in vain as long as she could speak; at last she fell into a lethargy, and dreamed of him, till she could dream no more; an everlasting sleep

Made in the USA
Lexington, KY
03 May 2019